Mine

THE ANTI-HERO

AMANDA MCKINNEY

HH TISEVICH

Paperback ISBN 979-8-9886030-6-1
eBook ISBN 979-8-9886030-3-0

Editor(s):
Nancy Brown, Redline Editing
Pam Berehulke, Bulletproof Editing
Gregg Sayers
Cover Design:
Damonza

https://www.amandamckinneyauthor.com

Dedication

For Henry
For Mama

Also by Amanda

THRILLER NOVELS:

A Marriage of Lies - An Amazon Charts Bestseller

When I Disappear

The Wife's Silence

In Her Own Words

The Widow of Weeping Pines: A Thriller Novella

The Raven's Wife: A Thriller Novella

The Lie Between Us: A Thriller Novella

* * *

ROMANTIC THRILLER NOVELS:

THE ANTI-HERO:

Mine

ON THE EDGE SERIES:

Buried Deception

Trail of Deception

BESTSELLING STEELE SHADOWS SERIES:

Her Mercenary (Steele Shadows Mercenaries)

Her Renegade (Steele Shadows Mercenaries)

Cabin 1 (Steele Shadows Security)

Cabin 2 (Steele Shadows Security)

Cabin 3 (Steele Shadows Security)

Phoenix (Steele Shadows Rising)

Jagger (Steele Shadows Investigations)

Ryder (Steele Shadows Investigations)

THE ROAD SERIES:

Rattlesnake Road

Redemption Road

THE BERRY SPRINGS SERIES:

The Woods (A Berry Springs Novel)

The Lake (A Berry Springs Novel)

The Storm (A Berry Springs Novel)

The Fog (A Berry Springs Novel)

The Creek (A Berry Springs Novel)

The Shadow (A Berry Springs Novel)

The Cave (A Berry Springs Novel)

The Viper

Devil's Gold (A Black Rose Mystery, Book 1)

Hatchet Hollow (A Black Rose Mystery, Book 2)

Tomb's Tale (A Black Rose Mystery Book 3)

Evil Eye (A Black Rose Mystery Book 4)

Sinister Secrets (A Black Rose Mystery Book 5)

And many more to come...

Let's Connect!

Text **AMANDABOOKS to 66866** to sign up
for Amanda's Newsletter and get the latest
on new releases, promos, and freebies!
Or, you can sign up below.

https://www.amandamckinneyauthor.com

Mine

In a world of power and secrets, passion is the deadliest weapon.

Astor

During the day, I'm a billionaire CEO in a designer suit. At night, I'm the man you call to make someone disappear. My life is a careful balance of power and secrecy, one I've spent years perfecting—until I receive a ransom note for my estranged wife, whom I've kept hidden away for her own protection.

Reluctantly, I accept an invitation to an exclusive party to get her back. But when the evening takes a dangerous turn, I take my rival's daughter as collateral.

Sabine

Being taken hostage wasn't on my to-do list. Despite Astor's cold, apathetic demeanor, I find myself completely captivated by the man. The problem is, I'm not the only one.

As tension boils over into passion, I realize the man who took me might also be the one who destroys me. Because in his world, love is the most dangerous weapon of all.

A seductive dark romance packed with steamy enemies-to-lovers tension, jaw-dropping twists, and a possessive anti-hero you won't forget.

***This updated version includes the **complete Anti-Hero series**—<u>two books</u> in one. No cliffhangers.*

Part One

Prologue

The Wife

THE MOON HANGS low in an inky-black sky dotted with a million stars. Endless, they seem.

Goose bumps rise on my arms as a gust sweeps over my nightgown, sending my long blond hair swirling around my face. The wind is getting stronger with each passing hour.

A storm is coming.

Peering at the ocean at the bottom of the cliff, I listen to the waves crashing against the shore. The sound reminds me of my own breath. Reminds me to breathe at all.

I close my eyes, rolling my wedding band around the base of my finger. On a deep, ragged inhale, I wriggle my bare toes deeper into the cool, thick dirt beneath my feet. I tilt my face to the sky and open my arms.

I'm flying, I think.

Yes, I'm flying.

I'm free, like a bird on the wind.

Suddenly, the air shifts around me. A chill. A presence.

He's here.

I freeze, the hair on the back of my neck prickling. My gaze drops to the garden that surrounds me, awash in silver moonlight.

Tears fill my eyes. From fear, or is it relief? Relief that, finally, all of this can be over.

I reach out, my long, skinny fingers fluttering against the breeze. I want to touch my flowers one more time. Just one more, just one petal.

"It's time," he whispers in my ear.

Yes. It's time.

A tear rolls down my cheek as I turn to face what I know will be the death of me.

One

Astor

I PULL a black balaclava over my head, followed by latex gloves on each hand. Moonlight sneaks through the treetops, dappling the forest floor in swaying silver spotlights. I'm careful to avoid each one.

I step out of the tree line and onto a narrow path of grass that skirts the back of the affluent neighborhood. No dogs tonight. Luck is on my side.

After a quick glance over my shoulder, I grip the top of the privacy fence and launch myself over. I land silently on the ground. After brushing a speck of dirt from my pant leg, I make my way to the back door of the three-story monstrosity known as the Knoll House, a nod to the former (very wealthy) owners who built it a century ago.

I pull a brass key from my pocket, unlock the door, and step inside. The house is dark.

Recalling the blueprint I studied an hour earlier, I stride past the kitchen, the media room, and the library, then quietly jog up the curved marble staircase.

A woman moans to the beat of slapping skin as I top the stairs.

The master bedroom is lit only by the dim glow of a television featuring amateur porn. On the California King ahead of me is a girl on all fours. Eighteen at best, with long red hair. On his knees behind her, a man in his mid-sixties with a protruding beer gut grips her hips as he thrusts into her.

She screams when she sees me.

"Get out."

I don't need to tell her twice. The girl hurls herself off the bed and sprints out of the room, stark naked.

The man scrambles backward, slamming his sweaty, flushed body against the headboard.

I pull the knife from my pocket as I cross the room. "Mr. Whitlock, I hear you've been sharing secrets."

"W—what? No. No. Who—who are you?"

I stop at the edge of the bed and stare down at him. "Are you a religious man?"

The blood drains from his face. He knows what's coming.

"Yes," he whispers, tears falling down his cheek.

"You have fifteen seconds to make peace with your death."

I turn my face and close my eyes as he begs for mercy.

Ten minutes later, I meet Cillian, my right-hand man, at the back gate of the home. He glances at the blood dripping from my knuckles, then at the knot swelling on my cheekbone. "Is it done?"

I nod, wiping the blade on my pants before slipping it back into my pocket. "The girl?"

"Paid her five thousand cash with a threat of framing her if she speaks. She's his mistress—prostitute, I think, and scared shitless—nothing to worry about. You ready for me to clean up?"

"Let me make the call first." I pull the SAT phone from my pocket and turn my back to Cillian.

I'm aware that I can't feel the lacerations on my knuckles or the contusions on my face.

I'm aware that my breath is calm, my pulse normal, my conscience unbothered.

I'm aware that the act of killing no longer affects me. And, in an ironic twist, this is what unsettles me.

The phone connects with a secure line to the US Department of Defense.

"Vice Chairman. It's done."

"Loose ends?"

"Taken care of."

"Great. I'll transfer the payment into your account within the hour. As always, it's a pleasure working with you, Mr. Stone. Expect your next package next week."

"Looking forward to it."

Leaving Cillian, I kill the call, hop the fence, and disappear into the shadows.

Where I belong.

Two

Astor

HANDS IN MY POCKETS, I stroll the empty halls of my penthouse suite. Aimlessly, as has become my habit on sleepless nights.

Rain ticks against the wall of windows that overlook Manhattan, the drops rolling down the glass in a distorted kaleidoscope of color. They remind me of long, skinny witches' fingers, slowly, sneakily reaching, eventually seizing everything I've built.

I watch each drop slither with aloof detachment. Same with the pops of lightning, the cracks of thunder that rattle the windows.

For a moment, I have a flashback of myself as a child, curled on my mother's lap, watching a thunderstorm with awe and wonder. But as quickly as the memory comes, it drifts away, like the smoke of a cigarette, cruelly reminding me that those days are gone forever.

It's only then that I'm jolted by a sharp pain in my forearm. I look down at my fingers that have slid up the cuff of my dress shirt, and at my nail that has dug into the flesh of my forearm. A thin line of scars mar my skin, each serving as a checkpoint to make sure I still feel. To confirm that I am not dead on the outside.

Only the inside.

There was a time when these detached emotions, disjointed flashbacks, and witless self-harm used to alarm me. To be honest, for a while I thought I was going crazy. That a life defined by monetizing murder had finally caught up to me.

But as the days went on, I accepted this temperament as inevitable.

I am fully aware that one day I *will* go crazy. That the ghosts of my past will find me, wrap their fingers around my throat—like the raindrops slithering down the window—and drag me into the afterlife. And when that time comes, all the money I've amassed over my lifetime—the homes, the cars, the jets, the yachts, the clothes, the priceless this, the exclusive that—none of it will matter. I will be judged solely on the decisions I made during my time on earth.

Isn't that an unsettling thought?

I find myself pausing as I step into the library. I do like this room. I like the smell of the leather couches, the musty scent of old books. I like the gold accents on the bar cart, the crystal decanters. The dim lighting, the thick red velvet curtains that block out the light. I have libraries in all of my properties, each a replica of the next.

Trailing my fingertip across the bindings of the books, I read each title. Most are first editions worth more than most people's cars.

All these *things.* So many *things* I have. Yet, still, I'm not happy.

Resigned, I shove my hands into my pockets and go to my office to check my email.

"Mr. Stone." Prishna's deep, sultry voice scolds me from the doorway.

Without turning or breaking my stride, I acknowledge my assistant with a dip of my chin.

I don't need to turn around to know that she is wearing the same floral robe she wears every night. That a pair of cream slippers cover her feet. That her long silver-streaked braided hair is pulled into a bun on the top of her head. That her caramel skin is sallow from lack of sleep, and that her strong, angular face is screwed into a scowl.

In her hands, she will be carrying a sterling silver tray with a porcelain teacup filled with chamomile. Next to it, a warm Medu vada, a traditional Indian food that looks like a doughnut but tastes nothing like it. Trust me on this.

Same tray, same cup, same tea, same doughnut-thingy, same scowl. Every goddamn night.

"You should be asleep," she says, frowning as she slides the tray onto my desk. Though Prishna—Pri for short—is younger than my forty-eight years by three years, she acts like my mother.

With a sigh, I look up and meet her catlike golden eyes, as intense as a sandstorm.

"Wandering again, I see," she says unhelpfully.

This has become our routine. Every night, I wander the suite until Prishna eventually gets sick of it and chases me down with a cup of tea that she knows I won't drink and a snack she knows I won't eat. This has been going on for so long now that I'm beginning to think this ridiculous pattern is more for her than for me.

"I've made an appointment for you."

This gets my attention. "An appointment for what?"

"With your doctor. Your insomnia is getting worse. I'm worried about you, Mr. Stone."

"Don't."

"Someone has to, and for reasons unbeknownst to me, the gods have chosen me for this task."

"Have they? Are you sure it has nothing to do with the grossly generous paycheck I deposit into your account weekly?"

She sighs, rendered speechless by frustration.

So, leave me. Someday she will, I remind myself, because they always do—in one way or another.

"I've also made an appointment with a therapist."

"What?"

"It's with a grief counselor. She specializes in the loss of loved ones . . . children, specifically."

I gape at my assistant as heat rises up my neck.

"It's been five years, Mr. Stone. If you don't find a way to deal with the trauma, it is going to manifest into something that will never be cured. It's time. You have an empire to run. Your mother would want—"

"That's enough!" The words echo down the hallway.

As if summoned from the depths of hell, Cillian breezes into the room, unaffected by my childish outburst. Or used to them, perhaps.

I throw out my arms. "Jesus! It's one in the morning. What the hell is everyone doing awake?"

Cillian is as alert as ever, still wearing the same suit he wore during our last meeting hours earlier. But now the top button is loose, and the sleeves are rolled up to his forearms. He'd almost pass for a respectable businessman if not for his tattoos, criminal record, and ability to kill a man using only his thumbnail.

Though Cillian left the life of a mercenary years ago to work directly under me, the fight still burns inside him. The old adage is true: you can take the man out of the war, but you can't take the soldier out of the man. He's the one who needs therapy.

"I hate to break up this little lover's spat," he mocks, "but something's come up."

I squint at Prishna. "It's time for you to retire to your room."

On a long, dramatic sigh, she turns and disappears down the hall, leaving a trail of attitude so thick you could grab it.

Cillian closes the door behind her and locks it.

Three

Astor

"WHAT'S GOING ON?"

Cillian clicks a button on my desk, sending the shades sliding over the windows to ensure privacy.

Something's up.

"Power up your monitors." He joins me behind the screens, but we don't sit. "Now bring up your personal email."

Cillian has access to my entire life. Every email, text, and phone call is filtered through him before it reaches me. I trust the man with my life—and I have.

"There." He points to an email with no subject. "That one. Open it."

The face of a pale, stunningly beautiful blonde fills the screen. The woman is gagged, mascara-stained tears rolling down her face. A thin line of blood runs from her left nostril, puddling on a severely swollen upper lip. She's wearing a white nightgown and is tied to a metal chair. She's staring directly into the camera.

Into me.

My stomach drops to my feet.

"Read the message."

I blink, tearing away from the photo and focusing on the words of the email. It reads:

YOUR WIFE MISSES YOU, ASTOR. I KNOW THIS BECAUSE SHE CALLS OUT FOR YOU IN HER SLEEP. SHE CRIES FOR YOU WHEN I HIT HER. SHE SCREAMS FOR YOU WHEN I FUCK HER.

MEET ME TOMORROW IN VEGAS, AT THE DUNGEON, AT TEN P.M. THE DOORMAN WILL BE EXPECTING YOU.

COME ALONE.

IF YOU ALERT THE POLICE, THE FEDS, OR SEND ANY OF YOUR MERCENARIES, I WILL SLIT YOUR WIFE'S THROAT AND LIVE STREAM HER BLEEDING OUT ON SOCIAL MEDIA FOR THE ENTIRE WORLD TO SEE.

I LOOK FORWARD TO SEEING YOU, ASTOR. IT'S BEEN A LONG TIME.

"Is the picture real or generated by artificial intelligence?"

"It's real," Cillian confirms. "I ran it through multiple programs. It's definitely not AI. That's Valerie for sure."

"Who's it from?"

"I don't know yet."

"Did you trace the email address?"

"Untraceable. The email was sent from a bogus account over a bogus IP address."

"Where are they?"

"I can't trace the location without a viable IP address."

I straighten, fold my arms over my chest, and stare down at the picture on the screen. "How the hell did someone find out Valerie is my wife?"

"Marriage records are public. Even though we made an effort to conceal it, anyone with significant hacking experience —which is pretty much half the population these days—could figure it out, I'm sure."

I squint at the email. "It's been a long time," I mutter, repeating the last line.

"So, it's someone you've met at some point."

"Which is completely useless information."

"Right. When was the last time you spoke to Valerie?"

"Seven months ago."

"When was the last time you saw her?"

"Longer than that."

"Was she still living in the safe house you set her up in?"

"Yes. She knows she's not allowed to leave—actually, that's a good point. Check the security cameras at the beach house where she was staying."

"Step back."

Cillian pushes me out of the way, which takes little effort considering the man is six-foot-five and as thick as a refrigerator. He sinks into the chair and begins opening multiple files and programs.

"Is she still on her meds?" he asks, his fingers flying over the keyboard.

"Yes. I get an update from her doctor every three weeks. He refills her prescription and takes a blood sample to ensure she's taking them."

"Good. How is she? I mean, mentally?"

"The same."

A dozen different views of my secret oceanfront property fill the screens. It's a small three-bedroom bungalow on a cliff that overlooks the Pacific Ocean, surrounded by twenty acres of gardens and manicured woods.

"Start with three weeks ago," I say. "That's the last time I received a communication from her doctor, who visited her at the house."

Cillian fast-forwards through the footage.

I watch my wife come and go. Outside, inside, back and forth, over and over again.

Small and painfully skinny, her long blond hair hangs in tangles down her back. The white robe she practically lives in is dingy and stained. In most of the footage, regardless of the weather, she's barefoot, her skin almost as pale as her robe.

She looks ethereal, ghostly almost, seemingly gliding over the ground as she walks.

Occasionally, she gestures to some phantom object in front of her, her fingers fluttering madly as if she's trying to communicate something. She walks the grounds, even in the night. When the camera catches her face, her eyes reflect like a cat's.

To say it's unsettling is an understatement. There is no pattern in her movement, no intention in her step. She simply meanders through the property for hours at a time.

As I stand there watching her, an eerie feeling comes over me. I see myself in her. Wandering aimlessly with a heart as heavy as a brick.

Day after day, my estranged wife cries as she walks, wiping away her tears with a wad of tissues she keeps in her pocket.

All alone.

Day. After. Day.

Guilt grabs my throat like a vise. The goddamn guilt I feel daily for sending her away like I did, for orchestrating a life of solitude. Even though I was only doing what I thought was best for her, the decision still plagues me.

"Fast-forward faster," I grumble, forcing myself not to look away from the woman I once got down on one knee for.

Suddenly, the screens go blank.

"What the hell?"

After clicking, checking, going back, and clicking again, Cillian looks over his shoulder, his brow cocked. "The cameras were cut."

"The cameras were *cut*?" I vehemently shake my head. "No. That's impossible. They're programmed to alert me if they ever turn off. Why the hell didn't it trigger the alert system here? Why didn't we get a text? Cillian, what the f—"

"I don't know, man. Stop. Breathe. I'm seeing this for the first time, just like you are. I'll look into it. I'll figure it all out. When was the last time the security system was serviced?"

I blink. My non-answer is answer enough.

He nods, then squints at the screen, hovering the pointer over the time and date. "The cameras went black at 2:16 in the morning, two days ago."

Two days. Someone kidnapped my wife *two* days ago.

Cillian leans back in his chair and scratches his chin. "The email isn't asking for money, so it's not a ransom kidnapping. They're simply asking for you to meet them . . . What if it's a trap?"

"To kill me?"

"Yeah."

"Don't worry, you're in the will."

"Whew." Cillian mocks wiping sweat from his brow, then falls serious again. "Do you have any idea who it could be?"

The list of men who want me dead—or at the very least, want revenge—is endless. Cillian knows this.

My company, Astor Stone, Inc., is a private investigation firm that operates in countries all over the world. Except it doesn't. The private-eye angle is a ruse to conceal that, in reality, my company is secretly contracted by the US government to conduct paramilitary missions domestically and abroad.

I oversee a team of mercenaries, hand-picked by me, who are ordered to do what our government can't—or is unable to, thanks to all the ridiculous red tape. In the simplest terms, we are hitmen, paid outrageous sums of money to run black ops for the government, with the understanding that they will deny all knowledge of us should one of us be exposed.

I've lost count of the missions I've overseen, of the men I've ordered to be killed, and killed myself. Of the enemies, their friends and family, who would want revenge. Like I said, the list truly is endless.

I crack my knuckles. "Well, there's only one way to find out who it is, isn't there? Las Vegas, here we come. Call Allan, have him ready the jet. We leave in the morning."

"Don't you mean we ride at dawn?" Cillian wags finger pistols in my face.

"Why does everything have to be a joke with you?"

"Because you are so damn uptight, Astor. I'd throw myself out the window if not for occasional comedic relief."

I bite back a dozen smart-ass responses because he's right. I am terrible company; I know this. I have one emotion—morose. Hell, I don't even want to be around myself half the time.

"By the way, what's the Dungeon?" he asks. "The email said to meet there."

"It's an exclusive bar under the Strip. Gambling, strippers, a Michelin-starred restaurant, secret rooms, every drug you could ever want, available in any form you could ever want it in. You know, your typical everyday blue-collar watering hole."

"You said *under* the Strip?"

"Yes, literally underground. It's an invite-only place. Has a secret entrance and everything. Very James Bond. Not many people know of it."

"Only the rich and famous?"

"Precisely."

"So, that tells us something about our crook—he has money."

"Or enough notoriety to get inside."

"You think he could be with the Mafia? Something like that?"

Shrugging, I consider the handful of missions my company has handled that involve Mafia-related crimes. I make a note to pull those files and study them on the flight over.

I begin pacing.

"Get some sleep, buddy." Cillian pushes out of the chair and makes his way to the door, unbuttoning his shirt. "We'll take care of this just like we take care of everything else."

I grunt and turn to the window. Silence settles in the room, yet I feel Cillian's presence lingering. When he finally speaks, his tone carries an ominous edge that makes me shiver.

"Vegas is where everything started, remember?"

"Yeah. I remember."

"Let's be more careful this time."

The door closes, and a heaviness like a ball of grease settles in the pit of my stomach. A foreboding that something big is about to happen.

Again.

Four

Astor

"I HAVE Astor Stone in the car." My driver, Mauricio, rolls down the window of our blacked-out SUV as we stop at a gated entrance.

It's only four in the afternoon, and the Vegas Strip is already shoulder-to-shoulder with tourists. Pitched voices and laughter mingle with a loud thrum of music from a club nearby. Bright, obnoxious light strobes from the rooftops, flashing against the gaudy mirrored buildings. Noise is all around us.

A crowd is gathered around the perimeter of the gate, mostly tourists and paparazzi trying to get a glimpse of who is behind the tinted windows. They think we're going to an exclusive bar frequented by celebrities, but instead, we'll drop several floors below street level to the Dungeon.

My backseat window slides down, ushering in a waft of hot, dry air that reeks of motor oil and food vendors. It was seventy-four degrees when we left New York this morning. It is now a face-melting ninety-seven degrees on the Strip.

I despise the heat.

I also despise Las Vegas.

In fact, I despise this entire goddamn trip.

The guard bends at the waist and studies me, his hand resting on the Glock on his belt. He's a short man but thick, with a cool, confident demeanor. Former military, my guess. Competent, in spite of his size.

Mauricio hands him my identification, along with his own. After scrutinizing both cards, the guard nods and passes them back.

Mauricio gestures to the black SUV behind us, identical to ours. "That vehicle belongs to Mr. Stone's security. One man; name, Cillian Mallas. He's with us."

"I'll need to check him too. Protocol."

"Understood."

After both vehicles successfully pass through security, we descend into an underground tunnel, where we are stopped at two more security checkpoints.

Finally, we arrive in a garage. Cillian parks next to us, gets out of his Tahoe, and slides into the backseat next to me.

I scowl at our almost identical outfits. We are both wearing tailored navy suits over white dress shirts. The only difference is the tie—he is wearing one, I am not. Instead, I've unbuttoned the top two buttons of my shirt to combat the heat in this godforsaken hellhole.

"Stop dressing like me," I mutter. "We look like twin toddlers at our sister's bat mitzvah."

"I packed the suit before I knew what you were wearing, you arrogant son of a bitch. Would you rather me change into the board shorts and tie-dye shirt I wore on the plane?"

"You mean the one with the barbecue stains? No thanks. Is everyone in place?"

Cillian radios each of the men, confirming their locations.

Screw our crook's demand to come alone. I never go

anywhere without security. Before Cillian and I even boarded the plane this morning, I had four of my West Coast mercenaries checking into Caesars Palace to begin recon work.

Always, *always* be prepared. I'd be dead a hundred times over if that were not my life's motto.

Cillian slides his radio into the inner pocket of his jacket. "We've got one on the roof, one at street level, and two walking every floor of Caesars, the Mirage, and the Bellagio looking for Valerie."

"If shit goes sideways, do not let anyone call for backup, understood? We've got enough men, and I don't want to bring any undue attention to this." I pull the pistol from my jacket and check the clip.

Cillian nods, then does the same.

I look up. "If you or I are not back at this car by eleven o'clock, we meet back at the jet when the smoke clears. I won't take off without you, and vice versa."

"Got it." Cillian glances at his watch. "I'm meeting with one of our guys in fifteen minutes. Meet you outside the Dungeon at ten?"

"Nine thirty."

"The email said to meet at ten."

"I want to throw off our host."

Cillian nods, then pauses, lingering on my profile.

"What?" I scowl. He always does this.

"Don't act like you don't know what I'm about to say."

My jaw twitches. I look away.

"Valerie was a mercy fuck that you accidentally got pregnant six damn years ago. The only reason you married her was because you knocked her up."

"I married her to protect my unborn child, Cillian."

"I'm not talking about Chloe right now. I'm talking about Valerie—the reason we're here. You need to take a second to do a cost/risk analysis before we go in guns blazing. You haven't even spoken to her in months. You locked her away, under heavy security—"

"Because she's my weakness, Cillian, according to my enemies. Not only was she a target, but she also needed more medical attention than I could give her. She also absolutely hated me. I did what I thought was best for her. And by the way, I'm sick of having this conversation with you. You've made yourself and your disdain for Valerie—and my decisions—clear since day one."

"I don't like her, Astor."

"I *know*."

"My point to all this is: does anyone need to die tonight—for *her*? For a woman you barely know and never loved in the first place? Look at everything we're doing. You've got four of your men's lives at stake, not including mine or yours."

"I take care of my own, Cillian. I married Valerie; therefore, I take care of her."

"You don't owe Valerie anything anymore. Doing this isn't going to bring Chloe back—"

"Say another word—another *fucking* word—and you will swallow this pistol. Do you understand me?"

Cillian shakes his head and shoves out of the car. "Crystal clear, boss."

Five

Sabine

BIRTHDAYS ARE the official worst day of the year. There, I said it.

Okay, fine. Maybe it's an unfair declaration. I imagine for most people, birthdays are celebratory. Happy. A time to reflect on years past and proclaim all those dreams and goals for the next twelve months.

For me, however, it's a yearly reminder of the vacancy that is my life. That it doesn't matter that I am a year older. I am still a hermit with no friends, no partner, no dog or cat—not even a plant.

It's a reminder that I'm still paying rent for an apartment the size of a shoebox, that I haven't upgraded my car in a decade, and that I still consider a bag of potato chips and a glass of wine a well-rounded dinner. That it is yet another year where no one—not a single person—will send me a Happy Birthday text, card, or gift.

It's all becoming a bit embarrassing and very Emily Dickinson.

So, when I wake, dreading the number on the calendar, I decide this birthday—*this year*—will be different. I will make an effort. I will try to look on the bright side of things. I will learn how to sit in solitude and thrive in it. (Also, I'm joining a Pilates class to help with those pesky fifteen pounds I need to lose).

With this renewed outlook, after breakfast, I walk my optimistic little self to the Forum Shops at Caesars and buy a skintight, cherry-red, off-the-shoulder cocktail dress. With it, I purchase a pair of diamond-studded Louboutins—as if the dress isn't gaudy enough. Then I treat myself to lunch and mimosas where I officially max out a credit card.

Delightfully buzzed, I make one final stop at my favorite sex-toy shop, Titty Titty Bang Bang. I have no shame in admitting that I have taken to electronics to satisfy my personal needs. Honestly, there's something very freeing about it. I don't have to suffer through bad dates or worry about sexually transmitted diseases.

The owner, Stormy (naturally), informed me just last week of a major milestone in my VIP membership. I have officially purchased every product in the store.

But that's not true. I haven't tried the growing selection of creature cocks that are displayed next to the Fantasy Erotica bookshelf. I draw the line at monster peen. A woman must have standards, after all.

After that, I wander back to my teeny apartment that overlooks the Vegas strip and take a three-hour nap, clutching my new dress like a life raft.

Evening comes swift and disorienting.

Sipping a fresh mimosa (this one peach), I spend an hour on my hair, treating, washing, drying, gooping, and then straightening until the black strands look like a curtain of silk down my back. I go for sexy and subtle with my makeup, like my mother taught me.

God rest her soul.

It's now nine in the evening, and as the mirrored elevator carries me down to the lobby, I study my reflection.

Despite the shopping spree, the champagne, and the overindulgent primping, I find myself slipping back into a somber state of mind. That damn discontent that comes with feeling that I'm not where I'm supposed to be in my life.

That somewhere in this crazy world, there is so much more for me.

Whatever. I shake it off. *I just need another drink.*

Six

Sabine

THE ELEVATOR DINGS, and the doors slide open to a crowd of drunken bachelorettes. Tiny plastic penises are everywhere. In their hair, around their necks, in their drinks.

A cloud of Victoria's Secret body spray crop-dusts the car as I sidestep two women comparing matching tattoos they'd just gotten. Both are laughing so hard that one drools, missing my new Louboutins by an inch.

I catch a glimpse of the new ink. On the blonde's forearm is an image of a salt shaker, and on her friend's, a pepper shaker. One reads: *Shoop Shoop A-Doobie*. The other: *Like Scoobie Doobie.*

I grin, then feel a pang of envy. (Of the friendship—not the tattoos, to be clear).

Gripping the small (fake) Chanel purse I have draped over my shoulder, I make my way through the crowd, ignoring the catcalls and whistles but secretly loving them. The dress just paid for itself.

"Good evening, Miss Hart." Jalen, a six-foot-seven former linebacker greets me as I approach the velvet rope barrier.

"Evening, J."

His gaze sweeps me as he pulls aside the rope for me. The crowd groans. Everyone wants access to this exclusive elevator.

"May I say you look ravishing tonight."

"You most certainly may." I wink, inhaling the scent of his cologne. Jalen wears the best cologne. Definitely not Victoria's Secret. "Thank you. It's my birthday."

"Well, a big fat happy birthday to you, then." Using the keycard chained to his wrist, he illuminates the screen next to the elevator. "Big plans?"

"Yes. I'm taking two weeks off work, starting tonight, and I've got the entire left side of the dessert menu being delivered to my room in exactly," I glance at my watch, "two hours."

The elevator door opens, and I step inside.

"Well, what a coincidence." He grins, blinding white teeth against deep ebony. "That's the exact time I get off."

"What?" I cup my hand to my ear, mocking deafness. "I can't hear you. I'm sorry, I can't—"

Jalen chuckles as the door slides closed.

I tap a screen on the elevator door and type in the code that was sent to my secure email thirty minutes ago. On a subtle chime, the elevator descends, passing the floor that houses the exclusive club that everyone thinks the elevator leads to, and dropping several floors below street level to an uber-exclusive underground bar that only the wealthiest and most powerful people know about.

When the doors open, the scent of sandalwood drifts into the car—the Dungeon's signature scent.

I don't recognize the guard, and this alarms me a bit. The Dungeon isn't the type of place to go alone, or at least, to be unknown by the staff. It's not that it's unsafe; it's that the men here have an inflated sense of ownership of everything around them, including the women. I've visited enough times that most of the staff know me—but not tonight.

A man steps out of the shadows as I hand my identification to the doorman/guard, watching me closely. I glance at the gun on his belt.

Something is different about tonight.

"Ballroom 107, Miss Hart," the monstrous man says in the deepest voice I've ever heard. "Down the hall, to your left, then make a right at the tee. You'll need a code to get inside." He presses a button, and a tiny card prints from under the lectern he is standing behind. "This number will be invalid in ten minutes. If you leave the ballroom, you'll need another card to get back in. Do you understand?"

"Yes. Thank you."

Usually, I take my time walking down the long red-carpeted hallway, appreciating the artwork and chandeliers that hang from the ceiling. Tonight, however, I'm eager to get to my post, and even more eager to get back to my room.

There is yet another guard outside of Ballroom 107. This one, however, is wearing a tuxedo and looks far less intimidating. I recognize him as Timothy, a frequent staffer.

"Good evening, Miss Hart." He smiles warmly. "You look stunning."

"Thank you. What's with all the beefed-up security tonight?"

Timothy shrugs. "They never tell us, and honestly, I don't ask. May I escort you inside?"

"No thanks."

I beeline it to the bar, scanning the dimly lit room as I do. Different night, same scenery.

The multiple-level ballroom is sparse with dozens of men in either tuxedos or fancy suits, and Barbie-sized women hanging on their arms, dripping in gold, diamonds, implants, and fillers. Cigar smoke floats on the candlelight. The focal point of the room is a roped-off poker table. Vacant, for now.

I take note that my red dress is the exact color of the carpet in the room. Kismet? Or a fashion disaster? I'm not sure which.

On my first-ever visit to the Dungeon, I was awestruck—and honestly, intimidated. But I soon learned that everyone who comes here is the same. Shallow, ostentatious elites living in a world dominated by material things. Well-groomed, carefully curated humans primed to take over the earth, here for no other reason than social status and profit. They are polite and cultured to your face, and vicious behind your back.

I can't say that I don't respect them, though. I do. It takes discipline to obtain and maintain that kind of wealth. It's just that when I speak to them, I feel as though I've landed on another planet. A fish out of water, I can play the part—and I play it well, if I do say so myself. Some nights I pretend I'm the lead actor in a Broadway play. Some nights I'm a real estate heiress, and others, the daughter of a tech CEO.

Tonight, however, I'm just going to be me. It is my birthday, after all.

"Miss Hart, good evening. I was hoping to see you tonight." Harold, the five-foot-one, seventy-something bartender slides a martini to the woman in front of him, then meets me at the end of the bar.

"Hey, Harold." I smile warmly. "How's the shoulder?"

The old man shrugs, rotating his right cuff. "Good as new. My last therapy session was two weeks ago."

"Good for you. No more sidewalk scooters for you, then?"

"No, ma'am. I've made a vow to never ride one of those things again." He jerks his chin to the far corner of the room where a group of men sit on leather couches. "Your man is here; did you see him?

"I did. Is Carlos behaving?"

I glance over my shoulder to where Carlos sits in a cream Giorgio Armani suit, one long leg crossed over the knee, a Scotch in his hand. His long brown hair is pulled back in his signature ponytail, and his skin looks even more tanned than usual. He sits with the aloof swagger he's known for, hardly paying any attention to the men around him.

"So far, yes. He just bought a few Cubans for himself and his crew. So far, that's all he's spent money on. I think they're about to start the poker game. Will you be joining him at the table?"

"No. I'm only here to ensure Carlos behaves."

"I heard it's a half-million buy-in tonight."

"Exactly." I roll my eyes.

Harold chuckles. "Carlos would be broke without you."

No—*I'd* be broke without me. Carlos's money is basically my money.

"By the way, you look stunning tonight. When are you going to let me take you on a date?"

I take in Harold's injured shoulder. He certainly fits my type: in need of help. I think of all my ex-boyfriends, and how, in every relationship, I stayed entirely too long. Why? Because I am a fixer-upper. Guilty as charged.

"Harold," I say with a smile, "I'd bore you to death. Trust me on this."

"Not looking like that, you wouldn't."

I snort, then sigh. "Is that all it takes these days, Harold? A skintight cocktail dress and a pair of Spanx?"

"In this town? Yes. But you see, Miss Hart, those women and their Spanx come and go as easily as the money in this room. Intelligent, polite, genuinely kind women like yourself are rare and meant to be worshipped."

"Okay, fine. You got me. I'll date you. Hell, I'll marry you if you keep talking to me like that."

"Perfect. How about we start by me buying you a drink. What would you like? The usual? Lemon Drop martini?

I smile. I have grown very fond of this man. "Yes, please, and let's make it a double tonight."

"A double, huh? What are we celebrating?"

"My birthday."

"No kidding! How many years of life are we celebrating?"

"Twenty-something." I wink. "And that's all I'll say."

Harold chokes. "My daughter is older than you."

"Family dinners will be awkward, then."

He laughs, then turns toward the couple stepping up to the bar. "I'll be back with that martini—and some champagne."

"Thank you."

I lean back in my chair, twisting the gold ring around my index finger.

Another birthday.

I sigh, tip back my head, and stare at the ceiling.

Wouldn't it be wonderful if something great happened tonight?

Seven

Astor

"I'M COMING DOWN WITH YOU," Cillian insists as we stride to the elevator, sidestepping the never-ending flow of drunken bachelorettes.

"They won't let you in."

"It's worth a shot. I can make myself invisible and be ready if you need me. Whoever you're meeting with knows there's no way in hell Astor Stone would go anywhere without security. He's got to be expecting it."

I don't argue because Cillian is correct. In fact, I want our host to know I'm not alone. That I will not follow his, or anyone's, orders. He, or she, wants something from me, and they won't kill my wife until they get it, whether I'm solo or have an army behind me. I've handled enough criminals to know this.

We're greeted by a monstrous man named Jalen, who, although I don't recognize him, knows exactly who I am. After checking identification, he gives me a card with a code and directions to the Dungeon.

Cillian passes this checkpoint.

The mirrored elevator drops us below ground level and opens to another man as imposing as the one upstairs.

"Astor Stone," he says, and just like Jalen, this one also knows who I am before I introduce myself. "You're early, but you're in luck. Your party is already here."

This time, I am not asked to show ID. Instead, I am asked to spread my arms and legs for a weapons check.

Cillian shoots me a wary glance. I give him a slight nod—*it's okay.*

I expected this.

Guard Number Two joins the party and pats me down, removing the pistol from my waistband. The gun is placed in a small safe, produced from behind a lectern.

"Your weapon will be stored in this safe until you leave. Please enter a passcode followed by the pound key. Only you will know this code, so please don't share it with anyone. Your weapon will remain under my guard until you return."

"Isn't that a reassuring thought." I key in a code.

"Thank you," he says. "Right this way."

Guard Number Two intercepts Cillian. "Sir, you're not on the list. Only Mr. Stone is permitted past this point. You can wait here."

I shoot Cillian a look over my shoulder when he begins to protest.

His fists clench at his sides. Watching me, he begins pacing like a wild animal.

I turn my back.

"Did you have a good flight over?" Guard One asks me.

"It would have been better if I knew who I'm meeting tonight, or at least what I'm doing here."

"My apologies, sir. My boss demanded complete discretion, as I'm sure you understand, Mr. Stone."

"Though I know little about your boss, I understand that

he weaponizes abusing women to lure his enemies. I suggest you either find someone else to work for or keep a close eye on your own."

The guard looks at me, a moment passing between us.

He refocuses on the path ahead. "You'll be playing poker this evening."

"Let me guess, the winner gets my wife. Well then, whiskey will be needed. Who do you talk to about getting a drink around here?"

"There is a barman at your disposal, sir, as well as every brand of liquor you can imagine. I believe the game is meant to begin the moment you arrive. Here we are. Ballroom 107."

A tall skinny kid offers his hand. "Good evening, Mr. Stone. My name is Timothy. They are expecting you."

As the guard disappears down the hall, the ballroom doors open.

I spot him immediately, sitting across the room, Scotch in hand.

Carlos Leone.

Eight

Sabine

I **FEEL** a shift in the air the moment Astor Stone walks into the ballroom. Like a hurricane sucking every molecule of energy into its vortex—if the vortex were made of flames, that is.

All eyes turn to the savagely gorgeous man in a navy suit.

The room falls deathly silent.

I am faintly aware of Harold's whispers of warning, but I cannot tear my focus away from the most darkly handsome man I have ever seen.

The rumors are true—and then some.

His body is tall and lean, his stride commanding and confident. A brooding sense of danger swirls around him like black smoke. Everyone moves out of his way, like Moses parting the Red Sea. The women gape like awestruck tourists viewing a priceless sculpture in an art museum, while the men hold on to them a little tighter.

His face is what strikes me the most—a contrast of razor-sharp jawline and soft, rounded, lush lips that make me lick my own. His eyes are as dark and perilous as night, slitted with a focus and intensity that reminds me of an animal seeking its prey. His hair is pitch-black and mussed just enough to suggest he doesn't give a damn what you think of him.

In short, Astor Stone is a mesmerizing combination of danger and sex appeal.

The moment my heart begins to beat again, I pull from memory what I know about the man.

Astor Stone, the reclusive founder and CEO of Astor Stone, Inc., is the only son of Evelyn Stone, an infamous New York district attorney who died tragically in a plane accident years earlier. There's not much about his father, and it's rumored he didn't have one present during his childhood.

Astor Stone, Inc. is an internationally renowned private investigation firm that handles cases from society's most elite and powerful. Rumors are that Astor is a cold, brutally savage businessman. For years, every top magazine and television network has tried to get an interview with him, multiple times. He declined every offer.

Rumors also say he's a billionaire.

I remember seeing a picture of Astor that went viral years ago after he made a rare public appearance at a charity gala for inner-city single mothers, where he donated five hundred thousand dollars. The mysterious Astor Stone was all the talk for months after that. Facebook groups formed around him, memes, GIFs; he was every woman's fantasy, and the envy of every man.

Then, like a ghost, he disappeared again.

He's older now. The sparkle is gone, replaced by a darkness that seems to scream from his soul.

The entire room watches him stride across the red carpet, steadfast and confident.

Across the room, Carlos stands, followed by his men, and I

see then that he is the center of Astor Stone's focus. And also, that both men do *not* look happy.

A tingle of warning slides up my spine. I don't know what's happening, but whatever it is, it's big.

Astor and Carlos meet on the elevated platform that houses the poker table in the middle of the room. No hands are shaken, no pleasantries exchanged. Only a few hushed words are shared between the men, as tense and rigid as their posture.

I look around at the crowd. Everyone appears to be as clueless as I am.

I turn to Harold and whisper, "What the hell's going on?"

"I don't know, but I'm assuming this is why the security has been so tight tonight."

Carlos snaps his fingers into the air. The dealer steps onto the platform, wearing a tuxedo with a red bowtie. Four others follow, all men wearing tailored suits, luxury watches, and designer wingtips. They look like replicas of Carlos himself. Then the area is roped off from us peasants below.

Astor takes a seat across from Carlos, facing me.

Our eyes meet like a clash of thunder. Goose bumps race up my arms, and my stomach flutters with a burst of butterflies.

He looks away, but then quickly back as if he needed just one more peek. This time, his gaze bores into me, shrewd and assessing. My heart stutters, followed by a rush of heat through my body. A visceral reaction.

The dealer momentarily steps into our line of sight, yet when he moves aside, Astor's gaze is still on mine. The intensity of it takes my breath away.

I swallow hard.

The dealer kneels beside Astor, demanding his attention. After a bit of back and forth, the dealer offers Astor a tablet, allowing him to transfer his buy-in into an assigned account so that he can join the game. Once satisfied, the dealer stands and addresses the table.

"The game is no-limit Texas Hold'em Poker. Each player at the table has deposited a five-hundred-thousand dollar buy-in. When the game is over, the winner will receive the pot via electronic transfer. During the game, please don't hesitate to raise your hand if you need anything, at any time. Our gracious host, Carlos Leone, has reserved a table barman and multiple waitresses who are at our disposal for the evening. We will take breaks every ninety minutes. If you leave the room, you will require a new passcode to get back inside. Are we all ready to begin?"

Carlos flicks his hand into the air. Though he's addressing the players, his focus is on Astor.

"In addition to the money," Carlos holds up what appears to be a hotel room keycard, "the winner gets what's being held in this room."

Astor doesn't react, his expression remains cold and stoic —but the tension in the room is stifling.

The game begins.

An hour passes quickly. Drinks have been served to the players, along with appetizers including shrimp, caviar, and baked brie with figs. Very fancy.

Carlos empties his plate, while Astor doesn't indulge in a single bite. His appetite appears to be fixed on something else —*me*. Our eyes have met countless times over the hour. So much so that I haven't moved from my spot for fear it will stop once I do.

I know the look, the linger. Astor wants me to know he's looking at me—and only me. And he also wants everyone in the room to know he's looking at me.

Remember what I said about the men who frequent this bar and their inflated sense of ownership, especially when it comes to the women? This is a perfect example. Astor is all but claiming me, the equivalent of a dog peeing on a tree.

But this time, this brazen egomaniacal advance doesn't bother me. In fact, it's making me hot as hell. So hot that my panties are damp under my dress.

Carlos has played carelessly, thereby losing many hands, spurring him into a pissy disposition that has required a new Scotch every half hour. Soon, I'll demand that the waitress cut him off. Astor, on the other hand, is an exceptional player.

The room, including myself, has been transfixed by the competition between the two men. Everyone else at the table appears to be a prop.

By the second break, I've had three glasses of champagne, which has given me a heady buzz. The game is down to three players—Carlos, Astor, and another gentleman. If Carlos keeps playing like he is, he's going to lose all his money, which means it's time for me to step in and do my job.

I grab my purse, cross-body it, and with confidence fueled by alcohol, diamond-studded fuck-me heels, and Astor Stone's ceaseless attention, I sashay across the room and onto the platform.

Astor's gaze follows me like a magnet.

I round the table, moving behind Carlos. Still watching Astor, I lean into Carlos's ear, and in no uncertain terms tell him to straighten the hell up.

Carlos swats away my hand.

Astor straightens, the muscles in his neck tightening.

When I begin to walk away, Carlos snaps his fingers to regain my attention. "Get me another drink."

I turn and cock a brow. "I will the moment you begin making better decisions."

Shocked and embarrassed, he surges from his chair. Astor does the same, sending his chair flipping back and tumbling off the platform, taking the red rope along with it and knocking down several pillars and a tray of appetizers.

The crowd gasps. A woman screams.

"This game is over." Astor's deep voice cuts through the noise.

"Leave us," Carlos demands of the crowd.

When no one moves, Carlos turns and opens his jacket, displaying the pistol on his belt. "I said leave us!"

The room is emptied almost immediately. Even the waitresses and Harold hightail it out. *Thanks a lot, Harold.*

The music stops.

"Lock the doors," Carlos demands of the doorman.

It is now, me, Carlos, Astor Stone, and three of Carlos's guards. Astor is alone. It's him against everyone else—and the odds are *not* in his favor.

This is also when I realize something very dangerous is going on here, and I'm caught, quite literally, in the middle of it. I take a step back, distancing myself from Carlos, but stop at the edge of the platform. I've seen him angry countless times but never this unhinged.

"Give me the key," Astor demands.

Carlos reaches into his pocket and tosses the keycard. Astor catches it in midair.

"She's not up there, though." A smug smile plays on Carlos's lips.

She?

She who?

"Where is she?" Astor growls.

"She's dead. Your wife is dead."

Nine

Sabine

WIFE? Dead?

What?

I didn't even know Astor was married.

My lips part and my heart begins to pound, little red flags screaming at me to get the hell out of this room—ASAP.

Carlos continues. "She killed herself, Astor. My men found her with a wastebasket liner over her head, tied at the neck. She suffocated herself to death."

Astor remains totally still like a statue—and it's absolutely terrifying.

Carlos tosses a photograph onto the poker table. It's of a woman lying on a bathroom floor, her long blond hair fanned around her head like a spiderweb. She's as pale as the nightgown she's wearing. Her eyes are closed, her lips a sickening blue. Next to her is a plastic bag.

Carlos then flicks a diamond ring into the air. It bounces several times on the table before settling right in the middle of the picture. Her wedding ring, I presume, based on the size of the diamond.

Astor glances at the photo. He plucks the ring from the table, slides it into his pocket, and then refocuses on the room in a way that suggests he's taking account of how many men surround him, and where each exit is.

"Where is she?" He refocuses on Carlos.

"Cut into a dozen pieces, chilled in a cooler."

My jaw drops. Still, not a twitch from Astor.

"I did you a favor, Astor." Carlos spits. "That woman was a miserable little slu—"

Like a flash of lightning, Astor leaps over the poker table.

I scream.

The men rush the platform, guns drawn.

Carlos lunges backward, but instead of attacking him, Astor grabs me, whirls me around, and yanks me to him while pulling a knife from his sock.

When he presses the blade to my throat, everyone freezes. I'm too stunned to breathe.

Carlos signals his men to stand down.

The guards discontinue their advance but keep their pistols pointed at Astor's head—and me, for that matter.

"You will regret this, Carlos. I promise you that." Astor's eerily calm voice vibrates through his hard chest, where he has me pinned. "By the time I'm done with you, you will wish you were dead."

"Let her go, Astor," Carlos growls. "She's not part of this."

"Neither was my wife."

His *wife*.

Astor jerks me into movement and begins dragging me across the room. I stumble in my heels, my knees giving out from both imbalance and fear. My eyes go wild, frantically looking back and forth between Carlos and his men.

Why aren't you helping me?

Why aren't you doing anything?

"If anyone makes a move—if anyone follows me out of this room or calls the police; if anyone breathes the wrong way—I slit her throat right here, right now."

My heart feels like it's about to explode out of my chest.

Why isn't Carlos helping me?

"Call your guards," Astor says. "Tell them to let us walk out of here without one word."

I stare at Carlos as he contemplates this—actually *contemplates* my *life*. Finally, Carlos pulls his phone from his pocket and messages the guards.

I am spun around and pushed out the door. The knife is lowered from my neck, and Astor's fingers splay into mine, gripping my hand so hard I wince in pain, half expecting one of my bones to pop.

"One word from you and I will kill you," he growls into my ear. "Do you understand?"

I nod, a whimper escaping my lips.

We fall into step together, hand in hand, striding down the same hallway where, hours earlier, I'd mused about how bored I was with my life.

We approach the first guard, a different one from when I checked in. I recognize him as one of Carlos's right-hand men. Lex something. He's watching us closely, his tattooed, calloused hand on his gun.

My body tenses, fearing he's about to kill us both.

He doesn't. Instead, he hands Astor a safe.

Astor inputs a code and retrieves a pistol, which he hides under his jacket. After that, we're allowed to pass, though it's obvious he's not happy about it. We go through two more checkpoints. Jalen is gone, replaced by another guard. He was my only hope.

We step out of the elevator and into the bustling lobby of Caesars Palace. Hand in hand, I follow Astor's lead as he slows to reflect a casual meander. We're smiling, laughing, kissing, and not a single person in the room knows that the man holding my hand has just threatened to kill me. It's like an out-of-body experience.

Out of nowhere, it seems, a monstrous man joins us, tall and muscular and even scarier than Astor. A tattoo peeks out from under his suit collar, giving me major mafia-kingpin vibes.

He offers me the briefest of glances before falling into step with us like everything is totally normal. Astor calls him Cillian.

We're led to a stairwell, where Astor and Cillian exchange a few hurried words, none of which I can discern due to the sound of the blood rushing through my ears.

Still gripping my hand, Astor jogs us down the stairwell several levels, then we enter an elevator that I didn't even know was there.

The mirrored door slides closed.

I stare at the reflection of the man next to me, gripping my hand.

Astor Stone, CEO, billionaire, sex symbol.

Astor Stone, kidnapper.

I blink.

What *the hell* just happened?

Ten

Astor

"YOU OKAY?" Cillian asks.

I drop into the leather recliner as the jet lifts into the air.

He sinks into the seat next to me, loosening his tie. "I asked if you were okay."

I don't respond.

"You are not made of steel, Astor, no matter how hard you pretend to be. The only woman you've ever married, and the only woman you've had a child with, was just kidnapped and killed. You have to be feeling something."

"I feel nothing."

He gives me a pointed look. "You did this when your mom died, and when everything happened with Chloe. You don't address death, and it's going to eat you from the inside out."

"My job is death. My entire life is death. Listen, Cillian. the bottom line is this—it's done. Just like this conversation."

I look away, swallow the knot in my throat, and close my eyes for a moment. My chest is tight, my hands clammy, and bones vibrating with adrenaline. I feel like I'm about to burst through my skin and rip apart everything in my path.

Grief is manageable. Yes, it's a cold and callous way to look at the end of life, but for me, it is the only way. Guilt, however, is a hundred knives severing my internal organs all at once.

Breathe, Astor. Fucking breathe.

Cillian is updating me on the men we still have stationed on the Strip, but the words aren't penetrating.

Breathe, motherfucker, breathe.

I focus on his voice and slowly bring myself back to center.

". . . so now I need to know who the hell this Carlos Leone guy is."

I wipe my palms on my slacks. Where to even begin?

Cillian glances back at the woman he gagged and tied to the seat in the back before takeoff. He sucks in a breath and sinks low into his seat.

"That's the same look my mother used to give me before she'd whip me with a belt."

I glance over my shoulder.

One diamond-studded heel is lying in the center of the aisle, the other dangling from a cherry-red toenail. Her mind-numbingly tight dress has ridden up her thighs, which, I'm sad to say, she's remedied by squeezing shut.

My gaze slides up her soft, tanned legs to the little shad-owed V between the dress and the crease of her thighs, and then to a trim waist and pair of perky, round breasts that make my dick twitch. To the long black hair that I want to fist, to the pair of red lips that make me want to chew off my own arm. To the cute button nose, and finally, to those hooded blue eyes that drew me in like a siren's call.

The moment I saw this woman, I had to have her. Period. It was like finding something that I'd been desperately looking for my entire life but didn't know I was looking for it. When our eyes met, one single word materialized in my head—

Mine.

During the poker game, I couldn't keep my attention off her. *Here I am*, her aura called to me. *You've finally found me.*

In the most inappropriate ways, and at the most inappropriate time, this stranger dominated me. It was both unnerving and incredibly intriguing—and sexy as hell. I can't remember the last time someone distracted me to the point that they had an advantage over me. This made me want her even more.

Though now, I'm guessing the attraction is no longer mutual, because the blue eyes that once held such longing are now murderous. Cillian's mother must have hated him.

I clear my throat and look away.

"Remind me again why you took her?" Cillian mutters.

"Because you'd be planning my funeral if I hadn't." I flatten my palms on my thighs to keep from fidgeting like I want to. "Also, she's going to be my ticket to get Valerie's body back."

Cillian takes a moment to speak. Only he knows about the clandestine trip to the location of my mother's plane crash, where I spent eight hours sifting through rubble in the pouring rain to find just one of my mother's bones, so that I could give her a proper burial. Only Cillian knows that I sat outside the medical examiner's office for eighteen hours straight, from the moment my daughter's body arrived, until the moment she was released to us.

Cillian thinks I don't address death. I do.

I bury it.

"How old do you think she is?" He takes another glance over his shoulder.

I shrug. *Jesus*, it's hot in here.

"She barely looks eighteen. It makes me uncomfortable."

I shift in my seat.

"Do you think she's Carlos's daughter?"

"Mistress, probably. Maybe wife."

"My bet's on his daughter. What's her name?"

I shrug again.

Cillian gapes. "You don't know the name of the girl you just kidnapped?"

"I'm sorry, I didn't know we had kidnapping protocol. Anyway . . ." I dismiss him with a wave of my hand. "Talk. She can't hear us."

He settles back. "I was asking about Carlos. Tell me everything. I know nothing about him. Start at the beginning."

"Carlos and I go way back."

"How far back?"

"High school."

"No shit?"

"No shit. He's always hated me—maybe I should say we've always hated each other. One of those ridiculous school-age rivalries."

"How did the rivalry start?"

"I fucked his girlfriend."

"That'll do it."

"Carlos and I both grew up the same way—dirt poor, in the slums of Brooklyn, with massive chips on our shoulders. The difference was that his grandparents had money. Carlos's mom was an addict. Eventually, the grandparents adopted him and his brother, Antonio, and moved them to the Upper East Side. We went to separate colleges but would run into each other from time to time. When my mother was elected district attorney, she was responsible for getting his brother locked up for tax fraud. Antonio killed himself in prison. She received several death threats after that, but none were verified. I threatened Carlos."

"So, this goes a lot deeper than sleeping with his high-school girlfriend."

I nod. "Not long after that, Carlos's grandparents died,

and he turned his inheritance into a real estate empire, buying and flipping lots in Las Vegas, where he settled. I haven't seen the bastard for years."

"Here's what I don't get." Cillian frowns. "The poker game was set up so that you could win Valerie back, right? But she killed herself before the game. So, why would he follow through with the game if she was already dead?"

"To mess with me. That's Carlos. He's a trivial little shit, a tit-for-tat kind of guy. I have no doubt he just wanted to see my face when he showed me her picture."

"That's messed up." Cillian rubs his chin. "Why kidnap her in the first place?"

I look away.

Cillian leans forward. "Astor, what did you do?"

"You know how I've been dabbling in real estate lately?"

"Yeah . . ."

"Well, I had my eye on a lot in Vegas."

"Let me guess, one of his lots?"

"*Almost* his. I paid a building inspector to, let's just say, exaggerate the faults of the high-rise he was using as collateral to buy the lot. When the deal fell through, I swooped in, bought the property, and then had his high-rise shut down for code violations. He sold it for dirt cheap, then I immediately bought it from that buyer and bulldozed it down." The corner of my mouth twitches. "Want to know what the building was named?"

"What?"

"The Antonio."

"You are a coldhearted son of a bitch."

"He shouldn't have threatened my mom."

"You're a twelve-year-old, do you know that? A stinky, pimply, insolent child wrapped up in overpriced Christmas paper."

I flick a piece of lint from my sleeve.

"Well, one thing I do know is that he's going to want *her* back." Cillian jerks his chin to the back of the fuselage. "She's obviously valuable to Carlos, considering he let you go, so that you wouldn't kill her."

"Agreed. That surprised me too. Find out everything you can on her—do it now."

"On it." Cillian begins to stand, but I grab his arm.

"I meant research on your laptop. Don't touch her. Give her a minute."

He cocks a brow. Cillian doesn't miss much.

I look away.

"She did have a purse on her," he says, popping open the overhead storage. "I took it off of her before tying her up."

As Cillian retrieves the black Chanel from the top rack, I'm vaguely aware of the grumbles of disapproval from the back. Curse words, though it's hard to tell through the gag.

When I open the purse, my first thought is how women can fit so many things in such tiny little bags. I hand Cillian her wallet, then sift through the other items.

"Her name is Sabine Hart," he says.

Sabine.

"She lives in Vegas, is an organ donor, and—holy shit—today is her birthday."

This gets my attention.

Cillian chuckles. "Wow, what a terrible birthday."

"How old is she?"

"Twenty-seven, today. Damn. I would have sworn she was younger than that."

I inwardly cringe. I could be her father . . . and why does this bother me so much?

He continues. "Credit card, credit card, debit, Starbucks card, spa card, and . . ." He frowns. "Some loyalty card from a place called Titty Titty Bang Bang."

I snatch the pink card and study it. Relief washes over me. She's not a stripper . . . but no less sexual. Interesting.

"It's a sex-toy shop." I toss it back.

Cillian wiggles his brows.

"Stop."

He laughs. "Okay, what else you got in there?"

I begin filtering out the contents, pretending that we're not going through her purse with the sick interest and excitement of a child opening a stocking on Christmas morning. No matter how large a man's ego, a woman will always remain a mystery.

- One tube of lip gloss: *Candy Apple*
- One tube of cosmetic concealer
- A toothbrush (but no toothpaste, which I find odd. Why have a brush without paste?)
- A flosser (Used—gross.)
- A tube of perfume named *Revenge*
- A small bag of honey-roasted peanuts
- One pack of cinnamon gum
- A handful of old cinnamon gummies (the little red bear kind) clinging to the bottom. Stuck to those is a small, crumbled sticky note. The handwritten script is faded and barely legible. It reads: *Money for lunch on the counter. You've got this. Love you.* Signed, *Mom.* I slide this one into my pocket.
- Next up, a tampon. I toss this to Cillian as if it were a ticking bomb. He scowls and swats it away like a gnat, sending it rolling down the aisle, landing next to her Louboutin. We don't dare look back.

- And finally, a smartphone, locked with a passcode, of course.

"Want me to go scan her face to unlock it?" Cillian asks.

"No. I told you to leave her alone."

He stares at me.

I sniff.

"Well . . ." Cillian clears his throat and refocuses on the driver's license in his hand. "I've got a place to start my research." He grabs his laptop. "I've got five hours. Plenty of time."

"No, we're not going back to New York. I'm not leaving this area until I get my wife's body and then punish Carlos accordingly. I want you to figure out where he is, contact him, and tell him I'll return Sabine as soon as he delivers Valerie's body."

"The address he sent the original email from has already been shut down, but I'll find a contact. When do we kill him?"

"Let me figure that out."

"Where are we going?"

"My little cabin in the woods."

"You have a cabin? Where?"

"On the outskirts of Tahoe National Forest."

"In Lake Tahoe?"

"North of it, but yes, around there."

"A mansion in the woods, then. Good. I could use some fresh air." He begins typing. "I'll have something on her shortly. What are you going to do?"

I glance in the mirrored ceiling at the girl tied up in the back. "I'm going to have a drink."

Eleven

Sabine

I HAVE BEEN GAGGED, restrained, tied to an airplane seat, then dragged into the back of an SUV, and tied up once again.

Did I mention birthdays are the worst?

We've been driving for hours now, well, technically, Cillian is driving, and I'm tied to the backseat. We're following Astor, who's in a midnight-blue Aston Martin. Because of course he drives a midnight-blue Aston Martin.

I'm guessing it's somewhere between 2:00 and 3:00 in the morning. I have no clue where I am or where I'm being taken, only that I'm going there against my will.

I have been kidnapped. _Kidnapped._

Never, in my wildest dreams, did I think this day would end up like this.

Over the course of the drive, my view from the backseat window has changed drastically. What started as interstate and suburbia is now a thick, endless forest. Translation: the middle of nowhere.

One thing is for certain. Mr. Billionaire Ass-hat Stone has an army at his disposal, at all times, day or night.

From the moment we boarded the private jet in Vegas to the moment we landed at wherever we are, people were waiting for us, eager to attend to our every need. Correction—*Cillian and Astor's* every need. I'm no more important than the discarded champagne bottles in the trashcans.

I have to pee. I'm dying of thirst. My wrists hurt from the zip-ties, and my head feels like it's caving in on both sides. I'm hypoglycemic and hangry, a very, very dangerous combination —for those around me, to be clear. In short, I am out-of-my-mind livid.

I've desperately tried to piece together an understanding of what happened tonight, and more importantly, why. This is what I've come up with:

- Astor and Carlos have some sort of beef with each other. (Duh).
- This beef has led to the horrific death of Astor's wife, and also the realization (for me) that Carlos has a much darker side than I could have imagined.
- I, being in the ultimate wrong-place/wrong-time scenario, have been kidnapped by Astor Stone, taken as collateral until he gets his revenge—I'm guessing, anyway. Basically, I'm bait, intended to lure Carlos to Astor, where Astor will then kill him and likely dispose of me in the same way.
- I have not been physically harmed (or worse), which means this isn't a dark-Mafia torture-the-captive scenario. There's my bright side.
- But in terms of being rescued, I am screwed because the only people who would miss me are my work colleagues. But because I'm technically

on "vacation," they aren't expecting me back for two weeks. There's my downside.

The vehicle begins descending a long, paved driveway that cuts through endless trees. Tall wrought-iron lampposts line the driveway. A gentle fog creates an orb around each light, reflecting off the black asphalt, wet from a recent rain. It's a jarring contrast to the Vegas Strip where I was just hours ago, though it feels like a lifetime.

I sit up in my seat, craning my neck to see what's ahead. Distant lights twinkle through the darkness. A house.

Finally, the trees open up to a large circular driveway.

A sign reads: STONE MANOR.

I gape at the log cabin beyond the driveway, nestled between towering pines. It's not large but is stunning, none-theless.

The entry is an A-frame walkway that leads to a pair of massive wooden doors with brass handles. The home is made of both log and multi-colored stone, blending seamlessly with the nature around it. Sweeping windows are everywhere.

The home is fully lit, which surprises me, considering how late it is.

Standing next to the front door like a sentinel is a tall, muscular man wearing a fitted black T-shirt and khaki tactical pants. His hands are clasped at his waist, next to a gun on his belt. He doesn't move as we approach, but I have no doubt he knows we're here.

Security, I guess.

Astor's car skids to a stop in front of us. He exits it, and strides inside without so much as a look over his shoulder, leaving the front door standing wide open. The guard closes it.

A rush of cool air scented with pine sap and lakeshore sweeps inside the cab as Cillian opens my door.

Goose bumps prickle my skin and, instinctively, I take a

deep inhale, my body unable to resist the fresh, earthy scent of real nature. I can't remember the last time I breathed real air that didn't smell of motor oil or pot.

The scent of water is strong, and I realize that this is not just a regular cabin in the woods. It's a lake house.

Cillian helps me out of the SUV while I wrestle with the hem of my teeny-tiny dress. Note to self: Never get kidnapped in a miniskirt.

"Welcome to Lake Tahoe," Cillian mutters, his first words to me.

Tahoe. I've always wanted to visit—but not like this.

Barefoot, I tiptoe across the cold stone walkway, still secure in Cillian's grip.

The guard eyes me coolly. There's something inherently lethal about the man, something that tells me he'd shoot first and ask questions later.

Cillian greets him as "Leo." I make a mental note of the name.

The interior of the lake house is as stunning as the outside.

Unlike its cold, callous owner, Stone Manor is warm and inviting. The aesthetic reflects Nordic architecture with long redwood beams against bright white paint, and splashes of indigo and cobalt to tie it all together. Plush brown leather couches, a massive stone fireplace, and all the upscale amenities. The focal point, however, is the view, illuminated by soft outdoor lighting.

I'm awestruck.

Floor-to-ceiling windows frame sloping pine-covered mountains that disappear into an endless lake. A full moon hangs low in the sky, its glow dancing on the black water below it. I imagine the view is stunning in daylight.

I am guided through the great room and down a hallway to a pair of wooden double doors. Cillian swings them open and clicks on the light.

The bedroom is larger than my entire Vegas apartment. Decorated in the same color palette as the living room, it boasts a four-poster bed and a generous sitting area in front of (yet another) fireplace. A copper soaking tub peeks from behind the cracked bathroom door.

"Make yourself at home."

The door slams shut behind him and locks from the outside.

I whirl around, my gag still secure, hands still restrained.

What? He's just going to leave me like this?

Panic jolts me into action. I lunge across the room and kick the door repeatedly, screaming until my throat burns.

It's no use.

Chest heaving, I turn around and stare at the room.

Are they seriously going to leave me like this?

Claustrophobia begins to mix with anger. My chest tightens, and suddenly it's hard to breathe.

What the hell have I gotten myself into?

And who *the hell* does Astor Stone think he is?

Twelve

Anonymous

CAREFUL TO STAY behind the tree line, I focus the binoculars, zooming in on the bay window that allows for the widest view of the bedroom.

I watch as she tries to unhinge her gag by hooking the fabric on the corner of the bedside table and yanking upward. Over and over she does this, tears streaming down her face. I can practically hear her screaming.

Next, she attempts to unlock the window with her bare toe, ripping her nail in the process, based on the wail that rips from her throat. Lastly, she tries to sever her binds by frantically rubbing them against the bathroom door frame.

When all efforts have failed, she begins pacing the room, mascara-stained tears rolling down swollen red cheeks.

I study every inch of her. Such an ugly, ugly creature.

While most probably see beauty, I see a foul black aura swirling around her like a cloud of stink. She's a troubled, weak woman. Pitiful.

Resigned, she walks to the window and stares into the dark night.

For a moment, I think she sees me. Adrenaline surges through my veins, and I shift my focus to the pistol tucked in my waistband.

I hold completely still, knowing my black balaclava and matching clothing make me almost invisible in the shadows.

Five seconds pass, six, seven. Finally, she turns away.

I slip deeper into the forest, creeping from tree to tree until I see him.

His pain is palpable, even from this distance. Still in his suit, he paces his bedroom, jabbing his fingers through his hair and clenching his fists. Like an animal, manic and unhinged.

I shift back to the accompanying bedroom. She is now trying to claw her way out of the binds.

So much pain, hate, and anger between them both.

I have to fight the urge to sneak in through the window and hit her. Break her nose, her jaw, blacken her eye, all while she's restricted and unable to defend herself.

A thrill comes over me, my pulse kicking.

I imagine grabbing her hair and slamming her face into the window, over and over until it shatters, the shards slicing through her cheekbones, into her eyes.

She gives up once again and drops onto the edge of the bed, where she slumps over and stares at the floor.

Such a useless woman. Such a waste.

My hand finds the folded picture that I keep in my pocket. I rub my thumb against the sharp edges.

A face, blurred and glassy, appears in my mind.

I pull the photo from my pocket, lower the binoculars, and stare down at the little girl with blond ringlets.

Licking my lips, I trail my fingertip along the curves of her face, her hair, her little body. The colors are faded from how many times I've done exactly this.

I tuck the photo back into my pocket and resume my place behind the binoculars.

"Soon," I whisper, tapping the pistol with my other hand. Soon.

Astor

"WHAT DID YOU DO WITH HER?" I demand, stepping into my office where Cillian has already set up shop.

"I locked her in the bedroom next to the master—yours, I assume. She's still gagged and tied."

I blink, my stride faltering.

Cillian scowls. "Don't give me that look. I don't know what the hell to do with a kidnapped woman."

"You don't know what to do with any woman, Cillian." I round to the back of the desk.

"*Exactly.* So, you handle her. Or have Leo handle her."

"Leo manages my properties, not my women, and he has plenty to do right now with the list of groceries and amenities you've demanded."

"Might as well live it up while I'm here. He's put on weight since last I saw him."

"Muscle, yeah. I noticed that too. You should have seen him when he first started working for me. The dude looked like the Rock."

"What happened?"

"Hurt his back on his third-ever mission for me."

"And you didn't just let him go?"

"I was looking for someone to manage my properties, so I hired him to do that. It's not an easy job. He works in solitary and is on-call 24/7 to prepare any of my properties before my arrival, and to get whatever I need while I'm there."

"What's it like to have an ego the size of Texas?"

"It's almost as exhausting as this conversation. What have you dug up on our prisoner?"

A grin tugs at the corner of Cillian's lips. "Well . . ."

"Well, what?"

"She's interesting."

"I doubt that."

"She's a genius."

I snort.

"Seriously. She got her master's degree in mathematics from University of California Berkeley and has made a name for herself in the math world."

"Sounds riveting."

"She's been nominated for a handful of national awards from the American Mathematical Society and the Mathematical Association of America. After graduating college, she moved back to Vegas—her hometown—and accepted a position with Sloane and Associates. She works there as a financial analyst." Cillian arches his brow. "In a nutshell, she's not just a pretty face."

"Hadn't noticed."

"Bullshit. The woman's a smoke show, Astor."

I grunt. "What else?"

"She's not married, and neither is Carlos. Which means she's not his wife. And FYI, Carlos's been married three times. His latest divorce was finalized last year. Oh, and he doesn't have any kids."

"I highly doubt that."

"Well, if he does, he didn't claim any of them."

"She's his mistress, then."

"Likely so. Also, she has some money."

"How much?"

"Seventy-five thousand in a savings account, and almost two hundred fifty thousand in stocks."

I can't hide my surprise.

"I'm guessing playing the market is a hobby of hers, considering she's a math whiz. But it's weird. Aside from random exuberant shopping sprees, she lives lean and invests most of her money."

"Surprising from someone who's only twenty-seven."

"I thought so too. Your twenties are when you're supposed to make all sorts of bad decisions, especially financially."

Frowning, I lean into the screen and scan the multiple hacking programs Cillian has open. "So, hang on, something's not adding up. How much does she currently make as a financial analyst?"

"Bingo. That's where things get weird. She only makes fifty-three thousand there, which she spends mainly on bills and groceries and stuff—her rent is astronomical. And the extra money doesn't come from her family; they're both dead and came from humble roots." He points to the screen. "But look here. She gets random large deposits from the same bank account. Fifty thou here, thirty thou there. She got one for seventy-five grand a while back, almost two years ago."

"Who from?"

"An offshore account connected to a fake business named Blum and Levy, Inc."

"A shell account?"

"Yep. She's definitely into something that's not entirely legal."

"That has Carlos written all over it." I straighten and begin pacing.

"Yeah, I thought so too. It could be bribe money. He's paying her to keep her mouth shut about their affair."

"This still doesn't explain why she's so important to him. Why he'd let me go to spare her life."

"Maybe he loves her."

I snort. "Yeah, right."

Cillian looks over his shoulder and studies me. "People kill for love, Astor. It's a real thing, even though you haven't experienced it."

"Have you?" I ask incredulously.

He looks away, and I get the sense that there's a story there. Though Cillian has been working for me for years, I've never asked about his personal life—and this reminds me what a shit friend I am. God, I hate myself.

"Anyway," he says, steering away from the topic of love, "I agree with you that she's probably his mistress, but I think he spared her life because he loves her. How could he not? She's a hell of a catch. Smart and insanely gorgeous."

"Oh, there's a catch, trust me."

"Want me to find it?" He grins, wiggling his eyebrows.

"*No.*" I respond far too quickly.

Cillian whistles.

"Stop. Don't. It's not like that." I cut him off before he can speak. "Now, what have you dug up on Carlos?"

"He's gone dark."

My jaw twitches. I expected this.

"One of the mercenaries we had stationed at Caesars found one of Carlos's guards, tied him up, and interrogated him. Got nothing."

"He must pay his team well. Where is the guard now?"

"Still tied up. They're just waiting for your orders to release him."

"Tell them to get a valid contact number for Carlos, and once it's confirmed that it's good, they can let him go."

"Will do. What are you thinking?"

I turn my back. "I'm going to give Carlos forty-eight hours to deliver Valerie's body in exchange for Sabine's."

Cillian follows me to the window, where a few yards away, under the watchful glow of a security light, a small pink cross spears up from the dirt.

"Is that . . ."

"Yes. I'll bury Valerie next to her." I clear my throat, turn away from the window, and crack my knuckles. "Anyway. Tell Carlos if he doesn't respond, we'll kill Sabine."

Cillian nods.

"What else do you have?" I ask.

"She has no criminal record, has never been married, and has no kids. Anything other than that, you're going to have to give me a bit more time digging."

"Do it. I want to know everything about her."

"Hey, I have an idea." Cillian leans back in the chair. "Why don't you just go ask her yourself?"

With a sniff, I stuff my hands into my pockets. "Good idea."

Cillian grins like he's won a battle. I suppose he has.

"I'm going to jump on a call with the guys holding Carlos's man. Once we've got a good contact number for him, I'll let you know. Also, what room do you want me to stay in?"

"Wherever you want. There are two bedrooms on the opposite end of the house, past the kitchen. One has its own outside entrance."

"I'll take that one. Is anyone else here aside from Leo?"

"No, and he won't stay the nights."

"What about Pri?"

I glance at my watch. "She should be landing in three hours."

"What did you tell her?"
"That we have a guest."

Fourteen

Sabine

INSTEAD OF WALLOWING IN VICTIMHOOD, I've decided to use my rage to cut through the plastic ties that bind my wrists. Having tried every sharp edge in the bedroom (and failed), I've moved to the bathroom, where I'm using the corner of the marble vanity.

According to the crystal clock on the armoire, it's now four in the morning. I am sick with exhaustion. My skin is clammy, my pulse fast, my head swimmy, my stomach turning. I need food, water, and sleep, but know none of that will come until I get out of these restraints.

With every passing hour, I grow more and more angry at the men who took me—and at the one who let me go. Clearly, Carlos is not the man I thought he was. It stings to admit that he threw me away so easily. What a fool *I* am. I'm both embarrassed and ashamed for being so naive.

I'm close to going into full-on rage mode when the *click* of the bedroom door lock pulls my attention. I straighten and freeze.

Swift, heavy footsteps cross the hardwood floor.

I expected Cillian. Instead, Astor Stone appears in the bathroom doorway, still wearing his suit and looking as irresistible and smug as ever.

I lunge away from the sink and rush him, my face beet-red from the fury simmering in my veins.

"Get this gag off me," I shout through the fabric, though the demand is slurred and garbled.

Unaffected by my outburst, Astor regards me closely, sweeping me from head to toe like I'm some rare, newly discovered species he's trying to figure out. It's a different look from the one I received when he first saw me at the bar. That one could be summed up in one word: heat. This one is more . . . cautious interest.

Under the harsh light of the bathroom, the difference in our ages is even more apparent. In the ballroom, I didn't notice the silver streaks of gray at his temples or the thin lines around his eyes. Astor Stone is all *man*—all ego and money and the kind of confidence that only comes from life experience. While I, on the other hand, could very easily pass for his daughter. I wonder if he notices this too.

He pulls a switchblade from his pocket, and with jarring speed and accuracy, slices the gag from my face.

The fabric tumbles down the front of my red dress, and it's then that I see the hem has ridden all the way up my thighs, stopping just below my ass. God, I *hate* this dress.

"How dare you." My lips are dry and numb, my voice like sandpaper. "Who the hell do you think you are? I have done nothing to you—and cut my damn wrists free."

"I will after you answer a few questions."

"I'm not answering anything. I don't deserve any of this. I want no part in whatever's going on here."

"You should've chosen a better lover then."

"*Lover?*" I squeak.

His jaw twitches.

"Lover? You're talking about Carlos?" A crazed, maniacal laugh bubbles out of me (mildly embarrassing). "Are you serious? I'm his *business partner*, you idiot—not his lover."

A perfectly sculpted brow arches, and I get the sense Astor's not used to being called an idiot. Well, that's too damn bad. I am a woman who has been pushed an ocean's length past her limit.

"His *business* partner?"

"Yes."

"What kind of business do you two exchange, Miss Hart?"

Hart. He knows my last name. Of course he does.

"That's another thing." I want to jab him in the chest with my finger, but my hands are still bound. "How dare you go through my personal things right in front of me. I want my purse and my cell phone back immediately."

"Not possible, but I can assure you both are safe."

"If you don't let me out of here, I'll escape."

"Also not possible. Every interior room in this house locks from the outside. Same with the windows."

Who else has he kept prisoner inside this house?

"Answer my question," he says. "What kind of business do you and Carlos exchange?"

I hesitate. My place in Carlos Leone's life is not something I'm prepared to discuss—with anyone. But I've spent a lot of time stewing over how Carlos did nothing to help me while Astor held a knife to my throat. So, screw it. Carlos obviously doesn't value me or my life.

"I handle Mr. Leone's financials. Confidentially."

"Bullshit. He's not on your client roster at Sloane and Associates."

"That's correct." *How much does Astor know about my life?* "Mr. Leone is not a client of mine. What we do is more, ah, behind the scenes. Off the books. I manage his personal assets."

"His *illegal* assets, you mean."

"Yes." Defiant, I cock a brow. I highly doubt Billionaire Stone's tax returns are squeaky clean.

"Explain."

"Why?"

Astor folds his arms over his chest. The suit fabric pulls against what appears to be a pair of cannons for arms. He's still holding the knife.

Again, I find myself hesitating, but figure if I give Astor the information he needs, he'll let me go. Probably. Maybe.

Probably not.

He blinks slowly, his patience waning.

"Mr. Leone hired—"

"Stop calling him that. The man kidnapped my wife."

"So, you two have a lot in common, then," I deadpan.

"Insulting me is only going to get you gagged again, Miss Hart."

"Fine. Carlos hired me to manage and handle his assets—he's terrible with money. I am the only person in the world who has total access to all of his financial accounts. I set them up, manage them, manipulate them as it serves him, et cetera."

"Who is Blum and Levy, Inc.?"

"A shell corp that I set up for him that he pays me through—which you already know, obviously."

"So, if what you're saying is true, you could empty every one of his bank accounts with a few clicks of a keyboard."

"It's more complicated than that, but yes, I could send him into bankruptcy, if that's where you're going with this."

"Or you could send him to jail if you testified against him."

"And send myself, for that matter, so that's never an

option. I willingly signed on to work for him, fully under-standing what it meant."

"Why? Why knowingly accept a job that could get you in trouble?"

"That's none of your business, is it?"

Astor's dark eyes squint, assessing me. He has a way of making me feel small, like I'm standing naked before him.

And why does this turn me on, this over-the-top domi-nant masculinity? Something about this man makes me hot as hell, igniting an unnatural desire I've never felt before. One that makes me want to do very stupid, very bad, very deli-ciously sexual things to him.

What *the hell* is wrong with me? My blood sugar must be negative zero. That's the only logical explanation.

"I'm sure Carlos has restricted your access to his accounts by now," Astor says, pulling me from my highly inappropriate thoughts.

"That's impossible."

"Why?"

"Only I know the passwords."

A heavy silence settles between us. Him assessing, assess-ing, assessing. Me lusting, lusting, lusting.

Get it together, Sabine.

I tilt my head to the side. "What are your intentions with me?"

"In simple terms? To use you, Miss Hart."

To *use* me.

"Turn around," he demands before I can speak. When I don't, his voice takes a sharper edge. "I said, turn around."

Like a dog in training, I obey, slowly turning like a balle-rina on a spindle.

Using his knife, he cuts the binds that secure my wrists. The moment the plastic falls from my skin, I spin around and slap him across the face. The sharp pop of skin against skin echoes against the bathroom walls.

I'm as shocked as he is. I don't know why I did it other than I'm hangry, overwhelmed, and out-of-my-mind confused, all at once. I've never hit another person in my life.

There is the briefest flash of surprise, but just as quickly, his eyes narrow. As if someone flipped a switch inside him, his expression heats like fire. *Now* he's looking at me the way he did when we first saw each other—times ten.

He begins flexing his fingers, shifting his weight. The cool, composed Astor Stone is gone. What stands before me now is a wild animal sizing up its prey—and I'm in trouble.

"You cannot keep me here against my will," I say, growing increasingly alert and wary of the sudden shift in him. "I will not be bait in a ridiculous game between two men with egos as large as their bank accounts. I want nothing to do with you, or with this."

My pulse kicks up as my emotions begin to boil over.

"You've kept me restrained for hours. I haven't been able to eat, drink, or pee this whole time. My *God*, I could eat a cow right now—no, an entire *family-size* bag of potato chips. I could drink a gallon of water, and I have a godawful headache. You are going to jail for this, do you know that? You *kidnapped* me . . ."

Though Astor is looking at me, he's not listening to a word I'm saying. His expression has gone so dark that goose bumps ripple my arms, so intense that the hairs on the back of my neck stand up.

I stop talking and stand totally still.

Slowly, he steps forward like a lion about to pounce. My instinct is to run, but instead, I hold my own.

My entire body braces for whatever is about to come, but nothing could have prepared me for what he says next.

"Slap me again."

I blink, rendered speechless by the request. Slap him again? The man wants me to slap him again? What the bloody *hell*?

"Slap me," he growls, his black-as-night eyes boring into mine. His chest is beginning to rise and fall heavily.

I've triggered something in him, something dangerous, something uncontrollable.

Something exciting.

His body begins to tremble. I *feel* the pheromones pouring off him.

"*Again*, Sabine."

The moment my palm connects with his face, his eyes flash with feral electricity. He grabs my shoulders, spins me around, and slams my back against the glass shower wall. My head bounces off the pane, the breath knocked out of my lungs.

I gasp as he pins my wrists above my head.

Fifteen

Sabine

MY LUNGS FEEL CHOKED, my heart like it's about to explode.

I'm pinned against the shower wall, my arms above my head, my wrists held in place by Astor's large, calloused hands. He's tall and hard against me, his body as strong as his presence. His smell, oh my God, his scent is an intoxicating mixture of woodsy amber and pheromones.

He has complete control over me, and I find it insanely sexy.

He lowers his face closer to mine, his eyes filled with both fire and madness. Like an animal tasting its dinner, he licks my mouth.

My brain short-circuits. My lips part.

As if he'd been waiting for the invitation, he spears my mouth with his tongue, sliding it against mine with delicious friction. My focus is split between the fervor of the kiss and the rock-hard bulge pressing against my pelvis.

I melt against him, heat pulsing between my legs. It's as if he's put me under a spell, and all I can think about is how it would feel to have him inside me.

He releases one hand from my wrists and uses it to yank the hem of my dress all the way to my waist. With one swift tug, the strings of my thong pop, and the fabric falls to the floor, tickling my bare legs as it falls. The feel of cool air against my naked skin makes goose bumps appear all over my body.

I am aching for this man.

Astor's eyes lock on mine as his fingers slide between my folds. "You're so fucking wet," he says, barely a whisper.

The only response I'm capable of is a flutter of my eyelashes. I arch into the touch, my body silently begging for more.

His finger slides over my engorged clit, sending a shock wave jolting through my system.

He exhales as if he's found the greatest gift on earth and buries his face in my shoulder.

I tilt my head to give him full access to my neck as he licks, kisses, and nibbles my ear. At the same time, he's slowly drawing tiny circles around my clit, officially destroying my last working brain cell.

To my shock, I feel like I could come—already. But then, as quickly as everything began, his finger freezes at the tip of my opening. He exhales and groans, then lifts from my neck, his gorgeous chiseled face filling my blurred vision.

Except now he looks pained.

Sixteen

Astor

IT TAKES everything I have not to rip the dress off this woman and bury myself between her legs. I'm hardly able to control myself as it is, without being in such close proximity.

If seeing her across the room dominated me, her slap undid me. I'm trembling from the inside out, wanting to fuck her raw, in every humanly way possible, until we are both unable to move.

I want to eat her. To devour every inch of her body.

I want to drink her. Every drop.

I want to come inside her, claim her. Listen to her scream my name over and over and over.

Something about Sabine Hart undoes me, makes me feel possessive and insanely protective, activating the most basic human desire to control and keep what's mine. In her case, what I *want* to be mine.

Mine.

And therein lies the problem, doesn't it? Because people like me can't have a relationship. In my line of work, women are a liability. Women become targets for my enemies. Love is, quite literally, the antithesis of what I do. The Achilles heel.

But damn it all to hell if Sabine isn't the most intoxicating creature I have ever been in the presence of.

Standing inches from her face, I drown in her eyes as they pull me like the ocean, an endless depth of fire and ice. Of pain and wanting. Of my life, or my death.

Her pulse flies under my fingertips. Her cheeks are flushed, her breaths short and ragged.

Mine are too.

I have never felt such a craving before her. In the endless desert that has become my life, Sabine Hart is a sudden mirage of sustenance.

What is this feeling? All I know is that I don't want to let it go—which is the other problem. I have made a deal with the devil. Her body for my wife's. No matter which way I spin it, Sabine's presence in my life is temporary.

So, maybe . . . maybe for one night—for *one* night—I can get whatever the hell is happening inside me out of my system. I can screw her mindlessly and then walk away.

That's all I need. Just one night.

But—no. No, no, no, Astor.

No.

Bad things happen when you take a woman for just one night.

Seventeen

ASTOR RELEASES MY WRISTS, sending my arms falling around my waist like dead weight. "Again," he says, low and menacing.

"Again? W—what?"

It takes a second to realize he's asking me to slap him again.

"No," I reply with exactly zero gumption.

"Again." The word rumbles through his throat. He's trembling again. "Hard this time, Sabine. *Harder*. Make it hurt."

"Why?"

"Because I need a reason to punish you. I need a reason to tie you to the bed and fuck you until you come so many times you forget your own name."

I am completely dumbfounded, unable to respond, unable to think, unable to breathe. I stare at him, gobsmacked.

When I don't slap him, his eyes slowly ice over.

Switch, *off.*

"Smart decision, Miss Hart."

With those words, Astor steps back, shoves me against the shower wall, turns, and walks out of the bathroom without so much as a glance.

My jaw drops. I stare at my flushed reflection in the mirror, unable to process what just happened. The whiplash of it all.

I listen to his brusque steps leave the room.

My heart is racing, my head spinning, my sex wet and throbbing.

The door slams shut.

What *the hell* just happened?

I hear a voice outside the room. Snapping out of my trance, I yank down my dress, dart out of the bathroom, and tiptoe in a jog to the door, then press my ear against it.

It's Cillian. "Whoa, man. You okay, Astor?"

"No."

Astor's angry footsteps fade down the hall.

There's a pause, and when the knob turns, I stumble backward.

Cillian peeks inside. He frowns as he looks me up and down, and I get the sense he's checking to make sure Astor didn't kill me.

Then he shakes his head and disappears, shutting—and locking—the door behind him.

An hour later, there's a knock at my door. I open it just as the manor's sentinel, Leo, disappears down the hallway.

In front of my room sits a rolling cart with a five-course meal.

The appetizer? A family-size bag of potato chips.

The main dish? A sixteen-ounce filet cooked medium-rare.

The drink? Exactly one gallon of water.

The dessert? A bag of cinnamon gummies (the little bear kind) and two painkillers.

Sabine

BELLY FULL, properly hydrated, and headache relieved, I find myself sitting lethargically on the floor, leaning against the bedroom door, doing what all lovestruck girls do—analyzing and dissecting every second of interaction between me and my new crush.

Yes, I said *crush*. Because in this crazy alternate universe I'm now living in, I have found myself undeniably infatuated with the man who just kissed me. Yes, the same one who *kidnapped* me.

Isn't it too early for Stockholm Syndrome? Forget love at first sight, is Stockholm Syndrome at first sight a thing?

And aren't I too smart for that, anyway?

The logical side of my brain is telling me to calm down and be rational about this. That the feelings I'm having are normal and are only because this is the most excitement I've had in years, doled out by a man who is insanely sexy and endlessly rich.

Of course I'm attracted to him. Any woman would be.

And by the way, why does sex have to be so complicated in the first place? So many rules, opinions, proper stages of advancement. Who says it has to be that way? Seriously, who? Why can't a man and a woman just have sex?

As for the illogical side of my brain, well, let's just say it involves a white picket fence.

Yep. I've totally lost it.

I pick at my cuticle (a nasty habit I've had since college) while my mind races.

Astor Stone is a cold, callous, powerful man, but so passionate. It's a heady juxtaposition. He threatened me, kidnapped me, and treated me like garbage. But the way he looks at me, kisses me, the desire, the need, the *fire*, the electricity between us, is undeniable.

And for the cherry on top, the man had a five-course meal delivered to my room, each dish exactly what I'd whined for during our argument.

So, despite the rough exterior, Astor is—dare I say—thoughtful. But also regretful, based on the pained expression after he kissed me. I'm guessing Astor is the type of personality who feels guilt from their inappropriate actions, and then obsesses over it until they do something to ease said guilt. (Hence the five-course meal.)

I have a feeling the term "rage and regret" has nothing on this man. What an exhausting cycle to live in.

As I sit here, replaying the last hour, I keep looping back to Astor's words: *"Because I need a reason to tie you to the bed and fuck you until you come so many times you forget your own name."*

He *needs* a reason. He wants to have sex with me but *needs* a reason. Because he's promised himself he wouldn't?

I get it. There are plenty of reasons why he shouldn't have sex with me. One being that I'm half his age and could be his daughter. But perhaps the biggest being that he just tragically lost his wife.

Or maybe it's not that he needs a reason, but that he needs to justify it, so that in the end, he won't feel guilty.

That's interesting.

I sigh, relaxing my head against the door, desperate for Astor to come back and finish what he started.

No man has ever made me behave the way I did tonight—like a willing and wanting slut with zero shame about it. I've never felt such an instant feral need for sexual intimacy. His touch alone turned me into a completely different person. Confident, uninhibited. I kind of like her.

Sometime around five in the morning, I get sick of myself and all my brooding, undress, and crawl into bed, naked.

Because sleep helps everything.

Sabine

I AWAKE, my subconscious hovering in that dreamless, confused state between sleep and wakefulness.

A man enters the bedroom. I must have heard the door unlock.

The tall silhouette is barely visible in the darkness. It's that time of morning right before the sun rises. *Always darkest before dawn.*

I can't make out the man's face, but there's no question that his full focus is on me.

Am I dreaming?

Without a sound, he crosses the room, stopping next to the bed. I am now aware that I am very naked under the covers.

A lock of hair is swept away from my brow. A knuckle gently caresses my cheek.

I want to reach up and grab his hand, hold it next to my heart. But the touch disappears, and my skin is left feeling cold and wanting.

The man sits in the armchair facing the bed. He leans back, settles in, and watches me.

I'm not scared. In fact, it's the opposite. I feel very, very safe.

Am I dreaming? I must be. Because why would Astor watch me sleep?

Speak, I think. *Say something.*

Instead, my eyes drift closed and sleep finds me once again.

Twenty

Sabine

DAY ONE OF MY CAPTIVITY: I slept like a rock for five hours.

Now, with clearer focus, I am sitting on the edge of the bed, listening to the rain tick against the window, trying to make sense of what has happened to me. I have been kidnapped and am the prisoner of a man whom I crave like the last box of Girl Scout cookies—Thin Mints, to be clear. Everything else is a jumbled mess of confusion.

I wonder what this day will bring, what Astor intends to do with me, how long he plans to keep me. And last, but not least, if he plans to kiss me again.

As if all this isn't enough to send a woman teetering on the edge of a mental break, mixed with these emotions is the sick realization that outside these walls, no one knows I'm gone. I have no friends, no family, and my boss thinks I'm on vacation. No one misses me. No one is asking why I haven't responded to text messages, or why I haven't come home.

It's eye-opening and very depressing.

A loud, brusque knock at the door sends my heart jumping into my throat. I grab the thin gray throw blanket from the edge of the bed, surge to my feet, and wrap it around my naked body just as the door unlocks and opens.

A woman breezes into the room, carrying a canvas bag over her shoulder. Her mood is almost tangible, as sour as the weather outside. While I'm shocked to see a woman at all, she is not surprised to see me. In fact, she's annoyed and making a concerted effort not to look at me.

Yes, I'm insignificant. *I get it.*

Older than me by more than a decade, the woman is extremely attractive with smooth caramel skin and long dark silver-streaked braided hair. She's wearing a pair of linen pants and a silk button-up shirt that emphasizes a pair of voluptuous breasts.

She drops the canvas bag on the coffee table in the sitting area and then turns to me.

My stomach drops to my feet.

The left side of her face is mottled with burn scars. The melted skin pulls her left eye downward, and it's the same with her lower lip. The effect is jarring—the kind of injury that's impossible not to stare at. One side of her face is supermodel perfect and the other, revolting.

A low rumble of thunder rolls through the mountains.

I look away but instantly regret it because she probably gets that all the time, and it probably makes her wildly uncomfortable. So, I refocus on her eyes, forcing myself to look there —and only there.

The glare I get in return leaves no question as to what she thinks of me.

"I'll be back in one hour to clean the bed," she says in a clipped tone.

Clean the bed? Is she the maid?

"Are those my things?" I ask, gesturing to the canvas bag.

"No."

"What is it then?"

"Toiletries. Clothes."

"For me?"

"Obviously."

"From who?"

"Astor ordered it to be done."

How nice of him.

"Where is my purse, my phone?"

"How should I know?"

I cock a brow. Okay, so the tone between us has been officially set—and it isn't pretty. Well, I can play this game too.

"Who are you?"

"My name is Prishna, but you can call me *ma'am*. I'm Mr. Stone's personal assistant."

"Okay, *ma'am*, can you please tell me why I'm here?"

"Don't worry. You won't be for long."

"What's that supposed to mean?"

And with that whisper of a threat, *Ma'am* turns and storms across the room.

"Hey!" I yell after her. "If you hate me so much, then let me go."

"Trust me, sweetheart, I wish I could."

The door slams—and locks.

Wow. Day one in Stone Manor and I already have an enemy.

Fantastic.

I turn on a floor lamp and then make my way to the coffee table. Inside the canvas bag is a handful of drugstore toiletries and cosmetics. The foundation and concealer are not my color, but I can make them work. The clothes consist of two pairs of baggy boyfriend jeans, each a size too large, and two ill-fitting sweatshirts—the kind a junior-high basketball player would wear to practice. Finally, two pairs of granny panties—nude—and one bralette, two sizes too small.

There's no question who did my shopping.

I begin folding the items back into place when, across the room, a silver sparkle catches my eye.

Frowning, I walk over to the picture frame resting on the bedside table.

The woman in the photo is in her mid-thirties with long blond hair and a soft pixie face. She's painfully skinny, reminding me of a '90s Kate Moss, but in the same way as Kate, she's uniquely beautiful. She's wearing a white silk dress, giving her an ethereal appearance. She's looking directly into the camera—directly at me. Around her neck is a gold pendant of one half of a broken heart. On her ring finger is a massive diamond. I recognize it immediately as the one Carlos tossed to Astor after showing him the picture of his dead wife.

This is her.

The wife.

Nerves tickle my stomach.

I look over my shoulder at the door, then back at the picture, absolutely certain the photo wasn't in the room when I arrived last night.

Twenty-One

Sabine

BY NOON, I've showered, brooded to the point of self-loathing, and paced the bedroom so many times my feet hurt.

I'm wearing the clothes I was "gifted"—a baggy gray hoodie, a pair of even baggier mom jeans, and a pair of flannel slip-on house shoes I found in the closet. Although I look like a fourteen-year-old boy, I feel marginally better. Definitely more confident than in the red minidress I plan to burn the second I get out of here.

I hid the photo of Astor's wife in the bedside drawer. I can't look at the woman whose husband I just kissed, even if she's no longer around. And I'm still uneasy about the whole thing. I'm certain the photo wasn't on the table last night. So, how did it get there?

Bottom line, I have to get out of this damn room before I lose my mind.

On a whim, I try the doorknob. It's unlocked. Someone must have unlocked it while I was showering.

For a second, I consider making a run for it, but then

remember that I have no phone, credit cards, or vehicle, and also that there is a thunderstorm raging outside.

Astor unlocked my door; I'm sure of it. Rage and regret, and all that guilt. So, I take this as an open invitation to look around my new prison.

Sheets of rain slash against the windows as I make my way down the hallway. The house is quiet with not a single light on.

Where is everyone?

Despite the ominous atmosphere, I am in awe of my surroundings.

I press my palm against the sweeping windows that line the great room. The pane is cool and an outline of condensation forms around my hand.

The view of the lake and mountains is exquisite in the daylight, even through the muted gray of the storm. Massive pine trees line a pebbled walkway that leads to a wooden staircase that disappears down a rocky cliff. Below is a large deck with a boat slip and a covered seating area with a full outdoor kitchen. The lake water is crystal clear, the bottom dotted with large moss-covered rocks.

At the top of the staircase, an American flag whips in the wind.

A patriotic man. Interesting.

Turning away from the window, I survey the room, zeroing in on a framed picture, then another, and another. An entire fireplace mantel of Astor's late wife.

In the middle, a small white candle burns brightly. It's the only light in the house.

I move from photo to photo, my stomach knotting tighter with each image. It's a shrine to her, and it's creepy as hell. In every photo, she is wearing the same half-heart pendant. There has to be at least a dozen pictures of her—*only her*. Astor is not in a single one of them.

Confused, I stare at the pictures, and for the first time, wonder how in love they were. After all, only a man who is madly in love with his wife would have so many photos of her everywhere. Am I stupid for thinking there was a genuine attraction between us? Or am I nothing but a rebound, an escape from the pain?

I turn away from the watchful eyes of his dead wife and follow the smell of coffee to the kitchen. Here I find Leo, the man who was standing guard when we arrived, and who later delivered a five-course meal to my room. He's stocking the cabinets full of food.

"Oh." I clear my throat, unsure if I'm allowed to speak. I'm not up to date on my prisoner/free-person protocol. "Hi."

He slides me a glance. "Hey."

Like last night, his expression is tight and hard, his demeanor rigid. He still has the five o'clock shadow, but today, his shaggy blond hair is slicked back, away from his face. Probably wet from the rain. He looks younger this way, and I wonder how close in age we are.

It would be far more appropriate for me to lust after Leo instead of his much-older boss. But then again, this alternate universe I'm suddenly living in is all Greek to me.

"Thank you for the food last night," I say, daring to move deeper into the room.

"It was ordered to be done, so it was done."

"By Astor?"

"Yes."

"Well, thank you anyway."

Clearly not one for small talk, Leo continues his work as I take in the space around me.

The kitchen is double the size of my Vegas apartment. Thankfully, there are no pictures of Astor's late wife in this room.

I take my time studying the lavish space, the marble counter-tops, the deep double sinks, the top-of-the-line appliances, the copper cookware hanging from the ceiling. I muse over all the wonderful dishes I could prepare in this kitchen, the hours I could spend in here cooking, listening to music, and drinking wine.

What a life Astor's wife had.

Leo closes the cabinet. "There's fresh fruit in the fridge, and the coffee is also fresh. Help yourself."

"Thanks. Do you think it's okay if I walk around?"

"I've not been told otherwise."

"Where is everyone?"

"Astor and Cillian are taking a meeting in Astor's office, and I'm not sure about Prishna. Have a good day."

I regard him closely as he gathers the grocery sacks. I find it interesting that Leo doesn't seem fazed that I am here, that his boss has kidnapped a woman and is keeping her hostage. I get the vibe that kidnapping is not the worst thing this man has seen.

After helping myself to fresh fruit, yogurt, and a delicious flaky croissant, I continue my stroll through Stone Manor, feeling much more clearheaded.

Next to my room are two massive wooden doors that I assume lead to the master bedroom, which I assume is Astor's room. I've been wanting to peek inside ever since Cillian dumped me in the next room.

The door is cracked, and the room appears dark.

Cupping my hand to my mouth, I call out a gentle *hello?* When I get no response, I slowly push open the door.

The walls are filled with stunning artwork, pops of color against deep mahogany walls. Massive plush rugs run over gleaming hardwood floors. More windows, these showcasing the mountains instead of the lake. The focal point of the room is a king-sized four-poster bed bathed in alabaster white.

Clean, slick, and sexy against the dark wood. The room is as impressive as the man himself.

I can smell him, and like Pavlov's dog, respond. A million racy thoughts pummel my head.

I feel both exhilarated and nervous being in his space, knowing I'm getting an exclusive sneak peek into a notoriously private and mysterious man. My pace quickens with my wish to see as much of the room as possible before getting caught.

There are more framed photos in this room. His wife, once again, is everywhere.

Once again, staring into my soul. Once again, making me feel stupid for thinking Astor's advance on me was anything more than an escape.

A sting of jealousy hits me hard and fast, and I almost laugh at how ridiculous I'm being.

The bathroom resembles mine, but larger. Marble, copper, and gorgeous. I open the vanity drawers and am surprised to see drugstore-brand skin and hair-care products. Billionaire Stone probably has unlimited access to the most luxurious brands, but he chooses the least high-maintenance products available. I find this endearing.

I notice that there are no female products anywhere.

The rest of the drawers are much of the same, until I reach the last one.

I squat down and survey the dozen little brown prescription pill bottles. Sleeping pills, all prescribed to Astor. None appear to have been used, or even opened.

A tortured billionaire.

I consider slipping a few into my pocket, but I think better of it and decide to move to the closet. Astor's clothes take up one-tenth of the space. A few suits, a few lounge outfits.

I smell them all.

At last, I come to a dubious door at the far side of the room. It's locked. Frowning, I step back and study the unusually thin mahogany door. I know it doesn't lead to the bathroom or the closet, so, where? I try the knob again, this time twisting hard. The door doesn't budge.

I snoop for keys but find none.

Fisting my hands on my hips, I chew my lower lip and study the lock. Suddenly, nothing in my life is more important than seeing what's behind that door.

A very, very bad decision.

Twenty-Two

Sabine

I JOG TO THE KITCHEN, grab a flat cheese knife from the croissant spread, and hurry back to the master bedroom. I slide the shaft between the mystery door frame, press, jiggle, and *boom*—the lock pops open.

My pulse kicks.

After a glance over my shoulder, I slowly push open the door, completely unprepared for what's ahead.

It's a baby's room, or more accurately, a little girl's room.

I gasp and cover my mouth.

Dolls are everywhere—plastic, stuffed, porcelain, each missing their heads. Some are completely mutilated, lying in a heap of their own stuffing. A leg here, an arm there. Fist-sized holes dot the walls, as if someone punched through the sheetrock, over and over and over again. The paint is a dusty pink, once a beautiful rose color, I imagine, but now dull and bleak. Duct tape runs over cracked windows that are spotted and dirty, hampering the already dim daylight from shining into the room.

A twin-sized bed sits flush against the wall, the pink comforter unmade, suggesting someone has slept in it recently. A pillow lying at the foot of the bed has been slashed repeatedly.

Though my head is telling me to run, I step deeper into the room.

There are many framed pictures, but this time, Astor's wife isn't the only subject. Most are of a beautiful little girl with long blond ringlets.

My heart pounding, I pick up one of the photos. Porcelain skin, white-blond hair, and dark chocolate eyes. The girl is almost an exact replica of Astor's wife, but the eyes . . . they are the same ones that bored into me the night before.

The frame drops from my hand.

Astor's daughter.

The picture shatters on impact, and I swoop down and pick up the broken glass, cutting my thumb. I hardly feel it.

My mind races.

Astor had a secret wife, and now a secret daughter. Where is she? And who destroyed her room?

What other secrets does this man have?

A drip of my blood drops on the picture. I swipe it away, then stick my finger in my mouth and quickly gather the broken frame—which would be clear evidence of my snooping.

With two handfuls of broken glass, I stand, whirl around, and run out of the room, closing the door behind me.

Movement out the bedroom window catches my eye.

Outside, Astor is standing with his back to the house. He's wearing a black jacket with the hood pulled up, standing in the pouring rain, unmoving, his head bowed. Alone.

I walk to the window and watch him, transfixed by the growing enigma that is this man. Somehow, I can *feel* his pain.

Rain pounds his shoulders. He doesn't notice.

Thunder rumbles overhead. He doesn't notice.

Slowly, he lowers onto his knees, doubles over, and drops his head in his hands. His body shudders with emotion.

He's crying.

I can now see what he was looking at.

In front of him are two small memorials surrounded by dozens of blooming daffodils. One is marked with a small white cross, obviously new. The other with an identical pink cross, dingy and faded.

One belongs to his wife, the other to his daughter.

Twenty-Three

Dear Butterfly,

My heart aches for you. Every hour, every minute, every second.

When I close my eyes, I see you, I hear you, I smell you, for you have been forever imprinted on my soul.

But I can't see you.

I can't hear you.

I can't smell you.

I can't touch you.

The absence of you is felt in every inch of this house, in the vacancy of my soul. In the death that now resides in my body, the nothingness that has become as much of me as my beating heart, in the hole that materialized the moment you left.

The moment I failed you.

The moment I failed myself.

The moment I died inside.

The moment my life, whatever it is now, became defined by grief, regret, and guilt.

I wish it had been me instead of you. Oh God, how I wish that.

I was not ready to say good-bye, in the same way that I was not ready to say everything I should have.

I will never forgive myself. Not now, not ever. Instead, I am now wholly prepared for my death, my fate, the end of whatever became of me the moment you forever left my life.

I welcome death because then I know the pain will be over.

I miss you more than words can say.

I hurt more than a million swords.

I love you, dear butterfly.

My butterfly.

I love you,

I love you,

I love you.

Yours forever,

Astor

Twenty-Four

BETWEEN THE MYSTERIOUS picture of Astor's dead wife in my bedroom, the ravaged baby's room, and then watching Astor sob in heartbreak, I have been jarred back to reality.

This is not a fairy tale. This isn't the beginning of the greatest love story ever told. This is a house of pain and death.

Finding an escape—*immediately*—has now become my sole focus. I don't care how attractive Astor is or how electric our kiss was, something creepy is going on here—and I want no part in it.

I hurry to my bedroom, dump the broken glass and the remains of his daughter's photo into the trashcan, and hide it with tissues. Then I gather what few belongings I have and shove them into the canvas bag. I don't have my purse, money, or phone, but I can't think about that right now. I have to leave. My instincts are screaming at me.

I rush down the hallway to the side of the house opposite of where Astor is currently having an emotional breakdown in the rain. I pass the kitchen, a library, a media room, and another closed door. Behind it, a woman is crying.

I stop. Backtrack.

The door is cracked, just barely.

Frowning, I peek inside.

Prishna is pacing beside the bed, weeping, muttering angrily to no one. Her hands are clenched in fists, her shoulders hunched, her steps heavy. Her body is shaking violently, her words incoherent.

Sensing me, she stills and looks up. Instead of lunging at me, as I expect, she stares with such an intense hatred that my blood turns to ice.

Her words from earlier trickle through my head. *"Don't worry, you won't be here for long."*

"I'm sorry," I whisper, backing away and quickly closing the door.

Get out, Sabine.

I feel him before I see him.

Astor stands at the end of the hallway, a frightening, sopping-wet silhouette. Though his face is shrouded in shadows, the closed fists tell me he's not happy.

I stand stock-still as he strides down the hallway.

My stomach drops as his face comes into the light. His cheeks are flushed, his eyes swollen and bloodshot—and completely mad. Rain drips down the side of his face. He sees the bag I have over my shoulder.

Shit.

"I want my purse. I want out of this place. Now."

"Do you?"

"Yes."

He grabs my bicep and drags me down the hallway. Stumbling, I pull the cheese knife from my pocket and hide it in my fist.

He pulls me into the library and slams the door behind us. The sound echoes through the quiet house. "Sit."

I'm dropped into one of the leather chairs in the center of the library.

I watch him storm across the room, grab a decanter of Scotch, and chug half the contents in one go.

He closes his eyes, takes a deep breath, then turns to me. "You were trying to run."

"No," I lie.

He crosses the room, stopping at the edge of my chair. "Give it." He extends his palm.

"Give what?"

"The knife in your hand."

"No."

A tense moment passes between us, the electricity between us crackling.

Astor kneels, grabs my knees, and parts them, shoving inside my personal space. His eyes aren't as cold and callous as they were before. Right now, they are dead. Vacant. It's haunting.

He lifts his chin and tilts his neck to expose the throbbing vein. "Then go ahead and kill me."

I can barely hear him over the blood rushing through my ears.

"Do it," he says, seething. "Get it over with."

When I don't move, he grabs my hand and presses the knife against his throat.

"*Do it.*"

"No."

"Do. It."

"No!" I jerk out of his hold and hurl the knife across the room.

It clatters to the floor, shattering the silence between us. My heart is pounding.

"What the hell is wrong with you?" I drag in a shaky breath. "What is *wrong* with you? Just let me go. Do you really think you're going to get away with this?"

His face inches from mine, he asks, "And who is going to come looking for you, Miss Hart?"

The words hit deep, right through my soulless little hermit heart.

"Both your mother and father are dead," he says, his words drilling in. "You have no siblings, no friends. You have no husband or boyfriend. You have no pet inside your shoebox-size apartment to bark or scratch at the door to let the neighbors know you haven't come home. From what I can tell, Miss Hart, absolutely no one will miss you. No one would ever care if you left."

"Fuck you."

His hand wraps around my throat. Squeezing, he leans in and brushes his lips over mine. My body begins to tremble.

"If you ever say that to me again," he whispers against my lips, "I will kill you."

I ignite from the inside out, every sexual sensor in my body surging to life.

"And if you ever try to sneak out of here again, I will find you and I will kill you."

"No, you won't."

The grip tightens, squeezing the breath from me, and all I can think about is how much I want him to have sex with me.

"Try me, Miss Hart."

His lips crash into mine, his tongue dipping inside. But this time, instead of frenzied passion, he tastes me with long, leisurely licks.

I lean into him, increasing the pressure around my throat, and kiss back, swirling my tongue around his, tasting the warm whiskey that coats it. The passion between us is unreal.

Using the hand that's not wrapped around my neck, he

cups the back of my head, fisting my air, repositioning my face so that he can dive deeper into my mouth.

My throat is on fire, my vision wavering, my chest constricting, my sex throbbing.

And just like last time, he suddenly releases me. I am quite literally seeing stars as he stands and brushes off his pants.

"Dinner is at seven o'clock in the dining room."

With that, Astor Stone saunters out of the room, leaving me breathless.

Twenty-Five

Astor

THE WOMAN MAKES ME CRAZY.

I can't think straight, I can't form a sentence, I can't sit, I can't stand. So, I'm pacing my office, trying to dispel the energy that is vibrating my bones, to keep myself from punching a hole in the wall, which is what I really want to do.

I'm sick at the thought that Sabine might have seen me outside. That she might have seen my weakness. My daughter.

I'm embarrassed and confused, mad at her, mad at myself.

What the hell was I thinking? Kissing her in the first place? Then telling her to "go ahead and kill me"—which, in that moment, I meant. Because if she killed me, I'd finally be out of the misery I live in day and night.

And as if that wasn't psychotic enough, I then proceeded to demand that she join me for dinner, because I can't leave her without knowing I'm going to see her again.

Since that kiss, Sabine has dominated my thoughts, then jumbled them up and thrown them into a blender.

I haven't slept. I've barely eaten, barely drank.

I should be thinking of my wife. Grieving my wife.

But I'm not.

Instead, I think of Sabine while I'm brushing my teeth, while I'm showering, while I'm pressing my nail into my forearm. I think of her while brewing coffee, answering emails, on my Zoom calls, on the phone.

This morning, instead of paying attention to the meeting I was in, I doodled her name in a notebook, surrounded by a dozen tornadoes. (I'm sure a therapist would have a field day with that one.) Then I imagined that name tattooed on my chest.

Yes, I am losing my damn mind.

Eyes closed, I take a deep inhale. Like always, Sabine's face materializes, those eyes, those lips. Her expression when I told her to kill me.

On a pained groan, I jab my fingers through my hair. She must think I am a complete psychopath, and she's probably right. I feel like I'm cracking. Something about Sabine makes me question every word out of my mouth, every move I make, every move I *don't* make. Makes me fantasize to the point of pain. Makes me dream. Hope.

Makes me fucking crazy because I know that it can never be between us. Because it never has been before. Because my life is too dangerous to allow a woman into my dark, sick orbit.

I know this because history has proven it to be true. I've lost everyone I've ever truly cared about.

And besides . . . what do I know about keeping a woman anyway?

Twenty-Six

Astor

"WHERE IS SHE?" I bellow to the empty dining room.

It is seven o'clock on the dot, and aside from Sabine's seat being unoccupied, everything is as I instructed.

The room is lit by a dozen candles. The shades are drawn. There are two place settings, one on each end of the dining table. In the center is a display of roses, next to it, a decanter of red wine and two crystal stemmed glasses. The salads are set, which will be followed by a five-course meal, hand-picked by me. This afternoon, I drove for over an hour to find the brand of caviar I wanted, and an extra twenty minutes for roses that didn't look like they'd been run through a shredder.

Prishna steps into the dining room, wiping her hands on her apron. Her braids are up in a bun, her eyes tired. Normally, setting dinner would be Leo's job. But for this, I needed a woman's touch.

"Your guest," she uses air quotes, "is trying to escape."

"She's *what*?" I gape.

"Trying to escape."

"How do you know that?"

"I heard her break the window in her room."

"Why the hell didn't you stop her?"

"Because I don't like her. Plus, it's dark outside."

"What difference does that make?"

"I don't like the dark. Also, it's your fault for not locking her door anymore." She cocks a brow.

It's true. I told Prishna and Cillian to leave Sabine's door unlocked. I couldn't stand the thought of her being confined to a small room day and night.

Actually, that's not true. I'd prefer that because it would mean that she is safe. But I also understand, from experience, that this is not optimal for either party involved.

"I want her out of this house, Mr. Stone," Prishna says firmly. "You can't bring someone into your life. You know that. I will not tolerate this."

"What, exactly?"

"Her. Here."

I shake my head. I can't deal with this right now. "Cillian!"

Cillian steps into the dining room a millisecond later.

I frown. "Where were you? Standing outside eavesdropping?"

"Don't flatter yourself." He blinks. "What's with the romantic dinner? And why are you still in your suit?" His eyes round. "Oh, you've got to be *kidding* me."

"It's none of your damn business—shut up," I snap. "Where's Sabine?"

"Astor, are you trying to impress—"

"Cillian, I swear to God I'm going to—"

"Okay, okay, okay." He chuckles. "I was just coming to find you."

He holds up a handheld video security monitor, which shows a live feed of Sabine climbing down the lattice below her bedroom. Above her, the window is shattered. She's visibly struggling to get through the cover of thick green vines that cover the lattice. Her baggy sweatshirt and jeans keep snagging every few inches. I notice she's barefoot, on top of it all.

"Fucking Christ." I jab my fingers through my hair.

Cillian grins. "It's been fun to watch. She busted the window hours ago, but then decided it was raining too hard to safely climb down. So, she waited, pacing the room like a wild animal. She's something else, boss."

From the kitchen, Prishna slams a cabinet door.

"Why the hell didn't you tell me? Why didn't anyone tell me? What have you been doing?"

"Watching her—and also bingeing Netflix. Hard to say which has been more entertaining."

"I'm going to fire you, Cillian."

"I'm half joking. I've been in my room working. I've got a bead on Leone."

"You do? You know his exact location?"

"Not yet. But our mercs got a valid cell phone number from his guard."

"Did you make contact?"

Cillian nods. "He has forty-eight hours to deliver Valerie's body in trade for Sabine's. I made that very clear."

"Good. I want you to add something to the mix. Contact him again and tell him that if we don't meet within forty-eight hours, I'll have Sabine empty his bank accounts and send him into bankruptcy, and then I'll use every single one of those bills to wipe my ass."

Cillian grins. "You got it." He pulls his phone from his pocket, and while leaving the room, mutters, "This just got much more interesting . . ."

Thinking the same thing, I hurry down the hallway and out the front door.

The storm has moved on, leaving a cool, clear night in its wake. My wingtips sink into the fresh mud as I pass through the garden and round the side of the house. Moonlight washes over Sabine's curvy body as she clumsily climbs down the lattice, ripping through the mess of vines.

Anger, and something else I can't quite pin, rush through me.

The woman is so desperate to get away from me, she's climbing down the side of my house. To where? Where the hell does she think she's going to go? Especially barefoot? Doesn't she know we're out in the middle of nowhere? And most disturbing—is it possible that Sabine is not as attracted to me as I thought she was? Of course she's not. She saw me sobbing like a child.

My hands ball into fists. *Stupid.*

Once on the ground, Sabine frantically smooths the hair from her face and looks around, not seeing me in the shadows. Then she spins around and sprints into the woods.

Damn woman.

My pulse thrumming, I stalk after her, my fists aching to hit something. Long shadows sway against the ground, the moon barely illuminating the dense forest that surrounds the lake house. She's lucky. Otherwise, she'd run headfirst into a tree.

I watch her weave through the dense forest, darting in and out of shadows. The woman is either going to break an ankle or cut open the bottom of her foot.

With each step, I grow angrier and angrier. At her for trying to leave, at her for *wanting* to leave, at me for assuming our connection would be enough to keep her here.

What a crazy thought. I kidnapped the woman, for Christ's sake. What did I expect? That she'd forgive me, fall head over heels in love, and stay with me forever?

Stupid.

For a moment, I lose her in the shadows but then hear, "Shit," followed by a dramatic moan.

Sabine then comes into view, her hands wrapped around the iron rods of the fifteen-foot fence that encases the entire property. Eight thousand volts of electricity hum through the top tier of the fence, though she doesn't know that.

I cross my arms over my chest and lean against the trunk of a tree, waiting for her to sense me.

It doesn't take long.

She spins around. In her teary eyes is a mixture of fear and white-hot anger. I understand this confusing combination. It is exactly what she does to me.

"Get back in the house, Sabine."

Pushing away from the fence, she hobbles angrily to me. If not for the anger and annoyance, I'd laugh.

"Don't ever put your hands on me like that again—"

"Like how?"

Chest heaving, she stops inches from me. Her long black hair falls in messy waves over her shoulders, a green leaf tangled in the ends. Her cheeks and the tip of her nose are flushed pink. Her blue eyes twinkle in the moonlight. I want to kiss her.

"Say you're sorry."

"*What?*"

"Say. You're. Sorry."

"Listen, sweetheart, you're in my house—"

"I will not go back inside *your* house until you say you're sorry."

Her defiance makes me want to tackle her and have sex with her right here on the damp forest floor.

"Say it, dammit!"

I spin around and begin pacing, my nails digging into my palms.

"Say—"

I spin back around. "I'm sorry, okay? I'm fucking sorry!"

I'm fucking sorry echoes through the mountains.

Sabine blinks, as shocked as I am by my submission.

Before she—or I—can speak again, I scoop her into my arms, thankful I don't get a fight. My entire body is trembling as I begin to retrace our path back to the house.

"Which foot?" I growl, looking down at her moonlight-stricken face.

She licks her lips, staring up at me. God, she is so beautiful in the moonlight.

"My right," she whispers. "I might have twisted my ankle."

Her arms tighten around my neck. She lays her head on my shoulder, and we walk the rest of the way in silence, in quiet understanding of the weight of my surrender. Still in shock at it.

"Astor?" she whispers as we near the house.

"What?"

"I tried to escape . . ."

"Yeah?"

"Do you remember what you told me you'd do if I ever tried to escape?"

If you ever try to sneak out of here again, I will find you and I will kill you.

When I don't respond, she says, "Well, I did . . . and you didn't kill me."

"The night is still young."

"Do you know why you didn't kill me?"

"Why?"

"Because you are as attracted to me as I am to you."

Twenty-Seven

Astor

NURSING A GLASS OF WHISKEY, I close out of my email and exhale, staring at the closed door of my office. Due to the unexpected change of dinner plans—i.e., Sabine trying to escape—I've decided to lock myself away and drink my dinner. Which, in an ironic twist, is only making me more irritable.

I'm sorry...

The two words have played on repeat in my head since I said them. I cannot remember the last time I apologized to someone. Probably to my mother, and she's been dead for years.

If Sabine has thrown me off-kilter thus far, I am now officially upside down.

It is a jarring and uncomfortable feeling.

I was so taken aback by my submission to Sabine that I had Cillian deal with her ankle. I regret this, as I seem to regret and question every single thing I do or say to Sabine.

Her ankle is fine, Cillian informed me after I'd texted no less than four times, demanding an update. For twenty minutes, I stewed in my office chair, staring at my phone, not liking how I felt knowing that *he* was tending to her instead of *me*. That he was looking at her, touching her, speaking to her. That she was looking back at him, close to him. Possibly falling for him instead of me?

Now it's all I can think about.

"Goddamn it!" I hurl my whiskey against the wall, shattering the crystal into a million little pieces.

Chest heaving, I lean forward, open a new search, and type: How to get a woman.

A slew of websites pop up that will surely get my computer flagged by the FBI. What the hell is wrong with people? Oh, wait, it's me. I'm the people.

Groaning, I close out of that search and open another:

How to keep a woman.

Same result—a dozen articles with very questionable strategies.

Maybe I'm looking at this all wrong. Maybe "getting" and "keeping" aren't the way to a woman's heart.

Frustrated, I scrub my hands over my face. "You are unbelievable, Stone."

How is it that I can singlehandedly run a billion-dollar business but am rendered ignorant when it comes to the opposite sex?

You are a complete idiot, I type into the search box. These results are actually on point.

After a few deep breaths, I type:

How to be in a relationship

How to make a woman happy

And finally,

How to love a woman

For hours, I pore over articles written by medical professionals and psychologists, engrossed by the content. For hours, I sit in awe of how much I've failed every woman I've ever been with. How unavailable I've been, both emotionally and physically.

No wonder I've never been in love. I'm a self-absorbed asshole with the emotional maturity of a fourteen-year-old. I feel embarrassed. Ashamed. Angry.

I find myself wondering what makes Sabine tick. What her favorite color is, her favorite flower, how she takes her coffee, how she likes to spend a Sunday morning. What I can do to make her so happy that she will never leave me.

Could it be possible?

Could Sabine be my soulmate, if there is such a thing? She makes me feel like there *is* such a thing.

The physical connection between us is undeniable, but that's just sex. Even a blunt instrument like me understands that. What gets me is the way she stands up for herself, the way she doesn't back down from me. The way she can see right through my bullshit.

Sabine is smart, witty, and fearless. And if all that isn't enough, I admire her for accepting a shady job with Carlos. It takes courage, grit, and an occasional bending of the rules to get ahead in this life.

I lean back in my chair, focusing on the article in front of me. One word stands out, one that has been repeated in every article I've read.

Communication.

Communicate, Astor.

Communicate.

The thought is as appealing to me as walking into oncoming traffic.

What if she doesn't like me after I communicate? What if

she runs away, hands over her ears, and then dies on the electric fence because death is better than spending another second with me?

After all, darkness taints every story I have to tell.

Twenty-Eight

Sabine

HE'S outside my bedroom door. I can *feel* him.

I'm now certain it was him the night before, watching me sleep.

He's come back three times since Cillian sent me to my room with painkillers and an ice pack. Each time, Astor's shadow darkens the crack of my open door. He stands there, unmoving and unspeaking, while I pretend not to see him. After a few minutes, he vanishes.

Now, however, he lingers.

The clock reads 11:37 p.m. I'm lying in bed. Moonlight streams through the windows, pooling on the hardwood floor and illuminating the room in a deep blue glow.

I want to scream for him to come to me. Lie with me. *Be* with me.

I don't understand the power this man has over me, but I know that I don't want it to go away. Astor's presence alone lights me from the inside out. Our chemistry is undeniable, my need for him all-consuming. And it's getting worse with each moment we're together, each time we touch. The sexual tension between us is already unbearable. I'm wild with arousal just knowing he's a few feet away, secretly watching me.

My gaze locked on his silhouette, I slide my naked body out from under the covers and sit up taller against the pillow.

He moves, ever so slightly.

Slowly, I spread open my knees, exposing myself to him.

My finger trails down my throat, between my breasts, down my stomach, settling between my legs. I'm already wet.

Opening wider, I dip a finger between my folds, slowly slide in and out, then add another finger.

My gaze never leaves his silhouette, thrilled with the knowledge he's watching me from the shadows. It is the most erotic, thrilling moment of my life. I don't know who this woman is, but I like her confidence, her unapologetic sensuality. I like the power she has over *him*.

Using my other hand, I begin massaging my breast, gently squeezing the erect nipple. Heat begins to build.

Watch me.

Watch me, my beautiful Astor.

Watch me come for you.

I slide the wet fingertip over my clit. A moan escapes me, the sensation spreading through my hips.

Slowly, I circle the sensitive nub, applying more pressure with each stroke. I am so turned on that my body begins to writhe in need.

I feel like I'm starring in my own little erotic movie, my own fantasy. But the best part is knowing what I'm doing to him.

I bite my lip and stroke harder, faster.

Watch me come for you, my beautiful monster.

My breath becomes shallow. The sensation begins to peak. It feels like all the blood has rushed between my legs, the drum-like throbbing building to an almost painful crescendo.

Faster, faster, faster.

I scream his name as I come.

Astor.

Oh God, Astor.

I drop my head against the pillow, pull my fingers up to my belly, and close my eyes for a minute to regain my composure.

When I open them, he's gone.

Twenty-Nine

Sabine

AFTER CLEANING MYSELF UP, I pull on a
sweatshirt and panties, and then crawl into bed. I lie there for
over an hour, daydreaming of Astor and all the things I want
to do to him. Wondering if he's masturbating now, thinking
of me, envisioning me too.

I'm desperate for him.

I've never felt this way in my life. Never needed something
so badly.

My *captor*.

Sighing at the insanity of it all, I roll over, and my heart
jumps into my throat.

On the pillow next to mine lies a pink baby doll.

Its head has been cut off.

Thirty

Sabine

THE MOMENT THE SUN RISES, I am showered, dressed, and striding down the hallway, creepy headless doll in hand.

Today's fashion-forward outfit includes (another) pair of baggy jeans (rolled at the ankles so not to trip over the hem), granny panties, and a white cashmere sweater. The sweater is rather nice, which leads me to believe Prishna included it by accident.

As usual, the lake house is eerily quiet. No television, no music, no voices, hardly any lights on.

I pass the kitchen, ignoring the pull of fresh coffee because I am on a mission. I bang on the door at the end of the hallway.

No answer.

I bang again.

"Prishna! It's Sabine. Open up. We need to talk."

Still nothing.

I turn the handle, surprised when the door drifts open. It was unlatched. "Prishna?"

The lights are off, and the bed is made. A small rolling suitcase lies on the floor, next to a pair of black ballerina flats.

I think I hear something on the opposite end of the house, maybe a door shutting, so I backtrack, veering into the kitchen for a cup of coffee. I'll have to confront her later. It's not like I have much else to do.

The bay windows frame a stunning sunrise. Beams of fuchsia, yellow, and orange spear up from the mountains like a postcard.

I set the doll on the counter. "Stay put," I say to it mockingly, then beeline it to the coffeepot.

I've just added creamer to my mug when Leo steps into the room, startling me. Everyone in this house walks like a damn cat. I wonder if "no noise" is one of Astor's rules.

"Morning." Leo joins me next to the coffeepot to refill his mug.

"Morning." I take a step back, giving him space. He looks much like yesterday, his hair slicked back, wearing khaki tactical pants and a T-shirt. But today, streaks of dirt color his arms, and his boots are caked with mud. He's been outside. Doing what, I wonder?

"Do you know where Prishna is?" I ask.

Leo shrugs, screws on the lid, dips his chin, and disappears down the hall.

Huh.

For a moment, I consider following him, but something outside catches my eye.

At the bottom of the sloped backyard, Astor is standing at the edge of the deck, his back to me. Ahead of him, the rising sun reflects in the lake, long streaks of light swaying gently on the ripples. I watch as Astor strips out of his T-shirt, revealing a chiseled, tanned back and shoulders that look like twin bowling balls. His wide chest fades to a trim, lean waist. I don't need to check to confirm that a six-pack is on the other side.

I don't know why I'm surprised. If there is one thing I can count on, it's that Astor gets sexier every time I see him.

I lick my lips as he slips out of his jeans and kicks them to the side. In nothing but a pair of black boxer briefs, he drops from the deck and wades into the crystal-clear water.

I've never wanted to be a fish so badly. Or ever, really.

After nimbly crossing the large mossy rocks, Astor dives into the abyss.

I notice the outdoor thermostat—48 degrees Fahrenheit. The water must be colder than that.

His strokes are long and fast, and I find myself studying the ripples his body makes in the water. Small at first, then bigger and bigger.

I compare myself to that water. Static and complacent until Astor barges into my life with all his mystery and arrogance. And then, just like the water, I am altered in a way that I am unable to stop. Unable to control.

As I watch the ripples, I wonder if, much as the water does, I should simply give in to it.

Astor fades out of sight. Swimming laps, I assume. Probably a billion—like his bank account.

Sipping my coffee, I consider my own body and wonder what he thinks of it. Is it good enough for him? Am I good enough for him?

Stop, Sabine. Push away the poisonous thoughts. My body is just fine. No man will make me think otherwise. Not even a ripped superhero like Astor Stone.

I sigh and turn to the doll on the counter. "You probably cut off your own head, didn't you? Years living with a man like that would make any woman go crazy. I get it, girl."

I make my way into the living room, wondering what

today will bring. Wondering what *tonight* will bring. The memory of Astor watching me climax sends a rush of heat through my body. I'm afraid that whatever this man does to me, whoever I am with him, is going to become very addictive.

My thoughts shift to the shrine of Astor's wife on the mantel. The woman who, although dead, has a very prominent place in this house.

I study each photo again, and the half-heart pendant necklace she wears in all of them. A gift from Astor? One of many, probably.

I'm envious.

She landed him.

She got him to marry her.

She bore him a child.

I pick up a picture of her in profile, smiling into the sunset.

What was it about her that Astor was drawn to?

There's no mistaking how different she and I are. While my hair is as black as a raven's wing, hers was as white as snow. While I'm curvy, she was skinny—*very* skinny. I'm tall, she was small. Even her smile was perfect, like she spent her entire childhood practicing it. Mine, on the other hand, looks manic half the time.

Astor's late wife was a trophy wife—and this is why I'll never be his.

"She's prettier than you are."

I startle, sloshing the piping-hot coffee onto my hand. I spin around to see Prishna standing too close to me. I didn't even hear her come in.

The sunlight streaming through the window shimmers on the burns on the side of her face.

"Yes," I say, swallowing the knot in my throat and regaining composure. "You're right; I agree with you. She is prettier than me."

"You'll never replace her."

"What makes you think I'm trying to?"

"I can see it in the way you look at him."

"He's a hard man not to admire . . . I'm sure you've noticed too, Prishna."

"I told you to call me ma'am."

"I'm not calling you ma'am."

We glower at each other, two alpha females in love with the same man, while the one who actually got him is forever memorialized in the framed picture that's clutched between my fingers.

"What was her name?" I slide the picture back onto the mantel.

"Valerie."

"How long were they married?"

"They still are."

"What?"

"Not even death could separate them. They were madly in love, Miss Hart. And he still is, *with her*." Prishna nods to the candle. "He lights this candle, just for her."

He lights it. A sick feeling rolls over me.

"He cries out for her in his sleep," she says, the words drilling into my heart. "But you wouldn't know that, and you never will. Because Astor never allows his whores to stay in his bed with him."

Bitch.

I pluck the headless doll from the counter. "Why did you leave this in my room last night?"

Her brows arch, and she appears surprised. Slowly, the anger drains from her face. She clears her throat and deflects from the question.

"It's not *your* room." She takes a step back.

"Correct. It's the room I'm being held prisoner in. Cut the bullshit, Prishna. Why are you messing with me?"

"I'm not."

"You didn't leave this creepy doll on my pillow?"

"No."

"Then who did?"

She takes another step back. Is she scared? Am I sensing fear in her?

I step forward. "Who did this?"

She looks down the hallway, toward Astor's office.

"Astor?" I scoff. "Did Astor do this? Why would he?"

"I didn't say that. But Astor controls everything in the house. If you weren't so blind, you'd see that. I need to go."

"No." I advance, desperate for more information. "They had a child, didn't they? Astor and his wife, Valerie?"

Prishna grunts and turns away.

"And she's dead, right? Their daughter is dead, right? How? How did it happen?"

Did Valerie wreck the baby's room? Driven mad by the grief of losing a child?

Prishna spins around, her gaze turning to ice. "Yes. She's dead, just like her mother. This family is cursed, Miss Hart. The less you know, the better."

Family.

I grab her arm. "Talk to me, dammit. What happened to their little girl?"

"That's none of your business," she snaps, yanking her arm away.

"Why do you hate me so much?"

"Because you're ignorant," she spits out over her shoulder as she stomps away.

I follow, though my head is telling me to let it go. "Of all the things I've been called in my life, ignorant is not one of them, trust me."

"You think you can make him love you." She turns around again, her face flushed. "Hear me, stupid woman. He loves *her.* Only her. When Astor finally gets sick of toying with you, you will be forgotten the instant you leave his sight. He does not care about you, not in the way that you wish he would, and he will never care about anyone like he did his wife."

"*No one would care if you left* . . ." Astor's words echo in my head.

"You are nothing, Miss Hart," Prishna growls. "*Nothing* to him."

With that final jab, she storms out of the room.

My heart pounds as I watch her walk away.

I feel like a fool, I feel uneasy, I feel a little scared, I feel like I want to run.

No . . . I feel like I want to cry.

The moment I get back to my room, Cillian appears in the doorway, all brooding and intimidating like his boss.

My eyes are red and I'm sure my face is flushed, but luckily I hadn't allowed myself to cry—yet.

Cillian frowns at the headless doll in my hand, then at the sweater I'm wearing.

I shake the doll. "Do you know who left this in my room last night?"

"You shouldn't have that."

"No shit! I don't want it! But someone put it here—along with pictures of Astor's wife, and as if that's not enough, I've been hearing whispers in the hallway."

He is stoic, wholly unconcerned and unaffected by my current emotional state. "I don't know why anyone would do that," he says simply.

I snort, then bark out a maniacal laugh. "Okay, well, it must be the Stone Manor ghost, then."

"Astor has requested your presence at dinner tonight. Seven o'clock."

"Has he?"

"Yes. He also wanted me to inform you of the electric fence."

"What electric fence?"

"The one that would have likely killed you if you'd made it to the top yesterday."

"The fence is *electric*?"

"Only the top."

I shake my head. "Bastard."

"Most of the time, yes."

"So, in other words, he told you to tell me not to even think about trying to escape like I did last night when I was supposed to be having dinner with him."

"In a nutshell, yes."

I cross my arms over my chest. "What else did he say?"

"My Catholic upbringing forbids me to repeat it."

I snort, then fist my hands on my hips. "Well, what am I supposed to do until then? There are no televisions in this place, and I don't have a phone or a computer."

Cillian glances outside. "It's going to be a nice day. Supposed to hit sixty degrees. Maybe go outside, take a walk. But stay away from—"

"The electric fence. I got it, I got it." I look over my shoulder and nod. "Maybe I'll grab a book from the library and read by the lake."

"Whatever."

"Hey, Cillian," I ask as he turns away. "What's on the king of the castle's agenda today?"

"He'll be in his office all day. As usual."

"Where is his office?"

"Adjacent to the library."

"Is it protected by electricity too?"

"Depends on his mood." He turns again.

"Cillian?"

"Yeah?"

"I mean this with all due respect, but . . . what the hell is wrong with your boss?"

Instead of the chuckle I thought I'd get, Cillian narrows his eyes. "Be careful not to judge someone without having walked in their shoes, Miss Hart."

I shrink, feeling like I've been reprimanded by my father. "One more question."

"What?" He sighs.

"How long does Astor plan on keeping me here?"

This time, Cillian hesitates, avoiding eye contact.

Finally, he says, "About twenty-four more hours, Miss Hart."

Thirty-One

Dear Butterfly,

I find myself consumed by death. Thinking of it, dreaming of it, fantasizing about it. Wanting it, craving it, needing it.

In a sense, I am already dead. Along with you, the light left from my life.

As I sit here at my desk, writing this letter, I find myself staring at my hands, studying them. They don't look like mine, or the way I remember them before you. It's as if they are someone else's, operating independently of my body.

I feel the same about my feet. My arms, my legs.

Everything is dying around me, detaching from me. My soul is slowly disintegrating, limb by limb, leaving nothing but a body that serves no purpose. Lifeless skin and bones, veins, muscle, and fat. Just insignificant things, like rocks or twigs.

I read once, somewhere, that our bodies serve no other purpose than to be the vehicle for our life. That our soul is our essence, who we really are. Something we can't see or touch but know is there. So, when the soul goes out of the body, it is rendered useless.

This is me.

Does your soul still love me? Wherever your soul is, do you still love me? Do you think of me?

Will I see you again? Somewhere up there? Or is this it?

What a sickening thought.

My God, I miss you, my butterfly. Words cannot describe the pain I feel.

I can't do this anymore. I don't want to. I don't want to live a life without you in it.

I love you. I love you. I love you.

My everything.

My whole entire life.

Astor

Thirty-Two

Sabine

CILLIAN SAID I have twenty-four more hours here. Until what, Astor kills me? Has one of his men take care of me? Or releases me, maybe? *Or* . . . falls in love with me.

The latter is what I've landed on because the former is too unsettling. I've decided that if I have twenty-four more hours with Astor Stone, I am going to make them count.

I feel invigorated by this decision. For once in my life, I am truly passionate about something. Motivated to actually put in effort, to work with purpose. To be triumphant in the end.

This must be the feeling people have right before a major change, I muse. Yes, I want *that*. I want change. I want this passion, every day, for the rest of my life—and I'm going to fight for it.

So, I start by going to the library, to Astor's office, unsure what I'm going to say or do but determined, nonetheless. The door is locked, of course, and I can hear him on the other side, on a conference call.

I linger for more than an hour, waiting.

Waiting.

Waiting.

Impatience finally gets the better of me, and I shift my focus to the vast library that surrounds me. The Stone Manor library houses books from every genre, even erotica. Many are autographed by the author, and many are first editions that I assume cost a fortune. I leave those untouched.

In the end, I choose three books to read outside.

A five-hundred-page biography of some famous World War II veteran. (To help me fall asleep should I try to nap.)

A self-help book that promises a better me in thirty days. (How about twenty-four hours?)

And last but not least, an erotic fantasy. Monster peen, here I come. (Pun totally intended.)

Guess which one I started first.

Cillian was right. It is a stunning spring day. I've been curled on a chaise lounge on the deck all afternoon.

It's the kind of weather that it's cool enough to be in the sun while snuggled under a blanket. The air is fresh, clean, and perfumed with an organic earthy smell that makes me want to frolic around the forest and pretend I have fairy wings.

It's a very freeing place, which is ironic considering the darkness of the home. While the forest feels light and happy, the lake house feels heavy and haunted, an angry energy vibrating through the walls. It's not only that someone is putting decapitated dolls on my bed, or that Astor's dead wife is memorialized in every room, but also that I can *feel* her everywhere. Lingering, watching, displeased by my presence.

I wonder if this presence (am I ready to call it/her/she/they a ghost?) is the reason Prishna looked fearful when I showed her the doll. Does she feel Valerie's presence too? Is that why she was crying and muttering manically in her room?

I can't stop envisioning Valerie in her deceased child's bedroom, dismembering the dolls, slashing the pillows, punching the walls. Such pain. Such madness.

It's unnerving.

And very, *very* nice to be outside.

The hours pass quickly, there under the sun, and it is now late afternoon. I'm in the thick of an MMF scene in my erotic fantasy book when I suddenly get the unmistakable feeling that someone is watching me.

I lift my gaze from the page and focus on the trees that surround the dock. Hundreds of them, dense and heavily shadowed. A million different places to hide. My stomach tickles with nerves.

I tune in to the sounds around me—the water lapping lazily against the shore, the wind rustling through the trees, the eerie isolation of the property.

I set down the book and sit up, then look over my shoulder at the lake house. Though the windows are dark, I see no one standing behind them, watching me.

Where is Prishna? Leo? Cillian?

A flash of black zips past the dock, followed by another, and another.

Bats.

I shudder in disgust. I've always hated bats.

Movement in the woods pulls my attention. For a second, I see someone—*something*—move behind a tree.

I surge to my feet, the book tumbling off my lap, my instincts telling me I'm in imminent danger. Just then, a tiny black bat hits the side of the dock and drops to the deck like dead weight. Writhing in pain, it flaps its wings wildly, and the shrieks coming out of it sound otherworldly.

Get the hell out of here.

I grab the blanket, the books, and turn to the house.

Astor is standing in front of a window, his dark silhouette

large and ominous against the shadowed background of his office.

I freeze and stare at the silhouette, and in that moment, I can't tell if I'm relieved or terrified.

Thirty-Three

Astor

"PRI, ARE YOU MESSING WITH SABINE?" I cross my arms over my chest and lean against the kitchen doorway.

Prishna wipes her hands on a dish towel as she turns away from the sink. She's prepping the dinner I requested she cook tonight for Sabine and me. And based on the sulky expression on her face, she's not happy about it.

"Define *messing with*, sir."

"Sneaking pictures of Valerie into her room, along with a doll's body from Chloe's room. And whispering outside her door. You know, creepy-ass things."

Prishna fists her hands on her hips. "Mr. Stone, why would I do that?"

"Because you don't like her."

"I don't like a lot of people."

I can't argue with that.

She continues. "But that doesn't mean I sneak into their bedrooms with," she uses air quotes, "creepy-ass things."

"You haven't been yourself lately."

"Nor have you."

I can't argue with that either.

"Did you ask Cillian?" she asks, placating me.

"He's the one who told me about it. Sabine mentioned it to him."

"Did he do it?"

I roll my eyes. "Cillian has his own demons that occupy 99% of his time."

Prishna shrugs. "Well, if he didn't do it, and I didn't do it, Sabine is either lying or we have a ghost in this house."

Ten minutes later, I find myself in my office googling—you guessed it—ghosts.

I have officially lost my mind. And I blame it all on Sabine.

But the thing is, ever since Cillian told me what Sabine said, I realized that since coming back to the manor, I've felt particularly unsettled too. More than usual—and not all because of Sabine's entry into my life. I get a weird, uneasy feeling as I walk through the hallways, the library, the master bedroom. An instinct, though I can't put my finger on what it's trying to tell me.

My ghost search takes me all over the Internet. Apparently, there are many people who believe in the afterlife.

Eventually, I land on something called a vengeful spirit. This is the spirit of a dead person who seeks revenge for a cruel, unnatural, or unjust death. The spirit will haunt the dealer of their death for months, sometimes years, following them wherever they go.

Considering I've made a career of killing people, it's safe to assume that vengeful spirits occupy a mile-wide radius of wherever I am standing. The article then goes on to say that, in certain cultures, a vengeful spirit is also defined as one who failed to receive a proper burial ceremony.

Valerie.

I reach for my drink and notice my hand is unsteady.

Must be tired.

I take a long sip, staring at the screen, the only light in the room.

Before I can stop myself, I click into the surveillance video of Valerie, days before she was taken, wandering the garden in the middle of the night. Before she died in an *unnatural way* and *never received a proper burial ceremony.*

A vengeful spirit . . .

Like a moth to a flame, I lean into the monitor, my chair squeaking against the silence of the room. I study her pale face, white nightgown, and long snowy hair.

Mesmerized, I draw even closer to the screen, feeling my pulse increase.

Valerie's lips are moving as if she's talking to someone. Her steps are unsteady, and she appears to be agitated. She lifts a long skinny arm and points to something just out of view of the camera.

Suddenly, she stills, completely frozen. Not even a strand of her hair is moving in the wind.

Is she scared? Or is she listening as someone responds to her?

"What is it?" I whisper, my heart pounding.

Like whiplash, her face turns to the camera, her eyes glowing unnaturally in the light.

I lurch backward, almost tipping over the chair.

Thirty-Four

Sabine

I BEELINE it to the kitchen the moment I step inside and out of the prying eyes of whatever—or whoever—was watching me from the forest. I was hoping to find Astor. Instead, I find Prishna there, surrounded by mounds of fruit, vegetables, and baked goods. She's washing veggies in the sink, her back to me.

Maybe she was the one watching me? From the windows, perhaps.

I toss my blanket and books on a chair and join her at the counter. "Hi."

Her disapproval of my presence is clear by both the scowl on her face and the sudden vigor with which she scrubs the potato.

The unforgiving natural light from the window illuminates how severe the burns are on the side of her face, and again, I find myself wondering what happened to her. What is her story?

"Is Astor still in his office?" I ask.

"Yes."

"Do you know if anyone is outside? Cillian or Leo?"

"It's not my job to handle their schedules."

"Were you outside?"

She rolls her eyes, gesturing to the activity on the counter. *Right.*

A moment stretches between us.

"Can I help?"

I refuse to allow this woman to intimidate me. As obvious as it is that Prishna hates me, the fact of the matter is that she is the only other woman in the house and knows much more about Astor than I do. In short, I want to pick her brain. Her miserable, rude little brain.

The spread on the counter appears to be ingredients for a very nice meal, and it hits me—Prishna has been put in charge of cooking my dinner with Astor tonight.

A wave of sympathy rolls over me. This woman is being forced to go shopping for, and cook dinner for, a woman she despises.

I pick up one of the washed tomatoes. "Cubes or slices?"

"Cubes," she mumbles.

I begin chopping. "I have a deal for you."

"What's that?"

"I'll cook this meal if you let me pick out my next round of clothes."

"No."

"Why?"

"Astor's orders."

"I won't tell."

She snorts. "Astor knows everything; I already told you that."

"Certainly not *everything*."

She cocks a brow. "*Everything.*"

"Well, do you promise not to throw a potato at my face if I

tell you I'm two sizes smaller than what you're buying for me?"

"Tell him that."

"Why?"

"Mr. Stone picks out your clothing."

"What?"

"Trust me. If I'd been given the task, you'd be wearing a trash bag, dear."

"He's picked out *everything*?"

"Yes. Every morning, I'm handed a detailed list and told to deliver everything on it. He makes every decision in this house, and his others. How many times do I need to tell you that?"

I consider the cheap toiletries and mismatched cosmetics. A man definitely wouldn't choose the correct color of concealer or be able to discern the correct size. Because men are, well, men.

Huh.

"So, is it safe to say your boss is a total control freak?"

Prishna says nothing, probably for fear of being reprimanded. I fill the silence by recalling an article I'd once read about controlling men.

- Isolates you from others
- Possessive
- Can be abusive
- Makes decisions for you
- Doesn't take no for an answer
- Demanding
- Snoops into your life
- Invades your privacy
- Uses intimidation

Check, check, check, check, *alllllll* the checks.

"Why do you work for Astor?" I ask. "It's clear you're not loving the tasks you've been assigned."

"That's none of your business, and you're cutting the cubes too small."

"Sorry."

As we fall into a steady rhythm, chopping and stacking, I study her.

Such an angry, unhappy woman. Why? Why work for such a demanding boss, especially if she hates the job? At first, I thought it was because she was in love with him, but now I'm not so sure.

So, why stay?

Then, like a wrecking ball, it hits me.

"Prishna . . ." I set down the knife and tomato and turn fully to her. "Are you here against your will too?"

Her hand freezes and she looks at me, taken aback by the brazen question.

"Did Astor kidnap you, like he did me? Is he forcing you to work for him?"

Heavy footsteps come down the hallway. Prishna and I turn as Cillian passes the doorway, frowning at something on his cell phone.

"Ugh, *Cillian*." Prishna groans at the trail of mud he's leaving on the hardwood floor.

"I'll help." I grab a dish towel and follow her to the hallway.

Shaking her head, Prishna kneels to pick up a clump of dirt. As she bends over, a necklace slips out from under her collar. Dangling from it is a gold pendant in the shape of one half of a broken heart.

It's the exact necklace Astor's wife is wearing in each of her photos.

<h1 style="text-align:center">Thirty-Five</h1>

Sabine

I AM SPINNING with so many conspiracy theories that I don't care if I get caught as I sneak into Prishna's bedroom while she's busy in the kitchen.

After seeing the pendant, I was so shaken that I politely excused myself under the guise of a headache. Though it wasn't really a lie as my head is suddenly pounding. The sleepless nights and unfamiliar surroundings are catching up to me. I know I need to nap to clear my head for tonight's dinner with Astor, but first, I need some answers.

Gently, I close the door behind me but don't latch it. The shades are drawn and the lamps are off. There's just enough light for me to see my way around.

My heart hammers.

I have no idea what I'm searching for, other than anything that will give me answers.

Why would Prishna have the other half of the heart necklace that Valerie wore before she died? What's the connection?

I recall from my pre-teen days that matching necklaces and

bracelets are a symbol of friendship. Were Valerie and Prishna friends? If so, how long had they known each other? Or am I in the middle of some weird polygamy cult where Astor is married to both women and gifted them the necklaces. I could totally see Mr. "Slap Me Again" being into kinky shit like that.

And also, *is* Astor holding Prishna captive? Just like he is me? Or is she being blackmailed for something and he's making her work for him?

I kneel beside the luggage. Inside, Prishna's clothes are folded at perfect ninety-degree angles, even her underwear. I grin when I find her pajamas. Two sets, one red flannel and one blue flannel, the kind you see in family Christmas cards. I can't see Prishna in matching flannel sets, but I guess like everything in life, there is always more than meets the eye.

I move to the bathroom where I find her toiletry bag. Nothing special, until I slip my hand into the side pocket and pull out a brown pill bottle of antidepressants. I get another pang of sympathy and recall my mom once telling me that behind most people's angry disposition is a broken heart. Who broke Prishna's heart?

Next, I find a tube of scar cream.

"Oh, Prishna," I whisper, shaking my head. The severity of her burns is well past what any over-the-counter ointment can remedy, but still, she tries.

Suddenly, I feel very bad for going through her things.

After replacing everything, I hurry out of the bathroom but find myself pausing at the suitcase, feeling a pull to search just one more time.

I run my fingers along the inner lining. My hand stops on a low-profile zipper.

A hidden pocket.

Inside is a long white envelope. The edges are worn, the color dingy. My heart hammers as I pull out a thick folded sheet of paper.

. . .

Certificate of Death
Decedent's Legal Name: *Prishna Anika Arya*
Age (Last Birthday): *40*
Cause of Death: *Cardiopulmonary arrest*
Contributing factors: *Chronic drug use*

"Oh my God."

I stare at the certificate—Prishna's *death* certificate. My hands are trembling as I reach back into the pocket where I find a blue velvet box, about the size of my palm. Inside, a small gold urn rests in a velvet pocket.

Thirty-Six

❦

Sabine

AFTER FINDING the death certificate and ashes, I hurry back to my room, then shut—and lock—the door.

If the real Prishna is dead, then who is the Prishna I've been talking to? And whose ashes are in the urn? The real Prishna's? Whoever that is?

I curse out loud, wishing I had my cell phone or any access to the Internet. I could use my sleuthing skills to investigate the name.

Frustrated, confused, and mildly scared, I sink onto the bed and pull in a shaky breath.

What the hell have I gotten myself into? What do I do now?

The answer comes instantly: Don't tell *anyone.*

I raise my head and nod. Don't tell anyone that you know about the devastation in the baby's room, or that you found a death certificate with Prishna's name on it.

Don't let anyone know you've been snooping. Because I

know that if I do, I'll be locked in my room again, unable to move freely around the house.

"Ugh." I drop my head in my hands.

My head is pounding. I feel nauseated and light-headed. And in a few hours, I am expected to have dinner with Astor. My *last* dinner with him.

Taking a deep breath, I decide that right now, Astor and this dinner are what I'm going to focus on.

Him.

Him only.

It will all be over soon, anyway.

I sneak into Astor's room, steal one of his sleeping pills, and jog back to my room, where I lie down and force myself to close my eyes.

Sleep, Sabine.

Everything is better after a nap.

Thirty-Seven

Anonymous

I WATCH her while she sleeps, the heavy rise and fall of her chest, the way her left eye twitches. She's dreaming.

My grip tightens around the scissors.

I study the vein running down the side of her neck, the gentle *thump, thump, thump* of blood. I imagine the mess it would be if I stabbed her right here, right now.

She stirs as if she can feel me. Her brows draw together in distress.

Quickly, I lift a strand of long black hair and thread it through the blades of the scissors.

"*Soon*," I whisper and snip.

Sabine

I'M jolted awake from my nap. Frowning, I sit up with the strangest feeling that someone is in the room with me, but I see no one. It's a different feeling than when I awake to Astor in the middle of the night. This is one of unease. Fear.

Must be the sleeping pill I took.

Blinking, I look at the clock. It's already six in the evening. Astor is expecting me in one hour. I'm disoriented, surprised I slept so hard. I make a mental note to steal more of those pills.

I push off the bed and walk into the bathroom. Staring at myself in the mirror, I frown.

"What the . . ." I run my fingers over a short patch of hair sticking out from the side of my head. It's as if someone cut a small strand out of my hair.

How the hell did that happen?

Could I have done that in some sleeping-pill sleepwalking scenario? Or is my hair starting to fall out and break from stress?

I spin around, expecting to see another headless doll on the bed, or the ghost of Valerie herself, sneering down at me with a pair of scissors in her hand.

But there is nothing . . . nothing more than a heavy feeling of doom in my stomach.

Thirty-Nine

Sabine

"YOU WATCHED ME LAST NIGHT." I cock a brow, sliding my napkin on my lap.

I'm referring to Astor watching me masturbate. Yes, it's a bold conversation starter, but it's my last night here. I'm bringing the big guns and focusing only on the man in front of me.

Not the death certificate, not who is putting creepy stuff in my room, not what happened to Astor's daughter, and not who (or what) cut my hair, and certainly not if I'm going crazy. Honestly, at this point, I've resigned myself to the fact that there is a ghost here, and he/she/it/they hates me.

So, right, it's going to be all about Astor.

We are in the dining room, sitting across from each other, under the glow of a magnificent crystal chandelier. The table is set with pristine porcelain dinnerware, linen napkins with gold rings, and crystal stemware. A lush green salad is centered in front of me, along with freshly baked bread and butter. A trio of candles burn in the center of the table, next to a decanter of red wine, half of which has been poured into our glasses.

It's an elegant display of opulence, just like the man sitting across from me, and so unlike me. I'm wearing the only clothes I have, baggy jeans and a white sweater, while Astor looks divine in a fitted navy suit. Casual—for a billionaire—and insanely sexy.

"Do you blame me for watching?" he asks, his hot gaze boring into mine in the way only he is capable of—like he is staring right into my soul.

I'm certain that Astor and I could be in a crowd with a hundred people, and he could still make me feel like the only woman in the room.

Before I can respond, he says hotly, "And by the way, close the door next time."

I blink, a rush of embarrassment coloring my cheeks.

Astor raises a brow. "Cillian is also staying in the house. You know this."

Oh.

Oh.

Does Astor care if another man sees me naked? Is that possessiveness I sense in his tone?

He stabs into his salad. "I'd also like you to stop wearing my wife's clothes."

"What?"

"You've been wearing her sweaters since you arrived."

I look down at the white cashmere sweater, then back at him. "No. Prishna gave them to me to wear. I had no idea they were your wife's. She said *you* picked them out."

"That's incorrect." He shoves a green leaf into his mouth and chews casually.

It annoys me how easily Astor can shift in demeanor. From crass demands and accusations one minute, to enjoying a salad and sipping hundred-dollar wine like he hasn't a care in the world in the next.

"Is it incorrect?" I ask, my eyes narrowed.

"Yes. I would never allow you to wear my wife's clothes."

I scoff. "I had *no idea* I was wearing her clothes in the first place. So, you're saying Prishna lied when she told me you picked them out?"

"I'd never call any of my employees liars. I'm simply telling you to stop wearing my wife's clothes."

I want to throw a fork at him. How can someone be so maddening and so addictive at the same time?

"Do you seriously think I would want to wear the clothes of the deceased wife of the man who kidnapped me?"

His head tilts to the side. "You hate your stay here that much?"

My mouth opens but hangs there for a second.

He and I both know I haven't asked to be released since my failed escape. He knows I have no friends, no family, no pets, no plants to go home to. It's just like he said, *No one would care if you left.*

He also knows of the undeniable sexual connection we have. A single minute with Astor Stone makes me feel more alive than all the years of my life combined. Why in the world would I want to leave that?

A grin plays on his lips. He's testing me. He knows exactly what he does to me—and he knows I hate that he knows.

"What do you miss?" he asks thoughtfully. "Of your life before me, what do you miss?"

"My mother." The response is instant. This wasn't the answer he was expecting—or I was expecting, for that matter. But it is the honest truth.

"Tell me about her."

"Well, she's dead."

"How?"

"Heart attack."

"I'm sorry. When did this happen?"

"During a home invasion."

His fork freezes in midair. He blinks.

"I know." I nod. "It's as tragic as it sounds, trust me. Are you sure you want to hear about it?"

"Yes."

"I was eight. Two masked men broke into our apartment in the middle of the night. My dad was at work—he worked the night shift at a local chicken plant. He passed away years ago from cancer. Anyway, I heard a commotion and ran out of my bedroom. One of the men had a gun to my mother's head, asking where her purse was. The other was ransacking the apartment. They got everything valuable, which wasn't much —just our electronics—and then they left. The second the door closed, my mother dropped to the floor."

I down the rest of my wine.

"And I've been dead inside ever since." I lift my glass in Astor's direction. "Cheers."

"Why?"

"Why what?"

"Why have you been dead inside ever since?"

"Because I did nothing to help her. I just stood there like an idiot. I didn't even try to stop them. I didn't try to help her."

As I'm speaking, Astor rises from the table, retrieves the decanter of wine, and tops off my glass. Then he returns to his seat and gestures for me to continue.

"Anyway, I didn't protect the only thing in my life that I really loved and that loved me back. I just stood there, a useless little girl who didn't stand up and be brave when I needed to be."

"You were eight."

"I was weak."

"Stop that."

"Fuck you."

He dips his chin in approval of my backtalk, or my gall, perhaps? Or is it pride I see? In the short time we've known each other, it has become apparent that Astor is attracted to strong, bold women. This works well for me.

I pick up my fork and dig into my salad. While he does the same, I find myself staring at him in awe.

Every second I spend with Astor, I become more curious about the enigma that he is. His mood is like an ever-swinging pendulum, and I am unable to hold on for the ride. On one end is someone with complete disregard for others and extreme mood swings, and on the other, a thoughtful gentleman with the ability to melt the panties off a woman.

"You're an incredibly complex person, do you know that?" I sip my wine.

"Yes, I do."

"Do you also know that you have some serious issues?"

The corner of his lip quirks. He swallows his bite. "Do I?"

"Oh yeah."

"Please." He waves a hand in the air. "Indulge me, Miss Hart."

"I'd love to. One, you're a selfish egomaniac with severe control issues."

He snorts in the middle of sipping his wine, breaks into a coughing fit, then wipes his chin and sets the wineglass on the table.

I fight a grin, then continue.

"You kidnapped me with no regard for my life or the consequences of it, for no other purpose than to make me a pawn in a game between two *billionaires.* From what I've seen, you treat everyone around you like they are on this earth for no other reason than to serve you, and you demand to be in control of every situation you're in, again, with no regard for the others around you."

"You're incorrect, Miss Hart. If I had no regard for you, you'd be dead."

I shake my head. "I don't think so, *Mister* Stone. I'm calling your bluff on that one. You'd like me to think that, but it's not the case. And this is the perfect segue into my next point. You've got a vicious temper."

"I'm aware."

"Then fix it."

"Keep going." He folds his hands on his lap, his attention suddenly laser-focused on my lips.

"Really? Are you sure?"

"Yes. Communicate with me."

"Of the two of us, you're the one with communication issues."

"I am also aware of this."

"You're also a very apathetic person, do you know that?"

"Yes."

"Why are you okay with it?"

"I kill people for a living, and I make a lot of money doing it. I'd rather have money than emotions."

I stab a fork in the air. "I knew your private investigation firm wasn't just solving mysteries."

"You're smart."

"So, money makes up for living a corrupt, soulless life?"

"Most of the time, yes. Are you done?"

"For now, yes."

"Good." He leans back. "May I counter your assessment?"

Well, this is intriguing.

I nod.

"Thank you. One, I treat everyone like staff because I have lost every person whom I've ever loved. Therefore, I choose to no longer attach myself to any other human being and not indulge in such weak emotions.

"Two, I demand control because no one can do my job better than I can. Period.

"Three, I have a temper because it serves as a release.

"Lastly, I kidnapped you because I couldn't take my eyes off you. Because I had a visceral, violent reaction when Carlos spoke to you the way he did. Because the moment you smiled at me, my entire world tilted, and suddenly nothing mattered more than tasting your lips. Are you going to eat your salad, Miss Hart?"

I am stunned speechless.

"Sabine, dear, are you going to eat your salad?"

"Uh—I . . . I don't really like salad."

Astor nods, rises from the table, and clears the dishes.

"You're so confusing," I whisper as he stacks the plates.

"I know."

I rise to help with the dishes.

"Sit."

I do. "No staff tonight?"

"No. I wanted to be alone with you tonight."

As my captor walks out of the room, I exhale and place my hand over my heart, now in a puddle at the bottom of my feet.

Forty

Sabine

ASTOR RETURNS from the kitchen carrying two gold-rimmed dinner plates.

The smell is heavenly. Veal parmesan, roasted artichoke hearts, and angel hair pasta, each portion plated like it's being photographed for a magazine.

He sets the plate in front of me. "Good?"

I look up. "Yes. God, yes. It looks amazing."

Pleased, he returns to his seat with his own plate. "Now I have an assessment of you, Miss Hart." He smooths the napkin on his lap. "You're a hypocrite."

It's my turn to choke on the wine.

"It's true. You judge me for killing people for money, yet the business you do with Carlos is corrupt and illegal, and you do it for the money."

"It's different."

"No, it's not."

"Yes, it is. One, lives are not at stake, and two, I grew up dirt poor and have vowed to never find myself in that kind of lifestyle again. The motivation to never be poor again is a strong one."

"The note . . ."

"What?"

"The sticky note in your purse."

"Ah." I look down. "Yes, that was her last handwritten note to me." *Money for lunch on the counter. You've got this. Love you, Mom.* "I carry it everywhere. Until now, you asshole."

"It's safe, I promise. What was she talking about when she said *you've got this*?"

"I had a math test that morning that I was stressed about."

"Ah." He nods. "That's telling."

"How so?"

"You turned math into a career."

"Why is that telling?"

"Because you subconsciously clung to that last moment. It's defined you."

"What's defined you?"

"Death. Back to the subject. What makes you think I grew up more comfortable than you?"

"Your mom was a hot-shot district attorney."

"She wasn't always an attorney," he says to clarify. "My mother got pregnant with me at age fifteen, and my father left not long after I was born. She was a waitress during my entire childhood. We lived under the poverty line in the slums of Brooklyn. One day she got sick of it, decided she wanted a better life, and put herself through college, through law school, all while working a full-time job and raising a child. It took her more than twenty years to become a respected district attorney. She never gave up."

"That's amazing. Good for her . . . I understand she passed away, is that right?"

"Yes."

"How did she die?"

"Plane crash."

Astor looks away, lost in memories. When he refocuses on me, he begins trailing his index finger over the rim of his wineglass.

"So. We have similar backgrounds and similar pain, you and me. We both grew up poor, we both lost our mothers tragically, and we both value money much more than any human being should." He lifts his chin. "You remind me of her."

"Your mother?" I can't hide my surprise. "How so?"

"She's the only other woman who's ever slapped me."

I grin. "Well. You deserved it."

"Yes, I did. Both times." He winks.

Electricity crackles between us. I feel my internal temperature rising.

"Speaking of that," I say, "I have one more thing to add to my assessment of you."

"Yes?"

"You have a kink."

"Impact play. A form of BDSM."

"Ah, so you're aware of it."

"Only since you."

I swallow deeply, suddenly feeling like my skin is on fire.

A moment passes between us, the silence deafening. He's staring at me as if waiting for me to say something, do something, but I'm so flustered that instead, I rip off a piece of bread and shove it into my mouth.

Dammit, how does this man turn me into a blubbering puddle of idiocy?

I swallow the bread and chug my wine.

"Eat your dinner," Astor says coolly, now back to his original demeanor.

I take this as the perfect opportunity to bring up Prishna

and see what Astor will—or will not—reveal. Will he tell me about the death certificate? The real reason she's working for him?

"I would, but the dinner is likely poisoned."

"Why do you say that?"

"Prishna cooked it, didn't she?"

"She did."

"She hates me." I cock a brow. "Yet another person who wouldn't care if I left."

"It really bothered you when I said that, didn't it?"

"Of course it did."

He doesn't apologize. Instead, he says, "Don't mind Prishna."

"It's impossible not to. She despises me."

"Prishna despises all women."

"Is it because she's in love with you?"

"No. Because she's afraid I'll replace her."

"Why don't you?"

"Loyalty."

"Loyalty to what?"

"To whom, you mean."

"You're such a dick."

"Slap me then."

"Ah, the kink returns." I wink. "Stop distracting me. Who are you being loyal to by keeping Prishna?"

"My wife."

"Your wife?"

"Prishna is Valerie's sister."

"Sister?"

He nods.

"But—"

"Yes, they're different ethnicities. Prishna is Indian; Valerie is white. Valerie's parents adopted Prishna when she was a child."

"Oh, I see."

I picture the necklace, the two broken hearts that come together as one. *Sisters.* They must have been close. Also, this partially explains why she works for him, but not why she stays.

"So, that's why Prishna hates me," I say thoughtfully. "She's protective of you and also grieving her sister."

"Perhaps."

I shake my head. "It feels like more, though. She seems scared about something or someone, and a bit unhinged—abnormally so. There's just something about her that makes me feel uneasy." When he doesn't acknowledge these accusations, I continue. "How long have you known her?"

"Six years."

The death certificate I found with her name on it says she died at age forty, which, according to what I assume her age to be, could very likely be six years ago.

"Where did she get those burns on the side of her face?"

"A fire."

"Yes, I gathered that." I roll my eyes so hard, I feel it in my brain. "I mean, like, what happened?"

"You'll have to ask her."

"You've never asked?"

"Why would I?"

"Oh, I don't know, to get to know your employees on a personal level?"

Now he rolls his eyes.

"You didn't even ask her sister, your wife?"

"Nope."

"You're unbelievable."

"Established."

"Okay, when did it happen? Do you at least know that?"

"A long time ago."

"Like around when you hired her?"

"Before then. Are we going to spend this entire meal talking about my assistant?"

"Fine. Just tell me this. Why would she tell me that *you* picked out my clothes—which were your wife's? Why lie about that?"

"I don't know."

"There's something strange about her . . . I just can't pin it down. And while we're on the subject, there's something strange about this house."

He looks at me from under his lashes. "Cillian told me about the doll and the pictures in your room."

"Yeah, I confronted Prishna about it, thinking it was her. She looked scared when I showed her the doll. She said—"

"Listen to me," he snaps. "You are safe here. You are safe with me. Nothing is going to happen to you, as long as I have you. *Ever.* You have my word, Sabine."

The image of Astor watching me sleep pops into my mind, and I realize then that he has not been watching me because he wants to. He's doing it to make sure nothing happens to me.

My captor and my keeper.

What a confusing combination.

Forty-One

Sabine

CILLIAN APPEARS IN THE DOORWAY. Astor is visibly upset at the interruption.

"Excuse me." He rises from the table. As he moves around my chair, he runs his fingertip along the back of my neck, leaving a trail of fire on my skin.

Just his touch.

With just *his touch*, I melt.

Astor returns quickly, his brows drawn with stress.

"Have you found Carlos?" I ask, assuming that's what the interruption was about.

"No. But we've made contact."

"Have you tried to call him from my cell phone? You could pin his location that way, I'm sure."

"He doesn't answer."

Ouch. That stings. I've given Carlos years of my life, and for what?

No one would care if you left . . .

My mood soured, I begin poking the veal. "Listen, Carlos

isn't going to resurface. He doesn't care that you have me, and that's clear. Me being bait isn't working out well for you, is it? So, if you're just keeping me here to toy with me, why? A man like you—with the wealth and lifestyle you have—can have any woman you want, and you don't have to hold her hostage."

"You think having money and notoriety automatically makes me a playboy?"

"Yes."

"You're correct. I cheated on Valerie more times than I can count."

"No offense, but I'm not surprised."

"None taken."

"And this kind of playboy lifestyle fulfills you?"

"No. Does your hermit lifestyle fulfill you?"

"No."

"So, endless women and endless solitude do not give us contentment."

Us.

"What do you think your life is lacking, Miss Hart?"

"Love. Yours?"

"Same."

We stare at each other with such intensity, such profound understanding, that goose bumps rise on my arm. And in that moment, I know—*I know*—my life is about to change.

"How is your veal?" he asks, although clearly hungry for something else.

"I could make better," I respond.

"You cook?"

"I know my way around a kitchen, yes."

"Then you'll cook for me tomorrow night."

"Will I, Master?"

"Yes."

"But I thought . . . I thought I was leaving tomorrow. Cillian mentioned I had twenty-four more hours here."

"I decide the length of your stay."

"So, I'm not leaving?"

"I just said you're cooking for me tomorrow night."

"Well, Captor, this will require a trip to the grocery store."

"Give me a list. I'll get it."

"What do I get in exchange for serving you, my lord?"

He has the same ravenous look as right before he kissed me in the bathroom. He stands, drops his napkin on his chair, and watching me like he's about to eat me, he walks to the end of the table, where I am still seated. He rounds to the back of me.

My heart hammers.

Soft fingertips graze the nape of my neck, gently pulling away hair from my face. Lips tickle the tip of my ear.

"What do you want?" he whispers.

You, I think but don't say it.

He moves to my other ear. "Seven o' clock, darling. Do not be late."

And then like a ghost, he's gone.

Forty-Two

Astor

CILLIAN STEPS INSIDE MY OFFICE, closing the door behind him. He takes a second to assess the room and my mood, both dark, before crossing the room.

"He's ready."

I turn from the window and fully face him. "Who's ready?"

"Carlos. He just messaged back. We have a meeting place arranged for tomorrow morning. You give him Sabine in exchange for Valerie's body."

When I say nothing—when I don't blink, don't move, don't breathe—Cillian frowns.

"You okay, boss?"

"No."

"What's going on?"

"No. I mean, no to the exchange."

He blinks. "I'm sorry—what?"

"You heard me. Tell Carlos he doesn't get Sabine back."

"But that's been the plan since the beginning. I—"

"He'll kill her. You know that as much as I do. She's nothing but a liability to him now."

And you care? Cillian doesn't say it, but it's written all over his face.

"What about Carlos?" he counters. "This is your moment for payback. You'll never see him again. You know that as much as I do."

When I say nothing, he grows impatient. "You're just going to let him go? Get away with kidnapping your wife? What about Valerie's body? Her burial?"

I look away.

"Boss?"

"The swap is off. That's my final decision. Now, leave."

Forty-Three

Sabine

I WAKE UP WITH A START, my skin hot, my breath short.

A bad dream?

No.

Him.

I lift my head off the pillow and see Astor sitting in the armchair, hidden by shadows. Both arms rest on the armrests, both feet flat on the floor. He's still wearing the same suit from dinner.

I look at the clock—3:11 a.m.

"What are you doing," I whisper, unsure if I am dreaming.

"Watching you sleep."

We stare at each other for a long moment.

Am I dreaming?

"Come here," I say, a throb beginning to pulse between my legs.

"No."

"I'm safe, Astor. You won't lose me like the others. Come here."

"Not tonight."

"Why?"

"Go back to sleep, Sabine."

I lay my head down, close my eyes, and fall back into a dreamless sleep.

Forty-Four

Sabine

I'M NERVOUS—BUT for the first time, it makes me smile. It's because I *care* so much. Because there's passion and pride behind the dinner I'm preparing for Astor.

I spend the morning meticulously planning the menu. This is difficult as I don't have access to the Internet to confirm ingredients. Around noon, Cillian appears at my doorway, demanding the grocery list, which, I assume, he passes to Astor.

I fix myself up the best I can with what I have, using every cosmetic in my possession. I even line my eyes and gloss my lips.

When I woke this morning, a stack of size large sweatshirts sat outside my door, each a different color. At first, I was confused, but when I smelled *him* embedded in the fabric, I realized they were Astor's clothing—not his late wife's—and that he'd delivered them personally.

I assume Prishna has been relieved of this duty. Thank God.

I choose the black sweatshirt, and instead of letting it hang limply around my hips, I knot the side, allowing for a sliver of exposed skin. Very '90s grunge.

I haven't seen Prishna all day—whoever the hell she really is. I've decided to push her out of my head because at the end of the day, what business is it of mine? Astor is my sole focus. *He* is what I want.

As usual, the lord of the manor has been locked in his office all day. Clearly, he's a workaholic. This doesn't surprise me. In fact, now that I know about his humble roots, his tireless dedication makes me proud.

I prep and prepare our dinner while dancing to old-school hip-hop, something with a fast beat to dispel the nerves. Also, wine helps.

I spend no less than an hour experimenting with place settings, wanting to choose the perfect set. I decide to go with black-and-gold plates and beveled drinking glasses. And instead of using the same long-stemmed candles from the evening before, I light an assorted dozen, placing them all around the room.

Dare I say, I've had a blast doing it all. The most fun I've had in a very long time.

Low, sexy instrumental jazz music hums through the speakers now, and I have just enough of a buzz to not have a care in the world.

It's 6:50 p.m., ten minutes before our arranged meeting time. I'm ahead of schedule.

Five minutes pass.

Ten.

Twenty.

Finally, quick, heavy steps echo down the hallway.

Butterflies burst into flight in my stomach.

Astor breezes into the dining room and subsequently takes my breath away. The billionaire CEO resembles a bronzed

Greek god in a tan linen suit that clings to his broad, muscular shoulders. Though the long work day is heavy on his face, his gaze immediately drops to the exposed skin peeking out from above my waistband.

"You're late."

"You look good in my clothes."

"Thank you. You're still late."

"I apologize. I had a call; it went longer than expected . . ." He sweeps a strand of hair over my shoulder, his gaze scanning my face like he's memorizing every line of it.

I look down in a feeble attempt to hide the blush creeping up my cheeks. "Are you ready to eat?"

His brow cocks.

"Food, I mean." I grin. "*Food,* Astor."

"Ah." He smirks. "Yes. I'm starved. I missed lunch."

"Sit."

"Yes, ma'am."

As Astor removes his jacket and settles into his chair at the head of the table, I slip into the kitchen and grab the first course.

"Caesar salad."

I slide the plate in front of him, admiring the shaved parmesan that is perfectly arranged on the lettuce. Each carving is the exact same size, placed equally apart. Next to it is a small serving of dressing, and next to that, two slices of garlic bread, fresh from the oven.

"Before you ask, yes, I made every bit of it—from scratch."

"Even the dressing?"

"Even the dressing."

This impresses him.

"I thought you didn't like salad."

"This isn't just about me."

He looks at me, our gazes lingering.

"Eat."

Astor waits until I'm seated. I pause until he takes a bite, desperate for his approval.

"That's all I get?" I squint. "Just a nod?"

"I haven't had the full course yet."

I stab my fork into the air. "You're lucky you're hot, do you know that?"

This earns me a chuckle, a deep, masculine sound that reverberates up my spine. I want to hear it again and again.

Astor devours the salad before I've taken my third bite. He wasn't kidding that he was starving, and it exhilarates me to know that I am able to remedy that need for him.

When I clear the plates and bring out the main dish, Astor looks up at me, a baffled expression on his face.

"What the hell is this?"

"Lobster mac and cheese."

"Macaroni and cheese? I thought you said you could cook. A seven-year-old could make mac and cheese."

"I'd be careful talking to me like that when there are knives within reaching distance. Just try it."

He sniffs, then picks up his fork.

"Make sure you get a piece of lobster in the first bite."

"Don't tell me how to eat."

"Then stop being such a pussy."

"That dirty mouth will get you in trouble, young lady."

"Here's to hoping. *Try it.*"

I hover over him as he chews, on pins and needles.

"Holy shit."

"I know, right?" I beam. "It's delicious. You owe me an apology."

"I already apologized once within the last fifteen minutes."

"Do you need to stretch before your second?"

Around another bite, he mutters (almost inaudibly), "Sorry."

Smirking, I return to the opposite end of the table and dig in. It's damn good. *I did good.*

Astor and I fall into an easy, comfortable conversation. Surprisingly so.

He has many questions about my education and accolades. I can tell he's impressed, and I feel proud talking about it.

I ask about his business and learn that it was built on the coattails of his mother, using her contacts and reputation to get his foot in the door. He has high respect and gratitude for her. A mama's boy, and I find this extremely endearing.

I also learn that Astor served in the military but left when he realized how many opportunities were missed by rules and regulations, restrictions written by politicians while sitting in their air-conditioned offices, most of whom have never served a day in their lives. Red tape, he calls it.

So, determined to fix a flawed system, Astor started his company when he was only twenty-seven years old, with the purpose of handling what the government is too inept to. He's driven by patriotism, greed, and an intense desire to honor his mother.

Astor has *two* helpings of my mac and cheese before dinner is over. For dessert, I serve a simple but classic chocolate layer cake with whipped cream and chocolate sauce. Between us, we've split a bottle and a half of wine, and I am comfortably buzzed—bordering on drunk.

"Thank you for cooking," he says, glancing up at me as I refill his wine.

"Thank you for enjoying it." I set down the decanter. "You should know that you make me feel alive. Not again—but for the first time ever."

He stares at me for a moment, and I can't quite read the expression. Then he removes his napkin from his lap, places it on the table, and pushes out his chair.

When he turns to me, his gaze is so intense that, instinctively, I take a step back.

"Make a decision right now, Miss Hart." His voice is deep, throaty. "I cannot take another second without being inside you." He closes the inches between us. "Consent or no consent."

I blink, thrown off by the brazen declaration. My pulse skyrockets.

"Right now," he growls. "Make a decision right *now*—"

"Yes," I breathe out, barely audible. "Please. I want it. I consent—I consent."

Like two magnets, our mouths collide. Frenzied and unbridled, his tongue thrusts between my lips. My clothes are thrown across the room.

With one sweep of his arm, he clears the table, sending food, plates, and priceless crystal shattering onto the floor.

My head spins as I'm grabbed by the waist and lifted onto the now-cleared table. He pushes himself between my legs, grips my thigh, and with one hand pinning me in place, wraps the other hand around my neck. His eyes are feral.

Goose bumps fly over my body.

"I will not ask for permission again. I will take you whenever I want you. I will not go gentle on you; this will not be sweet, soft, or sensual. I will fuck you exactly how I want to and for how long I want to do it for. Do you understand, Miss Hart?"

"Yes," I whisper, his words like gasoline to the heat already raging between my legs.

"Good." He releases me. "Now lean back and spread your legs."

My heart roars as I lean back on my elbows, lift my bare feet onto the table, and open my legs for him. There is no thinking, no questioning; I don't care if this is crazy, or wrong, or whatever. I have completely lost myself in this moment, in this man, and it feels so freeing.

He begins undressing. "I want to watch you finger-fuck that beautiful pussy like you did two nights ago."

Like an obedient puppy, I lick my finger, spread my legs wider, and slowly begin stroking back and forth. I'm already painfully throbbing, my body literally screaming out for this man.

His neck flushes with heat as he kicks off his shoes.

"Fuck it harder." His voice is now shaking.

He's as crazed as I am, and I love what I'm doing to him. I feel powerful, wanted, needed. Sexy as hell.

Watching him, I dip my finger in and out, shocked at how wet I am. I add another finger, and another.

The vein down the side of his neck throbs as he slides off his shirt, revealing a chiseled, tanned chest and an insanely sculpted six-pack. His hands tremble as he lowers his pants, then his boxer briefs. His erection springs out, long, thick, and veiny.

"Dear God," I whisper, thrusting harder now, unable to control my own fingers. I'm already going out of my mind, and he hasn't even touched me yet.

Gloriously naked, Astor picks up the silver dish of chocolate sauce and hovers it over me. "Are you ready?"

"*Yes.*"

I bite my lip as he dribbles a thin line onto my chest, between my breasts, down my belly, to my lips where it drips down my hand. The warm, thick liquid spreads over my body, sending tingles rippling over my skin.

The silver dish is tossed over his shoulder. Chocolate splatters across the wall.

"Stop," he demands, pulling my hand away from between my legs.

"What do you want from me?" I ask.

"Everything." He shoves me back against the table and pins my wrists above my head. "To start, I want to taste you before I fuck you."

Folding over me, he licks the chocolate from my aching breasts. With the hand that's not pinning my wrists above my head, he gently rolls my nipple between his fingertips.

I begin whimpering. "Fuck me, Astor. *Please* fuck me."

"I'm not done with dessert yet."

I groan as he licks down my sternum, my stomach, and finally between my legs. But he teases me, circling the outside of my folds, driving me absolutely wild. I am physically aching for him to be inside me. Just when I can't take another minute of the torture, his tongue slides over my clit.

It feels like an electric shock. My entire body jolts as he suckles the swollen nub.

Writhing against the table, I pull my hands from his grip and plunge them into his hair, moving my hips to the strokes of his tongue. I feel as though I am having an out-of-body experience, having never felt this kind of pleasure in my life.

Astor devours me like it's his last meal.

"I'm going to come," I whimper in a voice that doesn't sound like my own.

"Not yet." He lifts his face, licking the chocolate from a pair of beautifully swollen, glistening lips.

My God, he is *everything*.

"Astor, please." My pulse is roaring, my vision wavering. *"Please—"*

Before I can finish begging, he grabs my hips and yanks me to him, and off the table. I'm spun around like a rag doll, shoved face-first against the glossy surface, my ass exposed to him.

I cry out as he spears into me. Tears spring to my eyes, the sudden rush of emotions too intense not to release. The pain is exhilarating, and I can feel myself stretching around him, greedily taking in every inch. His nails dig into my hips, and before long, my body gives in, relaxing into his strokes and pushing back into him as he thrusts.

"Good girl. That's a good—*fuck*, Sabine."

He folds over my back, dips his finger in the bowl of whipped cream, and rubs it on my lips. I open for him, sucking the sweet vanilla from his fingertips.

We're both sweating, panting, molding together as one.

"You are so fucking sexy," he breathes into my ear. "You make me crazy."

He lifts off my back and presses so deeply inside me that I cry out, and then he wraps a hand around my stomach, pressing his thumb against my throbbing clit. With his other hand, he lubricates his fingertips with whipped cream and slides a finger between my ass cheeks.

Filled by his erection, I gasp as one finger rubs my clit while the other gently begins to circle my asshole.

I am floating. There's no other word for it. The sensation coursing through my body is the most intense I've ever had in my life.

I whine his name helplessly, unable to take another second of whatever the hell this man is doing to me.

"Say my name again," he demands.

I do, again and again.

"You are mine, Sabine Hart. You belong to *me*." The snarl in his tone is both terrifying and sexy as hell.

He's fucking me so hard now that with each thrust, the table inches forward and my forehead bangs against the polished wood.

"No man will ever touch you again. Do you hear me? You're mine, Sabine, mine, mine. *Mine*."

"Yes, I'm yours, Astor. I'm yours, I'm yours . . ."

"Do you want it, baby? Tell me. Do you want it?"

The pressure increases at my opening.

"Yes, please, I want it," I cry out. "Do it."

"Say my fucking name!"

"Do it, Astor! Do it!"

His finger slips into my asshole.

I come instantly, screaming his name as he screams mine.

* * *

I am unable to move or speak as I lie sprawled out, facedown, my upper body on the dinner table, my feet on the floor. My body is languid, loose, satiated beyond my wildest expectations. I am completely drained of energy and coherent thought.

The sound in the room slowly begins to register and I push myself up by my palms and turn around, still gripping the table for support.

Astor stands a few feet from me.

I watch as he gathers his designer suit and priceless shoes.

I watch him dress.

I watch him round the table and head for the door, not sparing me a single glance.

"Where are you going?" I ask.

"I never stay with a woman after, to be clear."

"I didn't ask it of you."

"Good. Now go clean yourself and go to bed."

"Yes, sir." I salute at his back as he exits the room.

Grinning, I slide onto the table, dip my finger in the chocolate, and suck it off.

Yes, sir, I think. *The tables are turning, aren't they?*

Forty-Five

Sabine

HOURS LATER, I awaken and find Astor sitting in the armchair again, watching me sleep—same as the night before, and the night before that.

Moonlight streams through the window, illuminating his beautiful profile.

We stare at each other for a moment, saying nothing, yet speaking a million words between us.

I smile.

His eyes twinkle, and to my surprise, a soft smile spreads across his lips. And with that beautiful image locked in my head, I roll over and go back to sleep.

Forty-Six

Anonymous

FROM MY SPOT hidden outside the window, I watch him watching her sleep. If he bothered to look outside, if he were self-aware enough to take one second to scan his surroundings, he'd see me.

She weakens him. It's disgusting. Astor is not the same man since she entered his life.

Anger spreads like heat over my chest.

I reach into my pocket to feel for the photograph, the snippet of hair. Next to it, I begin stroking the black wings of the dead bat.

My pressure increases, my strokes faster and faster as I watch him watch her.

Hatred, like a rolling simmer, bubbles inside me.

I dig my index finger into the bloody mush of the bat's neck where I decapitated it earlier. I begin finger-fucking the puffy flesh while imagining jumping through the window and strangling them both.

I pull my hand out of my coat, stick my fingers into my mouth, and suck the blood.

"Soon."

I spit a string of bloody mucus against the window.

"Soon."

Forty-Seven

Sabine

THE NEXT MORNING, I find Astor's office door open —actually *open*. This is the first time, since I've been here, that the door has not been shut and locked.

He looks up when I walk in. As usual, he's wearing a suit, but today, the top button of his white shirt is undone and he looks more relaxed. Or relaxed at all, I should say. Somehow, he's even sexier.

And just like that, a gentle tingle spreads between my legs. My very, very sore legs.

The office is as stunning as he is. Masculine with hard lines, deep mahogany, sweeping windows framed by blood-red velvet drapes. The desk he's sitting behind is quite literally the largest I've ever seen (just like him).

"Yes?" he says in greeting, and I swear he's concealing a smile.

"I want to go out."

Astor sets down his pen, leans back, folds his hands over his lap, and regards me closely. "Why?"

"I'm going stir crazy."

"Where do you want to go?"

"Into the nearest town, wherever that is."

"Okay."

I can't hide my surprise.

"Cillian will accompany you."

I scoff. "Seriously?"

"Seriously."

"Why can't you accompany me?"

"I have meetings."

"Fine."

A moment ticks away between us. He's wanting more of me, I can tell. A comment about our explosive sex the night before, or perhaps an invitation to do it again. I give him neither, reveling in every second of his wanting.

Finally, he lifts the phone from his desk. "Cillian, I need you to accompany Miss Hart for the afternoon. Take her wherever she wishes to go, and do not leave her side."

Astor slides a credit card across the desk. It's black, of course. The coveted black AmEx card.

I grin, sliding it into my pocket. "Thank you."

"You have ninety minutes once you arrive."

"An hour and a half to shop? That's ridiculous."

"One hour, then."

I roll my eyes. "Fine. Ninety minutes."

Cillian appears in the doorway.

Astor stands, rounds his desk, and hands me a cell phone.

"This isn't mine."

"Right. It's mine—one of mine, I should say. Yours for the day. The password is 0524."

I gape at him. "My birthday."

He nods to unlock it. When I do, I find one contact— him.

"I want *my* phone, Astor."

"No."

"You are a little sh—"

He grabs my waist, pulls me to him, and leans into my ear. "Careful, my dear, or it will be two fingers next time."

"Careful," I whisper back, pressing my cheek to his. "Or there won't *be* a next time."

With that, I yank out of his hold, peck him on the cheek, and saunter down the hall.

* * *

Though the drive takes an hour, the scenery is worth it. The sky is a brilliant sapphire blue, the sun blanketing budding mountains in a warm, crystal-clear light.

I roll down the back window and hang out my head like a child, allowing the wind to whip through my hair.

Cillian put in his earbuds almost immediately after beginning the journey, signaling to me that he didn't care for small talk. Which was just fine with me because I don't want to either. Why? Because I'm sleeping with his boss, and we all know when you have a secret like that, the less you say, the better.

We arrive in a town that looks like a postcard. Small, quaint, and deceptively casual. Luxury stores are everywhere. It's what I imagine Aspen to be.

Cillian walks a few feet behind me as I take my time meandering down the cobblestone sidewalks. There are a few times I even forget that he's there. I wonder if he worked as a bodyguard in his past life. I could totally see it.

I buy new clothes, toiletries, and cosmetics, plus a pretty candle to light in my room.

I could live like this, I find myself thinking several times. I could live as Astor Stone's captive. What a mind-fuck. Feminists would hate me.

Thinking of his wife, Valerie, I wonder how many times she did the very same thing I'm doing now. Walking these same cobblestones, visiting the same shops, using the same card, all while feeling grateful to be under Astor's control.

I stop short in front of a store called Twiddle Toys, gaping at the doll in the window. She stares back at me with dead eyes and a shy smile. It's the same doll that was placed next to my bed, except this one's head is still sewed on.

I push into the store, ignore the saleswoman's greetings, and look around, recognizing nearly everything. It's almost an exact replica of the baby's room in Astor's home.

Valerie shopped here for the daughter she would soon lose.

A wave of sadness rolls over me. I can't imagine losing a child.

My stomach sinks with guilt.

She's dead, I remind myself. She doesn't care that I just had sex with her husband.

But her ghost does . . .

I shake away the thought and hightail it to a coffee shop across the street.

I've kept my eye on the clock like a maniac, careful to stay within my allotted time of ninety minutes. I only have twenty minutes remaining when I spot a fancy jewelry store on the corner. The devil awakens on my shoulder. Grinning, I push through the glass doors.

Cillian doesn't join me. Instead, he waits outside, taking his millionth call of the day.

A beautiful salesclerk with long blond hair, aqua-blue eyes, and impossibly long legs greets me with a warm smile. She offers champagne, which I accept (obviously), and before I know it, Barbie is guiding me through each counter, describing in detail each glittering piece of jewelry. Each piece has a story. Each piece, priceless.

I want them all. Every single one.

I'm on my third glass of champagne when a loud trill vibrates through the air. It startles us—me and the salesclerk—and takes me a moment to realize it's the cell phone in my pocket.

"Excuse me."

I slide out the phone and click it on. But before I can lift it to my ear, I hear Astor's voice bellowing from the other end. He is *not* happy.

"What *the fuck* are you doing?"

His scream is so aggressive that a rush of adrenaline shoots up my spine, both fear and embarrassment coloring my cheeks.

Barbie's eyes widen. Humiliated, I turn away and step into the corner like a whipped dog.

"Answer me, goddamn it, what are you doing? You were supposed to be home eleven minutes ago!"

Home.

My gaze darts to Cillian, now chatting with a young woman outside.

Have I really been in this store for over an hour? How many times did Barbie refill my glass? More than three?

Shit.

"I'm sorry," I whisper-hiss. "I'm—we're still here, in town."

"I know exactly where you are, and it's not here where you should be."

Great. He must have the cell-phone location tracker turned on.

"Why are you so mad?" I ask, baffled at the emotion and wondering if there is something else going on. Because who would be *this* mad at tardiness?

"Why am I—Sabine, if you're not standing in my office in fifty-three minutes, I swear to God, I will—"

"Okay, okay." I disconnect the call and sprint out of the store.

Forty-Eight

Sabine

DURING THE DRIVE back to Stone Manor, my emotions are all over the place.

I feel anxiety that I'll get "home" and my small bag of belongings will be on the stoop, next to a note that reads *go away and never come back*. I feel disappointment because I have, once again, royally screwed things up. And lastly, I feel anger because *he* has made me feel these emotions.

It's a jarring realization of how crazy I am for this man, and how much emotional power he has over me. With him, I am both my most confident, bold self, and also my weakest, most insecure self. It's a confusing—and maddening—combination.

By the time I storm into his office, I've settled on one emotion—anger—and so has he.

Astor surges to his feet the moment I enter the room, rage in his eyes. His suit jacket is off, his sleeves rolled up to the elbows. He advances hotly, rounding the desk.

Do not back down, Sabine.

"How dare you speak to me like that?" I snap, my voice quivering.

Oblivious to my words, he's scanning my body from head to toe like he's checking for something. It's then that I realize it isn't *all* anger; it's also fear. Astor is checking to make sure that I am okay and not hurt.

His words from our first dinner trickle through my head. *I've lost every person I've ever loved.*

"That will never, *ever* happen again, do you understand me?" His fists clench as his eyes meet mine. "You will be home when I tell you to be. Is that clear, Sabine?"

I cross my arms over my chest. "Astor. We need to talk. Things need to be addressed."

He scoffs.

"No. Don't do that. This is happening, whether you like it or not. It's time. We're dancing around so many things. And for what?" I toss his phone and black card on the desk. "I'm going to put my things in my room, and in ten minutes, I want you to meet me in the library. Bring a bottle of wine. I need a damn drink."

Before he can protest, I turn on my heel and walk out of the room with my head held high.

It's time.

* * *

An hour later, I'm staring out the window, now black with night, with a sick feeling in my stomach.

Astor and I have hit a pivotal moment in whatever is happening between us. I'm sick because I feel like it's slipped out of my control, and that whatever this undeniable connection is between us will end before it's even really begun.

The hair on the back of my neck rises as Astor closes the library doors and quietly crosses the room.

I don't move, keeping my back to him. My heart begins to pound.

I feel his body stop behind me, all brooding, hostile, irresistible masculinity.

"Sabine," he says softly, gently sweeping my hair off my shoulder.

I close my eyes, exhale, and turn.

His eyes are bloodshot, heavy. He offers me one of the wineglasses in his hands. "Is red okay? I can get white if you—"

"No. It's fine." I take the glass, aware of—and surprised by—the nervousness emanating from him.

"Do you want to sit?" I gesture to the loveseat just behind us.

But I don't join him. I can't sit. Too many emotions.

I take a long, deep sip of my wine, and begin.

"What has happened here is crazy; I know it, and you know it. I am very aware that I haven't asked to leave since that first day. I'm very aware that some sick part of me is okay with what happened . . . because it's brought me to you."

Though his face is a mask of stoicism, the emotion in his eyes gives him away. The thick walls surrounding Astor Stone are beginning to crack.

"I think it's safe to say that neither of us expected to have the crazy connection that we do—and I know you feel it, so don't even act like you don't. And now, after the most incredible sex of my life, as things seem to be suddenly spiraling out of control, I have questions—*a lot*—and I expect you to answer them. Do you understand?"

"Yes."

"Good. Thank you. First, a comment more than anything . . . a demand, really. I will not tolerate you speaking to me again the way you spoke to me on the phone today."

His jaw twitches.

"Astor."

"Fine. I won't speak to you like that again. But I need you to listen to me. I only want what's best for you."

"I understand, but you need to learn how to restructure your requests so that they're softer and less demanding. And you also need to understand that sometimes I might not agree with you, or with what you think I need."

He exhales. "Sabine, all I can think about is the possibility that something might happen to y—" He shakes his head, still unable to verbalize his feelings for me. "I can't—"

"Then you're wholly missing the beautiful thing that's happening between us right *now*—in *this* moment. Not everything is bad, Astor."

"Life has taught me otherwise."

"Your life isn't done. And neither is mine, for that matter. So, Astor, let's talk like grown-ups, okay?"

He slowly nods.

"Now . . . for starters, I want to know about the little girl's room adjacent to your bedroom. I broke in and saw everything."

Closing his eyes, he takes a long, measured inhale. A solid minute passes before he finally speaks.

"It belonged to my daughter, Chloe. She died five years ago."

"I've gathered that much—and I'm so sorry . . . What happened to the room? Who marred her pictures, the walls, the bed, broke the windows, decapitated her dolls?"

"I did."

I blink. "*You* destroyed her room?"

"Yes. Over the course of a few years, yes."

"Why?"

He releases an exasperated, frustrated growl, then discards the wineglass, sloshing half of it onto the table. I'm afraid he's about to bolt.

"Talk to me, Astor. Why did you do it?"

"Because I can't handle it!" He explodes, the yell echoing off the walls.

The pain behind his eyes slices into my soul.

He drops his head into his hands. "I don't know why I did it," he says, his voice weak. "I have bad nights. I don't sleep. I can't. I . . . think of her. Of what happened. Constantly. It haunts me. I have to release it somehow."

I sit on the edge of the loveseat, next to him. "Tell me what happened to her."

He picks up his wine and chugs the entire glass in one go. I take the empty glass from his hand and slide it onto the table.

"Her name was Chloe. She was the light of my life, after my mother. She went to school one day and never came home. She was found facedown in the sewer, two miles away."

I cover my hand over my mouth.

"The police believe she fell through an open manhole in the alley next to her school. The workers were gone for the day and the area wasn't even roped off."

"They *believe*?"

"It was never confirmed. The two cameras outside the exit weren't working. There is no photographic evidence of the fall."

"What did the medical report say?"

"That her injuries were congruent with a fall."

"But you don't believe that's what happened, do you?"

"No, I don't, but the lack of visual confirmation isn't why."

"Why, then?"

"The medical examiner's report stated that there was a lock of her hair missing. Right up front, a thick section, like someone had intentionally cut it off."

I gasp, my hand flying to the side of my head.

"What?" He looks at me, startled.

"I—I took a nap yesterday and when I woke up, I swear a piece of my hair had been snipped."

"*What*?" He surges to his feet.

"Right here." I find the small section of short hair. "See?"

He bends down and studies it. "Impossible." His face pales. "I—I sit in your room all night. It's impossible."

"It happened during the day; I took a nap. I could be crazy . . . my hair has thinned and maybe I brushed too hard, but it really looks like a blunt cut." I don't tell him that it also could be related to the sleeping pill I stole from his vanity.

"Come here." Clearly upset, Astor grabs my hand, pulls me into his office, and closes the door behind us. I follow him to his desk where he has multiple monitors set up.

Frantically, he begins clicking open screens and keying in passwords. "What day was it?"

"Yesterday."

As he pulls up what appears to be a grid of security camera footage, my head spins.

Is it a coincidence that a chunk of his daughter's hair was cut on the day she died, and now, my hair has been cut? Is the same person who killed Chloe out to get me now?

"Tell me what we're looking at." I lean over his shoulder.

"I have twelve cameras throughout the property. If anyone sneaked in, it will be on camera."

We sit in silence as multiple feeds run on fast-forward.

He pauses on this morning and leans back in his chair.

"The only people on this property have been Cillian, Prishna, and Leo, aside from you and me." He shakes his head, and then, obviously thinking the same thing I am, says, "Neither of them killed my daughter and cut her hair, so it can't be the same person. I had all of my associates tracked thoroughly on the day of Chloe's death. Leo was in California, Cillian was on a mission in South America, and Prishna was with me the entire day, assisting with a virtual conference I was attending.

None of them did it, and they're the only ones who've been here."

"Aside from the ghosts."

He looks at me.

"I'm half joking."

He blows out a breath and scrubs his hands over his face. "I'm going to send Prishna to the beach residence to begin packing Valerie's things, and I'm going to tell Leo we don't need him anymore. That way, it will just be me, you, and Cillian in the house."

"Hang on—let's loop back to Chloe. Why didn't the cops think her hair being cut was significant?"

"Chloe had cut her own hair before. Several times, actually. They said she could have done it that day at school—which she'd done, twice."

"What do you think happened?"

"I believe she was taken from school and then killed and dumped, and whoever did it wanted me to know it was no accident, so they cut her hair."

"Why? If someone wanted you to know she was intentionally killed, why not do something less subtle than cutting a piece of hair?"

"To make me wonder, exactly like I am. To make me go crazy, exactly like I have." He rubs the back of his neck. "Sabine, because of what I do for a living, the list of people who would want to torture me is quite literally endless. I've run missions involving the most dangerous drug cartels in South America, terror cells in the Middle East, and against former Soviet guys who are some of the most ruthless men I've ever come across. And the families, children, associates of all those men—they'd all want a piece of me. Believe me, I spent years running my own investigation behind the scenes, sending my own men to investigate leads. Nothing stuck."

"So, you've just accepted it?"

"If by accepting you mean becoming a self-loathing insomniac who destroys my daughter's bedroom instead of my wrists, yes."

"And by keeping anyone close to you under lock and key. Just like you're doing to me, just like you did to your wife."

"Precisely." He looks up at me. "Yes, I get it. It's a trauma response, but I don't care. It's the only way I know to keep you safe."

"It's unhealthy."

"Almost as unhealthy as you pretending like you're the one in control here."

"What's that supposed to mean?"

He stares at me for a moment, weighing whether to continue. "Sabine, if you really want to talk, okay, but you might not like what I have to say."

"Try me."

"Your feelings for me are misguided."

"That's a bold statement. How so?"

"Your obsession isn't with me, it's with fixing me. You saw immediately how messed up I am, and instead of distancing yourself from me—as you should—you've become obsessed with fixing me."

I open my mouth to snap back but hesitate.

He continues. "Do you know why? Because you still carry the guilt of not helping your mother, of your inaction the night of the break-in—when you were eight years old, Sabine."

I go stock-still.

I think of all my broken ex-boyfriends, and how, in every single relationship, I stayed entirely too long. I labeled myself as someone whose weakness is trying to fix everyone, but it's only half right. Astor is right. I stay because I feel guilty abandoning someone who needs help—because of what happened with my mother.

Astor takes my hand and pulls me to him. "You see,

Sabine, you and I aren't as different as you think. Our lives are molded by pasts we refuse to let go of, and our motivations and decisions are clouded by guilt."

I stare down at him, tears welling in my eyes. "So, what are we going to do?" I whisper.

Astor pulls me onto his lap and gently cups my chin. "Kiss me."

Forty-Nine

Sabine

"SO, we're going to just fuck it all away?"

Despite the incredible sex we just had, I find myself irritated that I allowed my lust for Astor to circumvent the problem, once again.

He rises onto his elbow and looks down at me, naked on the hardwood floor. "What do you mean?"

"I asked what we were going to do about us, and instead of answering me, we had the kind of sex that I'm pretty sure is illegal in most countries."

"You didn't seem to mind it when you were screaming my name."

"I'm not being funny. I'm asking, are we just going to fuck away this gray area of us, or worse, pretend it doesn't exist? And then what? Go back to our regular lives?"

He sweeps a strand of hair behind my ear. "Be patient with me."

"Be patient with you?" I gawk, feeling heat rise up my neck. "Are you serious?"

I push off the floor and begin yanking on my clothes. My cheeks burn with embarrassment.

Astor stands, his naked body glorious. "Sabine, stop. Come here."

I swat away his advance and begin pacing. "I still have so many questions, and you just want sex. Geez, Astor, you are so incapable of handling anything serious that involves actual communication."

"Sabine, please." He slips on his boxer shorts.

God, why does he have to be so damn sexy?

Stop, stop, *stop*.

"Who is Prishna?" I glare. "Who is she really?"

Astor stills.

"Aha." I jab a finger into the air. "I *knew* it. I found a death certificate with her name on it hidden in her suitcase."

"You've been doing a lot of snooping."

"Of course I have. I'm bored out of my damn mind. Answer my question—and I also want to know all about your wife, your marriage, everything."

He blows out a long breath. "This is going to require another drink, then."

After grabbing a bottle from the bar cart, Astor refills his wineglass and tops off mine. Then he sinks back onto the loveseat and crosses one leg over his knee.

"I'll start at the beginning. I met Valerie at an event in Las Vegas. I got drunk, fucked her in the back of my limo, and two months later, she called me up—she got my number from a business colleague—and told me she was pregnant. I didn't even remember having sex with her."

"Because you were so drunk?"

"Because it was so insignificant."

"Ouch."

"You know the most surprising part? I was elated—but

not about Valerie. I was elated that I was going to have a child."

"I don't think that's particularly surprising."

"No? Why?"

"You care. A lot. Astor, you have *a lot* of passion pent up inside you. I can see it in your eyes, feel it in your touch. Which is why you're so miserable. You're an extremely emotional person but refuse to acknowledge it. Do you know what you need?"

"You. Again. Right now."

"No. You need a journal to write down your feelings—you know, instead of decapitating baby dolls."

His lip quirks.

"No one has to read it, and if you don't know where to start, write it like a letter, to no one in particular, and just get it all out."

"I'd rather cut out my own spleen."

"I don't doubt that, but please, just think about it. Start writing, and I'll bet you'll find yourself opening up."

"I'll think about it."

I grin, settling next to him on the loveseat. "Thanks for indulging me, at least."

He winks.

"Back to the subject. Have you always wanted children?" I ask.

"Absolutely not. My job doesn't allow for it. But when I heard that she was pregnant with my child . . . I don't know, it was like something lit up inside me. Hope that there could be something wonderful in this dark, black, dreadful world I live in, day to day. But that feeling was fleeting, almost instantly replaced by the most intense fear I've ever experienced. Me having a child would make me vulnerable to my enemies. The child would have a target on its back from the day it was born. So, I knew I had to keep the pregnancy a secret, and I didn't know if I could trust Valerie to keep this secret, so I married her."

"So that you could keep her close, under your watchful eye."

"Right."

"That feels drastic."

"Does it? I impregnated her. I felt like it was my duty to protect her and our unborn child."

"You have a very skewed sense of chivalry, do you know that?"

This earns me a half smile.

"Then what?"

"Well, I married her and moved her in with me, and I tried to make it work. Honestly, it wasn't hard because every time I looked at her growing belly, I felt excitement and joy—two feelings that were very foreign to me. I tried to force a loving relationship between us. She tried too, I think. But it didn't work."

"I find that hard to believe. You can be very persuasive."

He takes a deep breath. "Valerie had severe depression, and the pregnancy only made it worse. She became more and more unstable. She started resenting me for taking away her independence and demanding she take a bodyguard with her anytime she left the house. We fought all the time. The kind of arguments that make you want to pull your hair out, you know what I mean? Like two insolent children, neither trying to understand the other's perspective, instead just screaming over each other. And that's when I abandoned hope that we might have feelings for each other. Instead, I began building a wall of protection around her and Chloe, thereby making Valerie dependent on me for survival. It was manipulative, but I did it to protect my child."

He looks at me, the guilt palpable. But as I listen, I can't help but remember Prishna's words . . .

"He loves her. Her only. When Astor finally gets sick of toying with you, you will be forgotten the instant you leave his sight. He does not care about you, not in the way that you wish he would, and he will never care about anyone like he did his wife . . . He cries out for her in his sleep, but you wouldn't know that, and you never will. Because Astor never allows his whores to stay in his bed with him."

"After Chloe died," he says, "Valerie became even more unstable. She'd barge into my office unannounced, screaming obscenities while I was in the middle of meetings. She tried to kill herself multiple times. It got so bad that I asked her sister, Prishna, to come stay with us." He clears his throat. "And this is where *that* story begins."

I tuck my leg under my body and turn fully to him.

"Prishna has her own demons. She'd become estranged from her sister and family a long time ago and began running with a really rough crowd. She was on a downward spiral and was having some major health issues when Valerie and I married. At the time, she was more than happy to help with Valerie because she didn't have much else going for her. So, I opened my house to her and gave her a fresh start at life, offered her a job."

"You gave her a fake identity."

"Correct. Prishna died and Asha was born."

"Asha? Why doesn't she go by her new identity?"

"She doesn't need to here. Cillian and Leo know about it, and also Valerie hated calling her sister by a different name. So, we all just kept calling her Prishna."

"Did Valerie not approve of what you did?"

"She was so self-absorbed by then, she didn't care. Having Pri around helped anchor her for a while, but eventually, Valerie wanted out of the apartment—and New York— because she said it reminded her too much of Chloe. So, I packed us up and we came back here. But this place reminded her even more of Chloe, because we'd vacationed here a few times while she was a baby."

"You guys moved into this lake house?"

"Yes."

"So, that's why there are so many pictures of her everywhere. This wasn't a vacation home, it was an actual home."

"Correct. And she put them up, to be clear."

"She put up pictures of herself?"

"Yes. She became obsessed with the thought that I was cheating on her and might leave her."

"Which you were."

"Right." He sighs. "So, she put little pieces of herself everywhere. It was one of the many strange things she did before she completely lost it."

"What about the locks on the outside of the doors?"

"That's another thing she did. I came home one day, and a handyman was here doing it. I asked her why, and she said because she wanted to lock up the voices."

"Jesus."

"Yeah. Anyway, we lived here together for months until our arguments started becoming physical."

"Physical?"

"Yes. She came at me with a knife once; I pushed her. It wasn't good. It became apparent that Valerie needed psychiatric intervention and away from me. So, I set her up with proper home care, security, an on-call medical team, and moved her to her favorite beach house that we own. And that's where she lived for years."

"Until Carlos took her."

"Right."

"He said she killed herself. Do you believe he's innocent in her death?"

"I do. As much as I hate the guy, I don't think he's a killer. And she'd tried to commit suicide countless times, so . . ."

"I'm sorry."

"No need for you to be."

"No, I mean . . . I'm sorry, but I don't fully believe you, and you should know that."

Astor frowns. "What?"

"I think you did love your wife, deeply. Hell, she's all around you, Astor. You keep her sister around you at all times, which is a little piece of her. Her pictures are everywhere—and you haven't bothered to remove them. You light a candle for her every day. I saw you crying over the memorial you set up for her outside, next to your daughter's. So, yeah, I think you still love her. I think you still might be in love with her. And I think her presence is still very much in this house."

Fifty

Dear Butterfly,

I can't hide it anymore.

Your absence has spread through my body like a virus. It's turned me into someone I hate.

I can't hide my depression. My grief. My sheer disdain for living in a world without you in it.

I can't hide it from her anymore.

She knows.

Astor

Fifty-One

Sabine

I WALKED out on Astor after accusing him of still being in love with his wife.

He didn't chase me. Instead, he yelled through the house for Cillian, demanding that he keep an eye on me for the next few hours. Then Astor stalked outside and disappeared on a four-wheeler, alone.

Now, I'm sitting on the patio wrapped in a blanket with a glass of wine in my hand and my feet propped up on the railing, watching his headlights as he scans the perimeter of the property. It's a cold, dark night. Cillian lingers in the shadows of the kitchen behind me, out of earshot but close enough to make sure someone doesn't sneak up and snip another piece of my hair—like someone did to Astor's daughter the day she died.

I don't know what to think of it all. To be honest, I'm a very exhausting combination of confusion, frustration, and head-over-heels in love.

"You're up late."

Prishna's presence doesn't even startle me as she steps onto the patio. My emotions are too drained to care about much.

"I could hear you crying." She leans against the railing, watching the headlights in the distance.

"Sorry for disturbing you." I roll my eyes.

She glances at the picture of Valerie I've put on the railing in front of me. The wife between Astor and me.

"You're in love with him," she says coolly.

"Yes."

"You need to stop."

"I can't."

I drop my head back and focus on the one star that is visible through the thick cloud cover. We stay like that for a few minutes, just her and me, with only the dim glow from a lamp somewhere inside illuminating the patio. Cillian must have turned it on for me. How nice of him.

Finally, she speaks—and it isn't at all what I expect.

"Valerie's family adopted me when I was twelve years old. Before then, I spent my entire childhood in an orphanage in Mumbai, after my mother discarded me at birth for not being a boy. When Valerie and Astor married, I was in my third attempt at rehab. While there, one of the patients set the building on fire. I barely made it out alive."

I recall Astor's words. *She was on a downward spiral and was having some major health issues when Valerie and I married.*

"When I got out of the hospital, Astor opened his home to me, in return for helping Valerie through her depression. A few weeks later, I learned that Astor had paid my medical bills and wiped my debt clean. He offered me a job, a new identity, a fresh start at life, and I've been working for him ever since."

"That's where you got your scars?"

"Yes."

"I'm sorry."

"Astor is a good man but very troubled. His need for control extends beyond rational thought. He locked up my sister like an animal. All her decisions were made by him. She couldn't make a move without his approval. He completely isolated her from the world, even from me most of the time. *He* drove her mad."

"After he moved her into the beach house, why didn't you move in with her?"

"Astor didn't allow it," Prishna says, her tone sharp. "By then, I'd become so engrained in his business that he said I was indispensable. Everything I own is in his name, everything I do is under his watch, every penny I spend is the money I earn from him . . . You once asked me if I was being held captive by Astor."

She takes a long look at me.

"Being captive isn't always as simple as being kidnapped. There are ways to hold someone captive that doesn't involve a lock and key. If you'd stop being so blinded by your own desire, you'd see that there lies a dangerous darkness within him, and also that his heart is already taken—and always will be. While you're busy snooping through the house, you're missing things that are right in front of you. Tonight, go look at his bed. Every night, he picks a daffodil, her favorite flower, and lays it on her pillow. He lies down next to it, staring at it, until he eventually gives in to the insomnia, and he gets up and paces for hours. He is still, and always will be, in love with Valerie."

"You're a liar."

"You're dangerously naive."

"Tell me then, if he is still so in love with his wife, why hasn't he kicked me out? Why does he tell me that *you* are lying when you say he gave you his wife's clothes for me to wear? Why does he kiss me? Why does he look at me the way he does? Tell me—*tell me*, Prishna."

"I don't owe you anything."

"You owe me common courtesy, woman to woman."

"This from the woman manipulating a grieving widower."

"*I'm* manipulating *him*? You've got to be kidding me."

"Astor is confused. He's grieving, and you're taking advantage of a man who has lost his mother, his daughter, and his wife." She turns away from the railing and looks at me with disgust. "You are poison, Sabine Hart."

She slams the patio door so hard that Valerie's picture falls from the railing and shatters at my feet.

I surge from my chair and chase after her but stop.

Stop, Sabine.

On the mantel, a candle burns around a dozen pictures of Valerie.

I want to scream.

Go look at his bed.

My heart racing, I run into the master bedroom. There, on the pillow next to his, is a freshly picked daffodil.

Fifty-Two

Sabine

WHEN ASTOR ENTERS THE BEDROOM, I'm lying in bed, crying, gripping the pillow so tightly that my knuckles are white.

Although the lights are off and the room is dark, I bury my head in the pillow because I don't want him to see me cry.

"Go away."

The mattress shifts with his weight, followed by a waft of fresh, earthy air.

Gently, he pulls my shoulder, rolling me onto my side. "Shit, Sabine. Please don't cry. Please stop."

"I can't."

"Dammit, please stop." His voice is quivering now.

He rolls me onto my back. I carry the pillow with me, covering my face.

"Sabine." He takes the pillow from my hands.

I blink up at him, swiping the tears from my cheeks.

"I didn't mean to hurt you, or make you cry tonight. I'm sorry. I'm so sorry. Please stop crying."

"Don't tell me what to do—just let me cry."

"Then I'll sit with you until you stop."

He lies down on the bed, facing me. For a long time, we stare at each other, saying nothing.

"I'm so confused, and I don't want to get hurt," I whisper.

"I don't want to be the cause of any of your pain, Sabine," he whispers back. "I am not in love with Valerie, and it breaks my heart that you think that . . . I admit, I don't know how to navigate this—you and me, and everything that's happening around us right now—and I'm afraid I'll fail miserably. But I do know that you are all I think about, minute by minute, hour by hour. That every moment we're not together, I'm thinking about when I can touch you again. Can I touch you, Sabine?"

I sweep my hand over the covers, resting it between us. He loops his pinky finger around mine, then exhales softly as if my touch alone is a relief for his pain.

"While I was outside checking the fence, I was thinking about us. About how the feelings you stir inside me remind me of my childhood when I didn't have a care in the world. Free and floating and hopeful . . . You told me I make you feel alive. Sabine, you make me feel like I'm flying."

Tears fill my eyes.

He inches closer to me.

"You deserve peace. You deserve to be kissed every day, to be reminded how beautiful you are, and how smart, and funny, and strong you are. You deserve the world, and a man who can give it to you."

He kisses my knuckles.

"I want to be that man. I am so sorry I've let you down. I can't promise it won't ever happen again, but I can promise that I'll try. Because you, beautiful Sabine, are worth it. You're worth all of it." He leans forward and kisses the tears from my cheeks. "I don't want to know what it's like to lose you."

"Then don't." I wrap my arms around his neck and pull him onto me.

There's something different in this kiss. The others were fueled by fire, by unrestrained wanting and needing. They served as escape valves, opening just enough to release years of pent-up steam and sexual tension. But this one . . . this one is soft and passionate. Emotional.

Slowly and gently, he undresses me while running kisses down my neck, my chest. Naked, I rise to my knees and remove his clothing. He lies submissive as I do, watching me with such adoration in his eyes that my heart stutters.

This is real. I feel it in the depths of my soul. Whatever is happening between us is real. *We* are real.

He lays me down and lowers on top of me, settling between my legs. He's hard and ready but doesn't penetrate me. Instead, he takes his time kissing me deeply, unrelenting, as if wanting to savor every second of the moment.

I run my hands down his strong, tanned back, sinking deeper and deeper into what has become my dreamland, my new favorite place.

Under him.

His hand slides between us, between my legs. I arch into his touch, my breath becoming shallow. I'm throbbing so hard, I can feel my heartbeat in it.

Needing him now like I need my next breath, I pull up my knees and open as wide as I can for him.

He removes his hand and cups my face. "You are so beautiful."

The thick head of his erection presses against my lips. My body shuddering, I want to scream for him to slide inside me.

Do it, already, I can't take it anymore!

But still, he takes his time, barely dipping in, slowly popping in and out, wetting the tip. He groans, almost sending me over the edge already.

"Open. Open wider for me, baby."

Desperate, I splay open my legs until my hips feel like they could unhinge.

"Good girl." Finally, he slides into me, closing his eyes in complete surrender. "I need you," he says, his words breathless. "Come here, come here. Closer, I need you closer . . ."

A tear runs down his cheek.

My body trembles as I'm wrapped in his arms and lifted so that every inch of our bodies is touching. He squeezes me like it's the last time he's ever going to see me.

On long, leisurely kisses, he begins to slide in and out, the slow pace driving me wild. We mold together, our arms wrapped around each other, our bodies and souls melding together, moving as one.

I can already feel my climax starting to build when he stops, fully inside me. He gazes down at me with such tenderness, such warmth, that butterflies erupt in my stomach. He presses deeper into me, deeper and deeper.

I moan as he burrows himself inside me. We are as connected as two humans can possibly be.

Staring into his eyes, I feel a rush of heat spread over my heart, and I can no longer control the unexpected emotions bubbling inside me.

"Astor . . . " Tears slide down my cheeks.

"This," he whispers, hugging me tighter against him. "This, Sabine. This. I want this, with you. All the time. Forever."

"I love you." My heart and soul speak, uncaring of the consequences.

For a moment, he stills, his eyes widening. Tears spill over the rims. Then he crushes his lips onto mine, our teeth clashing as we kiss. He begins moving again, faster, faster, as if unable to handle what is happening inside him and I am the release.

Me.

Not her. *Me.*

The headboard bangs against the wall, the bed squeaks, the mattress moves.

I close my eyes, feeling like I'm floating.

You make me feel like I'm flying . . .

"You're mine, Sabine. Say my name. Mine," he whispers huskily. "Say my name. Mine—you're mine; say it." He's desperate, unhinged, shaking through shuddering breaths. "Please be mine. Please be mine, please, Sabine, please, please, please—"

I cry out, digging my nails into his back as I climax.

"Astor, I'm yours. I'm yours. Oh God, I'm yours, I'm yours . . ."

Fifty-Three

Anonymous

MY HEART THUNDERS in my ears. It feels like I'm one hard beat away from it jumping out of my skin. A bead of sweat drips down the side of my face as I grip the closet door, cracked just enough to see the bed bathed in moonlight.

With each thrust, the headboard hits the wall. *Bang, bang, bang,* the sound like a shotgun going off in my head.

My teeth gnash with such force I hear them grind, even over the panting across the room.

The photo in my hand crinkles, the lock of hair in the other, hanging limply from my fingertips and damp from my sweat.

I begin shaking.

As she screams his name, I picture myself bursting out of the closet and putting a bullet between their eyes.

Fifty-Four

Sabine

AS I FALL ASLEEP, Astor slides his arm out from under me, carefully lifts off the bed, and slips out the door without a word.

This time I wait for him to come back, knowing that he will. And he does, around two in the morning.

He settles into the armchair.

"I don't like that you leave me after sex," I whisper from the pillow.

"I don't like that I can't control myself with you."

"So don't."

My words from earlier echo through my head. *I love you . . .*

Do you love me? I think. *Say it. Say it now.*

A long minute stretches between us.

"I can't do this much longer, Astor. Emotionally, I can't handle this."

When he doesn't respond, I roll over and pretend to go to sleep.

Fifty-Five

"WAKE UP."

I hear the door closing. Footsteps. Movement around me. My eyes fly open.

Astor, looking impeccable as always, breezes past the foot of the bed and yanks open the curtains. Bright, crystal-clear light washes over the comforter.

I blink several times as I sit up, the haze of sleep still heavy in my head. "What's going on?"

"I have an event to go to in New York tonight. You're coming with me."

"An event?"

"Yes, a charity gala, to be specific." He ties back the curtains. "A black-tie event."

A black-tie event?!

"Hang on. Are you taking me as your prisoner or as your date?"

"You're no longer my prisoner. We both know that."

"So . . ."

"Yes—my date."

"Was it really that hard to say?"

"Almost as painful as that smart mouth you have on you, Miss Hart."

"You like it. So, a date, like, out in public?" I cock a brow. "You didn't even go out in public with your wife."

He turns from the window and rests his hands on his hips. "Correct. You've obviously driven me completely mad."

"Only you could ruin a potentially romantic comment, you know that?"

A grin tugs at those luscious lips as he meets me at the side of the bed and runs a knuckle down my cheek. "You've ruined me, Sabine Hart."

Butterflies awaken. Everything is good. Last night, I confessed that I loved him, and everything is okay.

Things are good.

"Well. Unless you want me to go as your fourteen-year-old little brother," I say, and he wrinkles his nose. "Because I only have baggy jeans and sweatshirts. I don't have anything to wear."

"Yes, you do. Everything you need is in your closet and bathroom. It's a four-hour flight. We leave in two hours." He glances at the gold Rolex glittering on his wrist. "I need to get some work in before—"

"Wait." I take his hand, slip out of bed, and onto my knees. I'm wearing only panties, and based on the immediate flush on his cheeks, he's pleased by this.

"Surely, you can spare a few minutes. The emails can wait."

"What emails?"

Grinning, I undo his belt. He's already rock hard by the time I unzip his slacks.

I take him in my hand, this gloriously beautiful muscle

that magically turns me into a confident, don't-give-a-damn, willing slut. A new side of me that I *really* like.

"God, Astor." I look up at him. "You are truly something else."

I slide my tongue over the engorged head of his penis.

"Damn, baby." He exhales, tipping back his head in ecstasy.

The fact that I can turn Astor on so quickly turns me on like nothing else.

"Still annoyed by this smart mouth of mine?" I ask, mocking him.

"No—God no, it's perfect, you're perfect, please—for the love of God—keep going."

I grin, then begin circling the tip with my tongue while gently stroking his shaft.

He moans, threads his fingers over my scalp, and takes a fistful of my hair. "Keep looking at me, baby."

My eyes water as I take him as far as I can, gagging on the sheer girth of him.

"Fuuuuck, Sabine." He growls, the veins popping out on his neck.

At the sound of my name, a switch flips inside me, and I am suddenly dripping wet and throbbing like a jackhammer. I suck frantically, chasing my lips with both hands, stroking him into oblivion.

His words are unintelligible as his whole body begins to tense.

"Sabine. I'm going to come."

Tears run down my face as I allow him to fuck my mouth.

"Can I come—"

"Yes."

With a guttural groan, he explodes in my mouth, shooting hot ropes of cum down my throat. I swallow it all—every last drop of it.

When I look up, Astor is gazing down at me, his face red, his eyes heavy with satiation. I wipe the corners of my mouth and wink.

"Jesus, Sabine."

Smiling, I stand. "How's that for a proper good morning? Now," I flick my wrist toward the door, "carry on."

"Oh, *hell* no."

I'm lifted off the floor and tossed onto the bed like a rag doll. I giggle as he clumsily rips off my panties and presses open my legs.

"You have the most beautiful pussy, baby, you're just so perfect. I want to taste every inch of you." Astor buries his face between my legs, slides his hands under my ass, and lifts me slightly. "Fuck my face, baby."

Moaning, I plunge my fingers into his hair while gently thrusting against long, wet strokes of his tongue.

"That's it, baby, that's it," he mutters while French-kissing my pussy with such fervor, I begin whimpering.

I writhe under him, my body feeling like it's about to explode.

His tongue slides over my clit, back and forth, then circles, circles.

My eyes flutter closed, and once again, I feel like I'm floating. "I'm about to—"

"Say my name when you do. You're mine, Sabine."

He clamps down, sucking hard while flicking the tip of my clit with his tongue.

I scream his name and come in his mouth. Wave after wave, I ride his face, whimpering, screaming, crying out. I lie limp as he licks me clean, swallowing every bit of my essence.

I'm hardly aware of anything as Astor rises from between my legs. When I open my eyes, I find him staring down at me, his lips plump and swollen, his eyes filled with emotion.

"Sabine Hart, you are going to be the death of me." He leans in and kisses me on the forehead. "Two hours, okay?"

"Okay."

I watch as he crosses the room. At the door, he stops, turns back, and smiles before closing the door behind him.

Astor Stone, I think, *you* already *are the death of me.*

I lie there for a minute, allowing myself to delight in the moment. Then, grinning like a child, I surge out of the bed and jog to the closet.

I gasp.

An off-the-shoulder black ballgown with a velvet bodice and a tiered ruffled skirt stares back at me. It reminds me of a black Cinderella gown. On the floor next to it are a pair of black heels with red soles.

"Oh my God." I drop to my knees and smell the shoes. Christian Louboutin.

My gaze shifts to a stunning ivory cashmere trench coat and wide-leg trousers. It reminds me of every classy rich woman I've ever seen sauntering down the streets of New York.

I'm staring at the pieces in awe when it hits me.

There's no way Astor got these last night or early this morning. Which means he prepared for this trip days ago . . . which means, he's wanted me to accompany him since day one.

I smile, shaking my head. Until Astor is able to communicate his emotions like a real grown-up, his actions speak volumes. I'm okay with that, I decide. For right now, I'm okay with that.

Men take work, after all.

I find a note in the pocket of the white trousers. It reads: *To wear on the plane.*

In the other pocket is another note, this one wrapped in

cherry-red strings of lingerie. It reads: *To wear under everything.*

I press the notes to my heart.

Astor picked these out, he did the shopping, he wrote the notes. Not Prishna, not Leo, not Cillian. *Astor.* Once my captor, now my (emotionally-challenged) Prince Charming. And me, his (slutty) Cinderella.

Could this actually work?

Could he and I work?

Elated, I move to the bathroom where rows of cosmetics and skin care are organized on the counter. All luxury brands.

Bracing myself on the sink, I stare into the mirror, my pulse flying.

A change is coming.

I can feel it.

My life is about to change.

This is it.

Fifty-Six

Sabine

WE TAKE Astor's private jet to New York—naturally. But unlike last time, I'm not tied to the backseat. Now, I'm Astor's guest—no, *his date.*

I feel like the leading lady in my own little movie as we board the plane together, Astor in his black tuxedo, me in couture cashmere. Just us. No Prishna, no Cillian, no Leo.

Our flight begins with an early dinner, an elaborate spread of meats, cheeses, fruits, vegetables, and, of course, lots of champagne. For dessert, we have sex, which is quickly becoming our favorite pastime. In a nutshell, it's *Pretty Woman, Cinderella,* and *Rochelle, Rochelle* all rolled into one little (big) trip.

The sun is just beginning to set as we arrive in the city. I slept the entire flight (sex with Astor really knocks it out of me), while Astor caught up on work.

Nerves bubble in my stomach as our limousine rolls to a stop next to a red carpet flanked by strobing spotlights. Everything is sparkling—the lights, the camera flashes, the dresses, the rings. People are *everywhere*, including dozens of paparazzi.

I smooth my clammy palms over the ocean of black dress that surrounds me.

Sensing my nerves, Astor slips his hand over mine. "Just be yourself."

I snort.

He squeezes my hand. "I can promise you three things tonight. One, you will be the most beautiful woman in the room. Two, every single person here is too caught up on what everyone else is thinking of them to judge you—trust me on this. And three, we will leave the moment you feel too uncomfortable, and we'll go find the biggest bag of potato chips you've ever seen in your life."

"Can we just skip to number three?"

Gently, he takes my chin. Astor is always impossibly gorgeous, but in a tuxedo? He's almost intimidating.

"I'll lead wherever you need me to," he says in that cool, confident tone that makes me melt. "I'll handle the small talk, the introductions, get you whatever you need. All you have to do is ask. Allow me to be in control, and I promise you'll feel comfortable. All I need you to do is stay by my side. I am your safe place, and you are mine. Do not leave me. Do you understand me?"

"Yes."

"Sabine . . ." The grip on my chin tightens. "Hear me—do *not* leave my side. I want you next to me all night."

"Yes, yes." I respond impatiently, only half paying attention as I survey the crowd. "I hear you. Do not leave; got it."

"Good. Now kiss me."

"You'll smear my lipstick."

"I'd like to smear it somewhere else."

"Stop."

He grins and pulls me in for a long, passionate kiss. I'm faintly aware of a car honking behind us.

"Astor," I mutter around his kisses. "I think they're wanting us to move."

"Screw 'em." Eventually, he pulls back and rubs his thumb over my top lip. "Don't leave me, okay?"

The vulnerability in his face tugs at my heartstrings. For all the brooding and controlling nature that warps this man, inside is a fragile human needing what we all do—love, trust, loyalty, and commitment, and really, really great sex.

"I promise," I whisper.

After a quick reapplication of lipstick, I take the white-gloved hand that appears when the door opens. Astor slides out behind me, and noise erupts. My senses shift into over-drive, assaulted by a sudden onslaught of flashing lights, shouts, and screams from women, all gawking at Astor.

He slides his hand into mine. I squeeze back, and in front of everyone, he leans into my ear. "Want me to lay you down right here and show these people how many fingers I can stick in your—"

I burst into laughter. Astor winks, grinning from ear to ear, and taps a kiss on my knuckle.

And just like that, the nerves dissipate, and I remind myself that I *am* worthy enough to be here.

• • •

The inside of the gala is like stepping into a dream—if I'd taken a hit of acid beforehand.

Everything is gold. Gold chandeliers, gold drapery, gold candles, gold-rimmed champagne glasses and plates. Even the flatware is gold. Massive displays of gold-dipped red roses perfume the ballroom. Sexy jazz music thrums from a twelve-piece orchestra in the corner, next to an elegant mirrored bar. Men in tuxedos move from circle to circle, posturing with their luxury labels and Barbie-sized wives.

The introverted part of me wants to perch on a barstool and people-watch for the entire event. Unfortunately, Astor has other plans. He is approached immediately, one tuxedo after another wanting to speak to the reclusive billionaire.

Watching Astor navigate small talk is both inspiring and enlightening. His public persona is very different from the man I see behind closed doors. This Astor is one of composed elegance. He offers just enough to make someone want more, then gracefully excuses himself, addressing the next person in line.

We fall into an easy rhythm. Astor introduces me, I smile, engage in a bit of witty banter, and then let him take over while I go back to my people-watching. He's never once released my hand, and he's right, I feel wholly comfortable because he is in control.

As I look around the ballroom, it's mind-boggling to think how far we've come, and how much my life has changed since Hurricane Stone blew into my life. I could lose myself in this, I think. Become addicted to the sex, the money, the power, the jealous looks from all the women. Little do they know the darkness that lurks under all the glitter.

We move through the auction items, talking, laughing, flirting. All eyes are on us, yet I don't feel insecure. Quite the opposite.

Let them whisper, wonder, gossip. Who cares? In a matter of hours, I'll be screaming Astor's name in a private jet while they masturbate to his online picture after faking an orgasm with their whiskey-dicked husband.

He's *mine*.

The drinks keep coming, one after another. It's almost as if someone has been assigned to serve only us. Before I know it, I've got a heady buzz.

"I need to use the restroom," I whisper, the moment there

is a break in conversation between Astor and the couple he's speaking to.

"They're across the room," the woman offers, eavesdropping. "To the right, down the hall, dear."

"Excuse me."

The moment my hand slips away, Astor grabs it back, squeezes, and gives me a hard look.

I know, I know, I subliminally tell him. *I'll be right back.*

Fifty-Seven

Sabine

I AM DRUNK.

Like, *drunk-drunk*.

I didn't realize it until I almost fall face-first into the bathroom stall door while lowering onto the toilet seat. The champagne has hit me all at once.

"Shit." Trying to relieve myself around my massive dress is almost impossible. How do people do this?

Mission complete, I wash my hands, squinting at the reflection staring back at me.

For absolutely no reason, I reapply lipstick, eyeliner, and blush, giving myself a clownish appearance. When I turn from the sink, I walk right into a pair of blonds who remind me of the stick figures I used to doodle in elementary school, as does the size of their dresses.

"Your nipple is out," I slur, pushing my way between them.

"What the—"

The other gasps in horror. "Oh my freaking G—"

Grinning, I push out the door, but then I wobble on my heel, which slaps the smartass smirk right off my face.

I'm turned around. Both ends of the hallway disappear into shadows. From which end did I come from?

A young couple is giggling in the distance, so I turn in that direction and sway down the plush carpet. The end leads to another hallway, and another, until I find myself back in the ballroom—on the opposite end from where I left Astor.

I don't see him anywhere. The lights have dimmed, and the crowd is making their way to the tables.

How long have I been gone?

"Ma'am."

A tall, attractive man with wavy blond hair rises from a barstool. Of course I wandered to the damn bar.

"Would you like my seat?"

"Uh . . ." I scan the crowd, and when I still don't see Astor, I shrug. He'll find me, and also, these heels are killing me, so *yes* I'd *love* a seat.

"Sure, thanks."

The man takes my hand as I awkwardly gather my dress so that I can perch on the teeny-tiny stool. He reminds me of one of the Marvel heroes from the movies. Handsome, but in a bashed-up kind of way. Not nearly as prim and proper as the rest of the crowd.

He's sexy, I decide.

"What are you drinking?" he asks.

"Just water for now."

"Water? Nonsense." He snaps his fingers to the barman. "Two glasses of champagne."

"And a water," I croak. "Please."

Mr. Marvel leans against the bar and smiles down at me. "I noticed you when you walked in."

"I didn't notice you."

His brow cocks, and he chuckles. "Name's Edgar."

"Sabine." I look over his shoulder, searching for Astor once again. A feeling of unease creeps through the haze of the alcohol.

"Where are you from, Sabine?"

"Vegas."

Where is Astor?

"Vegas, huh? You must be a performer with that body."

Ick. And no, I manage a billionaire's illegal assets, you twat. Correction—*managed*. As in, past tense. Now I have sex with a man who kidnapped me and pretend it's totally normal.

Where is he?

The champagne and water are delivered, although I don't reach for either. Marvel picks up his drink and rests the other on the back of my stool.

Again, I scan the crowd, suddenly beset with an awareness, an instinct, that sends a chill racing over my arms.

Sabine, do not leave me.

I turn back to the bar and am gathering my dress to stand when Edgar is suddenly yanked backward. His bar stool goes flying. He gasps, his eyes round like golf balls as he is lifted off his feet and thrown to the floor like a bag of trash.

All eyes turn to us.

I practically fall off the stool as Astor fills my vision, his face mottled with hives, his eyes wild with rage. "Time to go."

"Astor, watch out!"

Edgar, now off the floor, swings a vicious punch, missing Astor's head by a mere inch.

A woman screams.

Someone yells, "Fight!"

Another cries out, "Call the cops!"

All hell breaks loose.

I stumble backward as Astor's fist connects with Edgar's

face in a sickening sound of crunching bone. Blood splatters everywhere.

The man doesn't go down at first. With a river of blood running down his face, he rushes Astor, sending him slamming against the bar. Glasses and bottles go flying, shattering against the walls, the floor.

I see the moment Astor snaps. The moment he turns into a different person. And it is terrifying.

Like a machine on fast-forward, Astor engages in some insane mixture of martial arts and street fighting. He delivers a devastating right hook, immediately followed by a fist to Edgar's stomach. As Edgar doubles over in pain, Astor grabs his head, rears back, and slams his knee into Edgar's face, sending his head snapping backward and his body launching into the air. Edgar hits the floor like a dead weight, his face a bloody mush. He's knocked out cold.

It's absolutely horrific.

Astor grabs me by the arm and pulls me across the floor, screaming at everyone who is rushing him.

"Stop," I yell repeatedly at him, pain rocketing up my shoulder.

He spins around and yanks me to him so hard that my head snaps back. "Shut up! This is your fault—I told you not to leave!"

One shoe tumbles off, then the other, as I am dragged outside. I'm vaguely aware of someone yelling, "Help her, help *her*!"

The limousine is already at the curb when we rush outside. A woman screams when she sees me, and it's then that I realize that Edgar's blood is all over me—even my face.

Astor literally shoves me into the back of the car and ducks in after me.

The car peels out, speeding down the road.

"What *the hell* was that?" I manage to choke out through heaving breaths.

Astor doesn't answer. I'm not even sure he heard me. His eyes are wild, his jaw locked, his neck flushed and speckled with blood. His chest is rising and falling heavily.

He looks like a monster. *An animal.*

"You were supposed to come back to me, Sabine." His threatening tone sends a chill up my spine.

"Astor." I gawk at him. "We were just talking."

"Never, *ever*!" he bellows, and I jump out of my skin. "Never again! You are *mine*, do you understand? You are mine, and I will treat you accordingly!" He grabs my arm and twists it so hard that my skin burns. "I love you, Sabine. I fucking love you, and it makes me fucking crazy. Seeing you with another man—I can't. I won't. That will never happen again. *Ever.*"

"Astor." A chilly calmness comes over me. "Get your *fucking* hands off me."

* * *

We don't speak the entire four-hour flight home.

Once inside the manor, I hightail it to my room.

Ten minutes later, Astor appears in the doorway.

"I'm done," I say, tears streaming down my face. "You lied to me when you told me you would never treat me like that again. I'm done with this, and I'm done with you. I can't handle the crazy roller-coaster mind-fuck that is Astor Stone. Tomorrow morning, I'm going home. Not that you'll care, right? Because if you did, you wouldn't treat me like that. Hell, you said it yourself—no one would care if I left."

Despite the anger, I break into uncontrollable sobs.

"I can't do this anymore, Astor. I'm done. I'm done with you."

And with those final words, I lunge forward, push him into the hallway, and slam the door in his face.

235

Fifty-Eight

Sabine

I WAKE to the sound of rain tapping against the windowpane. A gloomy grayness colors the room, matching my mood. A sick feeling of dread washes over me like a thick black cloud.

I'm done. The words I'd yelled to Astor the night before hit me like a punch in the gut.

I wince, rolling my shoulder. If he would have yanked me much harder, he would have pulled it out of its socket.

I lift my head. The armchair at the foot of the bed is empty.

Astor never came back. It's the first night he didn't watch me sleep.

My stomach rolls.

I stare at the chair, a glaring symbol of the vacancy now between us. Of the end, of the nothingness I feel inside.

Shut up! This is your fault—I told you not to leave!

I'm done . . .

I press my palms to my eyes, which feel like a pair of sand-boxes. I have no more tears. I cried them all out last night.

The despair is so sickening that I can't take it. So, I do what I always do. Push it aside and plan my next step.

I'm leaving tomorrow . . .

That's what I'd told him, so that's what I'll do. I'll pack what few belongings I have and get the hell out of here.

Refusing to acknowledge that I am about to vomit, I force myself to sit up.

I gasp.

Dozens of black leather boxes stare at me from every surface of the room.

I recognize the label from the jewelry store I visited during my short trip into town. The store where Astor first screamed at me for not being where I was supposed to be, when he expected me to be there.

I throw off the covers, pad across the room, and pick up the first box. Inside is a pair of diamond earrings, and in the next is a diamond tennis bracelet. The next contains a pair of gold bangles.

I place my hand over my mouth. These are the pieces I spent time admiring while perusing the glass cases. Every piece that the saleswoman showed me then is here now, right in front of me. Astor must have called the store and purchased every single thing the saleswoman said I liked.

There are at least a dozen boxes in the room.

My stomach flutters as I move to each box, the contents of each more stunning than the last.

When I come to the end of the Easter egg hunt, I notice something on the seat of the armchair that once held the man who told me he loved me.

I love you and it makes me crazy. Seeing you with another man. I can't. I won't . . .

This box is different from the others. It's large and velvet with a gold clasp.

I pick it up, my hands trembling.

My heart stutters as I open the box. It's the piece I spent the most time lusting after. Their "showcase" piece—aka, the store's most expensive piece of jewelry. It reminded me of Astor and me, of me with him and him with me. Of death to self and pain, followed by a beautiful rebirth.

"Oh my God . . ."

My heart pounding, I carefully lift the necklace and gape at the diamond butterfly pendant with a sparkling red ruby in the center.

A notecard lies underneath it. It reads:

I would care if you left.

Fifty-Nine

WITHOUT PLANNING what I will say, what I will do, if I'll kiss him, if I won't, I run out of the bedroom while securing the necklace around my neck.

My feet skid to a stop the moment I fling the door open.

Astor is sitting on the floor, his knees up, leaning against the wall. He's still in his tuxedo. His hair is mussed, his eyes bloodshot and sallow. He's ghostly pale.

Astor might not have watched me from the armchair, but he never left me.

He surges up, his face riddled with nerves, sadness, and such desperation that my heart cracks.

"Astor."

"Can I kiss you?" The question comes out breathless in one long word.

Tears fill my eyes. "Yes."

"Oh, baby." He cups my face in his hands, tears filling his eyes too.

The kiss is the kind of toe-curling, butterfly-inducing,

sweep-you-off-your-feet kiss that leaves you dizzy and breathless. Like he's a desperate, starving man, and I am his only nourishment.

There is no lust in this kiss, no feral need for intimacy. This kiss is wrapped in agony, in need, in gut-wrenching despair.

"I'm so sorry," he whispers between kisses, his voice cracking with emotion. "I am so, so, so sorry."

His tears wet my cheeks.

"Me too. I'm sorry too." I pull away. "Astor, thank you for the jewelry, but I—"

"No." He takes my hands. "Don't thank me, and before you protest, you're keeping it. All of it. I'll buy the entire store if you want. I'll do anything you want. Can I please talk to you? Will you talk to me?"

I nod, pulling in a breath to steady my racing heart.

"Sabine, I am so sorry. I apologize, with all my heart, for speaking to you that way."

He squeezes my hands, and I can practically feel the pain radiating through the tips of his fingers.

"I'm so sorry for everything I've put you through, but more than that, I'm sorry for making you question, even for a second, my feelings for you and how much I love you. That's what hurts the most. I have failed at being the man I should be and *need* to be for you. When I saw you that first time, it was like something in my soul recognized you as a vital piece of my existence. I can't lose you."

Tears roll down his cheeks.

"Just please—please give me a second chance. Please don't leave me. Sabine, *please*. My beautiful butterfly, please don't leave me."

"Oh, Astor." I release his hands and cup his cheeks. "I love you too. I love you, I love you, I love you. We're so screwed up, but I love you."

I'm lifted off the floor and squeezed so tightly, it reminds me of a child hugging their mother.

"We'll make it, okay?" he whispers in my ear. "I want to do this, with you. I want to make it work. Today is the first day, my sweet Sabine. Today, okay?"

Just then, Cillian appears at the end of the hallway.

Astor and I look at him and freeze.

The expression on his face is jarring. Something is wrong. Very, *very* wrong.

"Astor," Cillian says. "We need to talk."

Sabine

"SHE'S ALIVE."

The two words detonate like a bomb between my ears.

Valerie, Astor's *wife*, is alive.

I stand there, in the doorway of Astor's office, as Cillian walks him through a message he just received from a woman who's supposed to be dead.

I'm not even certain Astor is aware I'm here. He's too preoccupied with the earth-shattering news. As if the world is just as stunned, a thunderstorm has erupted, sending rain slashing across the windows.

"I don't understand," Astor says, shaking his head. He's even paler than when I opened my bedroom door and saw him on the floor.

"It's real. I validated it. The email was sent from the secure account that you set up secretly for her years ago for emergencies."

Astor leans in, studying the screen. "Did you check the IP address?"

"Yes, it's registered to Blum and Levy."

"Carlos." He grabs a mug off the desk and shatters it against the wall. "That *liar*. He still has her. She never died. That son of a bitch."

Astor begins pacing, his shoulders hunched, his fists trembling at his sides.

Cillian watches him, frowning. "She must have somehow gotten into Carlos's personal computer or phone and reached out that way."

"When was it sent?"

"Two hours ago. I've pinned the coordinates to an abandoned airport hangar about an hour north of here, out in the middle of nowhere. It was previously used for helicopters and small planes to conduct search-and-rescue missions in the mountains, but the facility was shut down a few years ago and the business was relocated." Cillian pauses. "If Valerie never committed suicide like Carlos said she did, why the hell did he tell you that? Why did he make you think that?"

"To get back at my mother." Astor shakes his head.

"What do you mean?"

"After she got his brother locked up, he committed suicide, in the same way Carlos said Valerie did. In jail, he wrapped a sack around his head and suffocated himself to death. I didn't even put it together."

"The picture he showed you of her dead on the floor must have been AI generated."

"*Stupid*, how could I have been so stupid?"

"Don't beat yourself up. We've got him now."

"Get your shit together. We leave in twenty minutes."

"*What*?" I rush into the room, no longer able to keep my mouth shut.

Astor spins around, his expression softening when he sees me.

Thunder rumbles in the distance.

"Leave us." He flicks his wrist at Cillian.

Cillian spares me a glance before closing the door behind him.

My pulse is pounding as I stride across the room and meet Astor behind his desk. Long gone is the broken, shattered man begging me not to leave him. Standing in front of me now is a resolute, tenacious mercenary ready to fight. A killer.

But this time, he's not fighting for me. He's fighting for his *wife*.

"What the hell is going on?" I snap.

"Valerie emailed me."

The sound of her name coming off his lips is like a knife through my heart.

"Are you sure it's her?"

"Yes."

"What did it say?" I look at the laptop sitting open on the desk. Next to it is a map, scribbled on by Cillian. *X* marks the spot. "I want to read it."

I push past him and squint at the email, which contains only one seemingly innocent sentence.

I'm going to be late tonight. Love, Valerie

"It's code," Astor says, scrubbing his hands over his face. "Because I believed her safety was at risk by simply marrying me, I set up a special communication system. We have several code words and phrases for her to use in different scenarios if she needs help. This one means she is in imminent danger and needs immediate help. Only she and I know the codes. No one else. Not even Cillian."

The thought of Astor going to such lengths to protect her is another jab to my heart. Prishna's words sneak into my mind like a deadly virus.

He is still, and always will be, madly in love with his wife

. . .

I'm speechless, staring at him like an idiot. It feels like my entire world has crashed down around me.

What does all this mean? For us?

Astor reaches toward me. I think he is going to pull me in for a hug and tell me everything is going to be okay, and that *I* am the only woman who holds his heart. Instead, he reaches past me, opens a drawer, and pulls out a pistol.

"We're leaving in thirty minutes."

"We?"

"Yes. I'm not leaving you here alone."

"What's your plan? Where are we going?"

"To get my wife back."

"Get *your wife* back?!" I throw out my arms. "Then what? That's it?" I gesture between us. "For us? That's it?"

"I made a commitment, Sabine." He snaps back, impatient, frustrated. "Her daughter—*our* daughter—was killed because of her relation to me. It's my fault. Everything is my fault. I can't just leave her."

"The guilt, Astor. It's going to kill you one day."

"What do you want me to do, Sabine?" he bellows.

I startle, reminded of the man last night who brutally beat someone for speaking to me. The man who dragged me out by my arm, like an insolent child, in front of a hundred people.

He throws out his arms. "What do you want me to do, huh?!"

"I can't believe this, I . . ." *I don't know what the hell to say.*

I shake my head, suddenly dizzy.

How the hell do I answer that question?

Sixty-One

Anonymous

I COULDN'T SLEEP last night. The anticipation of today was too great, too exciting. Everything is in place. Years of waiting for the perfect plan, the perfect opportunity, the perfect time. It's finally here.

It's time.

I pull the picture from my pocket and peer down at the image one more time. The sweet smile. The blond ringlets. The sparkle in her eyes. So full of hope. Little did she know . . .

On a deep inhale, I slip the photo back into my pocket.

Carefully, I reach into the other pocket and gently wrap my fingers around the small clear syringe.

It's time.

After taking a quick breath to recenter myself, I enter the room.

Astor and Cillian look up from the map they're hovered over, covered in red lines and circles, all paths leading to a large *X* in the middle.

"Pri." Astor frowns at my boots, which are speckled in mud. "Where have you been? You okay?"

"Yeah. I was outside when I got your text to come here. Sorry. What's going on?"

"Cillian and I have something we need to attend to immediately. Sabine's coming with us. Instead of going to the beach house and gathering Valerie's things like I asked you to, I want you to stay here and wait for orders." He turns to Cillian. "Bring the car around. Sabine's in her room. I'll grab her, and we'll head out."

Cillian nods and exits the office.

"When will you return?" I ask, sweeping my long braids into a ponytail.

"Not sure. Just make sure to stay on your toes while I'm gone. Keep an eye on the property."

"Don't worry," I say with a smile. "Everything is in good hands, Mr. Stone."

Sixty-Two

Sabine

I'M STARING out the rain-slicked window with my arms crossed over my chest. The landscape behind the glass is a distorted prism of bleak colors, swirling together in chaos.

It's exactly how I feel inside.

Yesterday, the view was pristine. Perfect. Today, everything is still there, but now it's all running together in blurred confusion, and like the rain, I can't control it.

Just like that, everything has come tumbling down.

I'm accompanying Astor to "save" his wife. Okay. Do I just wait in the damn car? Then what? What the hell does he think is going to happen when the three of us are together?

How is he going to introduce me to her? Or is he going to introduce me at all? Am I going to be discarded at the nearest bus stop? Because I sure as hell know that he will not discard her. Not with the guilt that plagues him.

For Astor's demeanor to shift so drastically—in an instant, from declaring his love for me to vowing to save her—shows how much he cares about his wife. To *not* save Valerie wasn't even considered. And I'm a total bitch for even thinking that, I know.

Maybe I shouldn't go. Maybe I should leave now and tell him to call me when it's all sorted out. Or how about don't call me at all. After all, he's married.

Holy shit—he's *married*.

I've slept with a married man. Told a married man I love him.

I am not Astor's woman. I am his mistress.

Sabine, the *mistress*.

I choke on the word when the air around me shifts. All at once, my body jolts to alertness, my senses piquing.

I am not alone.

Before I can turn around, a hand covers my mouth and the tip of a blade presses into my lower back, piercing the skin.

"Not a word," Prishna hisses in my ear.

She jerks my head, presses the knife deeper into my flesh, and like a bridle on a horse, she guides me out of the bedroom and into the hallway.

My gaze frantically darts for Astor, but I know he's still in his office, at the opposite end of the house.

Adrenaline surges through my veins.

I thrust my elbow backward, connecting with Prishna's stomach. She grunts, relaxing her hold just enough for me to lunge forward.

"Astor!" I scream but my throat is too constricted. His name comes out in nothing more than a desperate squeak.

Prishna tackles me from behind, knocking the air out of my lungs.

We tumble to the floor, me at a disadvantage because I fall facedown. I try to twist, try to fight, but she grabs a fistful of my hair and slams my face into the hardwood floor. Fireworks burst behind my eyes. A blinding pain ricochets through my head, followed by a dropping feeling in my stomach.

The prick of a needle barely registers before everything goes black.

Astor

"THE TIRES ARE SLASHED."

"*What?*" I look up as Cillian strides across the office.

"All four, slashed. Fresh, best I can tell."

"On the Tahoe?"

"Yes—and your car is gone too."

My stomach drops.

"Where's Sabine?" I croak.

"I don't know."

I lunge out from behind the desk and sprint down the hall, yelling her name. With each vacant response, my pulse beats faster.

Is Carlos here? How did he get past the security cameras?

I burst into her bedroom.

A half-packed bag lies on the bed, a glass of water on the nightstand.

There's an energy in the room that sends a chill up my back. Something bad lingers here. Something evil.

Screaming her name like a madman, I check the bathroom, the closet, even under the bed like a fool.

"Check every room in the house."

"On it." Cillian spins on his heel and jogs down the hall.

My heart roaring, I pick up the black sweatshirt lying on the bed—my sweatshirt—as a million thoughts run through my head. But there is only one that matters.

I need to find her. Period.

Taking the shirt with me—no clue why, other than it feels like a piece of her with me—I jog out of the room and meet Cillian in the foyer.

"She's not here."

"Outside? The dock?"

"No. And Pri's gone too."

It's as if the world suddenly stops spinning and a little echo of a voice materializes in my head.

"Pri hates me, Astor."

"Pri wants me gone."

"She makes me feel uneasy."

"Pri said you *gave her Valerie's clothes for me to wear . . ."*

In a dizzying revelation, everything comes together at once.

Prishna took Sabine. She put Valerie's things in Sabine's room, she's been watching Sabine from the woods, she cut Sabine's hair—because she's one of the few people who know that Chloe's was cut in the same way.

Prishna—one of my most trusted associates.

It's too much to comprehend at the moment, the why and how of it. Only one thing matters, and that's to get Sabine back.

"She's got her," I croak out. "Pri's got Sabine."

"I never liked that woman, boss. Never."

I pull my cell phone from my pocket and call Pri's number.

It goes to voice mail.

Again. Same result.

I feel like I'm going to throw up.

I try one more time, praying she answers and tells me something innocent, like Sabine asked her to take her somewhere. But I know, in my gut, that's not true.

"Fuck!"

A rush of rage blows though my system.

"Where are you going?" Cillian barks as I push past him.

"To find Sabine."

The garage smells like fresh exhaust. Wherever Prishna is taking Sabine in my car, she's only just left. The only other vehicle, the Tahoe, is sitting on four flat wheels.

I sprint across the garage, rip off the vinyl cover, and stare down at the blacked-out Harley I haven't ridden in years.

After Valerie and I moved to the lake house, she enjoyed taking hours-long drives through the mountains on the bike. The doctor had advised us to do it. Said fresh air and sunshine would help her depression. I haven't had it serviced since. Honestly, I hate the thing.

Cillian frowns, striding across the garage. "It's raining, boss."

"Do you have another suggestion?"

"Yeah, give me ten minutes to switch out these tires for spares."

"We don't have ten minutes. The rain is going to wash away the tire tracks from the car—maybe already has. I'll lose her if I don't have fresh tracks to follow."

Cillian jabs his fingers through his hair, clearly disliking this idea.

I focus on the bike. I know, at the very least, I should check the battery and fluid levels, but I don't have time. I figure I'll ride it as far as it takes me, then follow them on foot if I must. That is, if the thing even starts in the first place.

I swing my leg over the bike and settle onto the seat with Sabine's sweatshirt on my lap. Cillian is already working on switching out the tires on the Tahoe.

It takes me a second to get my bearings. After engaging the choke, I turn the ignition.

The lights click on—dimly, but on, nonetheless.

Hell yes.

I take a deep breath and place my hand on her sweatshirt, then whisper, "To whoever is in charge of this crazy universe, I'm calling in a favor right now."

I close my eyes as I squeeze the clutch and press the start button. The engine roars to life.

I look over my shoulder at Cillian, who's as surprised as I am.

"Well, son of a bitch," he says with a grin.

Slowly, I back up, wobbly, still rusty on driving this hog.

Cillian meets at the garage door and hands me a helmet. "Don't die, brother."

"Bring some extra firepower," I say, securing the sweatshirt to the back. "I have a feeling we'll need it."

"One step ahead of you." He gestures to the guns and ammo already stacked on the floor next to the Tahoe. "Go get your girl."

I slide on the helmet, shift the gear, and press the throttle.

Sixty-Four

Sabine

THE MOMENT I REGAIN CONSCIOUSNESS,
a wave of nausea hits me like a Mack truck. It's so intense that
I feel like I've been pushed off a hundred-foot bridge and am
falling through the air. With it comes a knife-like pain in my
forehead, the combination so gnarly that I can't open my eyes.

Am I dying?

Am I already dead?

I become vaguely aware of a vibration under my body. A
bump, then another, and another, then the damp smell of
earth around me.

I'm in a car, and it's raining outside.

Groaning, I try to move, but my hands are bound at my
waist. Memories slowly trickle in.

Prishna shoving a knife into my side . . .

Prishna attacking me . . .

A needle piercing my neck . . .

My heart begins to pound.

"Bitch," I spit out.

A low chuckle comes from the front seat. "That's calling the kettle black."

I blink wildly, subconsciously demanding that my brain level out the blurred vision. Whatever Prishna knocked me out with is lingering in my system like a date-rape drug. I turn my head and feel something slide down my collarbone.

Astor's necklace. The beautiful butterfly necklace.

Where is he?

Is he *okay?*

Prishna glances over her shoulder. "Don't try to move. It's useless."

"Why . . . why, Prishna?" My voice is weak and gritty. It's hard to think, to speak, let alone piece together what the hell is happening.

"You were completely unexpected, Sabine."

Prishna's tone is eerily calm, which is even more unsettling. Whatever plans she has for me, she's confident in them.

"The moment you showed up at the lake house, I began observing you. I'd arrived hours before Astor thought I did. Immediately, I wanted you gone. I knew you'd be a distraction. I knew you'd fall in love with him, just like my sister did, and every other damn woman who crosses his path."

"You did it all, didn't you? Put her picture in my room, the dolls, you cut my hair . . . told me he was still in love with her . . ." Another wave of nausea rolls over me. My God, this is awful.

"Yes, and when scaring you away didn't work, I figured I'd make Astor think you were going crazy—just like Valerie did —and he'd send you away, just like he did her."

"My hair . . . you cut it to spook him because you knew his daughter's hair was cut on the day she died, didn't you?"

"Her name is Chloe," Prishna snaps.

"You're a bitch."

"No, I'm a survivor."

"Why do you have me now? Where are you taking me? Just kick me out of the car. Let me go; you'll never see me again."

She shakes her head with a chuckle.

"Why not?"

"Because I realized I could use you."

"How?"

"Do you remember me telling you about my childhood?"

I vaguely recall the conversation Prishna and I had on the patio when she told me her mother discarded her for not being a boy. That she grew up in an Indian orphanage, with very little, before she was adopted by Valerie's parents.

"Being thrown away by my parents had a profound effect on me—I know this from all the therapy I was forced to go through in rehab. I turned to drugs to cope; eventually got addicted to heroin. I don't remember half my life. You see, Sabine, every child needs a fair shot in life—and it begins with a loving parent."

"I don't understand what this has to do with me."

"When Astor and Valerie had Chloe, she was discarded as well. Not in the same manner as I was but discarded emotionally. Valerie had severe postpartum depression, and Astor worked all the damn time. He was never around. Chloe had no parents. So, I stepped in and mentally adopted Chloe, just like I'd been adopted, and I raised that beautiful little girl. *I* raised her. Without me, she wouldn't have had a fair shot at life."

Prishna's tone darkens.

"Because of my sister's and Astor's negligence, Chloe died. She *died*, Sabine, at *five* years old. I'd given her a shot at life, and they took it all away. Valerie and Astor have blood on their hands—it's all their fault."

"I'm sorry, Prishna, but—"

She continues as if she hadn't heard me. She's emotional, distant. Mad.

"I carry that little girl's picture around with me all the time, her ashes in my suitcase." Prishna's voice is trembling. "I wouldn't have stayed sober without that little girl. She was my everything. I miss her so damn much."

So, it was Chloe's ashes in Prishna's suitcase.

She bangs her fists against the steering wheel. "And she's dead because of their negligence!"

The vehicle shifts, and we begin climbing a steep mountain.

"If you hate Astor so much, why did you stay with him? Why did you keep working for him after Chloe died?"

"Because he made it impossible to leave him!" she yells, unhinging right in front of me. "You, of all people, should understand that, Sabine. This is what he does. He manipulates or blackmails you, and you don't even see it, and before you know it, you're forever indebted to him."

Astor's and Prishna's words echo through my head . . .

"Prishna was on a downward spiral and had some major health issues when Valerie and I married. So, I opened my house to her and gave her a fresh start at life, offered her a job."

"After recovering from the fire, I learned that Astor had paid my medical bills and had wiped my debt clean . . . I've been working for him ever since."

"But you see, Sabine," Prishna says, "you can only be a prisoner if you're unable to find an escape. Finally, I've found mine—and you're it."

"How?"

"You'll see soon enough. Astor will go to the ends of the earth to find you, and I'm counting on that. And then, finally, I'll be free."

So, I'm bait.

Bait.

At the end of this crazy, insane journey, I'm still only bait. My entire life can be summed up in my being a means to an end.

Useless.

I realize then that this is my fate. I've been useless ever since I did nothing as two men broke into my home, driving my mother to a fatal heart attack.

I am still that useless little girl who didn't stand up and be brave when I needed to. Who will die without ever making an impact on anyone's life.

No one will remember me. In the end, Astor was right.

I was such a fool to think otherwise.

I drop my head on the seat and begin to cry.

Sixty-Five

Astor

I DRIVE like a madman over the dirt roads, slicing through the sheets of rain, fishtailing around corners, almost blind by the rain streaking across my helmet. I am out-of-my-mind psychotic, a feral combination of rage and desperation driving me past the brink of insanity.

All I can think is, *Sabine has to be okay.*

She *has* to be.

I can't lose her. Not now. Not before I've made things right. Not before giving her a chance to see who I can be for her.

Sabine can't be Valerie. I can't let another woman down. I can't lose another person in my life without making things right.

Sabine can't be my mother. I can't lose the only other woman I've ever loved.

And finally, Sabine can't be Chloe. I can't lose the light of my life *again*.

I cannot fail her like I have everyone else in my wretched, warped, screwed-up excuse of a life.

Sabine has to be okay.

She *has to be okay.*

There can be no other outcome.

Because I will burn down the entire fucking world if she's not.

Sixty-Six

Sabine

"WE'RE HERE."

With a jolt, the car stops and the engine shuts off. The deafening pounding of rain fills the cab.

I raise my head from the backseat. I must have slipped out of consciousness from the drugs Prishna gave me. Though the headache and nausea are still there, I feel less like I'm on a roller coaster.

The front door slams shut, and the back door opens. A rush of cool, wet air rushes inside. I breathe in deeply. *Clear my head of this haze.*

Prishna grabs my shoulders and yanks me upright, pulling me toward her. I groan with the movement, feeling like I might vomit and secretly hoping that I do—right on her shoes.

"Come on, come on," she says as I find my footing on the muddy ground. "*Jesus*, come on," she growls now, unhappy that *she's* getting wet.

Finally, I straighten, my back feeling like a knotted rope. I wobble, unable to get my balance with my hands tied at my waist.

God, I feel awful.

Blinking through the rain, I take in my surroundings. We are on the top of a mountain, looking down on miles and miles of thick forest. In the middle of nowhere.

Prishna's long silver-streaked braids fall over her face as she grabs hold of my arm. Her eyes are slits, her pupils large and black. The scars on her face glisten under the rain running down her cheek. She looks like an animal.

I'm spun around and forced to walk. Dipping my chin against the rain, I focus on the ground to steady myself.

One step, two step, three steps. *Don't fall.*

We cross what appears to be an old parking lot. The concrete is stained and fractured. Long blades of grass spear up from the cracks.

The rain is relentless, pelting my shoulders, my head, dripping off my nose as I shuffle like the prisoner I am across the concrete.

Ahead is a large metal garage with two large bays. An airplane hangar—abandoned, based on its condition. Lines of rust mar the sides, resembling long streaks of blood. One garage door is covered in spray paint, mostly gang signs. A row of long, narrow windows line the top. It's dark inside.

Faded below the graffiti is a symbol of a helicopter's wings and the words: *S&S Search and Rescue.*

What the hell are we doing here?

I am sopping wet as Prishna pulls open a heavy metal door with a cracked window.

She drags me inside.

Dimly lit by a dozen smudged skylights, the space is even larger than it appears from the outside. Trash is everywhere. Torn shopping bags, wrappers, tattered shop rags mingle with drifts of leaves scattered across the concrete floor. Stains mar the floors, the walls, the large beams that serve as support. The air is stale, tinged with old motor oil and must.

It's completely empty—except for a gleaming black helicopter sitting outside the back bay, and two people standing in front of it.

My heart drops to my feet.

Sixty-Seven

Astor

I ABANDON the motorcycle halfway up the mountain, so they won't hear me coming. Breathless, I sprint through the forest, branches and thorns ripping my clothes and clawing at my arms. It's still storming, but the canopy of leaves overhead provides a decent shield so I can at least see where I am going.

The outline of the hangar slowly comes into view.

I press harder, faster, my breath coming out in short, ragged gasps. I can no longer feel my burning quads, constricted lungs, pounding heart. I've slipped into a robotic state of mind, programmed with only one goal: *Get Sabine before it's too late.*

As I breach the top of the mountain, I don't pause at the clearing. There's no time.

Double-fisting my gun, I hunker down and jog across the cracked concrete, skirting the side of the metal building. Best I can tell, I've come up on the back side of the hangar. A black helicopter sits on the small landing, just outside a bay. I'm careful to avoid being seen.

Cillian either hasn't arrived or had the same idea I did—ditch the vehicle and sneak up the mountain. There's no telling where he is. If Cillian doesn't want to be seen, not even a thermal-imaging camera could spot him. The man is a ghost.

I strain to hear anything from the inside, but the sound of rain drumming against the metal roof drowns out everything.

Thunder rumbles in the distance as I round the corner of the building.

Parked in front is my Aston Martin. The back door is standing open. No one is inside.

I squat next to the metal door that serves as the main entry and debate my options—which are extremely limited. Only two, really.

One, I wait for Cillian and we breach together. This is the smartest option.

Or two, I breach alone. The quickest option—and therefore the one I go with.

Staying low, I open the door, raise my gun, and lunge inside.

My pulse skyrockets as the scene unfolds around me.

Carlos is holding Valerie, his gun pressed to her side. My wife, back from the dead.

My *wife*.

Her appearance is jarring. She's sobbing, her face red and mottled. She's wearing a dirty housedress that stops just below her knees. She's even skinnier than I remember, her weak frame emphasized by Carlos, who towers over her by more than a foot.

Carlos, on the other hand, looks like he's ready for war. His long brown hair is tied back in a slick ponytail. He's wearing a pair of khaki utility pants and scarred brown boots. He smirks when he sees me, while Valerie's jaw drops.

Next to them, Prishna is holding Sabine, a knife to her throat. Her eyes fill with tears the moment she sees me.

My gaze darts back and forth between the two hostages.

My wife and the love of my life.

An impossible situation.

I try to understand the scene around me.

Prishna and Carlos are working together. It's almost too incomprehensible to process. I trusted this woman. Prishna has been working for me for over a decade. I gave her a second chance at life, opened my home to her, my life, both professionally and personally. I think of all the things she has access to, everything she's overheard, things she's read, printed, arranged. She knows my entire life.

Which is exactly why she got the drop on me.

Fucking idiot, and fucking bitch.

My eyes lock on Sabine, my sweet, beautiful butterfly. Her forehead is red and swollen, and a thin trickle of blood runs down her neck. Rage blows through my veins.

"Let her go." I shift my stance, pointing the sight of my pistol between Prishna's eyebrows.

"Who?" Carlos asks. "Your wife or your whore?"

Prishna laughs.

"Pri," Valerie croaks, barely audible. "What are you doing?"

"Something I—*we*—should have done a long time ago."

"You're my sister . . . stop. Stop this. You're not thinking straight."

"*I'm* not thinking straight? You haven't had a single straight thought in years. Your incompetence as a mother is the reason Chloe is dead."

At the sound of my daughter's name, I snap. "Will someone tell me what the fuck is going on here?!"

Carlos tilts his head to the side. "You know exactly what's going on here. You set this up. Last week, you offered me a swap—Valerie's body for Sabine. And here I am, ready to collect."

Oh shit.

Sabine's eyes widen with shock, with pain.

The betrayal she must feel, the foolishness.

No, no, I did it before, I want to scream. *Before I fell in love with you.*

My stomach curdles, and suddenly I feel like I'm losing control.

"Stone," Carlos says. "You and I go way back. You're the one who started everything when you went behind my back and fucked Valerie, my first girlfriend, my first love. Then you went and married her just to put the final nail in the coffin."

Oh God. I look again at Sabine.

I lied to her and told her I didn't know Valerie before our "one-night stand." I said it because I didn't want her to think there were real feelings between Valerie and me. Because there weren't. There never was.

Sabine's lips part, and her face pales.

Oh shit. Shit, shit, shit.

Carlos continues, his gritty voice like a goddamn hammer to my eardrums. "But it doesn't stop there, does it, Stone? As if that wasn't enough, your mother killed my brother. She's the reason he's dead. Honestly, I should have done this back then."

A mad chuckle bubbles out of him. His eyes grow wild.

"And even then, you *still* don't leave me alone. You go and destroy my most profitable real estate venture, costing me almost everything I'd worked for."

"Money can be replaced."

"My brother can't."

"Neither can my daughter."

"I didn't kill her, Stone. You know that. I've done a lot of shit in my life, but I don't kill kids. Trust me, I'd happily admit to it at this point if I did."

Valerie hangs her head, sobbing uncontrollably.

Carlos glances at her. "You have a way with women, don't you, Astor. Every woman who enters your life meets a tragic end, don't they? Your mother, in a plane crash, Valerie loses her daughter, and now Sabine, standing here with a knife to her throat. And Pri? Look at her. You made her hate you so badly, she's willing to do anything to get out of your clutches."

"How much is he paying you, Pri?"

"More than you ever would, Stone." She glares back. "Enough to go away and start a new life somewhere."

"In fairness, our partnership is new," Carlos says to clarify, like I give a shit. "When you took Sabine, I staged my men outside your penthouse in New York. There, they confronted Prishna on her way to meet you in the Tahoe. Using her was a backup plan in case you'd already killed Sabine. We struck a deal rather quickly. Her job was to deliver me both you and Sabine—if she was alive—and in return, I give her freedom from *you*. So, here we are. You get Valerie, I get Sabine, and we all walk out of here and never see each other again. Rivalry over."

"You think I'm a fucking idiot? You'll kill Sabine the second you get her. She's a liability to you now."

"Hey, I'm trying to be civil here. Technically, I could have just taken both women the moment Prishna showed up with Sabine, but I wanted to give you a fair chance to hold up your end of the deal."

"Liar. You have me here because you want to see me squirm."

"Fine, you got me. Now, I'm done with all this chitchat. I'm going to take Sabine and give you your wife, and if you interject, I'll kill both Valerie and Sabine right now and make you watch."

The second Carlos reaches for Sabine, I lunge forward.

He sends three warning bullets into the ceiling, shattering a skylight.

"Stop!" Sabine screams. "Just stop—everyone stop!"

I freeze in place, my heart roaring.

She turns to Carlos. "Take me. Just do this already." She looks at Valerie, the mess of a woman. "Give him his wife and let them go. Just let them go . . ."

Sabine's voice whispers in my ear as if she's standing right next to me.

"I didn't even try to protect the only thing in my life that I really loved and loved me back. I just stood there. A useless little girl who didn't stand up and be brave when I needed to."

No. *No, no, no, no.*

Sabine is going to offer herself as a sacrifice.

"No!" I yell, my voice cracking. "Sabine, no, you don't have to do this, you—"

"You are a liar, Astor!" she screams belligerently, the veins bulging in her neck and forehead. "Everything was a lie! This whole time, you planned to give me back to Carlos!" She bursts into tears. "Just take me, Carlos! Get this done. Give Astor back his wife and just take me!"

Tears fill my eyes, the torment of seeing Sabine's pain too overwhelming.

A sinister grin splits Carlos's face. He drops his gun from Valerie's waist and shoves her forward. She falls to her knees, sobbing like a child.

Then Carlos grabs Sabine from Prishna, pulls Sabine to him, and puts a bullet between Prishna's eyes. Her head snaps back, her long braids flying in the air as her body locks up like a plank and drops to the floor.

Valerie screams, curls into a fetal position, and covers her ears.

Cillian appears in the shadows of the doorway, his gun drawn.

"Stand down!" I scream, knowing Carlos will do to Sabine exactly what he just did to Prishna if Cillian threatens him.

Valerie begins clawing her way across the concrete, her hair covering her face, her weak, shattered voice saying my name over and over and over. I want to scream at her to *shut up*.

Carlos begins dragging Sabine backward toward the helicopter. There are no tears or fear now. She simply lifts her chin, as if accepting her fate, and mouths:

I love you anyway.

"Stop!" I press the barrel to my temple. "Let her go and I will kill myself, right here."

When Cillian moves, I scream at him to remain where he is.

Carlos stops, his brow arching.

"It's what you've always wanted, right?" My voice is shaking. "It's what this whole thing is about. You want me to suffer, to die, that's the bottom line. It's not about Sabine; it's about me. I trade my life for hers."

The realization hits me hard. I *will* die for Sabine, and I would do it over, and over, and over again.

Carlos's chest begins to rise and fall with excitement. He likes this new plot twist. It's *exactly* what he wants.

"Release her," I say, my voice booming over the rain, "and the moment my man takes her," I jerk my chin to Cillian, "I'll pull the trigger. You'll get to watch me die right here."

From the floor in front of me, Valerie looks up and reaches a skinny hand at me. "No, no, no, no, no, no."

"Deal."

Sabine is released.

Everything goes deathly silent.

Her eyes lock on mine as she slowly steps out of his hold.

I love you, I love you, I love you.

Cillian appears in my peripheral vision.

My heart feels like it's about to explode.

I love you, I love you, I love you.

Cillian takes Sabine's hand.

I love you, I love you, I love you.

I close my eyes and begin to squeeze the trigger.

"No!" Sabine lunges toward me.

Carlos raises his pistol.

Pop, pop, pop!

Sabine's body flies backward, hitting the concrete with a sickening thud.

I scream, lunge across the floor, and drop to my knees next to her body.

More gunshots explode around me. Windows shatter, metal splits.

"Sabine, Sabine, Sabine!"

Screaming her name, I frantically run my hands over her motionless body, stopping on the growing pool of blood on her abdomen. I rip off my shirt, press it to the wound, and apply pressure.

"You're going to be okay, my baby, you're going to be okay." My tears drop onto her face, sliding down cheeks that are growing paler by the minute. "Open your eyes, Sabine. I'm right here, I'm right here."

Valerie is clawing at my clothes, screaming my name, trying to pull me away.

In the growing pool of blood under Sabine's lifeless body, a sparkle of light catches my eye. I pluck the butterfly pendant from the blood and clutch it in my fist.

"My butterfly, my beautiful butterfly." I begin sobbing uncontrollably. I can't breathe. I can't move.

The chaos drowns to a dull roar, and I suddenly feel like I'm floating, staring down at myself and Sabine from some weird omniscient place.

Cillian grabs my shoulders and drags me backward, pulling me away from her body.

"He's got the place rigged with explosives!" he yells over my harrowing scream of grief. "Carlos never meant for any of us to get out of here alive. Come on! She's dead, man—come on! Leo's waiting for us outside! We've got to get out of here!"

I fight like a rabid dog, but it's no use.

"She's gone, Astor, she's gone! We've got to get the hell out of here!"

Tears stream down my face as I scream her name over and over like a dog being gutted. The name of the only woman I've ever loved.

My beautiful, beautiful butterfly.

Sixty-Eight

Astor

Two days later . . .

"MR. STONE?"

Hands in my pockets, I lift my head and turn from the window I wasn't looking out of.

The psychiatrist, Dr. Gorran, a short portly bald fellow with comically large hands, is standing by the door of the waiting room. I don't like him. I don't know why.

They'd asked me to wait at the end of the psychiatric wing of the hospital, in a room that appears to be a patient room they've transformed into a caregiver information hub. It's small and suffocating and smells like burned coffee.

Gorran is followed by another doctor, this one I haven't met. She's Asian, tall and svelte, with a sharp angular haircut that sweeps her jawline.

Gorran must have called my name several times before I responded, because they're both frowning at me in a concerned manner. In the same way everyone looks at me since I arrived at this godforsaken place.

"Mr. Stone, this is my colleague, Dr. Wu." We shake hands. "Dr. Wu is a neurologist who has been working with Dr. Stevens on your wife's case."

I nod. Over the last two days, I've met enough doctors to last a lifetime.

Dr. Wu steps forward. "Would you like to have a seat?"

"No. Thank you."

She dips her chin and focuses on the laptop in the corner, where she proceeds to key through several log-in screens before asking Gorran to hit the lights.

The room goes dark.

Gorran hovers next to me, a thick file in his baseball-mitt-sized hands. This is his thing, I've noted, expert invader of personal space.

A black-and-white X-ray of a human brain pops onto one side of the screen. Next to it is another.

Using a laser pointer, Dr. Wu begins.

"These are the MRI scans taken of your wife's brain this morning. The image on the left is what we consider to be a normal brain in a healthy individual the same age and sex as your wife. The image on the left is your wife's. As you can see here," she waves a little red dot across the screen, "your wife has markedly less white matter than the image on the left. Specifically, thinner cortexes in both the frontal and temporal lobes. It's important to note that thinning cortex is normal in aging, but your wife's is out of the norm for her age."

"In a nutshell," Gorran says, "this advanced thinning can cause the lobes to misfire, so to speak. In your wife's case, the frontal lobe is responsible for vital functions like memory, judgment, fine motor skills, and social appropriateness. The temporal lobe is responsible for memory too, but also regulating emotions."

"That's right." Wu clicks to another side. "What I see in your wife's images are congruent with Dr. Gorran's diagnosis of moderate to severe schizophrenia. In combining what we now know about abnormalities in her MRI, along with Dr. Gorran's assessment, our team recommends increasing the dosage of the medication Dr. Gorran has already prescribed, as well as adding . . ."

Dr. Wu rattles off several drugs I've never heard of, ones that I will spend hours researching this evening, just like I did the others, and just like I did when we received Gorran's life-changing diagnosis.

She asks, "When, exactly, did your wife's mental health issues begin?"

Almost immediately after she agreed to marry me, and I locked her in the house to guarantee her safety and the safety of our baby. But I can't say that, of course, so I dance around it.

"After we lost our daughter, Chloe. Literally, that day, she went to lie down in bed and never got back up. For days. She was never the same after that. I thought she was sick, honestly, but the doctor said she wasn't. And from there, she went downhill drastically. She never wanted to leave the bed. She was diagnosed with PTSD and severe depression shortly after."

Wu nods. "The exact cause of schizophrenia is unknown, but it is often triggered by a very traumatic episode, such as losing a child. Her diagnosis of depression was not wrong; it just likely advanced into her current condition."

When no one says anything, Gorran flips open his note-book. "As you know, your wife was in severe psychosis when you brought her in to us, as well as dehydrated, likely from her captivity. She also had several contusions on her body. As of this morning, her blood tests and urinalysis have come back normal, and the medication has relieved her psychosis.

Considering these things, we are looking at a release date of tomorrow."

He closes the notebook and looks at me.

"You and I have already spoken about this, but I want to reiterate that I strongly suggest that your wife be transferred to an inpatient psychiatric facility for at least a few months to get her medication—"

"No. As I already told you, I will take care of her."

His lips form into a thin line. "Okay then, Mr. Stone. I want to warn you that while we are going through the process of finding the ideal dosage and medication for a psychiatric patient, the patient can have relapses, anger issues, severe depression, suicidal thoughts or actions, or in some cases, be bedridden while dealing with side effects."

"I understand."

He turns to Dr. Wu. She is studying me so closely that it makes me itch.

"Okay." He sighs, obviously displeased with my decisions. "I'll have the medical equipment rep see you before you leave. She'll get you set up with everything you need for in-home treatment—hospital bed, wheelchair, bathing necessities, an IV stand if needed, etc." He glances at his notes again. "I understand you have refused to meet with our aid worker about setting up a nurse for daily visits."

"Correct. Valerie already had a medical team and nurse working with her for her depression. I've given their information to the nurse and signed a release waiver for your files to be sent to them."

An awkward pause hangs in the air.

Dr. Wu clears her throat. "Mr. Stone, do you have any questions about your wife's images or her diagnosis?"

"No."

"Okay, then." She logs out of the laptop. "It was a pleasure to meet you, Mr. Stone."

Dr. Gorran closes the door behind Dr. Wu and turns to me, his brow furrowed. I say nothing and stare back, a game we are quickly becoming bored of.

"Are you okay?" he says finally.

No response.

"If I may, sir . . ." He takes a deep breath. He's exasperated by me, and I don't blame him. "I've seen this many times before with caregivers who have themselves also been through a traumatic event. I see the markings of significant dissociative disorder in you. This happens when a person disconnects from their thoughts, feelings, memories, or sense of identity. It's a coping mechanism. But, Mr. Stone, please hear me. If your trauma isn't dealt with and addressed head-on, this disorder can turn into something that can greatly affect personal and social relationships, and in the most dramatic cases, lead to a full-on mental breakdown."

Gorran drones on, and all I can think of is how I want to put a bullet between his eyes.

The gall of this man. He's standing there talking to me about my trauma? *My* trauma. The dense twat doesn't get it. My concern isn't about me—it's about the trauma I've caused everyone around me.

Valerie.

Sabine. My dear, dear, Sabine.

My fault.

It was all my fault.

I swallow the knot in my throat. "Thank you for your time," I say, cutting him off mid-sentence because I can't take another word from his mouth.

Gorran nods and takes a step back, clearly disappointed in me.

Get in line, motherfucker.

Instead of waiting to be dismissed, I push past him and stride down the hall. And as with every other time, the chitchat stops, and all heads turn in my direction. I can feel the nurses' eyes burning into me as I hunch my shoulders and contemplate breaking into a sprint and hurling myself through the window at the end of the hall.

I hate this place.

Dipping my head, I push into Valerie's room. I fall back against the door and close my eyes.

I see Sabine. Every time I close my eyes, I see her.

Her face, those eyes, her smile. Her body as it flew backward. The blood pooling on her stomach.

The pain on her face as she took a bullet to save me.

Sabine saved *my* life.

It is all so twisted and messed up. It should have been me who died. It should have been *me* who saved *her*.

The guilt is unbearable, eating me from the inside out. Day and night, hour by hour, minute by minute, it shreds my insides.

You worthless, useless, pathetic excuse for a human being.
You should be dead. You *should be dead.*
You *deserve to die.*

A gentle cough pulls me back to the moment. My eyes open. I look at my wife, her little bird body tucked in the hospital bed.

One foot is hanging off the side. She keeps doing that.

I walk over and slide her thin white ankle under the sheet. Bracing myself against the mattress, I lean in. "Valerie."

Her hand flutters, and she coughs again. She speaks, but not often, and when she does, it's only two or three words at a time.

I hover there for a while, watching her chest rise and fall in shallow breaths.

I've failed everyone in my life, yes, but here lies my redemption. Here, in front of me, is one person that I can commit to helping. Here, I can begin to make up for all the wrongs.

My hand trembling, I sweep the snow-white hair from her forehead, seeing Chloe in her face. My beautiful, sweet baby girl.

If I could go back in time, what I would change. So many things. For starters, I would have spent more time with my daughter, loving her, pinching her cheeks, making her laugh. Holding her hand.

I lay a hand over my aching heart.

If I could go back in time, I would have pressed the cops harder to continue their investigation after ruling it an accident. I would have worked harder on my own investigation. I wouldn't have given up.

I don't have Chloe anymore, but I do have her mother, a woman I owe just as much. A woman I have vowed not to give up on. Not now.

"I'm here for you," I practice saying. "I'll be by your side. You are not alone, Valerie."

The door opens, and the nurse shuffles in. I quickly straighten, sniff, and gather myself. Her name is Marsha. She's blunt, competent, and unemotional. She's the only staff member here I don't want to punch in the face.

I step aside as Marsha takes Valerie's vitals.

"Has the doctor spoken to you about your wife's delusions?"

"Yes. Well, no, only that she's had them. I've heard her muttering things, but I can't make them out. Why? What specifically is going on?"

Marsha readjusts Valerie's pillow. "She keeps calling out for her daughter." She straightens and looks at me. "I'm sorry for your loss—I don't think I've told you that."

"Thank you."

The nurse nods, then continues. "When she isn't crying for her, she appears to be cursing someone."

A tingle spreads at the base of my spine. "I'm sorry—what? Cursing someone?"

"Yes. Angrily."

I frown. Valerie read Chloe's medical examiner's report and knows about the missing lock of hair, but she accepted the officer's analysis that Chloe had likely done it herself, as she'd done many times before. Valerie didn't draw the same conclusion I did—that someone had killed our daughter and that the missing lock of hair was meant to be a message.

"Who was she cursing? Did she say a specific name?"

"No, but to be clear, I didn't get the vibe that she was addressing someone in particular, just that she was, like, asking the universe why it happened. Anyway, I tell you this so that you don't worry if it happens at home. This is very common. She is on a lot of medication, and it's going to be a while before everything evens out."

I nod and thank her, but a feeling of unease slithers into my stomach like a warning, the heavy dread of something to come.

When Marsha leaves, I tuck the sheets around Valerie—very tightly around that one damn foot that keeps slipping out—and turn back to the window.

And once again, and forever, I think of Sabine.

I love you anyway . . .

And of how she must have felt when she learned that I'd made a deal to trade her for Valerie. How she must have felt when she realized Valerie and I had more history than I'd admitted to.

I love you anyway . . .

I suddenly feel like I'm going to throw up. I lunge to the bathroom and gag several times, but nothing comes out.

Swallowing the spit, I return to the room and begin pacing

to distract the feeling of death inside me, which has become a natural state of my body since Sabine died.

At two in the morning, my legs can't take another pivot in this godforsaken room, and my thoughts can't take another second of mulling over my mistakes.

Instead of replaying every word Sabine ever said to me, I decide to do something about it, focusing on her advice: *You need a journal. Start writing out your feelings. No one has to read it; it will just give you an outlet.*

I grab the notebook from my bag, a pen from the side pocket, and drop onto the world's stiffest couch. I pick up the black sweatshirt, press it to my nose, inhale, then set it on my lap.

After another deep breath, I begin writing a letter to Sabine, the first of what I fear will be many over the coming months.

Dear Butterfly,

My heart aches for you. Every hour, every minute, every second.

When I close my eyes, I see your face, I hear you, I smell you, for you have been forever imprinted on my soul.

But I can't see you.

I can't hear you.

I can't smell you.

I can't touch you.

The absence of you is felt in the vacancy of my soul. In the death that now resides in my body, the nothingness that has become as much

*me as my beating heart, in the hole that materi-
alized inside me the moment you left.*

The moment I failed you.

The moment I failed myself.

The moment I died inside . . .

"Astor."

I startle at the sound of Valerie's voice. My gaze shoots up from the notebook, and I realize I've been crying.

I close the notebook and jump up, quickly wiping my cheeks with the back of my hand.

"Yes?" I rush to her side. "Are you okay?"

Valerie slowly turns her head. Though she's looking at me, there is no focus. It's like she's looking right through me. Still, I get the sick feeling that she knows.

"Who was she?" she whispers.

She knows.

What do I say? *Her name was Sabine. She was my beautiful butterfly.*

"Who was she?" Valerie whispers again.

My love.

My light.

My reason for breathing.

My beautiful butterfly.

My everything.

"No one, Valerie." *Not anymore.* "Go back to sleep."

Sixty-Nine

Astor

IT'S three in the morning when the hospital room door creaks open. I'm sitting on the couch, my elbows on my knees, watching Valerie breathe.

It's Cillian.

I quickly lift my finger to my mouth. I don't want him to wake her.

He nods and jerks his chin to the hallway.

Quietly, I step outside. "What's going on?"

He glances furtively at the nurse behind the computer a few yards away.

"She can't hear us," I say, suddenly very aware that something is wrong. "What's going on? Speak."

"She's not there."

Every single hair on my forearms rises.

"What do you mean? Who's not there?"

"Sabine. Her body was not in the hangar when the crime scene techs did their sweep. Only two bodies were found, both confirmed to be Prishna's and Carlos's. There is no trace of Sabine Hart anywhere in that hangar."

"I don't understand." I'm suddenly breathless. "I don't fucking understand." My lungs feel like they are squeezing in on themselves. "She was dead, right?"

The look of doubt on his face makes me snap.

I grab his collar, lift him off the floor, and yank him to me.

"Right, Cillian?!" I bellow, and the nurses turn in our direction. "You pulled me off her because she was dead. You told me she was dead!"

"Astor, *stop*—calm the hell down." He jerks out of my hold and pulls me into an empty room and closes the door.

"Yeah." He begins pacing. "I thought she was dead. But the fact is that her remains are not in that hangar. I talked to the responding officers—had to bribe one of them for information; you'll get that bill. He told me when the explosive went off, only one side of the building burned. The other collapsed but was largely still standing. Technically, she could have gotten out if she was still alive. They're being super tight-lipped about it all . . ."

His voice fades. The room begins to spin, and I feel like I'm falling through a big black hole.

I reach forward, grasping for the wall, a second before everything goes black.

Part Two

Seventy

Astor

I SWAT at the mosquito buzzing around my face as I quietly close the car door. The cicadas scream at my arrival, their pitched whines like needles piercing my ear drums. The air is stifling, heavy with humidity brought on by a late afternoon thunderstorm. Already, I begin to sweat.

It's suffocating. Like being in a sauna.

I squint into the setting sun, hanging low in the sky, hovering just above the mountain peaks.

Per usual, I check the driveway for signs of recent tire tracks or footprints. When I find none, I scan the dense forest that surrounds the cabin, drifting from shadow to shadow. Miles and miles of nothing but rugged, dangerous wilderness.

A perfect place to hide.

Which was the point, I guess.

With the envelope clutched in my hand, I begin walking up the long dirt driveway, my boots crunching against the loose rocks. Massive cypress trees line the path, their long, crooked branches silhouetted by the setting sun. Spanish moss drips from the limbs, swinging in a breeze I can't feel.

I kneel down and study the trail of little paw prints set in dried mud. I've seen them several times now, and after taking pictures and studying the wildlife in southern Louisiana, I know they belong to a bobcat who must live nearby. It makes me uneasy. He's getting more confident. Soon, he'll be comfortable enough to climb onto the porch.

I grit my teeth and stand up, the t-shirt and jeans I'm wearing already damp with sweat. I hate this place. I don't know why anyone—in their right mind—would live here.

This particular region of western Louisiana is part of a dense, untamed forest known as the Piney Woods, and is marred with countless swamps and bayous. It's home to multiple dangerous species like panthers, wolves, and alligators, just to mention a few. It's a brutal untamed wilderness. Stubborn and unrelenting.

Just like the woman I'm visiting. . . . Though is it called visiting when the other person doesn't answer the door?

My pulse starts to pick up as the driveway curves and the tiny two-bedroom log cabin comes into view. Each time I visit, Sabine has done something new to the home. Last week she replaced the rotted planks on the wraparound porch. This week, she's added a swing bench next to the front windows. Potted begonias are everywhere; overflowing in a mismatch of pots. The bright red compliments the deep green of the shutters she painted three weeks ago.

My heart starts to pound, as it always does, as I walk up the four crooked porch steps that I've ascended what feels like a hundred times.

The cabin appears to be dark. No movement behind the glass.

I glance at the rusted Jeep parked to the side.

She's here.

She's always here.

My palm slides over the brass door knob, and like always, my brain tells me to just break in. To breach. To grab my beautiful butterfly, pull her into my arms and never let go again. But my heart reminds me, however, of Sabine's stubborn independence, and of the pain I'd put her through.

She needs time. Obviously, she needs time as she hasn't returned any of my phone calls, texts, emails, or opened the door.

I love you, anyway.

Those words—her words.

I love you anyway.

Those were her last words to me before being gunned down, after offering herself to Carlos as a sacrifice.

Let Astor and his wife go, and take me.

My *wife.*

Frozen, with my hand on the doorknob, Sabine's face flashes behind my mind's eye. The shock and pain in her eyes when she learned that I had made a deal with Carols *before* falling in love with her. The deal that said I was willing to trade her body for Valerie's.

I love you, anyway, she'd said, despite it all, in her final moments. In Sabine's worst moment, she still loved me.

The four words have haunted every minute of every day since then.

A knot grabs my throat, desperation clinging to me like a noose around my neck.

She needs time, Astor. Give her time.

I release the knob, and raise my hand and knock.

An eerie silence settles around the woods as I wait for the woman who has my heart to open the door.

To give me one more chance.

I knock again.

Again.

Again.

Again.

"Sabine," I whisper, dropping my forehead against the door. "Please, Sabine. Please open the door."

I wait for another five minutes before conceding. I kneel down, laying the envelope on the welcome mat, as I always do.

Then, I back away, tell her I love her, and retrace my steps back to my rental car.

Seventy-One

Sabine

SITTING with my back against the front door, I listen to Astor's footprints fade down the driveway.

On a long exhale, I close my eyes and drop my head in my hands.

For three months this has been going on.

Like clockwork, twice a week, on Saturdays and Wednesdays, Astor shows up at my cabin. After I ignore his knocks, he lays a letter on my doorstep and disappears, leaving me with my heart in my throat and my stomach on the floor.

At first, I was shocked that Astor knew I was alive. And also that he knew I'd left my Las Vegas apartment, and moved to Louisiana. But then I remembered he's Astor Stone and his entire life revolves around espionage.

Every time he visits, I wonder if it will be the last. If not, I wonder when he will give up.

I wonder when *I* will finally give up on *him*.

The last three months of my life have been horrific.

There's no other word for it. I wouldn't wish it on my worst enemy.

After Astor left me bleeding out on the airport hangar floor, I dragged myself across the concrete as the building burned around me, passing by the dead bodies of Prishna and Carlos. By the time I made it outside, the first responders had arrived. After strapping me onto a gurney, they rushed me to the hospital, where I was treated for a bullet wound.

I was extremely lucky, they'd said. The bullet had gone through my lower abdomen, but miraculously didn't enter the abdominal cavity. Instead, the bullet had lodged itself behind the pelvic bone, in the buttocks, without causing any damage or fracture. According to the doctors, it was a miracle.

It didn't feel that way.

Once released, I went back to my Las Vegas apartment, promptly packed my belongings, and using a large chunk of my savings, purchased an isolated cabin in the one place I was certain Astor Stone would never visit. The Deep South.

I was wrong.

I'd bought a burner phone (so that he couldn't track it), rented a U-Haul and drove myself here.

At that time, my entire being focused around one thing: to never speak to Astor Stone again. The anger and betrayal I felt was all-consuming. The hurt, devastating. But the worst part was knowing that while I had been left for dead, Astor was back with his wife, tending to her physical and emotional wounds.

I could never—*would never*—forget that I had been offered in exchange for her, then forgotten the moment she reemerged in his life.

I know Astor loves me. And I also know he doesn't love her—not in the way that he loved me. But this fact doesn't console me.

I've learned that, when the inevitable storm hits, being let down by the person you love the most outweighs the love you share when the waters are calm. Because that's when we need them the most—not in the calm before the storm, but when we're drowning. Anyone can love anyone when things go as planned. It's in the chaos that relationships are either bonded or broken.

And Astor broke me.

It wasn't forty-eight hours before he showed up for the first time. He sat on my doorstep for hours, calling my name, begging me to answer the door.

That night, he slept on the doormat, while I slept on the other side of the door.

The next morning, Astor tried again, for hours, to no avail. When he returned four days later, he was prepared for me not to answer.

This time he brought a letter.

Four days after that, the same thing—another letter.

For three months I sit against the door and wait until he leaves, with tears streaming down my face.

In the beginning, the letters were gut-wrenching apologies, leaving me in a puddle of tears on the floor. But, as the season has changed, so too have the letters. Today's reads:

Dear Butterfly,

One of my favorite books is The Art of War.

One of the key principles of this book is that a war must be won before it's begun. Decisions are made in forethought, not as a reaction to events that have already happened. It's about selectively choosing to win, regardless of the hurdles before you, and preparing accordingly.

I will win you back, regardless of time or circumstance. I will not give up on you, or on us. I will wait for you for as long as you need. My success—our success—is predetermined and my focus is singular. You.

My reason for waking up is you.

My motivation for continuing to live is quite simply: You.

You will accept me back, Sabine. Because I am yours, and you are mine. We are written in the stars, in my heart. Tattooed on my soul.

I will not stop. I will keep showing up.

I will continue to prove to you that my love for you is eternal. Until one day—one day—you will open that damn door and allow me the opportunity to be the man you've always needed me to be.

You, Sabine, have my heart. Please allow me the honor of holding yours once more.

Yours now and forever.

Always waiting,
Astor

Seventy-Two

Astor

IT'S HALF past eleven in the evening when I pull up to the beach house.

Cillian's SUV is parked next to Leo's beat-up Ford. A dim light glows from the kitchen window.

I roll to a stop on the opposite side of the cottage and cut the engine.

Per usual, I sit glued to my seat for a full minute, dreading facing what lays beyond the four walls ahead of me. I gaze at the moon, surrounded by a million twinkling stars. From my vantage point on the cliff, they seem so close that it feels like I could reach out and touch them. I wish I could. I wish I could spread my arms, ascend into the sky and just be free.

Free from myself.

A silver beam of moonlight stretches across the black ocean below. It's a still, quiet night. Cool for late summer.

When I'd purchased the cottage a decade ago, it was meant to be a vacation home. Surrounded by twenty acres of dense forest and a lush garden, the two-bedroom home sits on a cliff that overlooks the Pacific Ocean. A small walkway zigzags down the side of the cliff to the shoreline. The moment I saw it, I knew it was mine.

After Valerie and I had gotten married and her depression and hatred for me became too overwhelming (for both of us), she moved here, under the care of a medical team. After that she and I rarely spoke or saw each other for years. Now, here we are again. Similar circumstances, although nothing is the same.

I drag in a deep breath, pocket my keys, grab my duffel, and step out of the car.

My back pops painfully as I slowly right myself.

The flight from the beach house to southern Louisiana is just over four hours, one way. So, every Saturday and Wednesday, I am in the air for a total of eight hours, and driving for a total of three. The bi-weekly trips have taken their toll on both my pilot and my body—but not my focus. If my body failed me, I would still find a way to make the trip. Every day if I had to. If that's what Sabine asked of me.

"Evening, Leo," I say over my shoulder, hearing him before I see him.

"Hey, boss."

Leo hikes up the sloped hill of the side of the house. Wearing all black, he's almost invisible in the night, aside from the long blond ponytail running down his back.

Leo's position within my company has morphed dramatically since he joined years ago. Originally, the former Marine was hired as a mercenary, but when he injured his back during his third mission, I hired him to manage my properties, where he is on-call 24/7. Now, he doubles as a security guard for the beach house to ensure there are no unwanted visitors—or threats. When he isn't monitoring the property, which is ninety-percent of his life, he's bartending at a local seaside pub. Leo is a simple man.

Rarely speaks, never complains, and is always on time. We get along well.

"All quiet?" I ask.

He smooths a hand over the top of his head. "All quiet on the loop, boss."

The loop is what we call the perimeter of the property, including all twenty acres and multiple entry points. It's a lot to monitor. His security job here entails the outside only. Inside, between Cillian and I, there is always someone here.

I glance at my watch. "You can cut out early, if you'd like."

"No, it's fine; I'm on until sunrise."

"You look like you need sleep, son."

Leo glances in the direction of his apartment, twenty miles away.

"Go," I urge. "Get some sleep. I'll do a perimeter check later tonight. See you tomorrow."

Leo dips his chin. "Thanks, boss."

Cillian is sitting at the breakfast nook when I walk in, a laptop in front of his face, a longneck bottle in his hand. I glance at the master bedroom at the end of the hallway and am relieved to find the door closed.

Cillian looks unusually tired and it's then that I realize my pilot (and my back) isn't the only person who's affected by my trips to Louisiana. The moment I found out Sabine was alive, I made Cillian, my right-hand man, the interim CEO of Astor Stone, Inc. so that I could be freed up to deal with something I've never dealt with before. Two women, one who owns my last name, the other who owns my heart.

Cillian looks up from his computer, blinks away whatever email he was engrossed in.

He leans back, looking me over, and picks up his beer. "Did she open the door this time?"

"No." I toss my duffel on the chair, grab a beer from the refrigerator and join him at the table. I'm in a shit mood.

Cillian takes a long drag off his beer.

We sit in silence for a moment.

Suddenly, Cillian frowns and leans forward. "What the hell is on your arm?"

I glance down at the swollen, oozing bumps that cover my exposed skin.

"Bug bites."

"Gross, man. They don't have bug spray in Louisiana?"

"There isn't a strong enough chemical on earth to keep away swamp bugs. Trust me on this. They're the size of my fucking fist."

After sleeping on Sabine's front porch after my first (failed) visit, I'd awoken to hundreds of insect bites, head to toe. I bathed in antihistamine cream for the following three days. Eventually, I just got used to them. Just like I've gotten used to wearing supermarket T-shirts, worn Levi's, and boots instead of suits every day. I can't remember the last time I wore a suit, or got a haircut. Even the five o'clock shadow I used to trim to perfection has grown into a full-on beard.

Yes, I am a shell of the man I used to be. I'm aware of this.

I just need to get Sabine back and everything else will fall into place.

"The swamps." Cillian chuckles and shakes his head. "She *really* didn't want you to follow her did she?"

"She knew I'd find her, just like she knows she'll take me back." I sniff.

"Not if you die of malaria first."

"I'll buy some spray," I say, exasperated.

Cillian's computer dings with another email, pulling our attention. One of the million emails intended for me that are now being handled by Cillian.

When he accepted the interim role, I wasn't sure how he would handle the demanding position. Turns out, Cillian is a shrewd businessman. Before now, Cillian's strength lay in his fists. The man was a born mercenary—a savage predator known for his brute physical strength. Now he spends his days on the phone with the United States Department of Defense and studying case files.

So much has changed.

Everything has changed.

"I was just typing up your daily summary," he says.

I dip my chin, and again, we fall into silence. Both too tired to talk about work.

"How's Valerie?" I ask, finally.

He blows out of breath, sinking deeper into the chair.

"She slept most of the day and night. She was really out of it when she was awake."

"So, normal, then?"

"Yes. And that reminds me—Charles sent over a few dates and times for you to meet with the attorneys he's vetted to help work on the divorce."

"I'll take a look, thanks."

After learning that Sabine was alive, I reached out to Charles, my main attorney, about navigating a divorce with Valerie. While in the ER, I made a promise to Valerie that I would be by her side while she learns to navigate her diagnosis, and I meant it. However, I understand that I cannot continue in a fake, loveless marriage while the love of my life is out there.

When Valerie and I got married, she signed an iron-clad prenuptial agreement, which I'm certain she didn't read. (And, admittedly, I didn't push her to do so). Valerie was much too eager to step into the "Astor Stone lifestyle" to care about much else. However, with her recent schizo-phrenia diagnosis, things have become muddy. Apparently, divorce becomes exceptionally complicated when it requires an attorney who specializes in the grounds of legal incapacity.

"Did she speak today?" I ask.

"Not to me, but I think she said a few words to Jackie when she came by for her daily visit."

Jackie is Valerie's home-care nurse. After interviewing dozens of candidates, I hired Jackie years ago, not only for her competency but also her no-bull attitude. Despite being barely five feet tall and two decades older than most nurses these days, Jackie walks into the room like she owns the place.

"Oh," Cillian continues, "and she left a 'how to live with someone with schizophrenia' pamphlet on the counter over there."

I snort. A pamphlet. Ha. Since Valerie was diagnosed months ago, I've read every article available on the subject. Even still, I feel completely out of my comfort zone.

"How were her vitals today?" I ask.

"High blood pressure again and a slight temperature. I think Jackie took some swabs or something," he jerks his chin to a piece of paper sitting on the counter, next to the pamphlet. "There's the summary of her visit."

We drink our beers somewhere in-between the comfortable silence that comes with being friends for so long, and a simmering tension from things unsaid.

Then, to my surprise, he says it . . .

"So. How long is this going to go on?"

Seventy-Three

Astor

I LOOK DOWN, twisting the beer bottle between my hands. I'm honestly surprised it took him so long to ask.

"Astor." Cillian leans forward on his elbows, demanding my attention. "How long are you going to chase a woman who doesn't want to be caught? How long are you going to put your billion-dollar company at risk for a woman who doesn't want to be yours? How long are you going to be the caretaker for a woman you don't love? How long, friend, are you going to juggle two women at the cost of everything you've worked for?"

I don't respond because I have no answers to the questions.

Cillian snaps closed his laptop and stands. "I'm going to head to the hotel. I'll be back tomorrow morning to discuss things that need your approval before I head to the New York office."

I nod as he walks out of the room.

I push away my beer. I don't even want it anymore.

As I walk down the hallway to the master bedroom, anxiety tightens my body like a winding rope. Dread, like a wall of wind, threatens to push me back while I drag myself forward. It's the way I feel every time I walk into the bedroom.

Like a prisoner walking to the electric chair.

I open the door.

The moonlight streams over the bed, highlighting my wife's emaciated body tucked under the covers, and her long blond hair fanned out over the white pillowcase.

I strategically placed two nightlights in the bedroom, allowing just enough light so that I could see without having to turn on a lamp when I check on her throughout the nights.

The moment my boot crosses the threshold, she lifts one finger and begins tapping it against the bedspread, as she does every time I step foot into this room. Her body still and eyes closed, her finger *taps, taps, taps,* faster and faster, as if she's matching the beat of my pulse.

Tap, tap, tap . . .

"Why?" she whispers hoarsely, still not opening her eyes. "Why?"

"Why what, Valerie," I ask quietly, stopping at the edge of her bed, though I know what she's going to say, because she responds the same way every single night.

Every *single* fucking night.

"Chloe." Her face screws into a painful expression. "Chloe, Chloe, Chloe . . ."

The sound of our deceased daughter's name off her tongue is like knives piercing my heart.

I try to console her as I always do, but it's useless.

I sink onto the edge of the bed, place my hand over hers. "You're having a bad dream, Valerie; wake up."

"Chloe, Chloe, Chloe . . ."

"Valerie. Wake up."

She begins thrashing under the blanket, unusually agitated.

Since the incident in the airport hangar and then being officially diagnosed, my wife hardly speaks to anyone but me. The doctors say it's likely a combination of PTSD and her body adjusting to the new medications she takes daily. During the day, she's mildly lucid, but in the nighttime, somewhere between sleep and wakefulness, my wife continually begs a response to one question:

"Why, Chloe? Chloe, Chloe, *why?*"

"VALERIE, WAKE UP." I gently shake her shoulders.

Her eyes flutter open.

She blinks, coming out of her dream.

Finally, she focuses on me, her brows knitted together. "What?"

"You were dreaming again."

My wife peers at me with the same dazed, confused expression she has every time we go through this routine.

"You were saying her name over and over."

"Chloe's?"

"Yes."

Valerie closes her eyes and drags in a long inhale. "I'm sorry."

"It's okay. Do you remember it this time? The dream?"

"You've asked me a hundred times, Astor. No, I don't remember any of the dreams. I don't remember even saying her name or asking why. I don't even know why I'm asking why."

I pretend to smooth the edge of the sheets while I wait for her to say more—hoping she'll say more. That she'll remember whatever it is that's trying to come out of her.

It's been five years since our daughter, Chloe, was found dead at the bottom of a sewer drain. An accident, according to the police. She'd fallen, they'd said. While Valerie accepted their final report, I didn't. I believe our daughter was murdered.

Valerie hasn't spoken of Chloe in years, until now. It makes me uneasy, unsettled, like the past is coming back to haunt us.

As it always does.

I pick up the empty porcelain cup from the nightstand. "I'll make you some tea."

"Hand me my book before you go, please."

Not long after Chloe died and Valerie went into a downward spiral, I gifted her a book about loss and grief. *To Grief and Back*, it's called. Valerie thumbs through it often and asks for it when she's particularly unsettled. Like now.

Minutes later, I return with a warm cup of chamomile tea. After helping Valerie sit up against the pillows, I click on the lamp. It will be at least an hour before she falls asleep again.

Every night, same routine.

She coughs and I notice she's more pale than usual.

"Do you remember that stuffed lizard she used to love?" Valerie asks, surprising me.

"Yes, I remember it well."

"You remember it was missing one eye? And I think even a toe. And then," she smiles fondly, "remember when I accidentally put it in the washer with Chloe's sheets and poured bleach on its back? Chloe was so mad at first, but then decided it looks like spilled milk, so every time they'd have a tea party, she'd pour him milk instead of tea."

Gentle smiles cross both our faces. Until losing a child I never knew that joy and sorrow could be felt simultaneously.

"She loved that thing," Valerie whispers, lost in memories.

"Carl."

"Oh my gosh, you're right." Her eyes round. This is the most lucid I've seen her in days. "That was his name. Carl." She chuckles. "What a terrible name."

I'd thought the same thing. We'd laugh about it together. The few times we laughed at all.

"Do you know where it is?" She asks.

"In our storage unit in New York. We boxed it up with most of our stuff."

"You mean Prishna boxed it up."

I blink, startled by Valerie mentioning her deceased sister.

According to her doctor, Valerie is suffering from short-term amnesia. She remembers everything before the incident at the airport hangar, and everything since waking up at the hospital. But nothing that happened inside the hangar.

Valerie doesn't remember seeing her sister get shot in the head, by Carlos, a man out for revenge. She doesn't remember me putting a gun to my own head, asking Carlos to take my life instead of Sabine's. She doesn't remember Cillian dragging me out of the burning building while I fought against him, trying to claw my way back to Sabine's bleeding body.

The only reason Valerie knows Prishna is dead is because after waking in the hospital, she kept asking for her. Eventually we told her that she'd passed away in an accident. We had a small funeral, and haven't spoken about it since.

A long moment stretches between us.

Then—

"Why don't you ever talk about her?"

"Prishna?"

"No. Chloe. Our daughter."

My body stiffens. "I don't know," I lie.

The reason I don't speak about our daughter is because the conversation always leads to one place: a fight between us.

Valerie shakes her head. "We should have sued the city, you know? It's their fault they left the manhole cover off."

"Chloe didn't fall into that manhole, Valerie."

"Yes, she did." Valerie snaps, emotions flushing her cheeks.

"Then how do you explain the lock of hair that was missing from her head?"

"She cut it herself! You know she did. She'd cut her own hair at least half a dozen times." Her speech begins to slur as her emotions rile. "I'd always tell you to put up the damn scissors. But you were never there—"

"That's enough!" My voice echoes against the walls.

The room falls deathly silent.

"I apologize," I say stiffly, and stand. "Please drink your tea, Valerie. It will help ease you."

I study my wife, unbelieving that we have been married for years, but still, and have always, felt like complete strangers. After having met Sabine and now knowing what real love is— the soulmate, can't-live-without-you kind of love—only emphasizes the absences of feelings between Valerie and me. We never loved each other. We married because I accidentally got her pregnant after drunken sex in the back of my limousine.

When I turn to walk away, she calls after me.

"Where do you go twice a week?" She asks. "On Saturdays and Wednesdays?"

I stop cold. "What do you mean?"

"Twice a week, you're gone for at least ten hours. Sometimes twelve. Where do you go?"

To beg for the love of my life to take me back.

"Work."

"Liar."

I frown, feeling a distant instinct awaken. Is Valerie beginning to remember what happened? Does she remember seeing me cry over another woman? Offering my life for another woman's?

I've spent hours considering how I would respond if Valerie asked about Sabine. I've landed on honesty. When the subject arises, I will tell Valerie that I am in love with another woman, and let the pieces fall where they may.

I clear my throat and look away. "You need to sleep, Valerie."

"I can't sleep now." She sits up, peels back the covers. "I'd like to take a bath."

Relieved to be away from the conversation, I quickly say, "I'll prepare it for you."

Seventy-Five

Astor

USUALLY, Jackie, the nurse, takes care of assisting Valerie in the bathroom. But as her nightmares have increased, a midnight bath is sometimes the only thing that will soothe her.

I stay close to the bathroom door, per the doctor's orders. Until we find the optimal dosage for her new medications, Valerie is considered a fall risk.

As she bathes, I pace outside the bedroom door, whiskey in hand. It's now one in the morning, and the buzz I've gotten is making me more tired.

"Astor?"

I stop, frown. Is that Valerie?

"Astor . . ."

I rush into the bathroom where my wife is standing next to the bathtub, naked. Suds slide between her protruding breast bones, down her painfully skinny, pale body.

My reaction is visceral. Pure disgust.

I lower my gaze to the floor. "You okay?"

"Come here."

Something in her tone sends a tingle up my spine.

"Are you okay?" I repeat, unmoving. "Do you need something?"

"Yes. Come here."

My heart starts to pound as I cross the marble floor, slick with splashes of water.

"Look at me," she demands.

I don't.

"I said, *look at me,* husband."

Her chin is lifted slightly, her jaw clenched in defiance.

"Have sex with me."

I blink. "What?"

"Have sex with me, Astor." Her tone turns whiny and desperate. "Like we did the first night. Please, I beg of you. Have sex with me."

She reaches for me and I recoil like a cat.

"No, Valerie. You're just tired—you're not thinking straight. You need sleep."

"No, I'm not—"

"Val—

"You are my husband!" her voice quivers with emotion. "And I want you to have sex with me."

She throws her arms around me, stumbles as she leans in and tries to kiss me. I turn my face and jerk back my chin, fighting the urge to throw her into the wall. Her grip on me tightens as she sloppily licks my neck, my ear. Her hands are trembling.

"Valerie, please stop." My voice quivers with emotion. "Please. *Stop.*"

She begins weeping, tears mixing with the trail of spit she's leaving on my neck. "You don't love me. I'm your wife, yet you don't love me."

I grab her wrists, yank them down and hold her in place. *"Stop."*

"No!" She yells, tears streaming down her face.

She's completely unhinged.

I stand frozen as my wife drops to her knees and begins unbuttoning my pants, while spurting sobs and tears.

"I'm your *wife*," she keeps repeating, as if convincing herself as much as me. "I'm your wife! We're supposed to do this. Please, Astor. We're *supposed* to do this."

She grabs my flaccid penis, pulls it out of my boxer shorts and sucks me into her mouth.

I close my eyes, wanting to vomit. When I can't take it anymore, I pull her face away.

"Lay down," I demand through a clenched jaw.

She does, her watery, desperate eyes locked on mine.

My heart roars as I lower on top of her.

She grabs my dick and guides it to her opening. I squeeze shut my eyes and drive into her, gritting my teeth so hard that pain shoots up my temples.

Stomach swirling, I thrust into her, over and over, until finally, she screams my name.

Immediately, I pull out, surge up, grab a towel and toss it to her. Turning my back, I step into the shower, turn the knob to scorching.

The second she leaves the room, I drop to the shower floor, cover my mouth with my hand and begin sobbing.

Seventy-Six

Sabine

IT'S A HOT, humid night. According to the forecast, a line of severe storms is expected to roll in around midnight. I can feel it in my hip. Ever since the incident, I feel atmospheric pressure changes in the exact spot the bullet lodged itself. I'm a walking barometer. Maybe I should join the circus.

I park the Jeep I paid three-thousand dollars for from a retired Army vet under an oak tree. Its leaves are wilted and brittle from the unrelenting later-summer heat. When I'd chosen Louisiana, I hadn't considered the humidity. A major misstep on my part. The upside is that I have curly hair now.

Next to me is a jacked-up Chevy with an American flag hanging out the back. The bumper sticker reads: *Hot Mess Express.*

I don't doubt it.

The neon sign above the door flickers as I cross the gravel parking lot.

Boots and Bourbon.

My second home.

When I first moved here, I didn't leave my cabin, aside from going to the grocery store, for six weeks. For almost two months I did nothing but lay in bed and cry. Trying to come to terms with what happened. Trying to push it all away. Trying to forget about him—and his wife.

The only thing that would get me out of bed was Astor's bi-weekly visits. I would drag myself to the front door, as close to him as possible without letting him in—physically and emotionally—then drag myself back to bed after he left.

Eventually, the need for human interaction crept up and I set out to find the nearest bar. I wasn't necessarily looking for friends, I just wanted to be in the presence of other living, breathing people.

Boots and Bourbon is so much of a southern cliche, that at first, I thought I'd walked onto the set of a movie. It's a real honky tonk bar with hardwood floors, walls covered in road signs, torn leather booths, and an old red jukebox in the corner. A pool table sits in the back, in front of a small stage where they host karaoke multiple times a week. (My new favorite obsession).

Tourists don't come here. This is a local's place.

Wearing a pair of jean cut-offs, a faded Madonna T-shirt, and flip flops, I saddle up to my usual seat at the end of the bar. The woman who used to wear cocktail dresses and Louboutins died in the airport hangar. That naive little girl is long gone—and I'm still trying to figure out who's taken her place.

"Hey there," Josh, the bartender greets me, wiping his hands on a towel. Covered in tattoos, Josh wears the same black T-shirt and torn jeans every day. He's the only regular here who hasn't asked me on a date, and because of that, I feel comfortable with him. We've fallen into an easy, surface-level friendship. One time, Josh asked why I turn down every man who approaches me.

Because once you've had Astor Stone, no one else compares.

"The usual?" He asks as a burst of laughter rings out from a trio of drunken cowgirls playing pool in the back. Betting one of them is *Hot Mess Express.*

"Please."

Josh pops the top of a cold longneck and hands it to me.

Along with jean shorts, I've also started drinking beer. I ordered my first for no other reason than to fit in (everyone around here drinks beer), but to my surprise, I found myself enjoying the cool, refreshing buzz it offers.

The juke box switches to an old country song and I lean back and watch the muted football game on the television mounted in the corner. This is my routine. After three beers, I'll sign the check, call it a night, and, on the way home, be proud of myself for actually leaving the house.

As usual, my thoughts slip back to Astor and anticipating his next arrival.

I knew after his first visit that he wouldn't stop. After all, Astor's identity has been built on loss, which has manifested into controlling behavior, demanding that those he loves be kept under lock and key. I think, somewhere deep down, the reason I fled the area was because I knew me leaving would hurt Astor the most. It's hard to keep tabs on something that's three-thousand miles away.

Astor has lost his mother and his daughter. Not to mention the hundreds of deaths doled out by him and his mercenaries. Death lives and breathes inside of him. The constant vigilance that comes with knowing that his loved ones are potential targets, combined with unaddressed grief, turned Astor into a callous man.

Astor quite literally cannot function if he believes someone he cares about is in danger, and he acts out of fear, walling them off from the rest of the world, while thinking he's doing the right thing. This obsession has had a profound ripple effect on those close to him. Both Valerie and her sister, Prishna, went to great lengths to get out from under Astor's thumb.

I struggle with it myself, part of me knowing how unhealthy it is, while another part of me revels in his obsession with me, counting the seconds until I can see him again, even if only through my peephole.

Sabine

I'M on my second beer when a man steps up beside me.

"Is this seat taken?" he asks in a southern accent almost as thick as the beard on his face.

I take him in, tall, thick, with kind blue eyes that sparkle with clarity—which means he's not drunk. Which means he's safe.

"Have a seat."

The man settles in next to me. I catch the scent of motor oil on his skin. An auto mechanic, then. A good guy to know when you drive a vehicle that was eligible for the "antique car" license plate.

"I've got twenty on the Razorbacks," he jerks his chin to the television, then leans in, "but don't tell anyone that. Name's Rick."

"Your secret's safe with me, Rick. I'm Sabine, and which one is the razorbacks?"

Rick snorts. "Not a football fan, then."

"No."

"The Razorbacks are in red; Louisiana is in white."

I glance at the LSU T-shirts that some of the men around the pool table are wearing. "Now I see why you want to keep that a secret."

Southerners are nothing if not loyal to the home team.

"Where are you from?" He asks.

"Las Vegas."

"No kidding."

I slid him the side-eye. "I'm not a stripper, Rick."

"Dammit." He winks, then asks what brought me to the Deep South.

Before I can conjure up a lie, I hear the door open behind us. A rush of warm air sweeps in, carrying on it a spicy, warm scent I'm very familiar with. A rush of awareness flies over my skin like a tidal wave. My pulse skyrockets and I suddenly find it hard to breathe.

I'm vaguely aware of Rick asking if I'm okay, but I can't speak.

It's not Wednesday or Saturday.

It can't be him.

My eyes are glued straight ahead as Rick looks over his shoulder at the man whose shadow sweeps over me like a blanket.

"Sabine."

My stomach falls to the floor.

Rick is now looking back and forth between us. "Uh, sorry, my man, but this seat's taken."

Flashbacks of Astor almost killing a man for speaking to me while at a charity gala in New York sends a shot of adrenaline through my veins.

Not again.

I'm just about to surge up and run away before the fight breaks out when I catch the glint of something gold.

Astor's tanned hand slides between Rick and I, those

strong, masculine fingers that can work miracles between my legs.

A gold Patek Philippe wristwatch is placed on the bar top.

"Not anymore," Astor says to Rick.

"Holy shit!" Rick gawks at the watch worth seven figures, then, like a kid finding a twenty-dollar bill, he snatches the watch, slips it into his pocket and shoots off the barstool, disappearing before Astor can change his mind.

Astor lingers behind me. The blood rushing through my ears is almost deafening.

"May I sit, Sabine?"

I say nothing because it feels like a rubber band has been wrapped around my lungs.

His cologne sweeps past me as he settles onto the stool. Every sexual sensor in my body awakens. Every memory of our time together, every feeling I had, every smile, every laugh, every touch, every sensation barrels into me with the force of a logging truck.

"Whiskey on the rocks," he orders from Josh, the barman.

We sit in silence until his drink is delivered.

I still haven't looked at him.

He takes a long, deep sip.

Suddenly, the lights flicker on and off, and Josh claps his hands, startling me.

"Alright everyone! Listen up! We're closing early tonight. Everyone out." He gestures to the crowd like cattle. "Come on, right now. Get up, get out. Your tabs have been covered, just get the hell out."

Frowning, I begin to stand. Josh looks at me, winks. "Not you."

It takes under ten seconds to clear the room once the promise of paid tabs has been made. Josh locks the door, turns off the "Open" sign, and returns to the bar.

"Can I get you anything else, Mr. Stone."

Mr. Stone?

"No thanks, Josh. How's Katie?"

With a spark of father's pride, Josh smiles. "She's doing good. Thank you." He swallows deeply and I squint at the hint of tears in the tattooed barman's eyes.

What is going on?

"Thank you, again, for everything." Josh clears this throat. "Okay. I'll leave you two to it. I'll be in the office, if you need anything. Help yourself to whatever you want behind the bar and don't hesitate to come get me." He lingers on Astor, then raps his knuckles on the bar, and disappears.

I look at Astor, the strong lines of his gorgeous face, the fire and determination in his expression.

"You paid him to watch me, didn't you?" I ask in barely a whisper because I'm still struggling to find my voice.

"I paid him to look after you as you wouldn't allow me to. I did what I had to do."

"No. You did what you wanted to do. I can take care of myself, Astor."

He leans in, his dark eyes twinkling under the dim bar lights. "I know you can, Sabine. And you're stronger than I am because I can't seem to take care of a single thing in my life without you being in it."

Astor

I'M TRYING to be calm and collected, but inside I'm dancing.

This is joy.

Sabine. Is. Joy.

Just being in close proximity to this woman is like taking a shot of the most addictive drug. She's intoxicating. The most beautiful thing I've ever seen, with no makeup, a head of messy, curly hair, and shorts that make me want to bend her over the barstool. She looks magnificent.

She looks like mine.

Mine.

The fact that Sabine hasn't slapped me across the face or ordered me to leave is a good start. She's trying to hide her emotions, but I can read my baby like a book. Sabine is equally flustered and curious, but trying to be mad.

She takes a deep breath, still processing my impromptu arrival.

I'm still processing, too. What happened between Valerie

and me in the bathroom was one of my darkest moments, but with it came a clarity like nothing else. I am taking care of the wrong person. I never want to touch that woman again. Regardless of my obligations to Valerie, which I know I somehow need to uphold, I am spending my time with the wrong woman. At that moment, I decided that I would not live another day without Sabine in my life. The next afternoon I was in my jet, on my way to Louisiana, on a Friday.

"Astor," Sabine says on a deep inhale. "There are one million things I could say right now. One million questions that I have. But I am . . ." she shakes her head. "I am overwhelmed and—"

"May I touch you?"

"*Yes.*"

I take her hand from her lap, wrap it in my palm. Electricity shoots up my arms. I stare at this hand that I love so much. I turn it over, stroke the back with my thumb. I don't want to let it go. And I never will again.

Mine.

With a knot in my throat, I ask, "Did you read my letters?"

"Yes," she says, her voice cracking.

"Sabine, I need to make sure you know that I meant every word of them."

"I do. And as much as I hate to admit it, I believe you." Tears fill her eyes. "It's been so hard Astor. I need *you* to know *that.*"

With my other hand I grip my whiskey glass, having to physically restrain myself from wrapping my arms around her. That's not what Sabine needs right now. She needs to talk, to get it out.

"I understand that you told Carlos you would trade me for your wife *before* we fell in love—I get that. And I truly do understand why you lied to me and didn't tell me that you and

Valerie had a past. Things happened so fast between us. I get it."

A wave of relief washes over me. I squeeze her hand.

Tears spill down her cheeks and her chin begins to quiver. "And when you put the gun to your head and were prepared to give your life for mine . . ." She begins sobbing. I try to pull her to me, but she swats away my advance. "No, Astor. I need to get this out. When you did that, I knew there was no going back. That I would love you forever. That you were my soulmate. That this was it. Whether I would have you for the rest of my life, or not, you were—you are—my one true love." Her tears increase, shattering my already broken heart. "And then when I woke up bleeding out on the concrete floor and you were gone . . . I can't explain the betrayal I felt. You'd left me. You *left* me, Astor."

"I didn't know, Sabine," my words come out in a breathy whisper as tears fill my eyes. "I thought you were dead."

"I know, I know. Hell, I thought I was dead too. But it doesn't take away the intensity I felt in that moment when you weren't there. It was horrific, dragging myself across the floor while bleeding."

Unable to take it a second longer, I stand, pulling her off the chair and into my chest. "Please." I inhale her hair. "Just let me hug you, please."

She fists my t-shirt. "I'm so terrified I'm going to feel that again," she cries into my chest. "That you're going to hurt me again like you did that day. I love you more than I can express and I am so scared that if I give into you again—that if I give you my heart again—that I am going to metaphorically wake up on the floor one day and you're not going to be there—again."

Tears roll down my cheeks. "I promise you, Sabine." I gently tilt her face up to mine. "I promise you with all my heart that's never going to happen again."

"Astor, you're *married.*"

I growl with pained frustration. "I'm filing for divorce; it's complicated. But I know—I *know*. It's impossibly complicated and I don't know how to navigate that piece yet, but what I do know is that I have to have you. You are mine, my beautiful butterfly. You are my true love and we have to be together."

"It's impossible."

"No. It's not." I pull her closer, desperation squeezing my chest. "Please don't make me leave. Be with me. Let me stay with you tonight, please. I'm begging you. I'm *begging* you, Sabine. Don't let me go."

Seventy-Nine

Sabine

HIS LIPS ARE on mine the moment we reach my front door. Desperate, hungry kisses, the intensity sucking the air out of my lungs. My body is trembling so badly that I can't insert the key into the lock.

"Get back."

Astor slams his boot into the door, sending it popping on its hinges. We crash into each other again, teeth gnashing, clothes flying. At once, everything comes back in one heady, dizzying rush. I remember the power this man has over me, his ability to obliterate all rational thought. His ability to consume me and become the center of my world with a single kiss.

Together, Astor and I are like two tornadoes colliding into one massive twister, this pulse-pounding, earth-shaking, mind-blowing feeling of being so connected to another human being. A jarring sense that despite everything that's crumbling around us, it is right.

We are right.

"I love you," he mutters against my lips, tossing my bra behind us.

"I love you, I love you, I love you . . ."

In nothing but our underwear, Astor palms between my legs as he backs me toward the wall. "My God, baby, you are soaking wet for me. Fuck, Sabine, I missed you so bad. Never again, never again . . ."

We don't even make it to the bedroom, or hell, the couch.

Astor shoves me against the wall next to the front door, his kisses hot and demanding.

Dangerously possessive.

Dangerously addictive.

I yank down his boxer briefs; he kicks them off.

He grabs my thigh and hikes up my leg. As I wrap it around his waist, he pulls my soaked panties to the side and spears into me with the force of thunder.

I cry out in both pain and pleasure.

Tears roll down both our faces, rolling around our kisses, as he fucks me against the wall with such intensity that a picture falls and shatters next to our feet.

In what feels like a matter of seconds, we come together, screaming each other's names.

Dizzy with euphoria, I drop my forehead onto his shoulder. He gently wraps a hand around the back of my head and for a moment we stand there, silent, chests heaving, just being.

Together.

Eventually, Astor lowers my leg and it takes a second to find my balance.

Astor guides me to the couch, hand in hand. I drop onto the cushion like dead weight.

"What can I get you?" he asks, standing over me, gloriously naked.

"I have no idea." I blink up at him.

He grins, then grabs the whiskey and two glasses from the kitchen and settles next to me on the couch.

For a long moment, we stare at each other with small goofy smiles on our faces.

"So." he says. "It's hot here."

Laughter bursts out of me. It feels good to laugh. "I've been waiting for that."

"Jesus, Sabine, why *here?*" He presses, mocking. "Why choose to move to the devil's armpit."

"I needed anything and everything that was *not* Astor Stone."

He pours a drink, hands it to me. "I deserve that."

I sip, lean back against the couch, aware how easily Astor and I have slipped back into "us." And in that moment, I can't believe I ever considered *not* allowing him back into my life.

There is no life without love like this.

"So when did you make contact with Josh the bartender, and what exactly has he been doing for you?" I ask, settling in. Comfortable. Happy.

"The second I found out where you'd moved to, I got on my plane and was here within four hours. I actually passed you on the road once, but I was in a rental car and you didn't notice me."

"No Aston Martin rental cars around here, huh."

"Nope. I've never seen so many trucks in my life. And by the way, that Jeep is a rolling death trap."

"You're a rolling death trap." I smirk. "Keep going."

"So I drove around to familiarize myself with the area and that's when I found the bar. Somehow I knew you'd eventually find it, too." He winks. "So I went in and struck up a friendship, you could say. Turns out Josh's daughter, Katie was born with a cleft lip. Recently, they had to pull her from school because of bullying, and his wife had to quit her job to homeschool Katie. She turned ten a few weeks ago. "

"That's terrible."

"Yeah, it is."

"But what did he thank you for? And why did you ask how she was doing?"

Astor takes a long sip of his whiskey.

"You paid to have her lip fixed, didn't you?" I drag a hand through my hair. "Geez, Astor."

"I did it for you. I couldn't stand not knowing you were safe. So I made Josh an offer, he accepted, and has been checking on you twice a day."

"Twice a day? *Every* day?"

"Yes. It's not what I wanted, of course, but I had to know you were okay."

When I don't speak for a long moment, Astor slides his whiskey on the table and turns his full focus to me.

"Ask...Ask, Sabine. We can't ignore it. The only way we're going to work through this is if we communicate about absolutely everything."

I nod, knowing he's right.

I set down my drink. "When you're not dropping letters on my front door, you're with her, is that correct? Your wife."

"Yes."

"How is she? Valerie?"

"Not good. Her health is waning and her mental health is even worse. She doesn't leave the bed most of the time, and doesn't speak to anyone aside from me."

"Does she know?"

"About us? No. She's suffering from short-term amnesia. She remembers everything before the incident and everything after waking up in the hospital. She doesn't remember anything that happened inside the hangar."

"Valerie has no idea you were willing to end your life for another woman?"

"No."

"Will she eventually remember?"

"The doctors aren't sure. It's trauma blocking."

"So is she happy? Or complacent, at least? Does she just think everything's good?"

"No. Since the incident she's been having terrible nightmares, calling out for Chloe and asking why."

"What do you mean, why?"

"It's almost like she's calling out to someone, asking whoever that is, why it happened. Maybe she's asking. I don't know. But when I ask her, she doesn't remember the dream or calling out. But she's definitely obsessing over Chloe's death, all of a sudden. The doctor said it could be the new drugs she's on—she's on a *ton* of new medications—or it could be that the recent trauma has brought everything back up." He drags his fingers through his hair. "Every time we speak about Chloe it ends in a fight."

"Because she thinks her death was an accident and you don't."

"Right."

"Do you think you'll ever be able to let it go?"

"Let go that I believe my daughter was murdered?"

"Yes."

"I don't know. I just wish I knew either way, definitively."

"Closure."

"Yeah, I guess. Yeah."

"You're much better at communicating, by the way."

"Thank you. I've been working on it. When I realized you were alive, I knew I would get you back, and I knew I needed to be the best man I could when I did. I need to be the man you deserve. I'm working on it."

"Good. I like it."

"I like you."

Sabine

FOR THE NEXT two hours we talk about *everything*. What happened in the hangar, what happened between him and me. We laugh, we cry, we hold hands.

"Come back with me," he says, sliding his now-empty whiskey glass onto the table.

I laugh, but when I look at him, his expression is stone cold.

"What? Are you serious?"

"Yes. In fact, I'm not leaving here without you, so you don't have a choice."

"Well there's the demanding asshole I once knew."

"I'm serious, Sabine. And I know, in your heart, you feel the same. No matter how screwed up the scenario, the universe brought us together and nothing's going to tear us apart again. Life is tough. Let's punch it in the face together."

"Uh . . ." I gesture dramatically around the room. "I own this house, I have a car, I have bills, I have things here, I can't just—"

"You're right," he deadpans. "I certainly don't have the financial means to take care of all that for you."

"Astor, you're crazy."

"About you. Pack your stuff. I'll tell them to have the plane ready in an hour."

He grabs my hand to pull me off the couch but I yank it away. "Where am I going? To the house you share with *your wife?*"

"Yes."

I laugh maniacally. "Oh okay, so we'll just all live together in one happy polygamous relationship."

"Sure, let's take some of the south with us."

"Stop it, I'm serious."

"Listen, I don't know, but I know I'm not leaving here without you. We'll tell Valerie you're the new housekeeper or something—"

"Boyyy," I mockingly raise my hand to slap him.

"You won't clean a thing, geez, I'm just trying to think of anything."

"You have lost your mind."

"Sabine, she doesn't know you. Not your name; couldn't pick you out of a lineup. It could work. Hell, I'll build you a house next door until we figure it out. Just please, come with me. You can't stay here another minute. Your hair obviously can't take it."

"I like my curly hair."

"I love it. I'm just trying to say anything to get you to stop spinning."

"You need therapy."

"I'm not arguing with that. And stop deflecting."

"Why can't I be the cook?"

His eyes sparkle. "You are an *incredible* cook." He chews on his lip. "But . . . if I tell her you're the new cook, she's going to actually order things for you to make for her."

"I do make a mean rat-poison pancake."

We both grin.

"Okay, so no on the cook."

"I'm telling you, Sabine, housekeeper is the way to go. It makes sense and you won't have to do anything."

"I can't even believe I'm considering this. . . . *but* . . . the lake house in Tahoe *does* have multiple bedrooms on the far end of the house, and one even has a separate entrance, so I wouldn't even have to go through the main house."

Astor clears his throat.

"What?"

"We're not going to the lake house."

"Where are we going?"

"To the beach house."

My brows pop. "You mean the teeny-tiny two-bedroom cottage on a cliff you told me about? The one that she lived in?"

"Yes. The doctor said it would be best for Valerie to be in familiar surroundings for the time being."

I shake my head. "This just keeps getting better and better."

"It's temporary, Sabine."

"Your marriage better be temporary."

"Everything is temporary," he pulls me in, "besides me and you."

"It's going to be tough, Astor."

"Life is tough, let's go punch it in the face together, my beautiful butterfly."

Eighty-One

Sabine

IT'S two in the morning when we arrive at the beach house. In a matter of hours, it feels like I've gone from one foreign planet to another. From the blue-collar swamps in Louisiana to mansions on the majestic northern California shoreline. It's also about twenty degrees cooler here.

What Astor's beach house lacks in size is made up for in the surrounding property. Though the home is on a cliff, it's surrounded by pristine forest and a garden that extends from the side of the house to the back. The cottage is warm and inviting, reminding me of an ideal romantic retreat, which is ironic, considering I'm arriving as Astor's mistress while his bed-ridden wife lies inside.

What are we doing? This is ridiculous. There's no way it can work. Right?

Astor shoves the car into park, pulling me from my spinning thoughts.

"Whose vehicles are those?" I ask.

"One is Cillian's—though he's supposed to be in New

York handling business. The other is Leo's. Do you remember him?"

"Yes, the shy, robotic house manager who resembles Chris Hemsworth."

Astor cocks a brow.

"Don't worry. You're much hotter—and richer."

"Phew," he mocks.

I wink, then, "what are they doing here?"

"When I'm visiting you, I have Cillian stay to keep an eye on Valerie, and Leo has been hired to look after the property full-time."

"Security detail?"

"Right."

"Valerie doesn't have an in-home nurse?"

"Yes, her name is Jackie, she comes during the days . . . although we've talked about extending her duties to stay overnight."

"That's a lot of people for a small house."

"Tell me about it." He looks at me, his face shadowed by the dark night. "You okay?"

I wring my hands on my lap. "I think so. Remind me of the plan again? We're going with 'housekeeper'?"

"I'll take any other ideas you have, Sabine."

We talked about it ad nauseam on the plane ride over, and decided that the live-in housekeeper was the easiest and most believable story.

"And I'm sleeping in the guest bedroom and you are . . . sleeping where?"

"I usually sleep on the couch, but I don't really sleep. But with *you* here," he wiggles his brows, "I'll definitely be spending more time in the guest room."

"What are we going to tell Leo and Cillian? They'll recognize me."

"Cillian knows everything and Leo is paid well enough to

look the other way, trust me."

"Money for loyalty?"

"Something like that."

"What will you do during the days while I'm," I air-quote, "cleaning?"

"Working." He looks down, the first sign of stress I've seen on his face. "Cillian has stepped up to handle my job while I figure things out, but I'm still involved in most everything. And . . . I'm behind on things."

"Because of me?"

"Yes. And you are completely worth it, Sabine."

"You are completely out of your mind, Astor."

"Just shut up and kiss me."

"Wait," I pull back, nibbling on my lower lip. "What if I can't do it? What if I hate it here? What if it's all too weird?"

"Then we'll go to a hotel, and I'll figure it out."

"No, you need to stay."

He threads his fingers through mine. "Sabine, I am taking this one hour at a time. We are together right now and that's all that matters. Now kiss me."

I lean in and take the intoxicating hit that is Astor Stone, and like the beautiful drug he is, just like that, my worry dissolves.

A cobblestone pathway leads to a rounded front door with a beveled window. The door opens to sweeping views of the Pacific Ocean. Though the cottage is small it's been remodeled to Astor's grandiose standards, with plush leather furniture, expansive rugs, and upscale amenities.

I'm just about to tell Astor how beautiful it is when I notice he's stilled next to me with a concerned look on his face.

"What's wrong?"

"Cillian is usually sitting right here, or in the kitchen. He always greets me. Something's going on."

Astor grabs my hand, pulling me through the house.

"Cillian!" He calls out, checking the kitchen. I'm pulled down a short hallway to the master bedroom, which is vacant. The bed is unmade and the sheets have been pulled back.

"I'm assuming this is Valerie's room?"

"Yes. And she's not here."

"And I'm assuming that's not good . . ."

We hurry back through the house and push out the back door to the garden, awash in silver moonlight.

It takes me a second to understand what I'm looking at. There are two people on the ground. Leo is kneeled next to Valerie and appears to be consoling her as she sits on the dirt in a stained white nightgown. She's hugging her knees to her chest and rocking back and forth. She doesn't appear to be responding to Leo, or even aware that he's next to her, for that matter.

She looks ghostly.

Cillian is on his cell phone, pacing by the side of the house. He looks just as concerned as Astor.

Astor drops my hand and jogs across the dirt. The moment Cillian sees us, he hangs up the phone and hurries over. He nods to me in greeting, obviously having been apprised of my arrival ahead of time.

I keep my distance, lingering behind them, my stomach swimming with nerves.

Leo turns to Astor as he approaches. His face is ashen.

"She's been like this for two hours. We can't get her into the house. We attempted lifting her, but she fought us off."

"*Fought you off?*" Astor gapes.

"Yes." Leo notices me and frowns. Unlike Cillian, he was definitely *not* aware that I was coming.

Astor kneels down beside his wife, says something in her ear. She stops rocking. I can't tell what she's looking at. A bush, a flower, nothing? Whatever it is, it has her complete focus.

"Jackie's on her way," Cillian says.

"No. Call her back. I'll handle it tonight. What are you doing here? I thought you left for New York this morning?"

"Valerie's health declined soon after you left. She actually called out for you. It was . . . disconcerting. I didn't feel comfortable leaving her."

"You should have told me."

"I knew you had things to attend to." His gaze flickers to me.

"Tell Jackie I'll call her tomorrow morning and we'll regroup. I'm sure the doctor will want to adjust her meds. I'll make an appointment as soon—"

Just then, Valerie turns her head. Her eyes meet mine and she immediately stops rocking.

"Who's that?" She asks Astor.

Everyone freezes in place, shocked to hear her speak.

"She's going to be helping us around the house, Valerie. Come on, let's get you inside."

Eighty-Two

Sabine

I'M PACING the guest bedroom like a caged animal while Astor makes Valerie tea and puts her to bed. I attempted to unpack, but when I put my shirts in the nightstand and grabbed a hanger for my panties, I realized I was far too anxious to complete even the most mundane task.

What *the hell* was that?

Valerie is substantially worse than I'd anticipated. Not to mention she looks extremely unhealthy. Emaciated to the point of skin and bones and when Astor carried her inside, she had this wheezing cough that sent a chill up my spine.

So far, my visit to Stone Cottage is not off to a good start. I didn't realize how unstable Valerie was, and also what a strong reaction I'd have to seeing her—Astor's wife.

When our eyes met, my reaction was immediate. Not fear, not unease, or guilt. It was resentment. Resentment for the woman between us.

And the feeling was mutual. Whether Valerie recognized

339

me or not, she didn't like my presence, that much was obvious.

Seeing him console her ignited a possessiveness inside me that I'd never felt before.

Astor is mine.

I am *his*.

I knew this wouldn't work. What was I thinking?

Needing fresh air, I open the windows and look out at the ocean. I close my eyes, listening to the sound of waves crashing against the shore below. A gust of wind sweeps into the room and I get a rush over my chest, the feeling that something is about to happen.

Yes, something is happening, I think, trying to console the apprehension I feel inside. Astor and I are beginning our life together.

The bedroom door opens and I spin around, more than ready to be in Astor's arms.

Though the stress of the evening is written all over his face, when he sees me, life sparks in his eyes and a smile crosses his lips. My heart swells.

"God, Sabine, I can't believe you're here," he rushes across the room, cups my face in his hands.

I grab his wrists and nuzzle into his hands, inhaling the clean scent of him.

Love is the most powerful thing on earth. No matter the darkness that surrounds two people, if they are madly in love, they will always find the light, together. In Astor's touch alone, my stress melts to joy.

We take a moment to just hold each other.

"Is she asleep?" I ask, pulling away.

"Yes."

"Are Cillian and Leo gone?"

"Yes."

"What was that about? Was that normal? Did something trigger her?"

"No. That was definitely not normal. She rarely gets out of bed, and when she does, she needs assistance."

"Has this happened before?"

"Not since coming back from the hospital. Her new medication is supposed to help mitigate these kinds of things." He scrubs his hands over his face. "She asked about Chloe, again. Something isn't right. Something is off."

"Did she say anything about me? Aside from asking who I was?"

"No. I explained to her that you were the new live-in housekeeper for now, and that was it. She didn't ask any more questions. Are you okay?"

"Yes." I run my hands over his arms. "As long as I'm with you, I'm okay."

He sighs and drops his head into the crook of my neck. "I'm so happy to hear that—you have no idea. I missed you, Sabine."

While our kisses at my cabin were frenzied and manic, these are deep, passionate, and savoring.

I wrap my arms around his neck. "I love you beyond measure, Astor Stone."

He looks down at me with such adoration that warm tingles spread over my skin. I smile and, for a moment, think I could cry. I have never loved anyone this much. I didn't even know it was possible.

"You're mine, Sabine. Forever."

"And you are mine, only mine. Forever."

We fall onto the bed, enveloped in the cool night air sweeping through the windows.

We make quick work of getting undressed, and once naked, he wraps an arm around my torso and pulls me deeper into the bed, like I weigh nothing at all.

How does this man make me feel so small, yet so powerful at the same time?

At that moment, nothing exists except for me and him. This is what I want, forever and ever.

Kissing wildly, Astor strokes me with his fingers, slipping his thumb over my clit. I'm already dripping wet and throbbing, desperate for him.

"You're so wet for me," he whispers between kisses.

I tilt my head back and thrust into his hand as he finger fucks me, one, two, three fingers, while his pinky strokes my asshole with each thrust. I arch my back, digging my nails into his shoulders.

I already feel like I could come but I don't want this to end so quickly.

I shove him off me, onto his back, and crawl on top of him.

Lifted on my knees, I hover just above his cock. His eyes flash with heat.

"You are the most perfect thing I have ever seen." His hands caress my breasts, his fingertips rolling my erect, aching nipples.

"Ride me baby. Take it all. Take all of this cock."

"Tell me it's mine."

"It's yours, Sabine. All yours."

I lower, popping his thick, swollen head in and out of my pussy, wetting the tip while driving him absolutely wild.

"You're killing me, baby." He groans.

Supporting my weight with my hands on his chest, I slowly lower myself down his shaft. We both moan in ecstasy. It hurts but feels so good at the same time.

"Hold on," I wince. "I need a second to adjust." He's so big I can feel him in my stomach and, finally, sink all the way down.

His words are unintelligible as I begin rocking my hips, rubbing my clit against his springy pad of hair.

The veins bulge on his neck. He grabs my hips and thrusts into me.

I cry out.

"That's it baby, take all that cock. It's yours, take it all, baby."

My body clenches around him as he lifts me up and down, sliding deliciously against my g-spot.

I grow lightheaded, lost in the euphoric haze that only Astor can give me.

He presses his thumb against my clit, sliding against it with each thrust.

"Astor . . ."

Warmth spreads between my legs, the sensation becoming almost unbearable.

"Look at me."

The moment our eyes meet, I come instantly, whimpering his name as the orgasm rips through me.

Dizzy and panting, I fold over on top of him.

"That was so sexy, Sabine." Before I can put together a coherent thought, I'm lifted off his cock. "Now turn around and sit on my face so I lick you clean. I'm not done with you yet, my beautiful butterfly."

Mindlessly delirious, I crawl onto him and turn around.

"Fucking gorgeous." He spreads my ass cheeks and licks me from clit to asshole.

A shudder ripples through my body. I take his thick, iron-hard erection in my palm, lick the pre-cum, then slide my tongue over the tip. He groans in pleasure.

The second I suck him into my mouth, his mouth clamps onto my aching pussy and fucks me with his tongue.

"Oh, Astor," my voice is ragged as I suck him harder, faster, unable to control the sudden rush flying through veins.

"Sit further back," he mutters, "sit on my face."

I shift back and press my pussy against him, smothering his face.

I suck him harder, desperately chasing my hand with my mouth.

"Fuuuuuuuck," he cries out as he orgasms, shooting thick ropes of semen down my throat. I swallow it all and just when he finishes, he sucks my clit into his mouth.

I come again, riding his face with each dizzying wave of my second orgasm.

We both collapse, chests heaving, skin sweating, delirious with satisfaction.

When I open my eyes and lift my head, I see a shadow pass by the cracked door that I was certain had been closed.

Eighty-Three

Astor

I CLOSE my eyes and inhale the scent of Sabine's hair. I smile and squeeze her tighter against me, pressing against her back until there is not a single part of us that is not touching.

She sleeps soundly, peacefully. It makes my heart happy.

I want this forever. Sabine and I, sleeping just like this, her close to me, wrapped in my arms where no one can hurt her or take her from me.

Again.

Not again—*never* again.

My jaw clenches at the terrible thought, followed by a wave of heat surging through my body. My heart begins to race.

I curse my body, desperately willing the anxiety to subside so as not to wake her.

Before Sabine, my anger—my rage—was my curse. Controlling it was impossible. Before Sabine, I lived a life driven by guilt, suppressed until it turned me into a stone-cold bastard. I believe I'm better on both counts. But since Sabine has entered my life, a new emotion has taken over. Anxiety. Controlling this has become my latest challenge.

Until now, I didn't allow myself to love anyone. Losing a mother, a daughter, and living a life surrounded by death shaped that decision. I couldn't afford emotions. They made you messy. But now that I've found myself deeply, madly in love with Sabine, the fear of losing her is all consuming.

It keeps me up at night. It steals my thoughts, my dreams, my ability to make sound decisions.

My entire world revolves around one single thing now.

Keeping her.

She stirs, and I close my eyes and take another deep inhale. But it doesn't help. In my mind's eye, I picture Sabine bleeding out on the floor, and Valerie dragging herself across the concrete screaming at me.

I break out in a cold sweat.

My phone vibrates from the nightstand, pulling me from the pending panic attack.

More calls, more texts, more emails.

More pressure.

I suddenly feel like I'm suffocating. As quietly as I can, I work my arm out from under Sabine and lift out of bed.

I run to the faucet, suck down ice-cold water until the heat subsides, then splash it on my face. I stare at my reflection in the mirror, a feeling of dread clenching my stomach, a feeling that I'm not in control of anything anymore.

Not of Valerie, the wife I've never loved, who now needs me 24/7, while I want nothing more than to never see her again.

Not of Sabine, the woman I'd take a bullet for, who is uncomfortable in her new surroundings. Not of Astor Stone, Inc., the company I've given my life to, only to abandon for love.

I grit my teeth, staring at my reflection.

Stop.
Focus, Astor.
Focus on what's most important.
I wipe my face, walk back into the bedroom.
In her, I receive clarity.
She is what's most important.
Everyone and everything else can go to hell.

Eighty-Four

Sabine

THE NEXT MORNING, I sleep in while Astor rises before daybreak and tends to Valerie, before settling in behind his computer to catch up on work, as he planned to do.

When I wake, I'm somewhere between relief to be with Astor again, and unease knowing that I'm a hallway away from his wife.

The sun is rising in a crystal blue sky. We slept with the windows open, and the room smells of sea breeze and blooming flowers. I should smile, appreciate the beauty around me, but instead, I find it all tainted—by her.

Astor's words trickle through my head. *One hour at a time...*

He's right. It's the only way we're going to make it through this.

So, this hour, I decide to take a long, hot shower. There, I revel in the delicious soreness between my legs, and find myself longing to be alone with Astor again.

After toweling off, I consider what a "housekeeper"

would wear. Knowing Astor, he'd probably hire from a company that demands their employees wear uniforms, but I obviously don't have that, so I pull on a plain, white t-shirt and the cutoff jean shorts he likes so much. I've decided that I'm not going to unpack. Not while she's here, or we're here. It's not home until Astor and I are alone—wherever that may be.

Hair still wet from the shower, I quietly open the door and peek into the hallway, not wanting to run into Valerie. The master bedroom, her bedroom, is directly across from mine, down the hall.

The door is closed.

Phew.

I don't see, or hear, Astor anywhere.

I tiptoe to the kitchen. There I find Leo stocking the pantry and I get hit with major deja vu. He was doing this exact thing the first time we met in the lake house. The difference then was that Valerie's presence was memorialized in photos. Now, she's here in person.

"Morning," I say.

"Ma'am."

I smile. "Please call me Sabine."

He dips his chin, continues storing groceries.

I help myself to coffee. "Do you know where Astor is?"

"In his office."

"I didn't know this place had an office."

"It's the door right next to the guest bedroom."

"Thank you." I sip. "So, uh, where's Valerie?"

"In her bed, per usual."

I notice the tray next to the sink. On it sits an empty cup of tea and half-eaten bowl of oatmeal. I wonder if Astor fed her, and again, I get that weird possessive feeling.

Ugh, this is going to be tough.

Just as I'm about to leave, the master bedroom door opens

and closes. I freeze, my heart leaping into my throat at the thought of running into Valerie.

Instead, a five-foot sixty-something woman barrels into the kitchen. She doesn't appear to be surprised to see me as she takes a water mug that was nearly her size to the sink and dumps the mostly melted ice cubes. Her silver hair is pulled back in a bun and she's wearing traditional scrubs, rolled up at the ankles.

"Mornin' Leo," she says with a hint of a southern accent.

Leo nods. At least he doesn't speak to her either.

She yanks open the freezer and, with bare hands, scoops handfuls of ice cubes into the mug.

"You're Sabine?" She says over her shoulder.

"Yes." My gaze flickers to Leo. Does he know we're telling everyone that I'm the housekeeper?

The woman turns, shakes my hand with wet, ice-cold fingers. I bite back a wince.

"I'm Jackie. Valerie's nurse."

"Nice to meet you," I smile, and can't decide if I like her or not based on this initial meeting.

And with that, she disappears into the master bedroom once again.

Eighty-Five

Sabine

COFFEE IN HAND, I knock on the door next to the guest bedroom.

"Come in," Astor yells from the other side.

The room is no larger than a walk-in closet. Cillian is sitting behind a built-in desk that lines one side of the room, and Astor is sitting on a bench seat under a window, balancing a laptop on his lap. The scent of fresh paint lingers in the air and I assume they'd recently renovated the space into a temporary office.

Cillian's over-six-foot frame dwarfs the desk. He looks both comical and uncomfortable.

"Excuse me," Astor says to Cillian as he rises from the bench. He grabs my hand and kisses me on the forehead. "Good morning, beautiful."

I blush, while secretly loving the display of affection in front of Cillian.

He motions me outside the room and closes the door behind us.

"How are you? Is everything okay?"

"Yes. Just wanted to say hi."

"How did you sleep?"

"Well, actually."

We step outside onto a small patio and follow the cobblestone pathway to the cliff, and away from prying eyes.

The sun dances on the ocean below us and there's a light breeze in the air. Back in Louisiana it's probably already eighty degrees. Here it's barely seventy.

We both drag in a deep inhale, clearing our lungs of the darkness in the house behind us.

"I have news," he says, turning to me.

"Good or bad?"

"Good. I spoke with my attorney today. We're going to begin the process of untangling everything in preparation for a divorce. He's putting together a whole team to deal with it all. I have a conference call with everyone next week."

I can't hide my surprise.

"How do you feel about that?" He asks, eagerly with a hint of desperation in his voice.

Astor is doing everything he can to keep me happy and make me comfortable in this crazy situation we've found ourselves in.

"I feel good about it—very good."

He smiles broadly and he brushes a strand of hair behind my ear. "Okay, good. But I do want to add—when Valerie was in the hospital, I made a promise to her that I would take care of her; that I would be there for her. It's important to me to honor that, but I can do it without being legally married. She'll have me and a medical team at all times."

"I understand, and I'm okay with that."

He sighs, his eyes trailing my face as if he never wants to forget a line of it. "God, I love you. I know this is hard, and it's going to be a long process, but we took a big step today."

I smile. "One at a time, right?"

"Exactly. Oh. And Cillian and I walked the grounds today and there's a spot we could build a little house in the interim for you to live in if it gets that bad."

"Are we going to be here that long?"

"I don't know. I'm just trying to think of anything I can do to make you more comfortable. I just . . ." his expression falls, "I don't want you to leave again."

"I'm not going anywhere. I promise." I chew on my lip. "So. Are you going to tell her? About us?"

"Not until she's more stable."

I nod. After seeing Valerie rocking back and forth in the dirt last night, I understand.

"Oh," he says, "and, before I forget, there's a new nurse coming today. She's going to stay overnight to help with Valerie, and Jackie will come by daily."

"I just met Jackie."

Astor smiles warmly. "Thoughts?"

"I'm not sure yet?"

"She can seem abrasive at first, but she's competent and knows Valerie's situation well."

"Then it sounds like she's a good woman to have on your side." I look around the gardens. "I was thinking. Since I'm technically the housekeeper," I roll my eyes with a smirk, "I wouldn't mind pulling my weight and doing things outside the house, like working in the garden. I don't like being inside."

"Hell, me either. I've spent many hours working from the back patio. I think that's a great idea." He glances at his watch. "I have meetings this morning and this afternoon, then I thought we could take a drive down the shore, have early drinks and dinner on a patio somewhere."

It takes everything I have not to jump up and down with delight.

"Like a date?" I smile.

"Yes." He runs his fingers through my hair.

"As long as this one doesn't end with you beating a man to a bloody pulp because he flirted with me, I accept."

Astor winces. "I promise that won't happen again. I'm working on myself so that I can be the man you need me to be. I'm determined to be better, and also determined to never lose you again."

Leo appears in our peripheral vision. He strides down the side of the house, then disappears down the stairs that lead to the shoreline.

"He's so serious."

"He's focused. Exactly what you want in a security detail."

"Okay, go manage your billions, Daddy Warbucks. I'm going to go play make-believe."

"Make-believe housekeeper?"

"Exactly."

He leans, a spark of heat in his eye. "You know, I was thinking we could get you a uniform and one of those feather dusters—"

"It's already in my Amazon cart—have you met me?"

He throws his head back with a laugh. "I love you."

"Me too. Go."

* * *

An hour later, I'm on my hands and knees in the garden, pulling weeds and clipping dead leaves. I've been enjoying the sunshine and fresh air so much that I've almost forgotten where I was. Until suddenly, I get the feeling someone's watching me.

I sit back on my haunches and look over my shoulder.

Valerie, in her white nightgown, ghostly pale skin, and ice-white hair, is standing in front of the window. Though her silhouette is blurred from the reflection of the sun, there's no question it's her, and she's looking right at me.

My gaze flickers toward the direction of Astor's office. When I look back at the window, she's gone.

I blink. Another silhouette appears in the window. The nurse, Jackie, squints into the sun, before finding me in the garden. Then, she yanks the curtains closed.

I frown at the window wondering if I imagined it. Just like if I imagined seeing a shadow pass by the bedroom last night while Astor and I were having sex.

A tingle of awareness sends a chill up my spine and, somewhere in the back of my mind, I get the sick feeling that Valerie is far more lucid than she's led Astor to believe.

Eighty-Six

Brittney

I'M LATE. I'm freaking *late* on the first day of my first big job. This isn't emptying bedpans in the geriatric unit. This is working for a billionaire—that's right, an actual *billionaire*. A really, *really* sexy one. Well, technically, I'm not working for him, but for his ailing wife. But still, I can assume being in this kind of social circle can open many doors for me that the geriatric unit can't. (Those doors open automatically).

And God knows I need an opened door right about now.

I glance down at the check-engine light glaring from the dashboard. Maybe Mr. Stone will notice it and offer an alternative form of transportation. Do rich people do things like that? See us poor peasants struggling and toss us a few hundos with a wink and a smile. After all, a couple hundred bucks to a billionaire is probably nothing.

I wish I had a couple hundred bucks right now. I'd buy a new pair of sneakers to wear on my shifts. People don't realize how important quality footwear is for a nurse. I learned that the hard way within my first week on the job. I've never had such aching feet in my life. I could barely stand in the mornings. My current shoes are threadbare, stained, and the tread is worn almost completely smooth, making wet surfaces as slick as ice—not good when you're emptying bedpans a dozen times a day. Well, not anymore.

The reason I got this job was because the nurse who had been originally assigned to assist Jackie (Mr. Stone's main nurse) had a rollerblading accident and broke her ankle, and I was literally standing there when the call came through. Rumor is Mr. Stone isn't the type of man to wait on anyone or anything—broken ankle or not—so . . . here I am.

Nerves tickle my stomach as I drive through the narrow, windy road leading to Mr. Stone's beach house—one of many of his homes, probably. To the left, endless ocean. To the right, massive, gated entrances with long paved driveways that disappear into the woods.

Astor Stone is so sexy. Like jaw-dropping, food-falling-out-of-your-mouth sexy. He's also much older than I am, by about thirty years.

I am nervous to meet him—to meet everyone.

I've never seen such a detailed case file. Apparently, Mr. Stone hand-picks the doctors and nurses for him and his wife —regardless if they are employed by hospitals, home health facilities, private practices, whatever—and pays them handsomely to do house calls. Or, like I'm doing, twenty-four-hour in-home care. Then, everyone has to sign a non-disclosure agreement. After that, we're given, like, a ten-page summary of what to expect, including passcodes for entry, names of people who we are allowed to let into the home, etcetera. Mr. Stone is *very* big on security. From the summary, I know there are several people whom I should expect (and allow) into the beach house. Mr. Stone himself, Mrs. Stone, two men who work for Mr. Stone, and a new housekeeper who will also be there 24/7. Maybe she and I can become friends.

I glance down at the GPS. Four minutes until my arrival.

I exhale, practicing my breathing. I'm extremely nervous. The only person I will know is Jackie, who has worked for Mr. Stone for years. And I don't even know her. I overheard she was none too happy about working with a twenty-one-year-old who is fresh out of nursing school. That's okay though. It's my time to shine. It better be, anyway, because I cannot afford to get fired from this job. My apartment manager made it clear that he will not allow any more late payments.

My Nissan sputters and jolts as I accelerate up a cliff that overlooks the ocean. This car is a bigger train wreck than I am. I got a deal on it because I went to nursing school with the salesman's dad. And by deal, I mean a hundred dollars off of a car that had already been slashed to below blue-book pricing. Nobody wanted it. I assume it has something to do with the rust on the hood and the dented backend.

I pass a sign that reads: Dead End.

"Destination is on your left . . . You have reached your destination."

I hit the brakes and come to a full stop in the middle of the road.

No way. This can't be right.

I check the GPS, confirm that it is indeed my destination, then look back at the house.

To be clear, it's beautiful, stunning even. It's just not what I expected—to say the least. I expected a fifteen-thousand-foot mega-mansion with rooms that sense your entry and automatically change the temperature to your personal preference. (Doesn't Bill Gates have something like that)? But this? This little quaint beach cottage looks to be no more than two bedrooms.

Where am I going to sleep?

The butterflies in my stomach turn into one big knot as I pull into the short, pebbled driveway. There are three—*three*

—other cars here. How can that many people fit in this tiny house?

When I get out of the car, a woman appears along the edge of the property, wiping sweat from her brow, and unintentionally transferring a streak of dirt across her forehead. She's wearing a t-shirt, jean shorts, and is absolutely gorgeous. Long, silky black hair, almond eyes, tanned skin.

I immediately feel inadequate. These people are rich and beautiful. Because of course they are. That's always how it works, right? Me, on the other hand? I'm what they call basic. I have basic brown hair, basic brown eyes, a basic body that's neither skinny or fat, just toneless and curveless. I'm the kind of girl people forget instantly. I'd make a great serial killer.

The woman's stride breaks when she notices me.

I smile and wave awkwardly.

"I'm the new nurse," I yell out the opened window. Geez, why yell? Why not walk over, or wait until she comes to me?

I am a freaking mess.

A warm smile spreads across her face as she crosses the lawn.

I get out of the car, smooth the purple scrubs I'm wearing.

"I'm Sabine," the woman says, stretching for a handshake but then pulling back when she notices the dirt all over her hands. "Yikes," she runs her palms over her shorts. "Maybe next time."

I laugh, and feel a bit of the tension release from my shoulders. There is a warm, kind, non-snobby aura around this woman. I like her instantly.

"Are you the housekeeper?"

A grin tugs at her perfectly pouty lips. "Sure am. Name's Sabine."

I exhale. "Oh good. I'm late. I wasn't sure—I didn't want to . . ."

"Don't worry. Astor—I mean Mr. Stone—won't bite. What's your name?"

"Oh. Sorry. Brittney Shaver."

"Lovely to meet you, Brittney. I'm assuming you're working with Jackie, right?"

"Yes. I'm the twenty-four-hour nurse."

"Great, she's inside."

"Okay, let me grab my bag."

My cheeks burn as the back door of my car creaks open with an ear-splitting metal-on-metal sound. I suppose because that's what it is. The old musty scent of the interior, that I've tried endlessly to eradicate, wafts out.

"First car?"

I grab my duffel bag, and slam shut the door with the heel of my sneaker. "Yes."

"Mine was a fuchsia four-door sedan with purple tinted windows, and the fabric on the ceiling had come unglued and hung down like drapes. I hung Christmas ornaments from it." She winks. "Come on in, I'll show you around."

Don't screw it up, I think as I follow the housekeeper inside.

Don't let them know your secret.

Eighty-Seven

Brittney

OKAY, so size does *not* matter, apparently. The interior of the home is staggering. The floorplan was obviously built around the view, with sweeping windows everywhere, showcasing the ocean below. The furniture, the paintings, the amenities, everything is high-end, sparkling, spotless, gorgeous. And priceless, I imagine.

"Well, that's the tour," Sabine mocks as we close the front door behind us.

I laugh loudly. Feels good to laugh.

Sabine chuckles. "It's small, but nice. You'll get used to it."

She takes me through the living room, the kitchen, and shows me the back patio and garden. Again, I find myself awestruck at the view.

Once back inside, Sabine gestures to two rooms at one end of the hall, both doors closed. I can hear a pair of deep male voices coming out of one.

"Mr. Stone's office is there, and that's the guest bedroom, where I stay."

She turns toward the opposite end of the hall. The sunlight doesn't reach this end. The door to this room is larger than the others, and is also closed.

"That's the master bedroom, where Val—I mean Mrs. Stone—stays. I believe when Jackie has stayed overnight before, she stays in there with her, and they always keep the door shut."

"She *stays* in there with her?"

I notice Sabine's demeanor has changed. Once warm and welcoming, she's now serious.

She nods, watching me closely.

"So, I'm going to *sleep* in there?"

"I believe so. There's a loveseat next to the bay window that pulls into a bed."

My eyes round. I did *not* expect to sleep next to the woman I've been hired to care for.

Suck it up, Brittney. You can do this. You have *to do this.*

Sabine clears her throat. "So, uh, yeah, Jackie's in there. So," she gestures to the closed door—*go ahead.*

She's not going to walk me into the room? I guess I shouldn't be surprised. She's the maid. But I did expect to meet Mr. Stone upon my arrival.

I've been here ten minutes and it seems like nothing is as I'd expected. This makes me uneasy. I don't like surprises.

"Okay. . . . Thanks."

On a deep breath, I banish my nerves, and walk to the closed door at the end of the hall.

I knock, and while waiting, look over my shoulder.

Sabine is watching me from the exact spot she left me. Her expression is hard and apprehensive, and she's wringing her hands. It's like she doesn't want to get any closer to the room.

Why, I wonder?

. . . And why do I have such a weird feeling right now?

Eighty-Eight

Sabine

BY FIVE O'CLOCK, I'm more than ready to put distance between me and the beach house. As we drive down the shoreline, and the distance between me and Valerie widens, the weight releases from my shoulders.

We find a come-as-you-are shoreside diner. Astor fits right in in his t-shirt, shorts and scraggly beard. I like this new Astor. He's in a space of recalibrating what's truly important to him. Designer suits, fifteen-hour workdays, and living a life driven by guilt are just a few of things he's letting go.

As I sit across from him, I pray that the loose cannon with a violent temper is long gone. Time will tell, I guess.

We drink, eat, laugh, steal kisses when no one's looking. It's the happiest I've felt in a long time. But as most good things do, it comes to end when Cillian texts Astor about something important that's come up with work. A potentially big new contract with the DOD, and Cillian needs to fly to DC immediately.

We rush back to the beach house and I realize it's like we have a child to take care of. Cillian, the babysitter, has to rush out, so we adapt accordingly.

When we arrive, Astor leaves me to check on Valerie, who is asleep in bed. It's just after ten.

After grabbing a glass of wine, I decide to take a quick shower to unwind, then maybe lose myself in a good book in bed.

I've just gotten out of the shower when I hear Astor sneak up behind me.

I grin at the expression on his face.

"I swear you have naked radar," I mock, toweling off my breasts.

"It's one of my superpowers, my beautiful butterfly."

"Good news with work?"

"Yes, a potentially big new contract."

"That's exciting."

"Mmm," he says, sweeping a hand over my hair.

"Is Valerie asleep?"

"Yes, and the new nurse, Brittney, is outside, eating dinner on the patio. Speaking of eating . . ."

Before I can swat him away, I'm lifted off my feet and set on the marble counter of the vanity. I giggle as he tickles his beard against my neck in the playful way that he does. And in the playful way that I do, I reach down and grab his erection, already wet at the tip.

I laugh. "You have the hormones of a teenager, Mr. Stone."

"That might be the greatest compliment you've ever given me." He winks, then drops to his knees, his hands trailing down my thighs. We're both smiling, both so happy, as he leans in and buries himself between my legs.

I tip my head back and inhale, threading my fingers through his hair as he french kisses my pussy.

I come fast and hard, convulsing against his face.

When I open my eyes, Valerie is standing in the doorway —and written in the condensation on the shower wall next to her is one word:

Chloe.

Eighty-Nine

Sabine

I SCREAM, so startled that it's impossible to keep in. Astor surges up, startled by my scream, and spins around.

I lunge off the counter, wrapping myself in a towel. My hands are shaking so badly, I almost drop it.

Astor positions himself between Valerie and me, consoling her like a child.

Despite our outbursts, Valerie appears unbothered and doesn't speak. Instead, she backs up on her own accord, her face devoid of emotion.

As Astor ushers her out of the bathroom, Brittney rushes into the hallway, ashen with fear of whatever just happened. She apparently heard our screams.

I dart out of her line of sight, but not before taking one more look at Valerie.

My eyes narrow.

Game. *On.*

Ninety

Sabine

ASTOR SPENDS the next hour in the bedroom with Valerie. I have no idea what they're talking about. Is he confessing his love for me? Is she demanding a divorce? Am I going to be asked to leave? Are we *both* going to be asked to leave?

Something isn't as it seems, that much is clear. According to Astor, Valerie is—*was*—bed-ridden. Due to both the strength of her new medications and her depression. But since I've been here, she's been up three times, once in the garden in the middle of the night, once standing in the window, and now standing at the bathroom door while Astor had his head between my legs.

Why didn't she respond like most women would? Yell at us, maybe slap us both across the face?

And what's up with her writing their deceased daughter's name on the shower wall? Was it a message?

I know Valerie has been obsessing over their daughter recently. Is she communicating something? Is it a clue?

Or is she just messing with us and trying to freak us out? Is this her manipulative way to toy with her husband and his mistress?

I saw the look in her eyes. Her focus was on *me*.

Valerie is not as sick as everyone believes. I'm certain of it.

Thankfully, Brittney didn't see what was happening. It was close—too close.

Restless, I wander into the kitchen where Brittney is washing a coffee mug in the sink. Although she's not washing it, she's scrubbing the same spot over and over as she's staring out the window. Her body is rigid, her shoulders up to her ears. Whatever she's looking at is upsetting her. I slide behind the doorway and watch her for a moment.

Her long brown hair is pulled back into a messy ponytail. Half the hair has almost worked its way out of the scrunchie. Her purple scrubs are at least a size too big for her body. She's shifting from foot to foot, obviously nervous about something.

What's she looking at outside? What does she see?

It's not surprising Brittney would be off-kilter after the commotion earlier, but it doesn't appear that's what's upsetting her.

It's whatever's out the window.

I think of Valerie, rocking back and forth on the dirt, her eyes locked on some inanimate object that none of us could see.

Then, the image of Chloe's name written on the shower wall flashes behind my eyes.

A knot forms in my stomach.

What have I gotten myself into?

Ninety-One

Brittney

"HELLO."

I jump at the voice behind me, dropping the porcelain cup. It shatters in the kitchen sink.

Shit!

I spin around. Sabine is standing in the doorway, frowning.

Shitshitshit.

"I'm so sorry, uh," I turn back to the sink and begin picking up the broken china shards .

Sabine joins me at the sink, studies me for a moment, then looks out the window, then back at me.

"Oh!" she exclaims, "You cut yourself. Stop. Brittney, let go of the cup—"

I look down at my hands. They're trembling. Sure enough, a line of blood is dripping down my thumb, mixing with the water as it spirals down the sink. I didn't even feel it.

"Here, let me . . ." Sabine lifts my hand and turns off the

water. She grabs a paper towel and wraps it around my hand while applying pressure to stop the bleeding.

I'm the nurse. *I* should be the one tending to my stupid little cut.

My cheeks heat. I'm humiliated.

It doesn't help that Sabine is studying me so intensely that it feels like a laser beam on the side of my face. I can't look at her. She's so beautiful and perfect, and I'm—I'm what? A freaking mess. A basic, boring mess who breaks a cup and cuts my finger and doesn't even notice it.

"You okay?" She asks.

"Yeah. Oh no," my pulse skyrockets, "I broke one of his cups . . ." I pull out of her hold and toss the bloody paper towels in the wastebasket. When I begin to pick up the broken china, she stops me. "Don't worry about it. He has a million priceless cups, trust me. I'll tell him I did it." She winks.

"Really?" I'm fighting tears. "You'd—you'd do that for me?"

"Of course. The next one's on you, though," she winks again, then falls serious. "So. Um. How are you doing with what happened earlier? Do you have any questions?"

"Uh *yeah*. What was that about? You screamed, he screamed, and Valerie . . . she was just standing there, in the hallway, white as a ghost. The case file said she hardly gets out of bed. I was told to never let her walk alone because she's still adjusting to her new medications—I got the impression she couldn't walk without assistance."

"That's correct. That was very . . . *very* strange. It wasn't normal, so I don't think you need to worry about it happening often."

"I feel bad. I should have been there."

"You have to eat dinner, right? It's unreasonable to expect you to be in the room with her every second of every hour."

I glance into the hallway. "Is he mad?"

"Astor?"

"Mr. Stone, yes."

Sabine winces for a moment and I'm not sure why. "No, Mr. Stone isn't mad at you. Again, I think it's understood that you can't be with her every second. But, I do want to ask . . . did anything strange happen today before dinner? Was she acting funny? Anything like that?"

"No. Well . . . I don't know what her acting strange would look like because I've only spent a short amount of time with her, but nothing happened that alarmed me."

"Did she get up at all?"

"To the restroom, but that was it."

"What about her medication? Did you administer any this afternoon?"

"Yes, of course. She takes medication three times a day."

"And you gave the correct dosage . . ."

My stomach sinks. Could I have mixed up her medication?

"I'm—yes. Of course I gave her the correct amount," I say, far too quickly.

Sabine's eyes narrow and just when I think she is going to press the issue further, she says, "Brittney. You're still bleeding."

"Oh." I look down at my thumb. The blood is now dripping onto the floor. "Sorry."

I can practically feel Sabine's scrutiny as I clumsily wipe up the blood from the floor.

She's frowning when I stand. "Let's get you bandaged up, and again, what happened today isn't the norm, so don't worry about it," she says referring to Valerie.

Little does she know, that's not what I'm upset about.

Ninety-Two

Sabine

AFTER SHOWING Brittany to the first aid kit, I retire to the bedroom, knowing I won't get a wink of sleep until Astor returns.

What a night. Between Valerie's—and now Brittney's—odd behavior, I don't know what to think anymore.

Just after midnight, the bedroom door opens and Astor walks in. I'm fully prepared for him to ask me to leave. Instead—

"She's asleep, finally. Took me over an hour to get her there."

I close my eyes and exhale. "Astor."

"I know, I know. For three months, Valerie hasn't left her bed unless I physically helped her. She literally hasn't been anywhere but the bed and the back porch, where I put her occasionally so that she can get some fresh air and sunlight. And now . . ." he begins pacing.

"Astor, she's more lucid than you think she is. I'm telling you, she's either not taking her medication or not nearly as bad off as she's led the doctors to believe. What did she say?"

"She seemed confused and disoriented . . . almost like she's not sure what she saw."

"What? Like, she doesn't believe she walked in on you with your head between my legs?"

"Yeah—I know; it's weird."

It is incredibly weird, but when I picture Valerie just standing there watching us with zero emotion—no yelling, screaming, hell, no punching her husband in the face—it aligns with her demeanor.

"So you two didn't even talk about it?"

"Not directly, no. She didn't directly ask about it, and so of course I didn't openly bring it up."

"Hang on. Valerie didn't ask a single thing about walking in on us?"

"Right. And, I sure as hell didn't bring it up. I was more focused on getting her lucid and back to the present moment."

"Well what did she say about writing your daughter's name on the shower wall like a lunatic?"

His eyes meet mine. "She said she didn't do it."

"What?"

He begins pacing. "Yeah. Just like she says she doesn't remember calling out for Chloe in the middle of the night, or asking why—whatever that means anyway."

I grab his arm. "Astor, I'm telling you, she's playing you. She's playing us. Who else would have written Chloe's name on the shower wall? It was her." When he doesn't agree with my theory, I press. "Valerie was standing there, plain as day, watching as I orgasmed. Of course she saw it. *Of course* she knows there's something between us. *Of course* she wrote Chloe's name on the shower wall. For her to act confused is exactly that—an *act.*"

"I don't know, Sabine. She was really out of it when we got back to the room. Disoriented, confused. I'm going to call the doctor first thing tomorrow morning. Maybe have Jackie come by; I think it's supposed to be her day off but I think we need her."

"You need to do more than that."

"What do you mean?"

"You need to address it with her again. For her *not* to go crazy after seeing you with another woman means she has ulterior motives for staying with you."

"Sabine," he shakes his head. "She's sick."

"No, Astor. I'm not letting this go. There is something else going on here."

We both stare at the door, as if she's going to reappear.

"How is the new nurse handling it?" He asks.

"That's something else . . . something is weird with her too."

"What do you mean?"

"While you were in with Valerie, she was staring out the kitchen window with this scared, nervous expression on her face."

"What was she looking at?"

"Nothing. I checked."

He frowns, then sighs. "She's going to quit."

"No, I don't think so. I get the vibe she needs the money. But it was . . . strange."

"Add it to the list."

"Right?" I take a deep breath. "So what now?"

"Honestly? I don't know, Sabine. Brittney is in there with her now, and she's going to come get me if anything arises."

"Get you where?"

"Here. In the guest room."

I exhale, shake my head. "I told her that's where I sleep. You know, me, the housekeeper."

He lifts his hands in surrender, as if the new nurse knowing we're having a passionate love affair is the least of his worries. "Let her think it, who cares. She signed a non-disclosure agreement. I couldn't care less what she thinks of us."

I agree because we have way too much else to think about it.

Another moment passes before I take his hand. "It's almost one in the morning. Let's try to sleep."

He snorts.

"*Try* being the key word," I urge but knowing damn well that neither of us will take our eyes off the doorway until the sun comes up.

Ninety-Three

Sabine

I WAKE the next morning to a note on Astor's pillow.

> *Fresh coffee in the kitchen, I'm in the office. FYI, Jackie is coming by this morning so she might be here when you wake. Yesterday sucked, but today is a new day. Let's punch it in the face together. I love you.*
>
> *PS. Sorry for cursing so early.*
> *PPS. You looked so hot sleeping.*
> *Love,*
> *Your young, hormonal teenager lover.*

I chuckle. I love this man so damn much.

After brushing my teeth and getting dressed, I grab a cup of coffee, and peek through the house, looking for Brittney.

The master bedroom is closed so I assume she's with Valerie.

I can't get Brittney off my mind. Something is spooking the poor girl and it's making me uneasy. Is it only Valerie and her strange behavior, or is it something else?

I peer out the kitchen window she'd been staring out of the night before. I decide that I'm going to search every inch of the garden that was in her line of sight today. What am I looking for? I have no clue. But there's something about her that piques my interest, and it starts with figuring out whatever she's so scared of.

Also, I feel bad for her. Brittney is in that weird, difficult young adult stage. Not a teen anymore, but also not a woman. She's riddled with anxiety, has money issues (as we all do at that age), and seems like she's one bad decision away from a breakdown.

God knows I understand that.

When I was around her age, I accepted an underground job to manage a millionaire's assets, illegally finding and securing financial loopholes for him. I had no idea at the time how that single decision would alter the course of my life.

Carlos, the man I worked for, was Astor's archrival from high school. Their feud heated up when Carlos threatened Astor after Astor's mother, a district attorney, sent Carlos's brother to prison for tax fraud. Astor responded by sending Carlos into bankruptcy, igniting their feud. Carlos then kidnapped Valerie and staged her death, with the plan to lure Astor to his. Thankfully, Carlos's plan was thwarted, but the aftermath left two people dead. Carlos and Valerie's sister, Prishna.

I linger in the kitchen. When Brittney doesn't emerge from Valerie's room, I make my way down the hall.

Astor is sitting behind the computer engrossed in whatever is on the screen.

"Where's Cillian?"

"Hey, you," he smiles, beckoning me with his finger. "He's in DC, handling business." He taps his thigh. "He'll be back tomorrow."

I settle on his lap. "He's a heck of a friend."

"I'm aware, trust me. I owe him a lot, and I will repay him."

"I have no doubt you will." I squint at the computer screen. "What are you doing? Is that Valerie's personal email?"

"Yes."

"How did you get into it?"

He slides me the side eye.

"Ah, that's right. You and all your gadgets and fancy software can hack into anything."

"Cillian helped before he left."

I chuckle.

Astor exhales, leans back. "Now that I've had time to decompress from what happened last night, I think Valerie's behavior could have been legitimate."

"You believe she didn't realize what she walked into? Your head was between my naked legs, Astor."

"I'm not saying that, but I think it could have confused her. I saw her brain scans, Sabine; I spoke to the doctors myself. Her illness is unquestionable and one of the side effects of her drugs is hallucinations; she knows this. She's told me frequently that she thinks she has them from time to time. So her reaction—or lack thereof—isn't what's bothering me."

"Then what is?"

"The fact that she wrote Chloe's name on the shower wall. It's almost like she's communicating in a way that she can't control."

"That sounds way too creepy and paranormal for me."

He doesn't laugh.

"Okay so what are you looking for in her email?"

"Anything. I have this nagging feeling that she's trying to tell me something. That we're on the brink of something." He shrugs. "Her email is the best place to start."

I nod, and together, we scan the emails.

"Have you found anything?" I ask, already bored with the correspondence.

"The most interesting thing so far is that Valerie was in communication with the local farmer's market. She wanted to begin selling the flowers from her garden and growing vegetables, and she wanted to understand how to get involved."

"Does that surprise you?"

"Kind of. According to Jackie and her doctor, Dr. Squire, she was content. Maybe not happy, but content. She went out whenever she wanted, with security, of course, but she lived her own life."

"Under *your* terms."

"It was for her safety, Sabine."

"Women need independence, Astor. When will you learn that?"

A moment passes between us as we both consider how Valerie's adopted sister Prishna, felt so suffocated under Astor's hold, financially and professionally, that she formed a shaky alliance with Carlos and went to great, murderous lengths to regain her independence.

I drag over a small stool and reposition myself on top of it. For the next hour, we drink coffee and filter through hundreds of emails, many between her and her sister.

Astor leans back. "I'm bored."

"I'd rather be back in Louisiana."

This earns me a laugh. He sighs. "There's got to be something here."

I'm just about to refill our mugs when—

"Wait." Astor squints, leans forward, studying a teeny-tiny

arrow next to one of her mailboxes. He clicks on it. A new folder opens up. Inside it is another folder.

"This is a hidden mailbox. She intentionally hid whatever's in this."

A password box appears on the screen.

My brows pop. The coffee can definitely wait.

After two failed attempts, Astor calls Cillian.

I watch as Astor pulls what looks like a hard drive from the drawer and plugs it into the laptop. Several programs pop up. Cillian walks him through each one.

Under a minute later, the program cracks the password and the folder opens.

Astor hangs up.

"What are you waiting for? Open it."

Inside are *hundreds* of emails between Valerie and someone named Annex123@gomails.com

We look at each other. My pulse picks up and I can tell by the little vein in his neck that his does too.

He clicks into one.

From: *Valeriej@gomails.com*
   To: *Annex123@gomails.com*

I can't wait to see you. I can't stop thinking about you or what our life will be like when we're finally together.
   Love, Valerie

"Oh, my God," I cover my mouth with my hand. Astor wasn't the only one having an affair.

I grab Astor's hand before he clicks into the response. "Wait. Are you sure you want to do this?"

"Is there any way I *can't* do this?"

"Fair point."

My stomach twists and I get the sick feeling we are about to open Pandora's box.

Astor clicks into the response.

From: *Annex123@gomails.com*
    To: *Valeriej@gomails.com*

Soon. I miss you too. The plan is almost in place. Be patient, we'll be together again soon. I love you so much.
    Carlos

Ninety-Four

Sabine

HOLY *SHIT.*

Astor and I gawk at each other.

"Carlos and Valerie were having an affair? *Carlos?* The man she accused of kidnapping her?"

Astor gapes at the email, his jaw slack in shock. Of all the things he expected to find, I'm positive his wife having a long-standing affair with his arch nemesis wasn't one of them.

I watch the red rise up his neck, his cheeks, all the way to the tip of ears.

My stomach sinks.

I don't want Mad Loose-Cannon Astor to come back.

He seethes, "I knew there was more to the story than Carlos suddenly wanting revenge for our long-standing feud. It never made sense." He drags his fingers through his hair. "I should have seen it. Valerie was in on her kidnapping from the beginning. She conspired to *kill* me."

He surges up from his chair.

"No!" I surge up from mine and grab his arm. "Stop.

382

Don't talk to her yet. You need to take some breaths. Calm down. We need to read these emails and understand *exactly* what was happening."

"I know what's happening. They both hated me, and wanted me dead. Period."

"Okay, but, you can't speak to her until you've calmed down."

My grip tightens around his arm. He's trembling.

Finally—*finally*—he dips his chin in agreement.

We refocus on the opened email on the screen, from Carlos to Valerie.

" . . . the plan is almost in place . . ." I read out loud, frowning. "It's dated almost a week before she was kidnapped by him. That must be what he's referring to."

"It was all a ruse. She was in on faking her own death, then reemerging and luring me to that hangar—where *you* almost died."

"And where *you* were *supposed* to die. But instead, Carlos died." I look at Astor. "So, Valerie lost both her sister, and the man she was in love with."

"I should have killed him years ago."

On a guttural growl, he lunges toward the door.

"Stop, Astor." I grab him with both hands and force him to look at me. He has the same look in his eye that he had when he almost beat a man to death for flirting with me.

It scares me.

"Stop. Not now. Take a deep breath. We need to understand everything before going to her. You cannot go to her like this. I won't allow it."

For the next two hours, Astor and I read hundreds of emails between Carlos and Valerie, highlighting a surprisingly passionate and emotional love affair, though they were rarely able to see each other due to Astor's control over her.

Together, Valerie and Carlos had one common enemy: Astor Stone.

As I sit here, reading emails next to him, I can't help but notice the similarities between Valerie and me. Valerie felt like a prisoner in her marriage, while I was an actual prisoner for a short period of time. After all, it's how Astor and I met. He kidnapped me.

I get a sick feeling that nothing is going to go as Astor or I planned.

Ninety-Five

Brittney

SO MR. STONE and the housekeeper are having an affair. I'm positive. I mean I'm pretty sure. One, they both appear to sleep in the guest bedroom together, so uh, yeah. Two, they've been holed up in Mr. Stone's "office" all day.

The more I think about it, the more it makes sense. Sabine has never appeared to be nervous in her role as a billionaire's housekeeper. In fact, it's the opposite. She seems cavalier about the whole thing. Like when I broke the glass, she didn't appear the least bit nervous about it, and when I first arrived, she told me "don't worry, Mr. Stone doesn't bite." It's obvious she knows Mr. Stone on a much deeper level than I would suspect a housekeeper to.

I'm not going to lie. For a split second—a *split* second—I considered calling a gossip column to see how much they would offer for some juicy gossip about the notoriously reclusive and oh-so-sexy billionaire. But I'm not a horrible person, so I quashed the idea.

Still, it's intriguing, and it makes me want to know more

about Sabine. How did she land him? What did she do? Who made the first move?

I wonder how common it is for rich people and their staff to have inappropriate relationships. Probably more common than you'd think, especially considering they have to sign a nondisclosure agreement in the first place, which basically removes the first barrier for the relationship right there.

As I stand in the corner of the bedroom, hands clasped at my waist, like a sentinel awaiting instructions from Jackie, who is taking Mrs. Stone's vitals, I wonder if Valerie knows. It's widely rumored within our circle that Mr. Stone and his wife are estranged, and have been for a long time. Regardless, it's an interesting dynamic in this teeny-tiny beach home.

Speaking of interesting dynamics. Jackie doesn't like me and that's being generous. But I've decided that I'm not going to let it bother me. I can't. I have to keep my focus.

Which right now, is really, *really* hard.

My gaze shifts to the windows. I scan the tree line in the distance, then the gardens. As soon as Jackie leaves, I'll go into the living room, which has a much better view of the property.

Nerves tickle my stomach.

Leave, Jackie, I think. *It's time to leave.*

Jackie looks over her shoulder, shaking me from my thoughts. "Brittney, please go make a cup of chamomile tea for Mrs. Stone."

She doesn't have to tell me twice. I'm out the door before she can even finish the sentence.

After closing the door behind me, I turn, and freeze like a deer caught in headlights.

Mr. Stone's office door is open.

And he is *gorgeous.* Even more than the rumors. He's so engrossed in whatever he's doing on his computer that he doesn't even notice me.

Snapping out of my trance, I shuffle out of his line of sight and hurry into the living room. My eyes lock on the windows.

Sabine is outside in the garden.

I don't want her to see me staring at her like an idiot so I hurry to the kitchen.

What was I supposed to be doing?

Oh yeah. Tea. Mrs. Stone. On it.

After putting water on to boil, I lean against the counter and watch the housekeeper as she settles in front of a rose bush with gloves and a pruning tool.

I watch the way she moves, efficiently and elegantly. With purpose. She oozes confidence, and I find myself deep in envy. What a life to be *innately* confident. I can't imagine. Confidence to me is akin to assertiveness. They both come to me as naturally as flirting. (They don't).

I study her body, the generous and feminine curves. My hand drifts to my boxy waist, my square hips, and I make a mental note to eat more carbs.

While I'm wearing a pair of ill-fitting scrubs and worn sneakers, Sabine looks effortlessly sexy in another fitted t-shirt and cut-offs. It's such a basic outfit, but at the same time, seductive. In fact, it's even more sexy because it's so casual.

How do I learn to do that?

I bet her mother taught her how to do her makeup, her hair, how to dress and act like a lady. Mine taught me how to drive at age twelve so I could take her to the liquor store when she was too drunk to drive.

I don't notice as the water begins to boil over because I am so engrossed in watching this mesmerizing housekeeper who landed a billionaire.

I decide then that I'm going to study Sabine, I'm going to take notes, and I'm going to become the woman I've always wanted to be.

Ninety-Six

Sabine

BY THE NEXT DAY, I find myself consumed with the woman at the end of the hallway. Reading Valerie's emails made me remember that this is a real woman, with all the troubles, pain, and ebbs and flows that all women go through. The emails Valerie had shared with Carlos were vulnerable, passionate, and at times, all too relatable.

She and I aren't nearly as different as I'd thought we were. Her words gave insight to a woman battling for happiness and contentment in a loveless marriage, eventually finding it in another person—Carlos. While the emails leave no question about her instability, there were also times of strength and perseverance in her words. Especially when it came to devising a plan to leave Astor. The emails I've poured over paint a different picture of the woman wasting away in the bedroom down the hallway. Valerie is smart, cunning, and manipulative.

Though Astor assures me Valerie's strange behavior is due to her condition and medication, I still believe she's playing him. To a certain extent, it's an act—and I've decided I'm going to catch her in it.

Valerie is sitting outside under the shade of the deck, gazing at her garden. Brittney is sitting next to her, staring listlessly just as Valerie is. Astor is in his office on a marathon conference call. Leo is nowhere in sight, and Cillian is in the New York office.

Hidden behind a window, I watch her. For twenty minutes, Valerie doesn't move. Not a twitch of her finger, not a lick of her lips. I'm not even certain she's aware Brittney is next to her.

Fraud. Of course she is.

Finally, Brittney gets up and whispers something to Valerie. I lunge into the pantry as Brittney comes inside and disappears into the master bedroom.

The moment I hear the master bathroom door close, I step out of the pantry and search the kitchen for something to justify going outside. In the end, I grab the broom—I am the housekeeper after all.

I glance over my shoulder to ensure Astor is occupied.

Nerves tickle my stomach as I step outside and quietly close the patio door behind me.

Valerie doesn't react.

Fraud.

Keeping my distance, I begin sweeping on the opposite side of the patio, my gaze never leaving her profile.

Not once does she break character.

I sweep harder, faster, loudly swiping the bristles against the tile, trying to get her to react to me.

She doesn't, and I get the feeling this is her way of dismissing me. I'm so unimportant to her that she can't even spare me a glance.

Anger begins to simmer as I move closer to the woman

between Astor and me. The reason he and I can't begin our lives together.

After another glance over my shoulder to confirm Astor's office door is still shut, I move next to her, mindlessly sweeping with each step. For a moment, I consider swatting her with the end of the broom.

Still, she doesn't move.

"I know you know I'm here," I whisper, leaning toward her. "I see you, Valerie. *I* see you."

Then, like a wave moving from her toes to the tip of her head, her body begins to tremble, yet her focus remains forward and emotionless.

Fraud. I want to slap her.

I get close enough to touch her. There is no way she can ignore me now.

Her breath becomes ragged, a wheezing rattle from deep within her chest.

"I see you," I hiss, leaning into her ear. "You can't fool me—

The patio door behind me opens, and I startle, dropping the broom and sending it clattering on the wooden slats.

I spin around as Astor steps onto the patio, frowning.

"Is everything okay?"

"Yes," I force a smile, then bend down and pick up the broom. "I noticed Brittney wasn't out here so I was just checking on her. She's, ah, her breathing seems tight."

Astor studies Valerie, noticing the hitch in her breath. He checks her forehead, then kneels in front of her.

"Valerie?"

She doesn't respond.

A long moment passes as he watches her breath. Eventually, he smoothes her hair, then stands.

"Okay. Come back inside," he says to me. "I'll get her back to bed and make her some tea."

I follow Astor to the door. Before stepping inside, I look over my shoulder.

Valerie has turned her head, watching us, and our eyes.

There's no mistaking the hatred behind them.

Yes, Valerie likes everyone thinking she's crazy.

Well, bitch, you've met your match.

Ninety-Seven

Sabine

"SCREW IT. CONFRONT HER." I close the door behind Astor.

He turns around, frowning. "What?"

"I think you should confront Valerie about her affair with Carlos."

"Really? That's the opposite of what you said a few hours ago."

"My opinion on the matter has changed."

"Why?"

"She's playing us and someone needs to say something."

Astor looks out the window where Valerie remains unmoving, staring into her garden.

"Why don't you believe me?"

"Why are you so sure she's faking?"

I fist my hands on my hips. "Why are you defending her? Jesus, Astor, the woman conspired to have you killed not four months ago! She's manipulating everyone, just like she manipulated you while she was with Carlos." This outburst feels good and I realize how badly I've needed it. So, I keep going. "How long are you going to take care of her? Even after the divorce?"

Astor's jaw twitches. "I made a promise."

"Yeah, well she made a promise to Carlos, and look how well that turned out for him. He's dead."

"What the hell am I supposed to do, Sabine?"

"Leave her!"

"I'm her conservator! She can't even care for herself. She has no one. Her mother and father are dead, her sister is dead… it's incredibly complicated. You wouldn't under—"

"Don't you *dare* tell me I wouldn't understand."

He growls, and begins pacing.

"It's your guilt coming back," I say. "You feel indebted to her because she had your baby, and a part of you blames yourself for her depression. You *have* to let it go—"

Brittney steps into the kitchen and stops cold, registering the vibe in the room. I take a step back, distancing myself from Astor—which is ridiculous because it's obvious that we are in the middle of an emotional argument that has nothing to do with housekeeping.

"Uh. Hi." She says, laser focused on Astor as if he's the second coming of Christ.

"Brittney, this is Mr. Stone."

Astor clears his throat, along with the foul mood from his face. He extends his hand with a smile. "Lovely to meet you, Brittney. Thank you for coming on such short notice."

Brittney's ears are so red I'm surprised they don't burst into flames. Inwardly, I smirk. I remember being just as awestruck the first time I saw Astor Stone.

As I take her in, it becomes glaringly apparent how young and impressionable she is.

I hope Valerie isn't manipulating her, too.

"I broke a cup," she blurts out as if someone jabbed her with a cattle prod.

I blink at the abrupt confession.

"I'm so sorry, Mr. Stone," she stammers and I can tell she instantly regrets the confession.

"Actually, it was my fault," I step in, unable to handle this cringe-worthy encounter another second. "I walked into the room and startled her, and she dropped it."

"Ah, well." Astor's lip twitches as he narrows his eyes at me. "In that case, I'll deduct it from your paycheck, Sabine. And as punishment for your incompetence, you can spend the afternoon washing the windows and then pressure washing the back of the house."

Brittney eye's pop.

I roll my eyes. He's enjoying this far too much.

"He's joking, Brittney," I mutter, "Or trying to, I should say."

Astor smirks. "I am. Don't worry about it for another second, Brittney. Accidents happen. Sabine has broken at least a dozen cups since working for me."

This time, my eyes actually roll back into my head.

Brittney exhales. "Thank you. Sir."

"By the way," he says, "I noticed two of your tires are low, and you're leaking oil."

"I am?"

He nods. "If you're comfortable with it, I'd like to offer you a company car to use while you're working for me."

Brittney's jaw drops and I'm shocked to see tears fill her eyes. "Yes, that would be—thank you *so* much."

Astor dips his chin. "Great. I'll have it delivered by the end of the week."

"Thank you, thank you."

I smile, wink.

"Okay, well . . ." Brittney beams from ear to ear. "I'll go get

Mrs. Stone back into bed. I think she's had enough sun. Thank you again. Sir."

The moment Brittney steps outside, I grin. *"Sir."*

"That's right. Don't you forget it." He closes the inches between us. "I'm sorry I snapped at you just now."

"I'm sorry, too."

He takes my hand, guides me into the hallway and out of view from Brittney and Valerie.

"And I think you're right that I feel indebted to Valerie for no other reason than she bore my child, and then we lost that child."

"It's a terrible thing for anyone to go through, but you can't let it cloud every decision you make. It doesn't define you."

"What would I do without you?"

"I shudder to think of it."

He chuckles, then falls serious. "What were you saying to Valerie when I walked out?"

I look down, begin chewing on my lip.

"Sabine," he sighs, "what did you say to her?"

"I told her she's not fooling me."

"Sabine."

"I know, I know." I scrub my hands over my face. "I shouldn't have. I know."

Astor sighs. "This isn't working, is it? You, me, her, here."

"No." I shake my head. "I think we can confidently say that, at this point."

He mutters under his breath and begins making the tea. "I think she might be getting sick, too."

I bite my tongue because I've already embarrassed myself enough for the day. Also, her cough is bad, so I can't say she's faking that.

I come up behind him, wrap my arms around his waist. "I'm sorry."

Astor turns on the kettle, lays his arms over mine and threads his fingers through my hands.

"It's okay. What did I expect?"

"I know. We were crazy to think this would work. Listen . . . I'll go to a hotel."

"No. We both will. I think we both need a night away. I'll speak with Brittney and make sure she's okay with staying more nights without a break, and I'll also ensure Jackie comes by during the day. The doctor is supposed to be here tomorrow morning and Cillian is due back this afternoon. All bases will be covered and we can leave tomorrow afternoon."

"Are you sure?"

He turns into my embrace and wraps his hands around me. "Absolutely. We need this."

I nod because I absolutely agree. The situation we're in right now is so screwed up that I'm afraid neither of us are thinking clearly.

We all know what happens when Astor isn't thinking clearly.

Astor

MY STOMACH IS in knots as I carry the tea down the hallway. Something's got to give. I can't please Valerie, Sabine, or my business in the way each deserves.

Cillian has taken a tremendous load off me, but I'm still involved in almost every decision. Valerie needs me full-time. Sabine needs me full-time—and I need *her* full-time. I'm getting the sick feeling that the other shoe is about to drop.

I push open the master bedroom door.

Valerie is sitting up in bed. Brittney is next to her, leaning next to her face.

I stop. Valerie is speaking again? To someone besides me? "Valerie?"

Both women turn to me. Brittney backs away from the bed.

Brittany's cheeks are flushed—though I don't think that's anything new. I'm beginning to think embarrassed is her natural resting state.

"Can Valerie and I have a moment, please?"

Brittney dips her chin and all but runs out of the room.

"Were you and the nurse just speaking?" I ask as he closes the door.

Valerie frowns, then sputters a deep cough. She shakes her head.

"But I'm sure I heard whispering when I came in."

She waves her hand dismissively.

I'm certain she and Brittney were speaking when I walked in. Why would she tell me they weren't?

She's playing you . . .

I slide the tea cup onto the nightstand. Usually, we'd have a pleasant surface-level exchange here, then I would leave. Not today.

"I know about the affair, Valerie."

"Which one," her eyes narrow, "mine or the dozen you've had while we were married."

"Fair enough."

"It doesn't matter anyway. He's dead."

I pause. "How do you know that?"

"What do you mean?"

"You told me you don't remember anything that happened that day."

"I don't. I saw it on the news days later."

I don't know what to say here. I'm sorry for your loss?

I sigh. "We never should have gotten married."

"Hand me the tea."

I lay the bed tray over her lap and set the tea on top. "I'm not mad about your affair. But I am confused."

"I don't know why you're confused. You married me because I got pregnant and then sent me away after my baby died."

"*Our* baby. I understand why you're mad and I understand your feelings. And I understand why you had an affair. What I don't get is why create such an elaborate scheme? You faked a kidnapping and your own death. Why not just divorce me?"

"You wouldn't have allowed it."

I open my mouth to respond, but close it. She's right. I wouldn't have allowed it, not only from a safety standpoint, but also because she knew too much about me, my life, our daughter, our home life together. I would have thrown more money at her, more leniency.

God, I am an asshole.

"Fine. Maybe you're right but wouldn't it have been worth a shot to ask? Carlos had plenty of money, so it's not like your lifestyle would have been affected dramatically."

"He *did* have money until you sent him into bankruptcy," she snaps, showing a hint of the woman I knew before our lives got flipped upside down.

"Okay—but this doesn't explain your sudden fixation with our daughter. Why did you write her name on the shower wall?"

"I don't remember doing that."

I groan in frustration. "You're not telling me something about Chloe. I know it. . . . I get the vibe you're not telling me a lot of things. Valerie, it's time. Talk. Start with why you staged your kidnapping but then emailed me weeks later for me to come save you."

Say it. Admit that part of your plan was to have me killed. Say it.

"Valerie—"

"Carlos couldn't handle me."

"What do you mean?"

"He didn't realize how bad my depression—my schizophrenia—was. It was apparent within days of us being together. I was a lot more than he could deal with."

I don't doubt that.

She begins twisting the comforter between her fingers and looks down, sadness—or is it regret?—washing over her face.

She continues, "At least with you, I had proper medical care.

"You're welcome," I deadpan.

She snorts. "Anyway. I told Carlos that I wanted to go back home and he allowed me to email you a location for you to come get me—the hangar. I swear I didn't know Carlos and Prishna were working together at that point."

"So you didn't conspire with Carlos to kill me that day?"

"No."

She's lying. I feel it in my bones. I want to press the issue, make her confess, but at the end of the day what difference does it make? What's done is done.

Resigned, I tuck the comforter around her and stand. "Try to go to sleep."

"Astor?" She calls after me as I cross the room.

"Yes?"

"Tell the maid to wash these sheets tomorrow. They stink."

"Fine." I turn away.

"Also . . . tell Brittney to come back in here. I like her. A lot."

Ninety-Nine

Astor

THE NEXT MORNING, I'm sitting on the front stoop waiting for the doctor to arrive. I don't want the doorbell to wake Sabine or Valerie.

I have a headache, and I never get headaches.

I'm rubbing my temples when I get the feeling someone is watching me. I look over my shoulder, and sure enough, Brittney is standing behind the front windows, staring at the driveway. But she's not looking at me.

I turn fully toward her, the movement earning her attention.

She blinks, startled. She hadn't even seen me. How is that possible?

I offer a crooked smile and wave.

She responds with the most awkward wave I've ever seen, then spins on her heel and disappears.

I surge up and push through the front door.

"Brittney?"

I catch her just as she's about to go into the master bedroom.

"Can I speak to you outside for a moment, please?"

She hesitates, then drops her hand from the doorknob and follows me outside.

She looks paler than yesterday. Her eyes are puffy and red as if she's either been crying, or didn't sleep last night.

"You okay?"

"Yes," she nods feverishly. "Yes, sir."

"Okay. Let me know if you need some time off."

"I don't. Thank you."

"Okay. . . . Yesterday, when I came into the bedroom after you brought Valerie in from the patio, was she speaking to you?"

Brittney frowns, searching her memory.

Jesus, what is it about this place and people forgetting things?

"Um, I can't—I don't think so."

"So, no? She wasn't speaking to you?"

"No."

" . . . Okay, so, to confirm, you two *weren't* speaking."

"I don't think so. Sometimes she mumbles, but . . . no, I don't think so."

Her cheeks look like they are about to explode into flames so I let her go, feeling zero percent better.

Dr. Squire pulls into the driveway in a dusty SUV with two kayaks secured to the top and a bicycle strapped to the back.

"I hope I didn't interrupt your vacation," I say as we shake hands. His white hair sparkles in the early morning sunlight, his gaze warm and sharp. If not for the slight limp in his gait, you'd never know the man was pushing eighty years old.

"Anything for you, Astor. You know that."

He pulls me in for a hug. His signature scent, Old Spice,

tugs at memories. Squire has been my doctor for decades and became Valerie's when she became ill, not long after our daughter, Chloe, died. A war veteran, Squire is the type of doctor who still believes in house calls, natural medicine, fitness to combat chronic illness, and a swift kick in the ass when needed. I have immense respect for him.

"I love this place," he says, taking a seat on the porch swing while I settle in on the wicker chair next to it.

"It's becoming haunted with bad memories."

He sombers. "What's going on?"

"Valerie isn't doing well. Physically or mentally."

"Give me the physical first."

"She had a deep rattle cough and was running a fever yesterday. She also gets short of breath on occasion throughout the day."

"During exertion?"

"No. Sometimes she'll wake up and it seems like she's struggling for air. But I'm not sure if it's related to a bad dream—she gets them almost every night."

"I'll give her a full exam today, and will take blood and urine samples. Pending those results, we'll take her in for additional testing."

"Thanks. And Jackie? Did you talk to her?"

"Yep. She'll be here soon. She's prepared to stay full-time with Brittney, if she needs to. How is Brittney doing?"

I find myself hesitating. "She's young."

"You were young once, too, remember."

I nod.

"Give her a chance. She was the top of her class. Now, tell me, how is Valerie doing mentally?"

I take a deep breath. "She's confused more than usual, and slurs occasionally. And sometimes she sees things that aren't there, and other times, appears confused about seeing things that are right in front of her."

He nods. "Both are common with schizophrenia. Seventy percent of people living with the disease experience hallucinations. I know she's aware of this, so that's likely a part of her confusion— she doesn't know what's real and what's fake."

"Is there any way she could be exaggerating her symptoms?"

"You mean faking?"

"Yeah."

"It's highly unlikely, especially considering the dosage of medicine she's on." He pauses. "It's a horrible disease, trust me. Has she opened up to anyone else?"

"Well, that's the other thing. She says a few things to Jackie, as you know, but I also caught her whispering to Brittney. When I asked her what they were speaking about, she denied it."

Squire spreads his palms as if he's not surprised. "All part of it, Astor. But let me ask, this nonverbal thing is new right? Just in the last months?"

"Correct. She's been off since losing our child years ago, but it seems exacerbated since the incident."

"How so?"

"After Chloe died, Valerie hardly spoke Chloe's name. Now, she's calling out for her in her sleep, asking why. And the other day she wrote her name on the shower wall."

Squire sucks in a breath. "That must be hard for you, too."

"It's hard for many reasons, one being that I feel like she knows something on a subconscious level and is trying to communicate it—"

"You mean, regarding Chloe's death? And the fact that you don't think it was an accident?"

"Right."

He pauses. "Be careful in trying to get her to open up

more. Don't push her, especially with something as traumatic as losing a child."

I drag my fingers through my hair. "I know, I know, I just feel like there's something there."

"Astor, with the amount of medication she's on, I wouldn't put stock in anything she says. We need to get her stable before pressing for any concrete information."

He puts his hand on my shoulder. "I know it's tough, especially for someone like you who needs to feel in control in every situation. Your daughter's death and everything surrounding it felt totally out of your control. Astor . . . I've told you a hundred times, I highly recommend that you begin seeing both a therapist and a psychiatrist."

"And I've told you a hundred times to go fuck yourself."

Squire chuckles, pats me on the back. "I'll never stop, Astor. It's my job to advise you on your health. What was the other thing? You said you had two reasons for Valerie bringing up Chloe's name being hard on you."

I exhale. "It brings back all the memories. Feels like it was yesterday that I lost my only child. My only blood."

"I can imagine. Especially what a miracle it was to have gotten pregnant again so soon after the miscarriage."

"What?"

Squire frowns. "You know . . . the miscarriage."

I blink, shake my head. "Miscarriage? What miscarriage? What are you talking about?"

The porch swing stills and Squire is frowning intensely, staring at me in a way that sends my instinct piquing.

"What, Squire?"

He blinks, having trouble finding his words.

"*What?* Speak."

"I . . . I thought you knew."

"Knew *what?*" My heart is pounding against my ribcage.

"When Valerie became a patient of mine, I had her doctor

send over her medical records. She miscarried the first baby you and she had, at six weeks."

My head begins spinning. An ice-cold chill snakes up my spine.

"Astor. Are you okay?"

"She—she never told me." Sweat breaks out over my skin, and my lungs feel like they are being squeezed from the inside out. "And I—I never joined her at any of the appointments... I didn't know—she didn't tell me . . ."

"It can be a difficult thing for a woman to go through. It's not uncommon for women to feel embarrassed and think it was somehow their fault. Again, it was a miracle you two were able to get pregnant again the next month, so soon . . . Astor— Astor, are you okay? You're as pale as a—"

I'm vaguely aware of Squire pulling me onto the ground and guiding me to lay down while I gasp for air.

"Breathe, son, breathe. Feel the ground beneath you, focus on the feeling of the ground beneath you..." His voice sounds like it's underwater as he guides me through a meditation to alleviate panic attacks. "...The ground is there to support you. Feel the ground underneath your heels, your calves, your thighs . . ."

I'm not sure how much time passes before I feel less like I'm falling out of an airplane and more like I'm in shock. I sit up, but remain on the ground.

Squire is kneeled beside me, his hand on my knee. He looks extremely concerned.

"You okay? You passed out on me. . . . Astor talk to me."

I squint, forcing my focus on Squire.

When I speak, my voice doesn't sound like my own. It sounds weak. "Valerie and I didn't have sex again until after Chloe was born. I didn't want to risk hurting the baby after she'd told me she was pregnant."

Squire's eyes widen. "Wait, so you had sex one time, the first time she was pregnant?"

"Yes. Oh my . . ."

"Breathe, Astor."

I swat away his hand, anger beginning to mix with the shock. "Valerie miscarried our child, and then got pregnant with someone else immediately after—and didn't tell me."

Squire's jaw drops. "I'm sorry—I just always assumed it was yours."

"So did I."

"So then . . . who's the father?"

The emails flash behind my eyes.

I can't wait to see you. I can't stop thinking about you or what our life will be like when we're finally together.
Love, Valerie

Soon. I miss you too. The plan is almost in place. Be patient, we'll be together again soon. I love you so much.
Carlos

Chloe was not my child.

She was Carlos's child.

One Hundred

Astor

THE TREE BARK spirals into the air as I slam my fist in the trunk. Over, and over, and over.

I want to kill Valerie. I want to go into the bedroom, wrap my hands around her skinny, pale neck, squeeze the air from her lungs and spit in her face as she takes her last breath.

My knuckle splits, igniting a fresh burst of fury through my veins. Instead of letting up, I hit harder, faster, a wild rage driving me in a way I haven't felt in years.

Sweat rolls down the side of my face, my chest heaves to pull in oxygen as my heart hammers against my ribcage.

When another knuckle splits, I pull back and double over, catching my breath.

Once the world stops spinning around me, I straighten and look back at the house, barely visible through the trees.

"Go take a long walk to cool off while I examine Valerie," Squire demanded once he was certain I wasn't going to have another panic attack. Then he said, *"and I highly recommend not bringing this up to her until she's stable."*

Not bring this up to her? It will take an act of God to not confront my wife about deceiving me into believing she was pregnant with *my* child while secretly having my arch enemy's baby.

Sabine is right. Valerie played me then, and is playing me now. She's nothing but a gold-digging, lying whore and it's my fault I didn't see it.

Staring at the beach house, fantasies of Valerie's bloody, broken body flash behind my eyes. I imagine all the ways I could kill her and make it look like an accident. Her voice materializes in my head, begging me to stop, to spare her life right before I take it in the most savage, brutal way.

The corner of my lip curves.

I feel the monster inside me begin to awaken. The one who almost beat a man to death for doing nothing more than speaking to Sabine.

What a fool I was to think I could change. What a fool I was to think that I could tame the monster.

He never left. He's right here, front and center once again.

And it feels good.

One Hundred One

Brittney

I'M STARING out the window when Sabine walks into the living room.

I turn away and begin wringing my hands. "Sorry. Jackie is with Mrs. Stone. Dr. Squire just left."

"You don't have to apologize for taking a break."

By the look on her face, I can tell that she has something to say to me.

Shit.

She knows.

My stomach drops.

"Let's sit outside, yes?"

I swallow the knot in my throat and follow Sabine onto the patio. Nervously, I search the garden while Sabine sits in one of the padded wicker chairs. I sit next to her. She hands me a glass of iced tea, one of two that I didn't even notice she was carrying when she walked into the room.

"So," she begins. "How are you liking it here?"

"Ah, it's—it's great."

"Yeah?" By her tone it's obvious she doesn't believe me.

"Yeah." I blow out a breath and lean back. "I'm just thankful to have this job."

"Has it been difficult finding a job? You're fresh out of school, right?"

I nod, but hesitate, embarrassed to open up to this beautiful, confident woman next to me who appears to have it all.

Sabine leans forward, resting her elbows on her knees. "What's going on, Brittney?"

"I'm just so afraid I'm going to mess this up." My chin begins to quiver and tears spring to my eyes.

She puts her hand on my shoulder.

"Cry. It's okay. I can tell you've got a lot bottled up. Let it out, girl."

I do, sputtering tears like a child. It feels good.

Sabine strokes my back the entire time. When I've gathered myself, she says, "If you're so afraid you're going to mess this up, then don't."

I snort, look at her.

"Meaning, just do your best every day. That's *all* you can do. Do the best you can with what you have. My mom always told me that." She pauses. "Also, take it one day at a time. Today, do the best you can. Tomorrow, do the best you can, and so on. Look at it as little steps at a time—not the whole staircase."

"Thanks." I wipe my nose with the back of my hand. "You're so smart."

"No, I'm not. I've made a million mistakes, and learned from them."

I take a deep breath, feeling better. "Money is just so tight, and it's like I'm living month to month barely scraping by."

"How old are you?"

"Twenty-one."

"You're so young. Don't be so hard on yourself. Everyone is poor at your age, trust me."

A moment passes, and once I think I'm in the clear, she says—

"Now, tell me what you aren't telling me."

I close my eyes and sigh.

"I see you watching for someone or something every hour of every day. What are you looking for?"

"Leo and I had sex," I blurt out.

"Wow." Sabine's eyes pop. She laughs. "Of all the things I thought you were going to say, that was definitely *not* it."

"Really? I just assumed he'd told you, and that's why you came out here."

"Nope. Leo's a quiet guy."

"Tell me about it," I mumble.

"Okay, spill it. What happened?"

I take a deep breath. "When he's not here, he works at Spittin' Suzie, a beach bar in the next town over."

"What a terrible name."

"I know. Anyway, about six months ago, I went with some of my girlfriends. Long story short, he and I went home together that night and had sex."

"Was it good?"

I cut her a look.

She laughs. "Okay, so that's a yes."

"*Very* good. It was only my—well, I haven't dated a lot."

"I see. Okay so then what happened?"

"That was it. He never called me, or texted, or spoke to me again. And the thing is, we had the most wonderful talk before we had sex. I felt a connection to him, you know? But then, he didn't even let me stay the night; told me he had to be up early in the morning and herded me out the front door like cattle. . . . I wasn't even fully dressed."

Sabine winces. "Ouch."

"Yeah. Tell me about it. So then . . . *ughhh.*" I bury my face in my hands in embarrassment. "A week later or so, I went back to the bar—I know, I know. Stupid. But I was just . . . I don't know, I was mad and hurt and wanted to see him."

"And how did he react?"

"He acted like he didn't even know me. He wouldn't even wait on me."

"Double-ouch."

"That's not the worst part. I kept going back, Sabine."

Sabine winces again, then puts her hand on my back. "We've all been there."

"I don't know why. I just couldn't get over it. Every time I'd pull into the parking lot, I'd tell myself, 'this is ridiculous. You're making a fool of yourself,' but then I'd go anyway. I *stalked* him, Sabine."

"Did he ever talk to you?"

"No."

"So then, when I got offered this job, I was so excited, because you know *Astor Stone.*" Sabine grins. "And when I read the case report I saw Leo's name. But I couldn't turn down this job. When I got here and saw him outside, I almost threw up. He has got to think I am *literally* stalking him at this point." I shake my head. "It's so hard. I really liked him. He's so, like, alpha military dude, you know?"

Sabine laughs. "Trust me, I know. . . . And, yes," she leans in. "Mr. Stone and I are in a relationship."

"I knew it!"

"I figured you did."

"How did it happen?"

"He kidnapped me."

I laugh so hard I break into a coughing fit.

Sabine deadpans.

"Oh my—you're serious."

"As a heart attack."

"So you're like living every dark romance book ever."

"Pretty much. Like a messed-up beauty and beast."

I laugh again.

"It's complicated," she continues, "as is anything worth having in life." She takes my hand. "Listen. The best way to get over a guy is to—"

"I know I know. Get under another one."

"No, Brittney, the best way to get over a guy is to fall in love with yourself." She smiles. "Come on, I have some lipstick that would look stunning with your skin tone, and dress that would fit you like a glove."

One Hundred Two

Brittney

I COULDN'T BE any happier if I were standing in Sephora itself. Sabine's beauty products are top of the line and I am *living* for it.

After trying on multiple colors and products, I decide that I like the cat-eye, something I've always wanted to try but never had the guts (or training) to do.

It takes four failed attempts to get it right. I can't believe what a difference a little eye liner, mascara, and blush makes.

"You have impossibly long eyelashes," Sabine gushes. "I'd die for them."

"I'd die for your life."

She snorts. "The grass is always greener, remember that. We all have our problems, no matter what you see on the outside."

I nod, then ask, "So, what's he like?"

"Astor?"

"Yeah."

She considers her answer. "He's a complex, complicated,

passionate man. He's incredibly smart, dedicated, and funny—both intentionally and unintentionally."

I laugh. "He kind of comes off as . . ."

"An asshole?"

"I was going to say stoic."

"He's been on his own for a long time and has lost a lot of people he loves. The pain has manifested in something . . . well, something I'm trying to tame, to be honest."

"I'm sorry to hear that. Men are so complicated. By the way, where is he?"

Sabine frowns. "Dr. Squire said he went for a long walk after their meeting this morning. I'm glad—he needs it." She refocuses on my hair. "Let me ask you, what was it about Leo that hooked you?"

"Besides the fact he was good in bed?"

"Right."

"Well, initially, his looks. He's the kind of guy that makes you want to know more about him and he has this super sexy dangerous vibe."

"Dark and mysterious."

"Yeah. All the women at the bar swoon over him. I'm not the only one he's taken home. I saw him leave with two other women on two occasions."

"Yikes. Okay, then let me ask you this: why would you want a man like that?"

"Fair point."

"Good. Think about that every time you see him. Okay, now let's talk about your hair..."

For the next thirty minutes, we discuss layers and high-lights, then sift through Sabine's clothes.

In a blue sundress, I stand in front of the mirror and stare at my reflection. My cat eyes, my glossed lips, my curled, voluminous hair. I don't recognize this woman, but I instantly love her.

Sabine steps back, hands on hips. "You look like a million bucks."

"I feel like a million bucks."

"Good. Now. Leo is outside on the north side of the house. Go outside and pretend to be taking a break, let him see you, then turn around and walk right back inside."

I grin from ear to ear then wrap my hands around her. "Thank you, Sabine."

"You've got this, Brittney. Love yourself first, and everything else will fall in line. I promise."

One Hundred Three

~

Sabine

I'VE JUST COME in from the garden when I hear an incessant *thud, thud, thud,* followed by something crashing against the floor. The sound is coming from Astor's office.

Has Valerie *completely* lost it? I picture her destroying the house in a fit of rage as I hurry into the hall.

But her bedroom door is closed.

I turn toward the office the moment something else crashes to the ground.

What the hell?

I rush into the room.

"Astor," I gape. "What are you doing?"

Standing on a chair, Astor is pulling down stacks of boxes from the built-in shelving above the computer desk. His face is flushed, his eyes puffy and dark. Toppled boxes scatter the floor, along with papers, old pictures, random knick-knacks.

Streaks of blood run down his forearms.

"Astor!" I whisper-hiss, quietly closing the door behind me so as not to disturb Valerie. "What the hell—get down!"

He appears to be in some sort of trance—and very, very angry. When he doesn't respond, I grab his elbow, and drag him off the chair.

He's unsteadied. His breath is coming in short, panicked pants.

"What's wrong?"

"It's not my baby."

"*What?*"

He refocuses on the boxes, eyes wild. "Chloe wasn't my baby. It was Carlos's."

"*What*—What are you talking about?"

He spins around, face contorted with rage. "What don't you understand about it's not my baby?"

I stumble back, startled, the reaction reminding me of the brutally savage man who once slammed me against the shower wall.

Seeing my reaction, his face falls. "Shit. I'm so sorry, Sabine. I'm so, so—*fuck!*" He scrubs his hands over his face. "I'm *so* sorry."

I inhale and square my shoulders. I will not allow myself to be scared of this man—*again*.

"You need to calm down and tell me what's going on."

In spurts of half-sentences, Astor repeats the conversation he had with Dr. Squire hours earlier.

I am so stunned that I gape at Astor for a full twenty seconds before speaking. His expression guts me. Behind the anger is profound hurt. Shame, embarrassment, regret.

"I want to kill her Sabine," he says, his chin quivering as he fights tears.

"No," I take his hands, pull him to me. "You will not kill your wife. I'm not going to let you. You have too much to live for, including me and the business you've built from the ground up. You won't get away with it, Astor, not this time. You can't ruin your entire life for revenge. She's not worth it."

"Sabine—"

"*No.* We are leaving this house this second. Don't even get a bag, let's go. Brittany's here and Jackie will be here later, and I think Cillian is going to be back soon. You need to get out of here."

"No." He jerks out of my hold and turns back to the boxes. "Not until I find what I'm looking for."

"What are you looking for?"

"Chloe's first baby tooth. Somewhere here, we have a box of sentimental things that we couldn't throw away but I can't find it—"

"We'll look later. Why do you need it now?"

He spins around, tears pooling in his eyes.

My heart breaks.

"I need to know—without question—that Chloe wasn't mine, Sabine. I'm going to have them do a paternity test on it. I have to know the facts. I *have* to know."

I swallow deeply. I can understand that. I look over my shoulder. "Okay, let's find it and then we're getting the hell out of here."

Ten minutes later, the door opens and Cillian steps inside with his carry-on luggage. His brows pop as he takes in both the mess and also the disheveled demeanor of his boss.

"Found it!" Astor surges up, a little baggie containing a white tooth secured in his hand.

Cillian looks at me, desperate for answers.

I exhale, shake my head—*too much to explain right now.*

Astor stumbles over the boxes, hands the baggie to Cillian. "Take this to Jenkins at the local FBI office. Have him run a paternity test on it and compare the DNA to Carlos Leone. He'll be in the database." Astor's voice begins to shake. "I need it done immediately. Tell him I'll pay him, tell him—"

Patience cashed out, Cillian interrupts. "Will someone please tell me what the hell's going on?"

"Chloe wasn't my baby."

"What?"

"And I'm going to kill Valerie."

Cillian's hands fly up. "Hold the fuck on—"

"I'm getting him out of here," I say quickly. "He'll call you on the way to the airport."

One Hundred Four

Sabine

ASTOR SETTLES into the seat next to me and drops his head back as the jet lifts into the air. It will be a short, one-hour flight to Palm Springs, where Astor owns several buildings, including a small, exclusive five-star retreat. Astor stayed mostly quiet on the ride to the airport, stewing in the passenger seat. I wouldn't let him drive. The stress of the recent months has spun him into a constant state of fight or flight, and no one can remain in that kind of headspace without a release. And history suggests Astor's release is violence.

How long can this go on? How long until he breaks?

His personal life is in shambles, his business is up in the air. If Astor snaps, he has everything to lose, and I can't let that happen.

It won't. Not with me in his life. I'm hoping this getaway will recalibrate and recenter him—and me, for that matter.

I slide my hand over his, careful not to touch his bloodied knuckles, now bandaged.

"I'm sorry."

"You've already apologized for yelling at me, and I've already accepted it. Let it go."

"Thank you, Sabine. You're my anchor. I don't know what I would have done if you hadn't been there."

"You wouldn't have killed your wife, Astor. Stop thinking like that. You are stronger than you think you are."

He swallows deeply, and looks away. He's not so sure.

"I've replayed the first month of mine and Valerie's relationship over and over in my head," he says. "I can count at least three times Valerie snuck out on her own, without security. I remember because we got in a huge argument after she returned each time, me trying to make her understand why she needed security, and she demanding freedom to live her own life. She must have met Carlos those times, and that's when she got pregnant. And then she stayed with me for money." He laughs a humorless laugh. "Little does she know, the moment I found out I was going to have a baby, I made Chloe —not her—my beneficiary."

"That was your instinct guiding you. You didn't trust her from the start."

"I didn't even love her. I loved my child." He squeezes my hand. "Do you want to know what's crazy? Knowing that Chloe wasn't mine doesn't take an ounce of the pain away. I loved that little girl so much and the fact that she wasn't my blood doesn't make a damn difference."

I stroke his arm as he struggles to compose himself.

"Can you imagine watching your husband cry over the death of his child, secretly knowing it wasn't his? Keeping that kind of secret from me that whole time? Deceiving me. All for money?"

"So you divorce her, Astor, and *forget* her."

He sighs and nods unconvincingly. I understand Astor has built an entire career around the notion of "an eye for an eye."

Hitmen don't believe in moving on until revenge is dealt and a body is cold. Hell, they're paid not to. But this time, Astor is going to have to accept it, and move on. I will not allow him to have Valerie killed.

I need to redirect his focus.

I turn his chin to me, forcing his attention on me and me only. "We know that the DNA results for the paternity test won't be in for two days, so until then, I am going to do everything in my power to make you relax. Let's decompress, talk, and make a plan, okay?"

"Okay . . . but we have to do one thing first, and then, I promise, I'll push it all aside for two days."

One Hundred Five

"DETECTIVE THOMAS." Astor stretches out his hand as a short, balding man rises from the booth.

"Call me Ben, Astor, geez." The man rolls his eyes with a laugh.

We shuffle aside as a trio of suits push past us, coffees in one hand, computers in the other. The coffee shop is loud and crowded with both tourists and locals.

"Ben, this is Sabine. Sabine, this is Ben Thomas. He was the lead detective on Chloe's case."

"Pleasure to meet you."

"Sit," Ben gestures to the booth.

We slide in and order coffees.

"How's retired life?" Astor asks.

"Boring."

Astor smiles, nods. It's apparent the two are friends. "People like us don't settle well."

Ben's gaze flickers to me. A warning glance? *Astor will never settle, sweetheart?*

He refocuses on Astor. "Okay, I'm intrigued. What's going on?"

"I want to reopen Chloe's case."

"No."

Astor scoffs. "Why?"

"One, I'm retired."

"So you'll connect me with someone else and then I'll pay you to work pro bono with him. What's two?"

"That case almost drove you over the edge, Astor."

"Have you lost a child, Ben?"

"No."

"Then you don't understand the length a father will go to get justice for their murdered child."

"Chloe wasn't murdered according to the evidence provided and the medical report."

"Fuck the evidence."

Ben snorts, folds his hands on the table and leans forward. "It doesn't work like that, Astor, you know that."

"I know that someone pushed my daughter into that manhole."

"No you don't. We've been through this a million times." He leans back, scrutinizing us. "I know you well enough that you wouldn't be here, wasting our time, if you didn't have new information. Tell me what it is."

"Chloe wasn't mine."

Ben's brows pop. "Really?"

Astor retells the story to the retired detective, and as he does, Ben remains still, unemotional, but incredibly attentive. Me, on the other hand? I become uneasy at the desperate tone in Astor's voice. He isn't thinking straight. He's running on emotions, not logic. It's embarrassingly apparent that Astor has no real reason for this visit, other than he can't let Chloe go. As I watch him speak, the flush that rises up his neck, the pitch in his usually stoic tone, I worry that he's becoming unhinged and sliding back into the old Astor. The one I don't care to ever meet again.

"While this information is shocking," Ben says, twisting his empty coffee cup around in his fingertips, "it's not enough to reopen a case. Astor, you know as well as I do, the only reason a criminal case was opened in the first place is because you used your influence to do so. They ruled it an accident almost immediately."

"It wasn't an accident, Ben. A lock of her hair was missing, which was meant to be a message, or maybe a threat, to me."

"It couldn't be proven, Astor. We—I—tried to link the lock of hair to the hundred names you provided me. Nothing connected. We even searched the database and studied old cases where the killer took a piece of the victim's hair. Nothing linked back to you or Valerie. Also, Chloe had a history of cutting her own hair. Lastly, the medical examiner's report stated that her cause of death was a brain hemorrhage, congruent with a fatal fall." He takes a deep breath. "Astor, there has to be a legal basis to reopen a case—you know that. A real, tangible piece of evidence that would warrant us to file a motion. Do you have that?"

Astor looks down, his jaw clenching.

"Find that missing lock of hair and then we'll have something."

When Astor doesn't respond, Ben leans forward, a pitied expression on his face.

I slide my hand over Astor's, under the table.

"Astor, hear me," he says. "You need to let this go. For your health, for your future happiness." He glances at me. "You need to let it go."

One Hundred Six

Sabine

WE SPEND day one of our "vacation," reading by the pool —and by reading, I mean Astor staring blankly into the distance with a closed book on his lap.

By day two, I'm sick of it. Astor has to snap out of this harmful trance he's in. So, the moment his eyes open, I demand that for the next twenty-four hours everything we do must involve either sex or alcohol. Preferably, both. Two things sure to calm Astor and return his focus on me—and me only.

I'm in the bathroom, getting ready for dinner, when Astor appears in the doorway. For the first time since leaving the beach house, his face is relaxed.

I smile, turn, and take him in. He's wearing a salmon-colored dress shirt, untucked, linen pants that do nothing to hide the bulge between his legs, and flip flops. Impossibly handsome.

He takes in the red lingerie I'm wearing.

"It's the set you got me on our first date, remember?"

"Yes." His eyes meet mine, the spark of heat unmistakable.

Well, hello. There's my man.

He advances, reaching for me, and begins running his hands over my curves. I abandon the eyeliner on the counter and wrap my arms around his neck.

"As much as I'd love to take you right here on this counter," he growls in my ear, "we have to be upstairs in five minutes."

I pull back, frown. "I thought we were doing room service tonight?"

"Not anymore." He smiles adoringly and kisses the tip of my nose. "I know I've been distant, and I want to make tonight special. For starters, I have a surprise for you in the closet."

"A little black dress?"

"A *very* little black dress." He playfully pops a palm against my ass. "You have five minutes, my beautiful goddess."

Ten minutes later, we arrive at the stunning rooftop bar. Everything is black, gold, mirror, and glass. The sun is just beginning to set over the San Jacinto mountains, spreading a golden glow over the desert below. A streak of pink clouds color the sky, fading into a deep indigo blue.

I'm so awestruck at the view that I don't immediately notice that we are alone in the bar, even though it's seven o'clock.

"Where is everyone?"

"Just you and me tonight, darling."

"You rented out the entire top floor of the hotel?"

He shrugs. "Easy to do when you own it."

"Mr. Stone," a blond bombshell greets us. "Wonderful to see you. I've got your table set up outside as requested."

"I can't believe you," I whisper as he threads his fingers through mine.

"Consider this an 'I'm sorry' for my behavior lately."

"Consider this my forgiveness." I raise his hand and tap a kiss on his healing knuckles.

Hand in hand, we follow the hostess to a round table sitting under the sunset. Behind it is an infinity pool that melts into the desert below.

A white linen cloth covers the table. What seems like a million candles surround us, on the table, on the floor, hanging from the pergola above.

"It's stunning," I say.

"It's you." Astor smiles, sweeps a strand of hair behind my ear. "Let's relax."

"Done." I wink.

* * *

Two hours, five courses, and two bottles of five-hundred-dollar wine later, I am delightfully drunk and endlessly happy.

Astor takes my hand, pulling me up.

"Ready for a swim, darling?"

I look at the sparkling blue water, then back at him. "I didn't bring up my swimsuit, darling."

"You don't need it."

I cock a brow, glance over my shoulder at the emptiness of the bar behind us. The waitstaff have obviously been ordered to leave us alone, making rare appearances to refill our drinks or deliver our food.

The corner of my lip curves with the kind of confidence that comes with having drunk a bottle of wine in under two hours.

Astor grins at my reaction, and begins unbuttoning his shirt.

Nerves tickle my stomach as he pulls it off and drapes it over the back of the chair, his eyes never leaving mine.

I begin taking off my jewelry, enjoying the strip tease in front of me.

The boxer briefs come off and, with a wink, Astor strides into the pool with a full erection, and a body chiseled from stone.

I laugh. "What I would give to have your confidence."

"So have it."

I snort. "Okay."

"It's that easy."

"Is it?" I look over my shoulder again, ensuring we are still alone as I grab the zipper on the side of my dress.

"Yes, it's that easy. Simply disregard what people think of you. Screw them, Sabine. Who cares? Screw 'em."

I tilt my head to the side, smirking. "Okay, big shot, screw 'em. Screw 'em all."

I slip out of my dress and lingerie and stand above him in nothing but six-inch red patent heels.

His eyes twinkle. He swims to me, beacons me with his finger.

Feeling gloriously free and surprisingly empowered, I kick out of the heels and kneel by him.

Astor surges out of the water, grabs my shoulder and pulls me into the pool.

We breach laughing, soaking wet and entangled in each other's arms.

Under the water, his hands trace my curves. "Nice, huh?"

Still laughing, I sweep the hair from my face. "Something like that."

His eyes sparkle with mischief. "Come here."

He guides me to the far side of the pool. There, he pulls me to him, spins me around, and presses my back against the side.

I yelp. "Astor!"

"The jets are strong aren't they?" A devilish grin crosses his face.

"Uh, yeah, and blasting against a very—*very*—private part."

"Relax."

"Astor—"

"Relax and close your eyes."

I laugh and close my eyes, blushing.

My senses heighten as his hands glide down my breasts, my curves, and cup my pussy, gently pushing me harder against the jet.

I whimper.

"Keep your eyes closed and relax," he whispers, trailing his tongue against my ear.

"I'm trying."

His lips slide over mine while, under water, his finger glides through my folds.

I exhale, feeling the world begin to drift away.

Once wet and ready, he repositions his thumb against my clit, and slips a finger inside me; one, then two.

"Now lean against me, my beautiful butterfly."

I do, allowing the whirling pressure to rush over my asshole while he finger fucks my pussy. Between the pressure of the water spreading me open, his fingers inside me, and his thumb smoothing my clit, I feel like a harem of men are servicing me. I imagine it, the taboo of it all, and find myself surging with tingles.

I drop my head on his shoulder and wrap my arms around. "Oh, Astor."

"Don't come for me yet baby."

Just as I feel like I'm about to explode, I'm lifted out of the water and placed on the edge of the pool. I lean back on my hands as Astor pulls up my knees and rests my heels on the lip just below water.

Strings of wet hair drape over my shoulders, snaking around my aching, naked breasts as I stare down at him, my throbbing pussy on full display.

"I want to taste you." He spreads my knees wider and massages my thighs. "Such a beautiful tight cunt you have. It's mine. All mine. Remember, Sabine, it's all mine."

Our eyes lock as he lowers into the water, lining up his face between my legs.

I thread my fingers through his wet hair as he feasts on my pussy, rhythmically lapping my lips, then circling my clit before clamping down and suckling, over and over again.

I moan, licking my lips.

Anyone could be watching us right now, and the thought sends heat surging through my body.

It's sexy as hell.

His fingertip circles my asshole. I moan, I lay back, breasts full and aching as the billion-dollar man ravages my pussy and explores me in the most intimate way.

I drop my head over the ledge of the pool, the twinkling lights from the buildings below sparkling like jewels in the desert. My gaze drifts from building to building, the hundreds of windows all pointing at us.

Between the sensation between my legs, the wine, and the head rush from being upside down, I grow dizzy.

I'm flying.

I feel like I've taken some sort of psychedelic drug.

It's glorious.

The orgasm rips through me wave after wave after wave.

* * *

I'm brought back to earth by the distant sound of a cell phone ringing incessantly.

Frowning, I lift my head, squinting from the head rush.

"What's that?"

"Cillian's direct line to me." Astor frowns. "I never turn it off. It's for emergencies only."

After helping me off the edge and back into the pool, Astor swims across the pool and hurries to the table.

Wading to the other side, I watch as his face drops.

He hangs up, looks at me.

My stomach sinks.

"That was Cillian. Valerie's very sick. We need to get back."

One Hundred Seven

❧

Brittney

STANDING IN THE CORNER, I watch Jackie administer Valerie's medicine. She's not doing well, alarmingly so. Over the course of the day Valerie's health has declined rapidly. Jackie hasn't left her side.

The medicine kicks in almost instantly, and Valerie falls asleep.

As Jackie notes the dose and time in her laptop, she says, "Where is your report?"

I blink. Report? I assumed since she's been here most of the day, I didn't need to be leaving an hourly report.

"Um—I, I was just about to do that."

"But you didn't." Jackie slides me the side eye. "Fine. Just update me now."

I clear my throat. "Valerie has been talking a lot of gibberish."

Jackie's pen freezes mid-air. She looks over her shoulder. "She's been speaking to you?"

"Yes—kind of."

"What has she been saying?"

"Mostly weird things that don't make sense."

Jackie nods. "That's congruent with what Mr. Stone reports. It's likely her new medication. Just respond to her in kind, and make sure she feels heard and safe and—"

Just then, Valerie opens her eyes, clutches her chest, and doubles over in pain.

One Hundred Eight

Sabine

IT'S midnight by the time we arrive back at the beach house.

Cillian opens the door as we rush up the walkway. The worry on his face is jarring.

"Tell me everything," Astor says.

I close the door behind us and look down the hallway. The master bedroom door is closed.

"The night you left, Valerie fell while the nurse was helping her to the bathroom, and had a lot of trouble getting up off the floor, even with Brittney's help. I was nearby, heard the commotion and came in, and literally had to pick her up off the floor. She was ghostly pale."

Hearing us, the master bedroom door opens and Jackie rushes out, Brittney close on her heels. Brittney is pale, too, wringing her hands in worry.

"I'm glad you're back, Mr. Stone," Jackie says quietly, meeting us by the front door. "I just got her to sleep, can we talk somewhere else?"

Cillian leads us to the kitchen where we stand awkwardly in a circle in the middle.

"I just told them about the fall," Cillian says.

Jackie nods. "Over the course of the last twenty-four hours, Valerie's health has deteriorated significantly. Dr. Squire has requested she be brought to the hospital tomorrow for testing."

"What do you mean deteriorated significantly?"

"She's having trouble balancing, she's having severe nausea, and appears to have visual disturbances. She's confused. It's as if trying to figure out who I am and why I'm there."

"That's how she's been recently."

"But worse now." Cillian confirms.

"Mr. Stone, I think it's possible that Valerie has had one or multiple silent strokes over the two weeks."

"Strokes?" He and I exclaim simultaneously.

The nurse nods. "Silent stroke symptoms match everything you've mentioned and that I'm seeing tonight: confusion, slurred speech, visual confusion, hallucinations, disorientation. Also, people with schizophrenia have a significantly higher risk of developing cardiovascular disease. In fact, they are three times more likely to experience sudden death from a heart attack than normal people."

"So what do we need to do?"

"I'll stay here tonight and tomorrow they'll run a litany of tests at the hospital. Dr. Squire took blood work when he was here last, so those results should be in soon. If she does have heart disease, there are many options to explore like medication, and even surgery."

Astor scrubs his hands over his face.

"How was she before she fell asleep tonight?" I ask.

"Lucid. Good. Much better than earlier today."

"Can I see her?" Astor asks.

"I'd let her sleep for as long as she can, but once she wakes, I can come get you, if you'd like."

"Yes, please."

Jackie nods, then motions Brittney to follow her back to the master bedroom.

"Are you good?" Cillian rests his hand on Astor's shoulder.

"Yeah . . . yeah. Go to the hotel, get some sleep. How are you? Everything okay?"

"Yeah. Lots going on with work, but nothing I can't handle. You handle this, I've got that."

"Thanks, brother."

The two embrace in a surprisingly emotional display of affection.

Cillian nods at me, then gathers his duffel from the kitchen table.

As he opens the front door, Astor calls out after him.

"Cillian?"

"Yeah?"

"Where's Leo?"

Cillian frowns. "Actually, come to think of it, I haven't seen him. I'll send him a text and make sure he connects with you before he leaves in the morning."

One Hundred Nine

Sabine

ASTOR WON'T SLEEP. Instead, he paces the room waiting on Jackie's next update. It appears that neither Jackie nor Brittney is sleeping either. Everyone is too wound up. I gave Brittney blankets and pillows to sleep on the couch in the living room, if she wanted to.

The house is suffocating. And Astor is at the center of all the tension. As I lay in bed, trying to go to sleep, I try to imagine what he's going through.

For the last three months, Astor has cared for his wife, ensuring she had access to top-of-the-line 24-hour medical care, 24-hour security, and anything else she needed. In the last few days, he has learned that his child, whom he believed was murdered, wasn't his to begin with. That his wife deceived him for financial gain. In the last few hours, he has learned that the wife he is now planning to divorce—as soon as possible—is in poorer health than any of us realized and will likely need much more attention and care going forward.

The whiplash of it all would be jarring for anyone, especially a man who needs control to feel stable. And right now, nothing is in Astor's control.

A loud boom of thunder shakes the windows.

Startled, I propel myself off the pillow and sit up. I'd fallen asleep. I look at the clock, then outside. Though it's already 9 a.m., it looks like midnight outside.

A flash of lightning illuminates the room just as Astor steps inside, holding two cups of coffee. He closes the door using the heel of his boot. The rain lets loose, coming down in sheets, slashing against the windows. It's as if Astor brought the storm with him.

"Morning," he says, a small smile forming as he looks at me. I don't smile back. Astor is as pale as the sheets I'm lying on. His eyes are bloodshot and puffy. He does not look good.

"Thank you," I take the coffee from his hand. "Are you okay?"

"Yeah."

"Liar."

"Yes." He sinks on the edge of the bed with a long exhale.

Thunder pops, lightning crashes.

"There are warnings and watches all over," he says. "Supposed to be multiple rounds of severe storms." My stomach dips at the sound of his voice. I've never heard him so weak. "I just got off the phone with Squire. He agrees that it's likely cardiovascular disease, and that she might have had a stroke, or maybe even more than one, over the recent months."

"Would that explain the odd behavior?"

He nods.

I look down, unsure what to say. I'm sorry? Despite this news, is the divorce still on? Or are you going to continue to control her medical care and pay for everything? Are you going to continue to live with her?

What about us?

"She's lucid," he says, shaking me from my thoughts. "We've been talking on and off all morning."

"About what?"

"I filled her in on what Squire thinks could be going on."

"What did she say?"

"Her biggest concern is that she doesn't want to be on any more drugs."

A moment passes.

"Did . . . did you say anything?"

"You mean did I tell her that I know Chloe isn't mine? No." His hand trembles as he slides his coffee on the bedside table, then he drops his head into his hands with a loud, frustrated groan. Alarmed, I set down my cup, raise to my knees and wrap my arms around his back.

"It's all I can think about when I look at her," he growls, "when I talk to her, when she speaks to me. I hate her so much. I *hate* her, Sabine." To my utter shock, Astor begins quietly sobbing. He's officially hit his breaking point. "But I can't say anything right now, right? I mean, Sabine, what am I supposed to do? Throw her out on her ass? She has nothing of her own."

He's right. It's an impossible situation, especially when he blames himself for her depression in the first place.

I hug him from behind. "Astor, take a deep breath." Tears well in my eyes. I stroke his arms, his back, resting my forehead on the back of his head. "One day at a time, remember?"

He drags in a deep inhale. Just as he's blowing it out, the door opens. Cillian, wet from the rain, fills the doorway, his large silhouette backlit by the hallway light.

A phone is in his hand.

"Astor. The paternity test results are in."

Sabine

THE *PATERNITY TEST.* We'd been so preoccupied with Valerie's poor health that the pending test results had slipped our mind.

Astor pushes off the bed, his face and eyes red from crying.

Cillian's brows pull together in concern. I wonder if this is the first time he's seen his boss cry. He looks at me. I shake my head—*he's not doing well.*

Astor reaches for the phone. Cillian seems to hesitate, a war battling in his head. But Astor snatches it.

"It's on speaker," Cillian informs us.

"This is Astor."

"Astor, hey, it's Nick."

Lightning flashes against the wall.

"I want to confirm that you wanted me to compare the DNA from the tooth to Carlos Leone's DNA, correct? C-A-R ..." He spells out the name.

"That's correct."

"Okay. Well, I did, and it's not a match."

"I'm sorry—you said it's *not* a match?"

"Correct. The father of Chloe Stone is not Carlos Leone."

Astor looks at me, wide-eyed.

"And, just to cover all the bases, you're definitely not the father either. I checked just to confirm that as well."

Astor's knuckles turn white against the phone. He begins pacing. "Well did you get anything useful at all?"

"Yes, actually, I did. I compared your," he clears his throat, "I mean Chloe Stone's DNA to everyone we had in the system, and got a hit."

I surge off the bed and take Astor's other hand in mine.

"Your daughter's DNA is a statistical match to a man named Leo Harrison."

The phone drops from Astor's hands.

My jaw drops—make that *unhinges.*

Leo?!

Chloe's real father is Leo—Leo, the man who has worked for Astor for a decade, first a mercenary, then as a property manager. Suddenly, it makes sense. In managing Astor's homes, Leo would have had unrestricted, continuous full access to Valerie at all times. And no one would have thought twice about him being in and out of the homes they shared.

Holy. *Shit.*

"Where is he?" Astor lunges forward and fists Cillian's shirt. "Where the fuck is he?!"

"I don't know. Man, you've got to calm down—"

"Where is he?!" Astor bellows, the veins bulging from his neck.

He pushes past Cillian and storms into the hallway, fists clenched, chest heaving.

Cillian and I rush after him.

Astor kicks open the door to the master bedroom, sending it popping on its hinges.

Jackie surges up and stumbles backward. Brittney runs in

from the living room, dazed and confused having been awoken by the screaming.

Valerie's eye's pop open.

"You fucking liar!" Astor yells, ripping the covers off her bed.

Jackie screams. "Stop! Stop!"

More cracks of thunder, pops of lightning. The sheets of rain create a loud white noise, adding to the ominous atmosphere.

"Brittney, go outside. Get out of here. Now." I grab her shoulders and push her toward the door. Eyes bugging, she stumbles out of the door in nothing but her socks.

Astor grabs Valerie and hauls her to her feet. Her pale, gaunt face panics as she tries to get her footing, tries to understand what the hell is happening.

"He's going to kill her!" I yell breathlessly to Cillian as he lunges into action and grabs Astor's shoulders.

"Let her go, Astor."

But Astor doesn't hear his friend, his nurse, or me. He's glaring at Valerie with wild, feral eyes, his face contorted with rage.

He grabs the collar of her night dress and begins shaking her like a rag doll. Her neck flies backward, her jaw clashing. "You lying bitch!"

"Astor, let her *go.*" Cillian yanks Astor back. He stumbles backward, into Cillian, as Valerie crumbles to the floor.

Jackie, now crying, rushes to her aide.

Like whiplash, Astor spins around and slams his fist into Cillian's face. The sound is sickening. The look on his face is terrifying.

I gasp and jump back as Astor delivers another devastating blow, without allowing his friend even a second to register what's happening. Blood sprays the wall behind them.

He broke Cillian's nose.

The two engage in a brutal fist fight, eventually falling into the hallway. Behind us, Valerie is screaming and Jackie is trying to calm her down.

I rush into the hallway, yelling at Astor to stop, hoping that hearing my voice will snap him out of it.

Blood runs down both their faces, dripping off their chins.

I'm vaguely aware of Jackie sprinting past us and out the door, as I continue screaming, trying to distract Astor.

Something in Cillian's eyes flash, a look that resembles the crazed one on Astor's face, and then, as if someone hit a fast forward button on him, he snaps, delivering a series of punches to Astor's torso and face that incapacitates him within seconds.

Cillian wrestles Astor to the ground until—finally—Astor lays limp.

"That's enough, *friend,*" Cillian growls, his blood dripping on Astor's cheek. "That's *enough.*"

Chest heaving, Cillian pushes off Astor, who he could have easily killed, and wipes the blood from his lips.

Astor stumbles to get off the floor, disoriented. His eyes are dilated, distant. One will be swollen shut in an hour.

He's extremely messed up.

"Leave us," he says weakly.

Neither Cillian nor I move.

"Leave us."

I look at Cillian for reassurance. After a moment, he dips his chin—*he won't hurt her now.*

I take Cillian's hand as he guides me down the hallway. Over my shoulder, I watch as Astor disappears into Valerie's room.

One Hundred Eleven

Astor

MY EARS ARE RINGING, my head feels like an over-inflated balloon, my stomach is nauseous, but none of that is going to stop me from getting the answers I need.

The answers I deserve.

I stumble into the bedroom. Valerie, still on the floor, screams at my bloodied and bruised appearance, and scrambles backward against the wall.

"I'm not going to kill you," I mumble, spitting a string of blood on the floor.

Valerie whimpers, covering her face with her hands.

"Stop." I kneel down and pull her hands away from her face. "I'm not going to hurt you. But I am done with the games—I'm done walking on eggshells. I'm done with you. You will talk to me, or I will throw you out of this house and leave you to rot in the woods. Do you understand me?"

Her wide-eyes flicker between the open gashes on my face.

"I know Chloe is not my child."

She blinks, shocked by this.

"Do you think you could keep something that big a secret for the rest of our lives?"

Her mouth opens and closes. She's stunned speechless.

"Say it, Valerie. Say his name."

"I can't," she sputters, trying to cover her face again, but this time, I grab her hands.

"Say it!"

"Leo! Leo, okay? It was Leo. He and I had sex when he'd visit. It just happened, and then . . . kept happening."

I let her go, falling back on my ass.

For a long moment we say nothing.

"I'm not mad that you cheated on me, Valerie. I'm mad that you deceived me about Chloe. I have one more question for you and if you lie to me, God help me." I inhale. "Does Leo know that the baby is his?"

Please say no, please say no, please say—

"Yes."

My fists curl and it takes everything I have not to blow a hole through the wall. Valerie deceived me, and now one of my most trusted associates has deceived me as well. Despite the fatigue from the fist fight, my adrenaline begins to pump again, the rage beginning to simmer in my veins.

"He flipped out when I told him—absolutely lost it."

"What do you mean he flipped out?"

"He lost his mind over it. It wasn't planned, obviously, it was a mistake, and he was terrified you'd find out and have him killed. So we agreed to make you believe it was yours."

My heart starts to race.

"But . . . but he—he couldn't take it. He was so worried you'd find out. He looks at you like a father, Astor. He loves you."

My head starts spinning.

No.

"He stopped eating, sleeping; he was going crazy with worry. He started talking about all these crazy things."

No.

"The day Chloe died, Leo—he didn't show up for work, and he stopped talking to me after that."

No.

She reaches out her trembling hands, grabs mine. "You've asked why I keep having nightmares about Chloe, and why I'm asking why. Well . . . Astor . . . I—I think Leo might have killed Chloe so that you would never find out. I think he did it to save his own life."

I don't remember the next few seconds.

When I wake up, I'm on the ground again, being restrained by Cillian while Leo's name rips out of my throat like a pig being gutted.

One Hundred Twelve

Sabine

THE FOLLOWING hours are the most intense of my life —and that's coming from someone who's been shot and left for dead. The tension in the house is almost unbearable.

Astor isn't himself. He hasn't slept since our short time in Palm Springs, and between the recent news and physical altercation, his mind and body are spent. He's not thinking straight. He's disoriented, manic.

As suspected, his left eye has swollen shut and looks like a big purple balloon. His entire face is puffy and speckled with the beginning of a dozen bruises. I can't imagine what his ribs feel like. He doesn't seem to care, however, and I wonder if he can even feel it.

Cillian, on the other hand, looks markedly less roughed up. He is the more experienced street fighter of the two, no doubt about it. He realigned his nose in the bathroom (not joking), popped a pain pill and acted like he was never hit at all.

Cillian won't leave Astor's side to ensure he doesn't do

anything that would lock him up for ten years to life. Even though they almost killed each other, Cillian is a calming force for Astor. I knew the two were close, but seeing them interact in such a dark time has proven just how unbreakable their bond is. Astor trusts Cillian unconditionally, the way a child would a father. And Cillian cares for and protects Astor as a father would a child. They are family, maybe not by blood, but by heart.

Both Jackie and Brittney are gone, of course, and will likely never return. I can't say I don't blame them. I was surprised that a line of police cars didn't show up.

After the scuffle, Cillian called Dr. Squire and informed him that Valerie wouldn't be coming into the hospital today, and instead, they'd bring her in tomorrow. Neither Cillian nor Astor are in any shape to be in public.

Valerie is in her room and hasn't stopped crying. I can hear her through the closed door, even through the storm raging outside. It hasn't let up. One round after another, a violent reflection of the disposition inside the home.

Me? I'm using my sky-high anxiety to plan, to come up with any idea to help the situation. I keep landing on one thing—Astor needs to get far, far away from this mess. Leave the country, even. Settle somewhere until he's processed everything. If that will even happen.

My gaze shifts to the storm raging outside. I remember when I was a little girl, my grandmother, my mom's mom, was diagnosed with cancer. Instead of hospice, mom moved grandma into our tiny one-bedroom apartment. Grandma died on the couch while mom and I were making breakfast one morning. Unfortunately, there was a delay in hospice returning to collect the body. We didn't feel right leaving her, so for hours mom and I tip-toed around the apartment, with a dead body on the couch, trying to act as normal as possible in the most screwed-up situation we've ever been in.

This feels like that, but amped up by a million percent. There are so many pieces of the puzzle to sort, so many traumas to deal with, and here we are, tip-toeing around the house, trying to deal with it all.

At midnight, Astor passes out at the kitchen table, his body finally shutting down. Soon after, Cillian falls asleep on the couch, and after peeking into Valerie's room to ensure she was also asleep, I decide to give rest a shot, too. I drop like dead weight onto the mattress, fully clothed, and fall asleep within minutes.

At one in the morning, I awaken to the low growl of an engine outside. I surge out of bed, slip into my sandals and jog to the kitchen. Astor is no longer at the table. Cillian is still passed out on the couch. The door to Valerie's room is closed.

I yank open the front door just as Astor backs onto the street in his Aston Martin.

"Hey!" I whisper-hiss, running into the sheets of rain.

When Astor doesn't stop, I lunge into the street, blocking his path.

I glower into the headlights until the window rolls down.

I have to swallow back a gasp. Astor's face looks even worse than before he fell asleep. The swelling, the bruising, it's hideous.

"Where are you going?" I snap, wiping the rain from my face. The interior of Astor's priceless car is getting soaked but he doesn't seem to care.

"I have to take care of something."

"Don't bullshit me. Where are you going?"

His eyes are as cold as ice. I've seen the look before, and whatever Astor is about to do, there is nothing to deter him from it.

"You're going to find Leo, aren't you?"

"I'm not going to kill him. I'm going to break into his apartment and look for the lock of hair that was cut from Chloe's head the day she died. If he has it, he's the one who killed her, and I'll take that to Detective Harris and they'll nail the fucker. And then, I'll be able to rest."

When I open my mouth to protest, he cuts me off.

"He did it, Sabine. I know. He did it to protect himself because he was worried what I'd do if I found out."

I can't blame him.

"Okay." I take a deep breath. "We do this together, Astor —everything together, you and me. Remember?"

"I don't want you to be a part of this."

"Too bad." I yank open the door and crawl over him to the passenger seat so that he couldn't peel away before I made my way to the passenger side.

We take off, speeding through the narrow road that skirts the ocean. Even with the wipers on high, it's hard to see through the rain.

"What makes you think Leo won't be at home?" I ask, buckling my seatbelt.

"He bartends when he's not on shift for me. The bar closes at two."

I remember Brittney telling me that's where she met him, right before their one-night stand.

"How far is his apartment?"

"Twenty minutes."

I look at the clock. "We better hurry."

One Hundred Thirteen

Sabine

THE APARTMENT COMPLEX is a rundown two-story brick building at the end of a cul-de-sac. The kind of neighborhood where you wouldn't want to be out past sundown. It strikes me as odd, considering how much Astor pays his employees, but then I remember that Leo spends most of his time bouncing between, and living in, Astor's many mansions. Why pay for something that nice when you spend most of your time in luxury, anyway?

The neighborhood is quiet, with only the roar of rain to break the eerie silence. Every room in the complex is dark, and not a single light is on in the surrounding homes. Everyone is asleep in their beds—where we should be.

We pull into the small lot.

"Oh no." I shake my head.

"What?"

"That's Brittney's Nissan."

Astor squints through the rain at the car parked at the end of the lot. "What is she doing here?"

"She and Leo have a connection—they had a one-night stand recently. She's having trouble letting go, to say the least."

"She told you that?"

"Yeah. We've become friendly. She is a sweet, young woman trying to find her way."

"Wow, the guy gets around, doesn't he?"

I nod. "She's probably here because of the fight earlier, to tell him about it, maybe."

"Well, shit." Astor looks at the clock. "He shouldn't be home yet. According to the person I spoke to at the bar, he's closing tonight."

"Let me see if she's in her car. Park there, and I'll be right back."

"No, let me do it."

I snort. "No thanks, Incredible Hulk, I'm pretty sure she never wants to see you again. Stay here. She's comfortable with me."

Astor grabs a poncho from the back of his car and hands it to me. I slip it on. "I'll be right back."

Dipping my face against the rain, I pull up the hood and jog across the parking lot.

Brittney is sitting behind the steering wheel scrolling on her phone. She nearly catapults through the roof of her car when I knock on the window.

Shocked to see me, she rolls down the window. When I try to shield the rain from dripping into her car, she rolls her eyes. "Don't worry about it, seriously. What are you doing here?"

"What are *you* doing here?"

"I . . . I" she stammers. "I came here to tell Leo about what happened. I heard Astor scream Leo's name, and I, well, I came here to warn him."

"Of what?"

"That something huge happened and Astor appeared very upset with him. What happened, Sabine?"

"A lot. But I can't go into all that right now."

"I didn't have your number; I wanted to call you. I've never seen someone so mad. I've never seen a fight like that."

I sigh. "I know, it was awful. I'm so sorry you had to see that." I glance over my shoulder. So, um, have you told Leo? Have you seen him?"

"No."

Phew.

She continues, "I went to the bar, but he was on a break, so I came here to wait for him until he gets home."

My heart breaks for her. She is madly in love with this guy.

"Where's Jackie?" I ask.

"I don't know. I called her after I left, asking what to do, and she told me to go home and not return to the beach house until she gives me the okay."

"Do you know if she called the cops?"

"I don't think so. She seems like the type of person to stay out of other people's drama, you know what I mean?"

"Brittney, listen, I need you to go home right now. Please."

"What's going on? What's going to happen?"

"Honestly, I don't know, but it's best for you to leave."

She glances in the rearview mirror at Astor's car idling behind us.

"Honey," I say desperately, "I need you to make a good decision tonight."

"Go home," she mumbles.

"Yes. On multiple levels, that's the best decision right now. One, what is Leo going to think of you waiting for him all night? And two, whatever Astor has to say to Leo is not your business. Okay? Here," I open my palm. "Give me your cell phone."

I program my number into her contacts. "That's my personal cell. I'll call or text you later and I'll let you know when to come back, if you're even willing to come back to work." I wink.

"Okay." She nods reluctantly. "Thank you."

"Be careful."

"You, too."

As I watch her pull onto the street, I get a weird feeling of something that resembles parental concern.

One Hundred Fourteen

Leo

I POP the trunk and set the grocery sacks next to the packed bags. I have ten more minutes until my break is over. I need to hurry.

After a quick glance over my shoulder, I transfer the perishables to the cooler, and the rest of the food to the dry bag. After slipping back into the truck, I count the remaining cash I have and sigh. It's enough for what I need to do, but that's about it.

I pull my phone from my pocket, click into the travel app and, for what feels like the hundredth time today, I confirm that my 5 a.m. flight is on time.

It will be tight. I have to work until past 2 a.m., then pack my remaining bags, then drive an hour to the airport.

Her face flashes behind my eyes, and I get the same sick feeling every time I think of her. Regret.

I am not the type of man Brittney Walsh needs, that much is clear. But knowing it doesn't erase the memory of our one, short-lived night together.

I'd had my eye on Brittney since the first time she stepped foot in my bar with her friends. The third time, with a churning stomach and sweaty palms, I made a move.

It was the first good decision I've made in what feels like years.

I was nervous. Me, the guy who spent years running special ops in the military, then running black ops for Astor Stone (only to hurt my back and be discharged from further missions).

There was just something about the girl that spoke to me. Pulled me in.

When we got to my place, we ended up talking for an hour before going to the bedroom. Brittney has this sweet, innocent outlook on life. She's a hard worker, an eternal optimist, and sees the best in people.

She reminded me of the type of woman I'd wanted my daughter to grow up to be—and that is something I haven't been able to stop thinking of.

I wanted all *that* in my life. Her, and everything that came with her.

It was the first time I'd had sex since Valerie—and it was the best sex I've ever had in my life. After we finished, I wanted to wrap her up, put her in my pocket, and carry her around with me everywhere.

But then, Valerie's face flashed behind my eyes, her threat echoing in my ear.

I'll never forget that day. I was in New York, working in Astor's penthouse, when she pulled me into the master bathroom. There, she told me that Chloe was mine, and that if I didn't go along with it, she would tell Astor and he would kill me. For years, I worked for Astor sneaking peeks at the daughter I knew was mine, while watching another man raise her. Knowing that if that man found out, I was as dead as roadkill. When she was feeling generous, Valerie offered me little mementos from Chloe; pictures, finger paintings, an ornament she made in pre-school, but it didn't help.

It ate a hole in my gut. The guilt of knowing I was deceiving the one man I looked up to, I admired. The regret of the decision I'd made with his wife.

I couldn't eat.

I couldn't sleep.

I became a closed-off hermit, rarely speaking to anyone, rarely leaving my apartment when not at work.

Then I met Brittney, and all the darkness seemed to float away. I felt happy. Real joy. Hope.

Then, it was gone. Next day, while at the beach house, Valerie started randomly calling out for Chloe. She hadn't spoken her name in years. And I knew she was going to tell him our secret.

Looking back, I think I knew all along. You see, nothing gets past Astor Stone. Not forever anyway. I've been biding my time, living a nightmare of regret since that day.

For the last three months, I've been saving every penny while devising my getaway plan. A plan that didn't involve dragging a sweet, innocent nurse down into the depths of hell with me. It was so hard to pretend that I didn't care for her. But what was I supposed to do? I knew I was leaving. And I knew, at the end of the day, I was no good for her, anyway. Men like me, who have done the things I've done, don't deserve love.

Astor will come for me, I know that, but I'm not going to make it easy on him.

In a matter of hours, I'll be out of here.

Somewhere far away from my mistakes.

One Hundred Fifteen

Sabine

THE MOMENT BRITTNEY'S car is out of sight, Astor gets out of the car. I have to run to catch up with him as he strides across the parking lot.

Astor pulls a thin silver tool from his pocket and picks the door lock in under ten seconds. Forgoing stealth and patience, he swings open the door and steps inside.

Heart racing, I glance over my shoulder before following him.

The apartment is tiny, scarcely furnished, and smells of must and mold. A loveseat sits in front of a television and a tarnished coffee table. A half-drunk bottle of beer sits in the middle. The dim orange glow from the security lights stream in through dirty, bare windows, pooling onto threadbare carpet. It's just enough light to see around.

The scarcity of Leo's belongings makes me sad as I picture the shy former soldier in my head. Leo lives a simple, solitary life. Not even a plant to care for.

Astor strides through the living room, checks the kitchen,

then pivots to the short hallway that leads to the bedroom. There, he checks the closet and the bathroom.

"He's not here," I state the obvious, punctuating how nervous I am. "What now?"

"We turn this place upside down looking for anything of Chloe's, especially an envelope or bag where he would have kept her lock of hair."

"Shouldn't take long," I mutter, looking around the bedroom, a single bed and a stack of boxes in the corner.

Keeping the lights off, we turn on our cell phone flashlights. We make quick work of searching the bedroom first, the closet, the bathroom. Then the living room and kitchen.

"Why do you think Leo has so little possessions?" I ask as I filter through the pots and pans.

"He went straight from the military, where he was deployed six months a year, to working for me."

"It's sad."

"It's his decision. Just like it was his decision to continue to take my money while he was fucking Valerie. Just like it was his decision to not tell me that my child was actually his. Just like it was his decision to watch me weep over her grave, and *still* not tell me."

A scraping sound outside the front door pulls our attention. We freeze, listen. A cat meows loudly, then fades away.

I blow out a breath and quickly replace the pots. "We need to hurry. We've checked everywhere. There's nothing here. Let's go."

"One more look."

Groaning, I push off the floor and follow Astor back into the bedroom. He rechecks the loose floorboards, the underside and backside of the bed, then puts his hands on his hips and studies the closet.

"One more look . . ."

I linger in the closet doorway as Astor filters through Leo's clothes and shoes as he did before.

"Come on, Astor, we need to go."

He turns, pauses, then looks up. We both freeze, staring at the small square covered cut out in the ceiling. A scuttle attic.

"I'll get a chair." I run into the kitchen, grab a chair and run back.

Astor climbs onto the seat and moves the thin panel cover.

"Hold my phone."

Astor pulls himself through the small space, then reaches down for the phone.

My heart pounds as I watch the flashlight bounce around until suddenly, it stops.

"Did you find something?" I whisper-hiss, wanting to get out of here.

After a minute, Astor lowers himself out of the opening.

"What is it?" I ask, staring at the brown manila envelope in his hand.

"I found it on top of the insulation."

My heart hammers as I follow him to the kitchen table. I hover my light above the envelope as Astor opens the flap and begins pulling out the contents, laying out each, one by one.

There are a dozen pictures of Chloe, from infancy to the age she died. A small beanie, the kind the hospital gives newborns. Multiple finger paintings ranging from smears to stick figures, drawn by Chloe.

Astor picks up one of the finger paintings and stares at it until his hand begins trembling. His face has grown flushed and that crazy, wild look in his eye has returned.

Two words materialize in my head.

Get. Out.

"Astor, take it and let's go; let's get out of here right—"

The front door opens.

Oh shit.

The painting falls from Astor's hands and he lunges into the living room.

Leo, dressed in jeans and black t-shirt, stops cold, startled. The blood drains from his face as he looks at Astor.

He knows.

Leo raises his hands in surrender and begins backing up. "I'm sorry—"

"You son of a bitch." Astor advances, chest heaving.

"I'm sorry. I'm so sorry. I'm sorry I didn't tell you. I didn't mean to get her pregnant."

Astor launches himself at Leo, slamming his body against the wall, and wrapping his hand around his throat.

Leo releases a gurgling sound and his eyes bulge with fear.

"You killed Chloe so I wouldn't find out. You *killed* her—"

Knowing that he's fighting for his life, Leo slams his fist into Astor's kidney and twists out his hold.

Astor pivots, delivering an uppercut that snaps Leo's head back. Leo doesn't go down, instead, his eyes flash with rage that matches Astor's.

Leo lunges toward Astor with a jab, which Astor blocks, one, two three in rapid succession.

Lightning flashes through the windows and the rain is so loud it sounds like a million bugs screaming in horror.

Astor answers back with a left cross into Leo's eye socket, bursting open his skin. Blood sprays everywhere. Like a robot, Leo isn't fazed. They fight like rabid dogs, punching, jabbing, rerouting and attacking again. Blood is everywhere, on the walls, on their clothes, dripping down their faces.

This fight is different from the one Astor had with Cillian. Cillian meant to debilitate Astor so that he wouldn't do something stupid. Leo, on the other hand, means to fight to death.

Astor swerves, missing a hook aimed at his chin and drives

his shoulders into Leo's stomach, sending him flying backward, both men tumbling to the ground. Astor gets on top of him and unleashes like an animal. Leo thrashes under his holding, jabbing him in the liver and kidneys but Astor doesn't appear to feel a thing.

"You killed her you killed you killed her." His screams are manic as he pounds Leo's face like a jackhammer.

"Astor!" I scream, "Stop, stop!"

Leo's body goes limp.

I lunge forward, grabbing Astor's shoulders, trying to pull him off but it's no use. Desperate, I grab Astor's face and scream in his ear as loud as I can.

Astor stops, looks at me, his eyes adjusting as if coming out a trance. Then, he looks down at Leo. A full minute passes as his brain begins to process what he's just done.

Astor doubles over Leo's body in uncontrollable sobs.

I begin crying too.

What feels like eternity passes until I am finally able to pull Astor to his feet.

We stare down at the body. We don't need to confirm he's dead.

I put my hand on Astor's forearm. "It's done. Let's clean up."

One Hundred Sixteen

Sabine

FOR THE NEXT FEW DAYS, Astor and I don't leave the beach house.

Valerie's medical testing confirmed that she has cardiovascular disease, which is common in patients with schizophrenia. She stayed overnight in the hospital and was released the next day with a slew of new prescriptions. With her came two full-time nurses (not Jackie or Brittney) who rotate out every twelve hours, and a doctor who visits daily. The next step will be surgery, although she's not stable enough for that yet.

Astor and I rarely speak about what happened at Leo's apartment, though it's a sick, dark cloud that lingers between us. Cillian "took care" of the bloody scene and erased any evidence that we were there. It's like it never happened. Well, aside from the sinking feeling in my gut I get every time I think about it.

I try to stay out of the way as much as possible, which I'm doing now, trimming hedges in the garden. It's a humid, cloudy day with the promise of rain on the horizon.

466

More rain.

The overnight nurse reverses out of the driveway, pulling my attention. Seconds later, the day nurse arrives.

I decide to take a break.

I pull my phone from my pocket.

"Hello?"

"Hey, Brittney, it's Sabine."

"Hey! How are you? How's Mr. Stone? And Valerie?" I can hear the hustle of the hospital behind her. She must be at work.

"Valerie's pretty sick."

"I'm sorry to hear that. How do you like the new nurses?"

"I don't know, really. I've just been staying out of the way as much as possible."

"I know one of them, Carla. Everyone loves her. She's been around for a long time and knows her stuff. How's Mr. Stone?"

"He's okay, trying to catch up on work stuff while dealing with Valerie's health." I take a deep breath. "So. How are things in geriatrics?"

"Today, a patient came in. Her name is Karen. She's in and out a lot. She asked for me specifically and when I went to see her, she'd knitted me a scarf."

"Oh, Brittney, that's so wonderful."

"Yes, I almost cried. It makes the bad days and bed pans worth it."

"You're something else, you know that?"

"Honestly, though? I'd rather be working for you again.
"

I chuckle, but it feels forced.

Ever since the night at Leo's, I've been sick about Brittney. Obviously, I couldn't tell her what happened, but I can't help that I want to. I hate lying to her.

"So, um, Leo still hasn't turned up?" She asks.

"No." My stomach sinks. "We think he took off after Astor met with him."

She sighs. "And you're still not going to tell me what they talked about?"

"Maybe someday." I swallow the knot in my throat. "Anyway, that's not why I'm calling. I wanted to let you know you should be receiving a package today. A few, actually."

"Really?" Her voice perks up. "From you?"

"Yes, ma'am." I smile. "If anything doesn't fit, let me know."

"Oh my gosh, Sabine—"

"Hush. Don't make it weird."

"Thank you *so* much."

"It's my pleasure."

And it really, really is.

Brittney and I speak for twenty more minutes, sharing stories about her patients. I cling onto every word, hoping she finds contentment and happiness in her day.

After hanging up, I go inside. Astor and Cillian are in the office on a conference call. The door is open.

I lift my hand. Astor smiles and dips his chin.

I motion that I'm getting a drink and ask if he wants one. He shakes his head, then winks. I smile back. We're trying.

After washing the dirt from my hands, I pour a glass of sweet tea.

The nurse steps out of Valerie's room, shakes her phone at me indicating she needs to take this call, then steps outside.

I haven't seen Valerie since she got back from the hospital. She hasn't left her bed and the nurses keep the door shut while they're inside.

Curiosity gets the better of me and, before I can stop myself, I tip-toe down the hall and peek inside.

Valerie is lying in bed with her eyes closed. Her cheeks are pale and sunken in, giving her a ghostly appearance. She's even more emaciated than she was a week ago. Multiple wires run from under the covers to monitors, which beep every few seconds.

I lean against the door, a wave of sadness washing over me. No matter how deceitful the woman was, no one deserves this.

I find myself metaphorically slipping into her shoes, thinking of her story.

Valerie got pregnant with Astor's baby and accepted an invitation to marry despite the lack of love between them. After miscarrying the baby, instead of telling Astor, she keeps it a secret and begins an intimate relationship with the young, handsome house manager to fill the void of a loveless marriage. Finding herself pregnant once again, Valerie sees an opportunity—make Astor believe the baby is his, and continue her lavish lifestyle, while secretly having multiple affairs, including one with her husband's archrival.

But the story doesn't end there. In an ironic twist, the child is tragically killed by the hands of his father, Leo, because Leo couldn't handle the stress of knowing that Astor might one day discover their secret and have him killed.

But now—

Chloe is dead.

Carlos is dead.

Valerie's sister, Prishna, is dead.

Leo is dead.

And Valerie is wasting away.

All because two people, who didn't love each other, committed to a life together out of obligation (Astor) and opportunity (Valerie). It's a twisted, cautionary tale of devotion to self over love.

As I study her, I wonder if it was all worth it. The years of lies and manipulation. If she could go back in time, would she do it all over again?

"Come."

I startle at the voice that came out of nowhere and look over my shoulder, expecting to see the nurse. But she's still outside on the phone.

When I turn back around, Valerie's eyes are open and fixed on me.

"Come," she beckons with a long, skinny finger.

Again, I look over my shoulder. Astor is still in his office, engrossed in the call he's on.

I step into the room. It reeks of antiseptic and bleach.

You're just the housekeeper, I remind myself. *She thinks you're just the housekeeper.*

"What are you drinking?" She asks in a weak and raspy voice.

I look at the glass in my hand, having forgotten I was even holding it.

"Iced tea. Would you like some?"

"Yes."

"Okay."

She tilts her head to the side. "What happened to your scars?"

I frown. "What?"

"They're gone. Where did they go?" She lifts a painfully skinny arm and taps the side of her face with her index finger. The loose skin around her bicep jiggles.

She thinks I'm her deceased sister, Prishna, who was once badly burned. She's completely delusional.

"They faded." I play along, recalling the scar ointment Prishna carried in her bag. "With the cream I used daily."

"I like the scars better."

An odd thing to say.

Valerie pulls out a thin gold chain from under her house dress. On it is the half-pendant of a broken heart. Her sister wore the other half around her neck.

Her face falls into deep sadness. "You understand, don't you?"

The hair on the back of my neck prickles.

"Understand, what?"

Valerie looks down, her eyes filling with tears.

Desperate to know what she's talking about, I step forward. "Understand what, sister?"

The beeps on the monitor become faster. Whatever she's talking about is making her visibly upset.

"Understand what, Valerie?"

The nurse's silhouette appears beyond shades that are drawn against the windows. She's still on her call, but making her way back to the front door. She must have gotten an alert.

I back up, heart pounding. "What do I understand?" I whisper-hiss. "What? Tell me."

Boots on the front porch. *Dammit.*

I turn to rush out of the room. When I reach the doorway, Valerie calls after me.

"Sabine?"

I freeze. She said my name.

My *real* name.

I turn.

Our eyes lock. What was once sadness is now ice-cold hatred.

She says, "Don't ever forget, beautiful butterfly, you weren't the first one on that bathroom counter."

The front door opens.

I spin on my heel and step out of the room. As I quietly close the door behind me, I take one more look over my shoulder just as Valerie closes her eyes and the machines begin to flash red.

One Hundred Seventeen

Sabine

IT'S BEEN two months since Valerie died.

After the small memorial we held for her, Astor and I flew back to New York to decompress. To begin healing and putting the past behind us. To my shock, this included Astor officially stepping down as the CEO of his company, Astor Stone, Inc.

He says he's done with darkness. With living a life shrouded in death. He wants to live a more simple, laid-back life centered around only one thing—me.

Though he was already handling the position, Astor appointed Cillian as the CEO of his company. Astor will hold the position of chairman of the board, stepping into that role after taking a full year off. Beyond that, he has hired a team of people to help manage his billion-dollar empire, to take much of the weight off his shoulders.

It's a reset, he said, and I'm damn proud of him.

Cillian is already making waves within the company, demanding his mercenaries enroll in additional classroom time that includes extensive lethal combat training—not surprising considering how easily he took out Astor. Much like Astor, he's a ruthless and efficient businessman, but unlike Astor, he wears t-shirts, tactical pants, and combat boots to the office.

I've grown to love the man.

Now that the dust has settled, we've decided to return to the beach house to clean it out before putting it up for sale. It's something we've both been dreading, but it needs to be done for both of us to move on.

Astor turns off the engine, leans back, and we both sigh in unison.

We *despise* this place.

The yard and garden is overgrown, half brown, brittle, and dying. Dead leaves speckle the porch and walkway. Autumn is in full swing in the Pacific Northwest.

The house smells old and musty, with a lingering anti-septic scent. It makes my stomach roll.

Astor takes me by the waist and pulls me in for a hug. "Thanks for coming."

"Everything together. That's our motto. Now. Let's get in and get the hell out."

"You don't have to tell me twice."

I open the windows as Astor puts on a pot of coffee and an upbeat playlist to help combat the dark, gloomy vibe that lingers in this godforsaken place.

I pause in Valerie's room, visions of her last moments alive sweeping through my thoughts.

"Sabine," she'd said, crystal-clear. In her final moments, the only thing that mattered to Valerie was making sure I knew that Astor had sex with her first. She was a troubled, ill woman, and I hope she's in a better place.

We spend the day packing what little belongings Valerie had, then emptying the cupboards, the refrigerator, the cabi-nets, removing paintings and pictures from the walls. We're donating all the furniture and have arranged for that to be picked up at a later date.

Packing is tedious and exhausting work, and before we know it, dusk has fallen on the horizon.

Astor and I decide to go outside for some much-needed fresh air. Hand in hand, we walk through the brown, brittle garden. Once full of life, now withering away.

The tip of the sun peeks out from above the ocean line in the distance. The temperature has dropped, cool enough for the couple walking hand in hand on the shore below to wear coats.

Simultaneously, Astor and I take a deep breath, and then laugh. We've become freakishly in-tune with each other. After all, we've been through hell and back.

He wraps an arm around my shoulders and, for a minute, we watch the couple below.

"That will be us someday."

Warmth blooms over my chest. I smile, rest my head on his shoulder.

Together, we watch the sun set.

One Hundred Eighteen

Sabine

WE'VE LEFT the master bedroom, Valerie's room, for last, neither of us wanting to spend the day wallowing in the darkness that comes with that room.

"I'll do the bed and nightstand; you do the bathroom," I say, "then we'll do the closet together."

"Deal."

I strip the bed as Astor disappears into the bathroom. I can smell her on the sheets, a rose scent tinged with antiseptic.

My stomach drops, a creepy sensation like fingernails flutters up my spine. Immediately, I want to leave, I know we can't until everything is packed up, and I'm *not* coming back.

Just get it done.

After haphazardly folding the bedding and shoving it in a box, I shift my focus to the nightstand.

The drawers are filled with used tissues and prescription pill bottles, and a dozen over-the-counter supplements. A pen and notepad, random cotton balls. Hand lotion, nail clippers, an eye mask. Once the drawers are emptied, I unplug and carry the lamp to the hallway, where we've stacked the easy-to-move furniture. Once back in the room, I pick up the hardcover book on the nightstand that Astor got her.

To Grief and Back, it's entitled. A #1 New York Times bestselling novel.

I open the flap, and find the pages still crisp, some even stuck together. I frown, recalling Astor saying Valerie never went anywhere without it. Did she even read it?

Curious, I flip through the pages until I get to the back flap, which is significantly thicker than the front cover.

My frown deepens as I examine the edges and discover that the interior paper of the back cover has been cut away and glued back down.

What the heck?

I glance to the bathroom. Astor's shadow moves along the wall as he packs up the vanity. I consider calling out to him, but something tells me to explore this privately.

My heart begins to race as I slide my thumbnail under the paper and peel up the edges that have been previously cut loose.

I pull out a thin stack of folded papers.

My hands tremble as I unfold each one.

The first is a copy of a communication between Valerie and a lawyer about divorcing Astor. The email appears to be a consultation of what the process would entail, including a layout of potential fees (which are insane), and how to contact him if she wishes to move forward. Next is a print of a photo captured from a cell phone, presumably Valerie's, of a piece of paper sitting on Astor's desk in his New York suite. The picture was obviously taken in secret, as the lights in the room are off and it's heavily shadowed. The photo is of a copy of a living trust amendment that indicates if he were to die, every penny of his estate would go to his child, Chloe—not his wife, Valerie.

I recall Astor telling me that he did this, and I remember him saying that Valerie didn't know.

He was wrong.

The next photo is a clause that says in the event Chloe passed before Valerie, the bulk of the estate is to be broken up among several charities, and one million dollars of his estate would go to his wife, Valerie. If they divorce before then, she gets nothing.

I gasp, the papers falling from my fingertips.

As they scatter in the air, a small ringlet of curly blond hair flitters to the floor.

One Hundred Nineteen

Sabine

6 Months Later,
Positano, Italy

"TELL ME ABOUT TODAY." The therapist, Allegra, smoothes her alabaster pencil skirt as she settles into her leather chair.

Astor looks at me and smiles. "It was a good day." He squeezes my hand. "We started with a long walk on the beach, as you've recommended."

"Great. Exercise first thing in the morning is optimal for people who struggle with anxiety. Good job."

Though we've been in Italy for months now, I still struggle with Allegra's thick Italian accent.

"And how are you sleeping, Astor?"

When he hesitates, I step in. "We have good nights and bad nights, but more good than bad lately. We found a cooking show that we both enjoy. We record it and watch it to wind down. No news, phones, electronics, just food."

Allegra laughs. "I remember you two said you had begun taking cooking classes together, yes?"

"It's more of Sabine showing me how to cook."

"Good, that's good. Wonderful bonding time. I must say, you two have come so far since our first visit."

Believe it or not, it was Astor's idea to begin therapy together. After Valerie died and we realized she was the one who killed her own daughter for Astor's money, Astor and I both agreed that we needed to get far away for a while, and needed to get help to process. To reset, unplug, recalibrate. Together we chose Italy, where Astor owns a villa (because of course he does), and one of the first items on our to-do list was to find a therapist to help work through the trauma together.

"And how is Brittney doing?"

I sit up, smile. "Wonderfully. She just flew in today and is coming for dinner tonight."

"Oh! That's wonderful," Allegra exclaims.

If you would have asked me six months ago what I would be doing today, I would not have said vacationing in Italy with Astor, and inviting Valerie's twenty-one-year-old nurse to visit, I would have laughed.

In the days following Valerie's death, we realized just how much she had been playing and manipulating us—even Brittney.

In the final week of Valerie's life, Valerie confessed everything to Brittney in small blocks of disjointed confessions, while sprinkling in delusional comments to throw Brittney off.

Brittney, assuming it was a combination of her new medication and illness, didn't feel the need to say anything because she assumed it was "normal."

To Brittney, Valerie confessed to killing Chloe after realizing she'd been left out of Astor's will. To Valerie, one million dollars was more valuable than her child. So she began planning. Valerie knew that by cutting a lock of Chloe's hair, Astor would assume it was a message from one of his enemies—exactly as he did—and would never consider her.

Valerie kept this a secret, even from her sister Prishna, who loved Chloe and raised her from infancy. I now understand why before Valerie died, she asked, *don't you understand?* She was asking Prishna if she understood why she had to do it. Perhaps guilt—or fear of what lay ahead—was getting to her in her final moments.

Brittney also felt tremendous guilt for not telling us about the confessions. Since Valerie died, Brittney and I have grown incredibly close, building a bond that feels a lot like one a mother and daughter would have. She, like us, is still processing everything that happened. We speak and text daily, and I look forward to every one of them.

It's amazing how trauma spreads to those around us, but even more amazing how love can heal it.

Allegra studies us for a moment with a smile. "For this session, I'd like us to begin a new phase in our therapy. Are you open to that?"

"Yes," we say in unison.

"I want you both to keep a journal—separate journals. Inside it, I want you to jot down moments that you feel your best. The happiest, or the most like yourself. It's important not to overthink it. Make it simple so that it doesn't feel like a chore. For example, today I felt most myself while jogging by the lake. Or, today, I felt happiest while sharing coffee with Astor. Or, taking a walk, seeing the sun set, smelling the rain, drinking a glass of wine." She winks. "Anything like that. Write it down."

"And what are we accomplishing with this," Astor asks, always having to know the whys behind everything. It helps him process, I've learned.

"When we go through traumatic experiences, sometimes

our observation skills can be altered. Meaning, we get locked into a feeling of doom, or flight or fight, and before too long, everything we look at is through that altered lens. This exercise helps rewire our brain to notice the little things that make us happy throughout the day, and I think you'll be surprised how many little things there are. Over time, your perspective shifts. That's the goal."

"I like that," I say. "Like a gratitude journal."

"Kind of, yes, but again, don't overthink it. Let's start now," Ana says. "What is something that happened today that made you smile?"

Astor and I look at each other.

Tears fill his eyes.

He places his hand on my growing belly, and together we say, "Feeling our baby kick for the first time."

One Hundred Twenty

Brittney

"HOLY SHIT."

I smirk and slide my hand on Leo's leg, sitting in the passenger seat.

Together we gape at the villa ahead of us, surrounded by lush gardens and greenery that envelopes the soaring stone walls. The side of the home stretches down a small cliff and literally disappears into a crystal-clear lake.

"I know," I say. "I think he bought it from, like, George Clooney or something."

Leo exhales, dragging his fingers through his hair. He's nervous, though he'll never admit it. And I can't say that I blame him. It will be the first time he and Astor have seen each other since Astor thought he killed him. If not for Cillian coming in shortly after to "clean up," Leo very likely would have died. Instead of finishing the job, Cillian gave Leo proper medical care and took him to his home where Leo laid low until the dust settled. Meaning, Astor settled.

Sabine told me Astor cried when Cillian told him Leo

was still alive. It was the next day Astor officially stepped down from his job as CEO, and decided to completely restructure his life—around his one true love, Sabine. Behind the mask Astor has worn for decades is an extremely emotional, passionate man who just wants a normal family life.

And slowly but surely, it's happening.

I park the rental car under the port cochere.

"You ready?"

I watch the Adam's apple bob in Leo's neck. He grips my hand. "Yes."

The moment the car doors shut, Sabine swings open the front door.

I gasp. "Sabine! You're showing!"

"Come here!" We embrace for what feels like a full minute, rocking back and forth.

Astor appears in the doorway and I realize Leo is lingering behind us.

For a moment, Astor and Leo stare at each other. Then, Astor steps out of the entry, rushes across the cobblestone driveway, and throws his arms around Leo.

Shocked, Leo freezes, his eyes bugging as he looks at me.

Sabine and I laugh.

"Wow, so he's . . ."

"Healing," Sabine smiles. "The guy has become a daily crier."

I laugh. "Wow, who would have thought?"

We watch Astor and Leo speak for a moment, though it's mainly Astor talking. Apologizing, I assume. But I also know that Leo has plenty to ask forgiveness for as well. Regardless, things seem to be off to a great start.

We watch as Astor leads Leo into the home, his arm around his shoulders. Leo smiles at me as they pass.

I exhale, put my hand over my heart. "That went well."

"I had no doubt. Come on, come inside. I'm so excited to see you . . ."

As always, Sabine and I fall into easy conversation as we step into the kitchen. Astor and Leo have poured themselves a drink and are outside on the patio, where, if I had to guess, they'll remain for a while.

Sabine pours me a glass of wine, while she opens sparkling water for herself.

"How much longer are you going to stay here?" I ask.

"Just a few more months, I think. We want to have the baby in the states."

"Do you know what it is?"

She smiles from ear to ear. "A girl."

I scream in delight.

Both men rush in.

Sabine and I laugh. "We're fine. Go away."

Once certain we are not being kidnapped by bandits, Astor and Leo retreat to the patio. No amount of therapy will remove the innate protector that lives in both men, and that's just fine with us.

We spent the next thirty minutes talking about all things baby, until Sabine switches up the conversation.

"Okay, tell me about you. And Leo. He still hasn't found a job, right?"

"Right, but he's applying every day. It's just that his skill set is so singular."

"Yes, most soldiers turned hitmen don't have a wide career path." I laugh, she glances toward the patio. "I wouldn't worry about that though."

My eyes pop. "You think Astor is going to offer him his job back?"

"I'd be shocked if he didn't. Okay, what else?"

My smile turns into a squeal as I lift my left hand.

"Oh, my God, you're engaged!" Sabine screams.

Again, both men. Again, we tell them to leave, and for the next hour, Sabine and I giggle like little girls while talking about our future.

A very bright, happy future.

About the Author

Amanda McKinney is the Amazon Charts bestselling and multi-award-winning author of more than thirty romance and thriller novels. Her books have received over fifteen literary awards and nominations, including the prestigious *Daphne du Maurier Award for Excellence*, and have been included in lists such as *POPSUGAR's 12 Best Romance Books*, and featured on the *Today Show*.

Text **AMANDABOOKS to 66866** to sign up for Amanda's Newsletter and get the latest on new releases, promos, and freebies!

www.amandamckinneyauthor.com